the book of moon

the book of moon

An Loúr ihn Géalach

k. rose quayle

Book design and production by K. Rose Quayle www.thebookofmoon.com

Published by K. Rose Quayle
Pittsburgh, PA, United States of America

The Book of Moon is set in Minion Pro 12/16. Cover and chapter plates are set in Kells-SD by Stephen Deffeys.
Author photos by D. Chalich.

ISBN 978-0-578-56598-9
Library of Congress Control Number:2019917357

Typesetting services by BOOKOW.COM

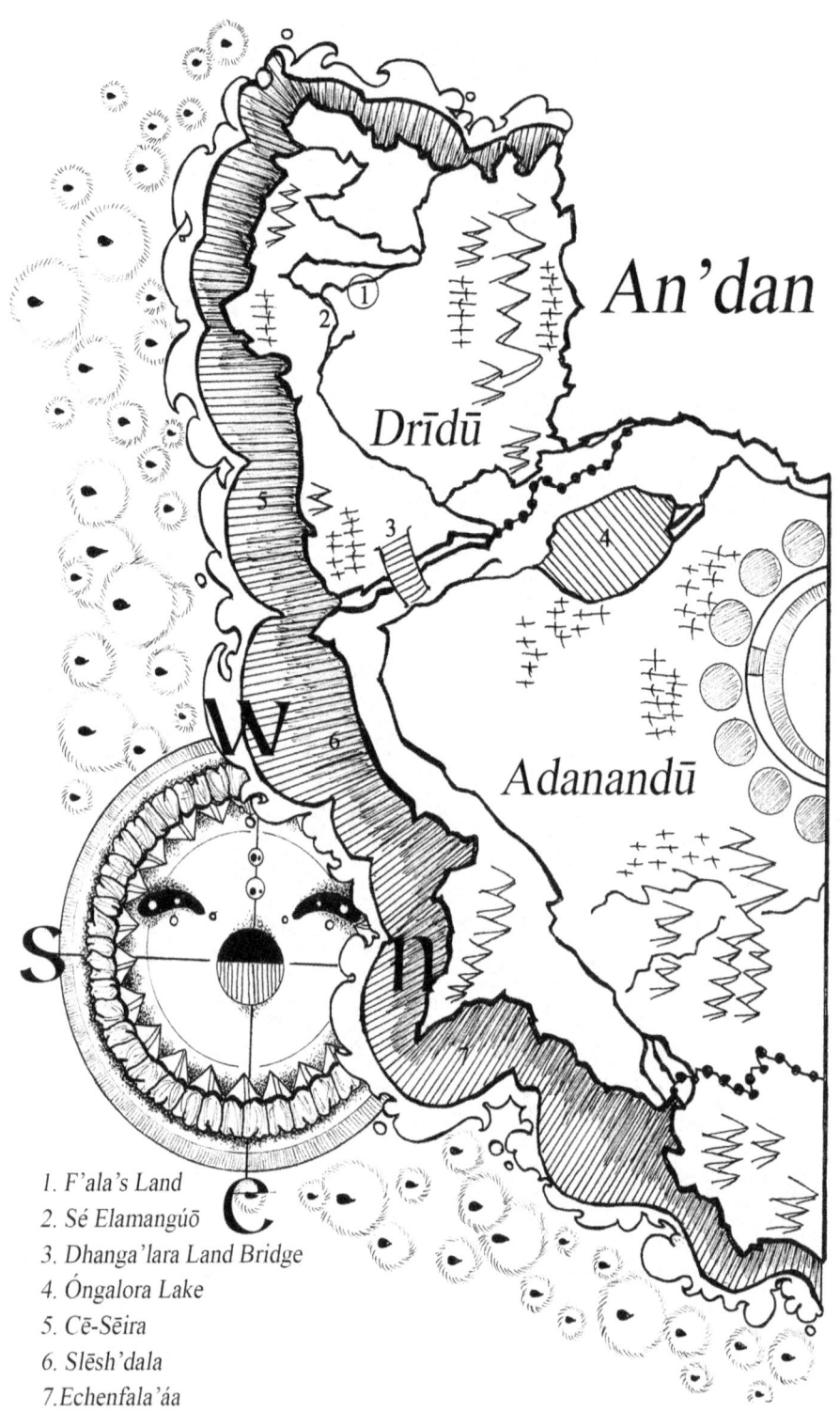

An'dan

Drīdū

Adanandū

1. F'ala's Land
2. Sé Elamangúō
3. Dhanga'lara Land Bridge
4. Óngalora Lake
5. Cē-Sēira
6. Slēsh'dala
7. Echenfala'áa

Ebūda

Peridūr

8. Gaú Bri'én
9. Prādha
10. Nandhacot
11. Ceshii-Ceshii

for *my* ah'sha
and,
with great love,
Michelle

Contents

Pronunciation Guide to Common Words

Análong	aan-yah-LON
Ebūda	eh-BOO-dah
Peridūr	pair-ih-DOOR
Adanandū	ah-dah-NAHN-doo
Drīdū	DRY-doo
Sé Elamangúō	syeh el-ah-man-GWOH
Pōcarū	POH-kah-ROO
Bri'én	bree-YEN
Rā-alta	RAY-ahl-teh
Sā'úū	SAY-yoo
Anan	ah-NAHN
Lān	LAYN
F'ala	faa-laa
Ā'dō	AY-doh
Mi'hal'ē	MIH-ha-LEE
Éē'shī	YEE-shy
Rāca	RAY-kah
Anshē	ahn-SHEE
Hor'ē	hor-EE
A'nō	ah-NOH
Sarshēl	sar-SHEEL
Caémba	kah-YEM-bah

Book One

rā-alta
1

standing at the end of the
world

*samala-én mah an dōn ihn
gaú*

UNBELIEVABLE.

The servants had asked me if it was the end and I had no reply more substantial than a wavering "I don't know." Privately, I wondered if anyone ever knew the end had come. Wasn't that something our elders liked to say in hindsight; *that they should have seen it coming*? I hoped not, because I'd never known until a thing was done and past that it had ended. And likewise, I didn't know now.

I gazed past the Palace veranda out over the thinning trees beyond the city wall, barely making out the soft, thinning canopies of the lower *bashō* plains that had already lost their cotton with the harvest still two months away. Looking down over busy Bri'ën, over the red-roofed temples, the Cāilon-da of selling the living and beyond that, the filthy slums; all so necessary to the holiness that was our sacred city. The faint, ever-present whir of the bōmen on either side of us lulled my thoughts back over these recent years, years in which our land, our beautiful Ebūda, had fallen under famine; an evil which spread suddenly and silently with the all-consuming, unrelenting power that can only feed from a place of plenty.

We *análong* were too young to remember the last time our land had suffered, too full to remember hunger and too fat with dreams to believe anything could ever happen to our happiness. We may have endured the hunger and the sickness, but when our hopes evaporated with the sea, the end of Ebūda began to near. But its eyes weren't hungry; they were already gone.

At first, we didn't notice the end had begun. The north had the most trouble, up in Peridūr at the shore of the Silver Sea. Word was sent to the Palace that the sea was growing smaller and no-one believed this. No-one at the Palace, that is. But *someone* did.

Then the harvest failed at the border of Adanandū, the centerlands. And harvests will fail on occasion, we said, thinking the next year would return to normal. But *someone* took note.

Then confusion swept over, and denial shut our eyes. The trouble wouldn't come to us, it couldn't possibly leave the north. Then the second bad harvest, the third dried up stream, the fourth bad harvest came and went, came and went. Well, what had they done up there in Peridūr anyway? Had they angered *Mi'á*? Certainly, *we* hadn't.

The next five seasons passed by with no rain in Peridūr, rain which normally floods and nourishes the fertile bashō plains and the *dūūcerfrūt* bushes. These were the very same plains and bushes all análong made their yearly treks to for gathering cotton to make cloth and to stuff up their pantries with dūūcerfrūt wares. It had only taken those five years for the great rains to die. Once there had been days and nights and weeks of rain so thick the curtain of water which fell over Bri'ën was nearly solid. No trade wagon coming from neither north nor south could get through until the season had ended. And when it had finished, the morning steam rose with the dust from the hot ground, turning into a wall of wet heat by midday that made the eyes filmy and clung on the skin for another few weeks until we wished the rain would return!

Unbelievable.

It only took nine years to collapse Peridūr. The lost harvests forced análong to use their grain and rice stores up. There were towns in Adanandū that sent food by darna-cart to help but this too had its end. Still, at that time hope lifted up the rest of Ebūda with the surety that Peridūr's problems would stay in Peridūr. Or maybe that was denial. In either case, during those nine years we looked away, *someone* saw.

Being so close to the Rivers Gōmōbarasū and Elamangūō, the southern análong in Drīdū benefit from a longer and more successful growing season year-round. When, in the fifth year of the drought ambassadors from Peridūr came to the Palace telling of a new sickness wiping out the high mountain tribes, they asked us to force Drīdū to give in to demands only they could supply. We análong, who had never in memory had reason to give in to greed, quickly learned to listen to it to survive. Suddenly *nendē* became obsolete in half of Ebūda. What was it good for except to burn and keep warm over? The rich could get no richer now; they stared at their wealth over their evening fires, unable to eat it. Our laws, given to us by the heavenly Guardians from the beginning of análong memory, were enforced, then compromised, then forgotten in the race to secure enough food.

The análong began to divide themselves, something strictly forbidden by the Old Kings of Ebūda after their ancient wars, that time long before us, before anyone now alive could remember. Elders through the many generations had warned us of such a time in a series of prophecy scrolls stored here in the Palace.

And as mortal things do, every generation believed in their hearts these things would never happen to them, right down to my own. Yet, *someone* believed. And because we did not understand the words of the scrolls, we paid no attention to those outdated suggestions. So, fifteen years passed since the first signs of drought. Now the highest mountain tribes in Peridūr were all dead, the sea was dried and gone, and análong everywhere north of the Palace were starving.

South to us, the análong of Drīdū, still largely unaffected, raced to build a wall across the narrow strait of land bridging them to Adanandū to protect their rivers. I suppose they thought they could wall themselves in from hunger. And as well, we were all too naive to believe they would do it. But *someone* wasn't.

Now there was no law against weapons as long as I could remember, and I don't think a law would have made much difference then anyway. Such a thing wouldn't have kept the future from coming. This, we didn't know either, but *someone, somewhere* did.

In Adanandū, a group of smiths began making and selling swords and bows and joined up with those northerners of the lowlands still strong enough to fight, calling themselves the Ebūdean Defense Army. Their goal was to press downward into the south and mix with the survivors to form a stronger, if smaller, Ebūda, one able to survive the famine. The análong in upper Drīdū refused to share from their hard-worked land and sent spies into southern Adanandū to protect their border but this only resulted in violence when they were caught. It was hard in those days to figure out who to side with. To those of us who were not allowed to leave the sacred city, the Army's mission seemed sensible at first to ensure the survival of our tribes until a year dragged on and it was clear the true purpose was only their own survival. Drīdū's border became more and more violent, and the análong began to call the army *NaÓma*, meaning "the death-bringers."

The NaÓma worked mainly as a string of smaller groups for easier travel. As these little bands made their way across the centerlands towards the south, picking up anyone able to hold a weapon, they quickly became caught up in superstitions and took over every village and town they entered, rousting out anyone they accused responsible for bringing on the famine. They might be sentenced for charming or conjuring, they may have no little dhana or too many little dhana. Whatever the NaÓma frowned upon gave grounds for these poor souls to be put to death with the villages' blessing. And after a time, análong became so desperate in some places that their thoughts began to turn backwards, and they looked on their neighbors' good intentions with suspicion; turning each other in for any reason to save themselves. And when the NaÓma ran out of resources to keep going, they took as they wanted and burned everything behind, leaving nothing to witness against them.

The constant travel and fighting with poor conditions took a toll eventually and made the NaÓma to fight amongst themselves. Then the sickness which killed off the high mountain tribes showed up suddenly among them (one of the servants told me "*It's because they stoled from the dead, nūaca. That's what give it to them. They cursed themselfs same and all around them too!*").

But they learned to leave a few victims alive to keep their own numbers; mainly little dhana who had been abandoned or orphaned outside their villages and could now be forced to pick up a sword and who followed willingly so they could be fed.

Then finally they convinced the most rural análong to sell one or two of their dhana to them in exchange for an elusive "cure" to the sickness. Brothers were sold to save sisters, sisters for mothers. But these cures were no more than bitter water.

Unbelievable.

All of these things happened within fifteen years.

* * *

Yet, was it so unbelievable? Could it be to me, this lost daughter of Perīdūr, this sole survivor of a cursed tribe Ebūda had worked so hard to forget? My own life could never have been described as anything *but* unbelievable. Had the world just caught up with my own existence?

But, kept safely away from all this in the sacred city in Adanandū on its walled hill, I could only observe the trees along the plain; see the thinning of the marketplace below the Palace and hear the whispers of servants and messengers as they dressed me and bathed me and made certain I had nothing to do for myself. The sick were forbidden inside the city walls; the starving had no strength for the long journey to Bri'ën. Even the deaths of my parents were told to me by a messenger passing through to the south. They were buried in the high mountains as I stood in the Hall of Mirrors by my servant, Sā'úū, wondering how I had come to be caged here.

I was the youngest of the Elders, the youngest in history and perhaps more importantly, the first and only female to ever be elected to the Council. There was no precedent; I had no claim.

Unbelievable.

It was a strange position; the highest appointment any análong could aspire to and one that I had never dreamed of or longed for. The Council of Elders came from a line of successions which traced back to the middle ages of our beloved country. These Elders (never more or less than nine in number) ruled with wisdom after the Age of Kings had died out with the old wars. There were many opposed to me; many who cursed the sacred city itself and swore it was the end of Ebūda the day I was given my staff and robes. For though Ebūda beholds a society where mothers and sisters and aunties take care of the dhana and fathers are seldom ever mentioned; the análong would hear nothing of letting a female lead them.

The nomination came from nowhere because no análong would claim the shameful responsibility afterwards. But somehow, I was summoned to the sacred city from my home in Peridūr to replace the Elder before me who had lived out his days in the chambers now belonging to me. How I came up to be mixed up in it to begin with was never discussed with me, even by Elder Anan.

Unbelievable.

That was exactly fifteen years ago.

Rā-alta
2

what magic cannot do

ban'á arra in'ga-tsō nē

"**I** do say we are quite likely the last generation of Ebūda," Elder Anan said as he dipped his nose into his cider mug. The words were only fact; his scratchy old voice hollowed inside the cup. "It's inescapable, nā. Gone are the days of the old banquets and festivals. This is the time of meager celebration and scant joy if ever there was, wouldn't you say, Rā-alta?"

Would I?

"Are they saying it's me?" I whispered into the bright morning air.

"Of course," Anan grinned behind his wrinkles. "You're a female! Nothing in Ebūda is more suspicious than that."

I scowled. "Be serious."

He put his mug down on the smooth stone ledge with a shaky hand and smiled vaguely and not without a bit of amusement. "You asked me, and I respect you far too much to tell you anything but the truth. Now, of course the análong blame you. They loved you yesterday, they hate you today. It's only fear. If they couldn't blame someone else, the análong would be forced to admit the wrongs they have done themselves and have let others do behind their backs," he blew his nose and blinked. "We have stayed out of the affairs of war for generations now and it looks like we are standing on the edge of a very bad turn. Nothing to do but brace for it, dhana."

I closed my eyes against the na'bōmen's faint breeze as it grazed along my neck with icy lips. I thought again to the days before, even the night before; a particularly salty meeting of the Council right below where we now stood which would foreshadow this moment between us.

It always seemed to me that there were much too many meetings where not enough of my opinion was ever discussed. But knowing I was no more than a very fortunate stranger in a forbidden world to my kind kept me from voicing much of it to begin with.

A messenger had come from Peridūr and called an audience of the other Elders and I to the Room of Words. We each shuffled in through the narrow stone doorway and sat in our places around that ample, circular table into which the prayers of our ancestors had been carved around and around in the grain. Under each of our respective bottoms, as it were, lay the words of our parts of the blessings we sang as we gathered.

Elder Corin stood. "If you would, *n'saō*." He held his arms out as if to conduct and everyone stood and opened their mouths to hum in pitch. A decidedly off-key note twanged from my left. "Tsōl, tsōl, tsōl, let's not do that. Elder Indhad!"

Silence fell as Elder Indhad gummed "Daaa?" faintly and nearly fell over in his place. Elder Corin swiped a tired hand across his face and I noted that like Bri'én, Elder Indhad's time was counted and coming to a close. "Rā-alta, would you please take over for Elder Indhad?"

I nodded and lowered my voice slightly, trying as I might to stretch my lips outward to master the Adanandū pronunciation of *dlah* rather than my softer, northern *chlah*. The syllables must be at just the right pitch to invoke the protective spell; if anyone fell higher or lower, we could bring about a curse. I dreaded singing the blessings for just this reason and held my breath each time in case disaster struck. In any case, Elder Indhad seemed grateful to sit down. Luckily, our harmonies intertwined into the usual invocation before we again took our seats where ancient análong did the same centuries before.

Once seated, Elder Corin called in the messenger to give his news. "And now, we may begin."

The messenger entered the room, bowed and took out a scroll from his short robe. "It is my regret to inform you that the dark illness has swept the north, saō. Análong are dying by the hundreds, our healers have not been able to stop it and now the NaÓma… they've…"

Elder Corin swiped the scroll abruptly from him and smacked him soundly over the head, for it is well known that messengers cannot read. He was telling us whatever he had overheard as it was being written, which is very poor manners. Elder Corin cleared his throat to read aloud:

"Elders, I greet you.

In the name of Mĭ'á, I pray you, send help to Peridūr as soon as you can. So many darna lay dead in the fields, their feathers cover the mountains. As far as I can see, there is no green left from this terrible drought. Our dhana are crying for food; the ground is not fit to plant in. We exist by what we carry up from the centerland border.

If you have any magic left at all, protect us from the NaÓma, for they have killed even the healers east of us (even into the north of Adanandū!) because no one can cure their ranks of the sickness. We fear they shall burn down our villages next as they have done to the west of us.

In good faith,

Ta- Dhemma, Andūasa village, Peridūr."

A collective sigh went up around the table. "*Magic*," Elder Hēda spat. "There is not an análong in all the plains and forests of Ebūda who does not think we are common sorcerers to conjure up rain with a wave of the tail! The magic surrounding this city is of the Guardians and is much too old and complicated to begin to explain to the likes of a common *Ta-*. Curing colds is hardly the business of the Council of Nine!"

"A *cold*, Elder! Our very race is dying out!" Elder Manahan, a darna himself, hissed back.

"Death from starvation! All Peridūr is starving to death from simple drought and all the consequences of it; nothing magical about it! Who in this room can bring in a harvest with no rain? Who can pull water out of the sky? Is anyone here the Creator? Let him stand!" Elder Hēda threw his blue robe back and pulled at the sky dramatically for effect.

The room fell silent. The welfare of families and peaceful relations between prefectures fell under my jurisdiction. Gathering my own robe's sleeves around me, I stood to address my fellows in the soothing tones I saved for addressing this bunch of cantankerous Elders old enough to be my grandfathers. "The cause hardly matters. Surely it is clear that the Council cannot cure disease or bring

rain. But, it is well known that disrespect will not soften Mĩ'ắ's heart to pour water down from the sky, either," I pointedly cast a glance round the room to which several nods met my eye.

"As the Palace cannot publicly sponsor any war with the NaÓma, I think what we ought to do is look at maintaining the comfort of the ill and dying now and protecting this city as the refuge it's always been. Haven't the grandmothers told us we must do all we can for the dying?" I smiled inwardly, knowing that often the most heated of arguments could be softened with reference to the grandmothers' sayings.

Elder Talishin rapped his staff against the floor. "Well said, saō Rā-alta, let us all be reminded of the wisdom of the grandmothers. However, while I agree with you, I find myself in a difficult situation. Brïën may be in the centerlands, but our longest border is on the south, which is still protected from these troubles. If we...*requisition* supplies from that prefecture, we would be depriving the southern análong of their stores. They argue that they have worked the land for generations and deserve its profits. And what if the famine extends into Drīdū? Is it not better to put our energy into preserving at least that part of the population so we are assured our legacy will survive this?"

"Or," Elder Talishin mused aloud, "Should Adanandū declare its independence from Ebūda and seal its borders before the NaÓma grow any stronger?"

Immediately Elder Corin struck the table and shouted for all he could, "Declare ourselves an independent country? Here now, a wall is being built on the main land bridge between Peridūr and Drīdū as we speak! We cannot let that nonsense go on. It will mean the death of anyone trying to flee Peridūr through Adanandū's southern border!"

Beside him though, Elder Anan, who enjoyed being cleverly awkward, noted, "Building a wall is not against the law."

Elder Corin shot back, "Dividing Ebūda is *against the law*. Capitalizing on the suffering and want of others is *against the law*, or have you forgotten the Law of Mercy and Justice? If that wall goes up there is no other way through the whole of Ebūda from north to south on foot. Any one of our own people, shanár or g'éalach would be trapped. At least the darna can fly over. If there are any left in the north to flee, that is!"

At this I cringed, for the darna were my adopted people; I was raised in one of their villages.

"Not if they cut a gateway out of it; put a door in," Anan retorted. "What do the grandmothers say about that?" he winked at me but suddenly my sense of humor died.

"Are you then suggesting one race of the análong is worth more than the other? Would you dare claim to the Council that the shanár of the south are above the darna of the north! Or that they should be punished for saving themselves? Do you wish to say that it's fine for the darna to fly into Drīdū but the g'éalach must perish at the cliffs of Peridūr?" Elder Talishin interrupted in outrage.

Elder Hēda waved his hand carelessly and quipped, "Or should we just magic them over this little wall to Drīdū?"

Anan sat back lazily in his seat and propped his head against his brittle hand. "Then, fellows, if we should not punish the southern análong for defending their land by any means, what do we do about the NaÓma who are also fighting for their own existence? Is it we who decide who should live?"

And then everyone rose quickly from their seats and raised their voices past any incoherent level. All that is, except Elder Indhad, who spent the rest of the meeting happily chewing on his sleeve.

"*N'nūaca*!" I shouted, rapping my staff against the table until they settled. "Like it or not, killing each other for whatever reason is absolutely against every sense of decency we have. What are we going to do about it?" But the room erupted again into heated argument and I quietly slipped out into the hallway to gather my own thoughts, knowing no answer was coming. After a few moments between the translucent walls overlooking the hidden gardens where the servants went for solitude, I felt a thin hand on my shoulder. Elder Anan had also escaped.

"Nothing will be done Rā-alta, nothing. The problem with law is that whether it is righteous or not, it is not a law unless someone upholds it. Look at us, just a bunch of cranky old análong in robes losing our voices as well as our eyesight. You're young; you could probably beat someone into submission with your staff, but I haven't had any fight in me since my eight hundreds!" He laughed and I groaned.

"It's infuriating, *nanē*, it's wrong. What is the Council going to do? Other than shout it out here in the palace? Peridūr is almost gone from the map!" I exploded in sheer frustration. Didn't they understand that though I would live locked in the Palace for the rest of my life, Peridūr was still my home? That though I was born a shanár, the darna would always be my tribe? No, of course they wouldn't. It was a secret only a few knew outside my village; a secret that died in the village of my birth. Only Anan and I knew the truth of where I came from.

"How true. And not that I'm changing the subject, but perhaps I could ask a favor of you." He said, eyes sparkling and mischievous. I waited for it; Anan was well-known for his mercurial requests. "Your dreams, the visions you mentioned a few months ago?"

My face grew hot in embarrassment as if I had been caught at sneaking in the Palace kitchens or sitting too close to my servant in the Tea Garden. It was true, I had been having strange nightmares for a while. I nodded carefully. "Always the same dream over and over. I had hoped you'd forgotten; I know I keep trying to."

"Of course not! I've been thinking about them night and day and I'm certain I know the connection. In fact, I knew it before you even mentioned it!" Here I raised my brow as I had indeed not mentioned it, and he prattled on without noticing. "I would advise a visit from Lān the dream-seer to discuss this in detail, get an expert opinion of sorts. That's exactly what I think should be done," he said. "Absolutely."

"Anan do you really think that's necessary, I mean we really don't have time for such pursuits right now…" But as his old wizened face fell underneath the plush folds of his headdress, I reached over and patted his hand reassuringly. "All right, the only promise I'll make is that I'll think about it."

He gave a little hop and smiled broadly so that his eyes folded up into tiny, happy, wrinkled slits; confident that I would acquiesce in my own time anyway.

"And that is better than no promise at all!" he exclaimed. Turning to lumber off down the hallway to his quarters, Anan suddenly turned with more spryness than one might suppose and added, "By the way, Lān will be calling sometime tomorrow afternoon. I would set aside the rest of the day if I were you."

Rā-alta

3

when the dreams died,
the dhana were no more

*sā'ét na'dhorúū óng'ma-da
an na'dhana tū-da tsan*

$\mathcal{A}$s was often the case, my morning was spent alone except for the company of my own servants. While they meant well and generally thought of things I needed and should have needed long before I ever did, they kept their certain distance from me. When I entered a room, eyes were cast down, laughter faded and smiles were fond but somehow wary. This was the price of rising above one's own class.

The younger servants took me down the tiny jeweled stairway behind the kitchens into the imperial baths, holding up the voluminous skirting of my dressing gown so I could step without tumbling head-first down onto layers of sapphire tiles set in gold. It was the delight of the Palace tailor to have a female Elder at his disposal to dress up, and this is exactly what he did. I was draped in all the newest and finest fabrics, all the brightest colors and in every jewel that could be found in Ebūda for all manner of meetings and ceremonies, court sittings and dinners.

I didn't hate it exactly; it was only that I was raised by darna, who had no need at all for clothing. And while they did find someone to make sure I had the most basic of coverings growing up, layers and headdresses and all those skirts were foreign to me. Dressing each day was the work of three servants who thought it absurd I should want to tie my own ribbons and slapped my hands if I tried to button anything. It was also the same three servants who helped me lower into the steaming water and gently push me forward so they could work scented oil into my skin.

I rested my head on my forearms over the edge of the tub and looked through the curtain. Being a female had its advantages: here in the open baths of rows and rows of alabaster tubs I had my own private toilet and fireplace curtained off to protect my modesty but sheer enough I could see through somewhat to the outside. Sometimes being surrounded by Elders over nine hundred years old was such a shame.

Wincing as a comb was dragged along my ear and caught at an earring, I sat right up uncovered when I heard a voice close by say in concern, "Are you all right, *āsa*?" Wrapping my arms around me, I squinted to see through the curtain, but the light was too dim this early to see well. I knew who it was though. Only one called me "your honor": Sā-úū, my g'ealach attendant.

I didn't answer my personal servant for a moment; the others were listening so intently even the birds in the rafters had stilled. It was frowned upon greatly for me to have a male attendant, but I always spoke carefully to him in front of the others and was never seen with him anywhere alone where others could not overhear if they wished. It was only that... I didn't want another attendant. And he didn't want another master. I wished the others could leave it at that.

I relaxed against the edge and laid my head down again. "*Shē'a*, Sā-úū, I'm fine. Just a tangle." And I felt, rather than saw him recede from the curtain silently and realized with a sudden, not unpleasant shiver that it wasn't just that I didn't want another attendant. Sā-úū wasn't only my servant; he was my *freedom*.

The laws of the Elders were old and resolute and utterly unfair to someone my age. Elders could never leave the city of Bri'én, they could have no home other than the Palace. They couldn't own land or hold money. Elders could never marry or have heirs. And this might not be so terrible for my nine hundred-year-old fellows who had lived much of their lives already by the time they took their staffs and were totally provided for in the Palace. But no-one had ever thought of how it would affect someone closer to three hundred. As they'd never had to before, no-one had ever thought of me.

So, they had taken me to the Palace to steal away my home, my family, my future, my life. My responsibilities and choices were gone underneath the weight of the law of Elders. Everything was done for me by servants and every moment I had to myself was never truly to myself.

But no-one could lock up my heart; it was free to dream, and in dreams I could be anywhere, with anyone I wished.

In the afternoon I sat by the fire in my room meditating when I heard Sā-úū's nails *click-click* softly along the corridor and stop at the door. With him came another sound, a hard *thump, thump, thump!* and an unfamiliar shuffling. Ah, the dream-seer must have arrived.

He lowered himself onto a chair by the window without ceremony and propped his chin on his hands, giving the impression of studying me behind the band of cloth covering his eyes. *So*, I thought, *the one who sees dreams is blind*. Then again, I had no right to judge anyone else's own particular brand of irony.

It was said that Lān himself could not dream; that the dreams he saw were those of all análong and that he could tell prophecies from them. It was fashionable for rich análong to employ him to tell them if they would have a son or if their crops would fail or if they'd find a good husband. It was even said that he was one of the Guardians of Ebūda; one of the twelve reincarnated beings from the world of the *gelim* put in charge to protect and guide us all until the time of *caémba*, the day we would receive souls.

But he didn't look much like a Guardian to me. It was true, no-one knew exactly what they looked like but throughout the Palace (and indeed, all of Bri'én) were murals and statues, mosaics and carvings of those sacred twelve spirits as shanár, darna, g'éalach or a combination of all three. But none of these incarnations looked like this young shanár in his eastern-style tunic and wrapped feet. His ears bandaged, his left cheek scarred, and his skirts trimmed with silver and gold, Lān looked to be no older than me.

"You're not going to offer me a place by the fire? Pretty poor manners for an Elder to a Guardian," he smiled slyly.

I didn't know what to say to such cheek, so I said nothing at all and clumsily helped him up to amble to the fireside stool which he sat down on- hard. But his smile never wavered. Rather he beamed all the brighter as I backed away and seated myself on the chair he'd just left. "What are you smiling at?" I asked, knowing Sā-úū was just outside the door but feeling unnerved anyway.

"You," he answered. "You're staring at me."

"I'm not!" I gasped. I *was*.

Lān laughed. "It's fine, I understand. It's not every day you Elders get to feast your eyes on a handsome young specimen such as myself. You can't help yourself, really."

I rolled my eyes. He was partly right, but I had quite enough to look at without his charity. "I believe Elder Anan actually sent for you."

Lān nodded. "He did. He mentioned a dream that has been bothering you for some months now. It's a common problem you know; dreams and nightmares. Everyone wants to know what they mean. I can help you, no problem at all."

"Hmm. And just so I understand," I looked at him sideways, "How is it you can help with dreams?"

"How can someone who is blind see dreams, you mean?" He leaned over and rested his cheek in his palm. "I will tell you: here." He tapped the side of his head. "I see the dreams of others in place of my own dreams. I've never dreamed on my own in all my long life, but every night thousands of dreams pass through this head and I remember them all. I remember yours, every dream you've ever had."

"I don't think that could be possible," I said gently.

"You used to dream of your parents. You could never see their faces; in fact you could only ever see their *feet*. You'd look up and call for them, but it was as if you'd shrunk; you stood no bigger than their toes. But still you knew it was them. Your mother had a good singing voice; your father wore silver rings on his ankles. But it was only a dream; you've never met your parents."

My heart caught in my throat and like a little dhana I immediately asked as if he could tell me all my heart's desires, "Was it really them? Do I look like them? Were they… looking in on me?" Then I felt stupid for asking. How would Lān know what I looked like? But he smirked and mused idly to answer my unspoken thoughts, "You've appeared in the dreams of another once or twice. Or more."

My eyes grew wide, but the smile faded from his face and he sat up. "But such are not the dreams I came all this way to discuss. The dream I was sent for, now that dream… shě'á. It is a dream you must *not* forget."

I looked down in disappointment. "How could I forget it? I dream of the white análong, the Guardian of Death. I can't understand; only dhana are able to see the Guardian of Death. I expected to die the first time I saw her, but I didn't. Then it came again and still I woke up. Then again and again and again. Every time, the dream becomes clearer. I only wish I knew what it was trying to say …"

"It is telling you of the past and of the future of your family," Lān said.

I pointed to myself, forgetting Lan couldn't have seen me. "You're mistaken I'm sure. I have no family, none at all."

"The dream is of your family; your *asama*," Lan repeated, and he began to trace along the stones of the floor with the end of his staff. "Your shanár family is gone," he agreed. "Your darna family is gone. Your Guardian family is... waning."

I sat very still, trying to determine if I'd heard right. *Tsōl*. Not possible. "My what?"

"In the dream there is a white análong she-dog sitting in a circle. Around her, the land is scarred and barren; dead. Around her, she lays down a set of twelve objects," he went on as if I hadn't asked the question, but I was too fascinated to stop him.

"Each of these objects represents a Guardian. The order that she lays them down in is the order in which the Guardians were born into this world or *will be* born into this world. First, there is a looking-glass," he seemed to be making the shape of it on the floor with his staff as he spoke, "which is the first Guardian, the keeper of the Gates of Ebūda who guards its gates and protects this world. The looking-glass is *A'nō*.

Beside the glass; a ribbon belonging to the most beautiful of Guardians, *Āe'rū*."

My ears pricked up; I had heard that name once long ago whispered amongst my cousins after an uncle had died. "Isn't that what they call the Guardian of...?"

"Death. She who ended her own life to preserve her beauty and was reborn again and cursed to forever remain a dhana." He went on, nonchalantly. "Next, the ball. It recalls the orbs of desolation *Hor-ōċō*, the Guardian of Despair is doomed to carry containing all the sins of Ebūda. Beside it, a bell: it rings out with the clarity of truth for its little Guardian who is named *H'orē*. Then,"

"A strip of cloth," I interjected.

"The cloth that binds the eyes that did not survive the journey to this life; a Guardian of Dreams..." Lan raised his head to face me but then looked down and resumed his tracing on the stone. "A quill, the Guardian of Love; a key, the Guardian of Creation. A pair of bound scrolls: the twin Guardians of Memory and Secrets, *Narū* and *Sada*. And a sword to divide all of Ebūda: it belongs to the last Guardian, *Úā'la*. She is the one who appears at the dawn of caémba."

And with that the dream-seer lowered himself back onto the stool and crossed his arms.

"But you forgot something," I pointed out.

"What did I forget?"

"A dūūcerfrūt and a staff. Who did those belong to?"

Lān looked towards the fire, his face suddenly drawn and older and the light from the flames seemed to grow cold. "The dūūcerfrūt is the emblem of the Guardian of Hope and it does not symbolize plenty as it does in this world, but rather hope during the time of great despair. The dūūcerfrūt is the symbol of the dhana you dream of."

I shook my head in confusion. That he even knew my dream was beyond belief but... "Tsō, that can't be true. White is the color of death. Why would the Guardian of Hope be the color of death?"

"White is the color of death to the análong. For us, these meanings are nothing. It is the constants of those things unseen that we put our concern to," He explained patiently.

"Tsō," I disagreed. "We *are* análong!"

"And the staff," he picked up his own and pointed it at me as though I'd not spoken, "belongs to the Guardian of Wisdom, the Guardian who walks with Elders."

I sat very still waiting for the next words, not moving even when the fire suddenly blew out. The light from the window behind me felt warm across my shoulders and still I waited, until all the busy little sounds from the halls faded behind the *thrum thrum thrum* of my heart in my ears. "Are you saying an Elder is a Guardian?"

Lan sat silently.

"Could Elder Anan be the Guardian of Wisdom? It must be!" Something like excitement and confusion rolled together lifted me off the chair and I turned to the window to open it as I had nothing more constructive to do with my hands in the face of this astounding news.

"Tsō," Lān's voice, low and tired interrupted. "*You* are the Guardian of Wisdom. It is you."

"Tsōl," I contradicted immediately. "Of course it's not. Do I look like a Guardian?"

"Aren't these halls filled with Guardians and none of them look like...?" he stopped, letting me realize I'd thought the same of him only minutes before. I felt silly and shallow. "How could you know I was a Guardian? Are you telling me that's what my dream is supposed to mean?"

"I know it because *I* am a Guardian. *I* am your brother, the Guardian of Dreams," he said simply as if it were as plain as the moons were fat. But there was sadness in his voice as he said it, and as incredible a claim as it was, something in me believed him and that same something in me was afraid.

"I don't believe..."

Lān wrapped the floor with his staff. "*Shēá*, you do. You don't recognize me in this life; indeed, you've never seen me before with your eyes. But then, how could you know me now? I was your *sister* in the last life. And still it hardly matters now, because I've come to tell you that there are still Guardians to come, Guardians who cannot be born into this world until you do what you were born to do. That is the meaning of the dream."

My head was spinning, and I sat back down on the chair to catch my breath. There was no reason for him to lie; to claim that either of us could be a Guardian was so fantastic it couldn't be lied about. No análong would dare. To even hope anyone would believe such a lie... then he must be telling the truth and yet, how could I possibly believe those words? "I don't understand...I'd know if I was a Guardian, wouldn't I? I mean, how could I not know if that were true?"

"Guardians are not magical beings the way the análong think of such things. Some have powers, true, but only over the things they have charge over. The Guardian of Death has power over things related to death; she cannot influence life. But for the rest, they are born into this world the same as anyone else. Their power is in the way they live," Lan explained.

"What were you born to do?" I wondered aloud.

"Find you," Lan leaned over and pinned me with his gaze. "At the appointed time, I was to find you to give you the meaning of the dream so you would know what you were born to do."

"Not everyone believes in Guardians," I pointed out. "Some say they're only stories; like the gellim."

"What does it matter what anyone else believes? You believe." Lān sighed in exasperation and spread out his hands. "Is it so hard for you to accept who I am, who you are? Is *this* all that you are in this life?" the dream-seer asked, pushing down on his staff as a crutch to help himself up. "Are all of your memories gone from our life before? Look at my face! Don't you remember when I shone? Can't you recall my light before I became dull and trapped within a mortal body?"

"But I *haven't* ever seen you before," I whispered, suddenly cold inside as if I'd eaten ice.

"Long ago before Ebūda was separated from An'dan you did; in the days when this world was one country before our family bargained for our lives by becoming Guardians of the análong. I was your sister before this Ebūda and now I'm your brother in this Ebūda, and I will be your family in whatever is after this Ebūda," he smiled lovingly, the feeling of warmth stretching up to where his missing eyes lay behind the cloth. "You and I are of the same kind; our very dust comes from the earliest of days."

A strange feeling crept into my heart; a warm sort of shiver from my knees right up to my shoulders like something large and unseen had picked me up in its palm and I wasn't sure if it would set me down or crush me. I was about to tell Lān that I had no brothers or sisters, that I was the only one left, but he went on.

"You were older than me before we were reborn; always trying to show me the wonder of the world below us, but I wouldn't look. Can't you remember? I wouldn't look when I had the means to see. Now we have siblings waiting to be born and they cannot be until you make up the mind of your heart to do what you were destined to do. I have found you and told you who you are; I am done. It is soon time for me to sleep and time for you to wake."

"But Lān, if I was a Guardian it would mean… it would mean I was meant only to die for the next Guardian to be born. If I was the Guardian of Wisdom, the staff, then the Guardian of Hope would be after me. It's not possible, I'm only-"

"Three hundred twelve years old, born on 16 Tsāi'in on the night when the moons dropped and touched the Cónpa mountains. Those curious creatures; every time a Guardian is born, they can't help but come have a look. All Guardians have their mark left by the moons." He pointed to the scar on his cheek.

I thumped the chair with my fist. "It's just not true! Isn't it enough to be locked up in the Palace for the rest of my life as an Elder? Do you think it's been easy for me? Don't you think I already do as I must for Ebūda? What else can I possibly do? Now you want me to just hand over my own life too?"

Lān's voice dropped and became deadly serious. "Don't act as though you were the first to be put to the test. No Guardian born in Ebūda comes into the world knowing their true name. It is only at our time of awakening that we're given the chance to decide the next Guardian's fate by deciding our own. I am your brother; I remembered who I was when I woke, and I also had to choose to take my destiny or not before you. I made my choice so that you could be born; so that you could be you! And now you must understand that from this moment you will either fight with your fellow Elders day in and out while the NaÓma tear apart all Ebūda or you will take up your name and do as Anan tells you.

Or not! Every Guardian has a choice. They may awaken to their true selves and know yet continue on as they were living as análong; turning their back on our family and the fate of this world. You expect life to be an exact science; it's not. I never thought I'd have lived this long and here I stand."

"And if I choose to be a Guardian…" I faltered, unsure if I wanted to know the answer, "How will I know what to do?"

Lan began to shuffle towards the door. "Anan knows. Anan knows what you must do."

"Anan? Elder Anan? What does he have to do with this?"

"He knows the story of your past and your future. He's always known," Lan smiled. He had pried the door handle and was already half into the hallway, deftly guiding himself around Sā'úū still sitting guard outside. "But wait!" I called, gathering up my skirts to follow. "What will you do now?"

"I am the Guardian of Dreams; a gateway for dreams to pass into Ebūda from the realms outside its gates. But the path has become corrupted, allowing evil and malice to influence the análong for some years now. I will block the path; I will end the dreams. Go to Elder Anan. When the dreams of Ebūda have dried up and the streets are filled with talk of it, you will know I have gone on and it is your time," he said quietly.

I watched him go in silence to the end of the corridor before pausing and calling over his shoulder, "Who you are does not have to change *you* so don't be afraid. Have the courage to become yourself. Your story has already been written without you; will you live its pages out or shut this book without a glance?"

Sā'úū fixed his gaze curiously down the corridor but said nothing as my guest departed and I was too transfixed to say anything to him. "Impossible," I whispered to myself, an impossible story and yet…my birthdate was another secret that no-one in all Ebūda but Elder Anan, myself and one other análong knew. I'd never told anyone, and I was certain they hadn't either. My darna parents didn't know my birth date so they decided on 5 Tsāi'in as close enough. Many times, over my life I'd heard speculation that a Guardian had been born that night of the dropping moons because no análong had been registered at the Palace for the 16th of that month. No análong that is, except me.

Had my shanár parents known someday I'd be a Guardian? Had Anan known? I could never ask them, but nothing was stopping me from asking him. I set off to do just that.

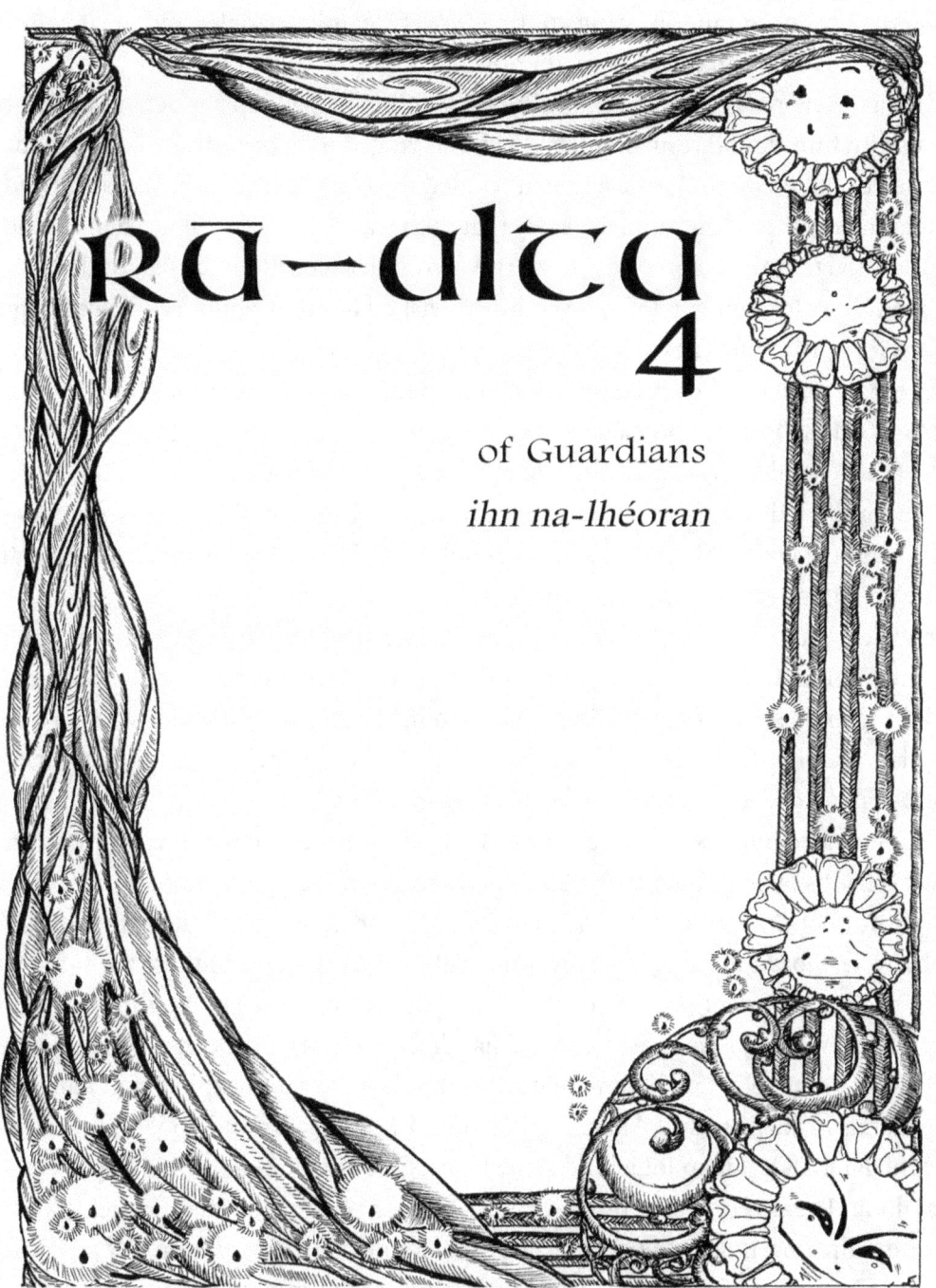

Rā-alta

4

of Guardians

ihn na-lhéoran

W HILE my quarters had high-ceilings and delicate, golden things, Elder Anan's chamber smelled of heaviness: spice, wood, the color of dark and age. Yet something sprightly diffused the main room in random sprigs of tiny flowers, gaudy spangles and great bags of incense sticks and it was this blend that so summed up Anan.

I looked away as he reached underneath the folds of his heavy outer robe and pulled out a long necklet hung with thin, round resin amulets. Each was ringed with beautiful gold braid but appeared to be scratched or dulled on the surface. Anan handed the chain to me and I was surprised at its satisfactory weight. Inspecting the amulets, I saw that each was a different color when turned a little in the light. And though unique and oddly beautiful, I couldn't see what they had to do with me.

As it seemed he wasn't going to tell me anything I wished to know voluntarily I went right into the matter: "How long have you known about me?"

"That's fine workmanship," Anan beamed unconcerned, and took them back into his own wrinkled hands. "Elder Rĭíd the Prophet himself carved these. You just don't see anything like this anymore," he mused, as all old análong do about the worth of things of the past.

I wasn't going to be distracted. "Have you known since I became Elder? Before? When I came here as a dhana to the Halls of Learning? What about *this*?" I waved my hands to indicate the Palace. "Was I made an Elder because I'm a… Guardian?"

Anan chuckled. "You give me too much credit; I have no idea why you were made Elder, but I agree with the nomination. As for how long, well, since you were born. Now sit down and let us do the natural thing in these sorts of situations." He held up a cup and motioned with his wizened eyes towards the fat steaming teapot left by his servant. I picked it up and obliged him, pouring myself a cup as well. Análong did not discuss anything serious under two cups.

Elder Anan wriggled into his seat to get comfortable and finished his tea. As I poured him a second, he warmed his hands by it and began his tale. "Now every análong knows the basic teachings of the world, the wisdom of the grandmothers," he winked. "And some know more than this, those like yourself who were chosen to learn the dangerous truths of Creation. But there are some truths even beyond this, such as the order of Guardians. And if you will hand me that lighting stick," (I dipped the long twig of timber into his hearth fire and handed it to him) "You can see that there is a secret here." And when Anan held it up behind one of the amulets the room exploded in amber light. I fell back on my hands in surprise and Anan laughed heartily. "Look around you!" he exclaimed and as I did, I saw the faint Dala-oúam longhand scrawl emerging on the walls of his chamber.

Reading along, I realized I had come across the order of the Guardians much like that which had been in my dream. But in the chronicle of the amulet, the Guardian of Hope came after the Guardians of Wisdom and Love. "But Lān told me the order, and Wisdom came after Hope so I don't understand. Who's wrong?" I asked.

"Your dream is a reflection of what you already know, and that is the same as every other análong. But we have all been purposely taught incorrectly. This has been so because the ancient prophets believed that in the future there would be wars against the Guardians and when the enemy came, they could be fooled into looking for the wrong Guardian. For above all, the Guardian of Hope must live. It is she who will bring caémba; she is the one who will save our kind."

His thin, papery hand shook as his eyes beamed at me. I nodded, fighting down the dread and excitement that came from knowing something would be unlocked within these words before me, the unveiling of something locked deep within myself that I might not wish to see. I took a breath and read from the wall:

"These are the words and the truth I, *dhinshū Rī-íd* leave to my descendant to guide you through the last days of Ebūda:

Of Guardians there are twelve; the seven Guardians of the air who are accountable for maintaining Ebūda and the five Guardians of the land, born among us who must live as lowly mortals until the time of their awakening. The seven of the air may take a physical form when they so choose but exist in the outer realms of dreams and wisdom, just beyond us and yet with us; in the space between the moons. The five of the land are conformed to the bodies of análong but are given a life much longer than ours, and these have been given charge to work together to attain immortality for the análong as is their agreement with the Creator.

As the Guardians came to our world in punishment from their previous life, each must also complete a task to redeem themselves. Each one of them is reborn into the order of the twelve in relation to their penalty, sometimes the attribute of it taking on physical form and sometimes only defining their task. Some will appear to us for only a moment to move time along on its path. Most will not know their own task, but rather must discover it and themselves as part of their mission.

I was told these things by A'nō, the Gatekeeper. Many years after our first meeting when he had given me our nation's language, the Dala, I came upon A'nō one night in the forest as I was hunting. He was standing at one of the Gates of Ebūda, listening to Time. I knew it was forbidden for an análong to hear such things, but I crept closer and closer until he heard my footsteps and closed the Gate shut. I was too afraid to run, and the Guardian walked up to me and challenged me, promising that if I defeated him, he would allow me to listen through the Gate. And though I was afraid of him, my curiosity won me over and I attacked him with all my might. We fought through the night and into the morning, pulling up tree roots and knocking over piles of stone left by the *t'landala*. When I thought I could go no longer, the Guardian fell to the ground and cried out. "You have defeated me, análong. Whatever spirit guards you is strong, for no análong has seen a Guardian of the air twice and lived. Come here to the Gate and hear." And when I stood at the door of the Gate, I heard all these words I leave to my descendent:

These are the tests of the last Guardian: Before their awakening, they must know their own name from their life before rebirth. They must discover their purpose of their own accord and in order to fulfill it, they must leave everything behind no matter the risk. But above all, the last Guardian born in Ebūda must live completely as an análong and show the best of their qualities against the worst of such. For that Guardian must prove to the Creator that the análong are fit to gain souls." I swallowed hard and paused, drawing a stinging liquid up into my throat.

Anan sat back and handed me another amulet which I took with trembling hands, afraid of what it might contain. *This is why*, I thought to myself, *This is why I don't want to be important. This is why I don't want to know Lān. It may not change who I am but it's changing who I know I am.* Disarmed, I did continue, but softly.

"If the Guardian of Hope is successful in her task, the twelfth Guardian will come who is called Úa'la. She will be reborn in the time of caémba to witness the judgement of the análong. And if it does not come, the Guardians will fade into the stars and stories of Creation with the other análong who have gone on to wait for their deliverance throughout the generations of Ebūda. Their dust will scatter all through Time.

Now, to the Guardian of Wisdom: should you be given these amulets I have inscribed my words on and read them aloud by a witness, you will have contracted yourself to this prophecy and the days which are coming. The white análong is coming." A thin, hard shudder made its way from my spine out through my hands and fingers so that they shook and dropped the pendant, immediately dousing the jewel-toned light and then flicking it on just as swiftly as Anan caught it mid-air and placed it back in my outstretched hand. I took a low breath and continued; my voice hoarse.

"For you, the trial is to find a caretaker, a *dl'ah'sha* for her until she has grown, for in your time there will be many waiting to kill her for their own reasons. She will be rejected in this world as is her penalty, so she will search for acceptance. But at all costs she must be kept alive until she knows who she is and what she must do. For the Guardian of Hope is the only remaining hope for the análong.

Āsa Naúaca Shanár Saō Rī-íd."

My fingers had turned a darker blue from clutching the amulet so tightly and then I dropped it in exhaustion onto the floor. I knew better than to question its validity; it was protected by old, old magic and as the entire necklace hit the old boards below me, fine dust rose lazily up over my clothing and filtered up into my nose.

"Nā – *tchihh!*"

"*Sdorii.*" Anan smiled as he blessed me. "Do you understand what you must do?"

"I… just…tsō. It can't be…how could it be?" I murmured to myself, not looking at him. "How can I understand something so great? Really…" I sighed heavily. "Is it *right* for me to believe it?"

"It's necessary that you do. The quest you will undertake now will lead you onto another path from that of an Elder. Not undertaking it will do so as well," Anan said very seriously. "That is the nature of choices: that which creates, destroys and that which destroys, creates. Declining to make the choice is still making a choice."

"And if I take this path, I'll create another but destroy the one I am on. Anan! I'm not old enough or wise enough to be a Guardian of Wisdom. And you've tricked me into binding myself to a prophecy! I don't even have a choice in that now!" *Not so wise to be tricked so easily, am I?* I thought.

The great words had faded from the walls and again Anan's chamber darkened from the bright washes of color to the dull flickering of a fading fire. "This was the proper way to tell you. I know the life of an Elder is too lonely for someone your age. The life of a Guardian will seem little better to you but in the end is so much more important than you could fathom and only another Guardian could truly explain it to you. That is why I called Lān. It was hard enough for you to grow up without your tribe and asama but it was also your fate as a Guardian," he explained.

"What do you mean, my fate? What else is there to know?" It seemed suddenly that my organs were pushing each other out of the way in an attempt to flee my body before any more bad news could befall me. The traitors.

Anan wiped his face with a gnarled, bejeweled hand. It was a motion of exhaustion, but he smiled regardless, albeit sadly. "It's time you were told and there's no easy way to do it."

He sat and gazed into the fire with a look of concentration. "The tribe you were born of was called the Tribe of the Damned in those days. They were known for their intelligence and their technology; they had devised the cleverest ways of collecting water and diverting it from the surrounding mountain tribes. They were so far beyond the rest of Ebūda, if you could have seen the inventions… it was unlike *anything* that had ever been seen. You carry that intelligence inside of you," he tapped a finger to his temple and smiled.

"But they came to use those inventions to further themselves at the expense of the mountain darna. The more they had, the more they longed for. Whatever it was: food, clothing, hadim, it was never enough. The Elders sent warnings to them to redistribute the water, but they ignored the messengers and refused to leave Cónpa mountains. The Elders became convinced that the tribe was a threat to Peridūr, that they were in danger of causing a famine. So, they made a plan to rid Ebūda of the tribe; to get rid of them. Do you understand?"

My hands, cold and clenched, seemed so large against my skirts. I understood; their deaths were planned. There were times in the Palace that I was aware, as one is aware of the sun outside a curtained window, that strong decisions were made beyond my awares; that a reality beyond what I could see was constantly being formed by those sworn to be honest with me. I nodded numbly.

"Three hundred and twelve years ago on sixteen Tsāi'in, I was ordered by the Elders along with four others to carry it out. We were to set the village on fire and contain it completely or risk public execution for disobeying the Elders. We were sworn to secrecy; no one could know that the Elders had allowed it, much less have ordered it. But I knew I had no heart to carry it out and I had only been chosen because I opposed the decision. If I died in the mission, it was no loss because then how could I tell if I were dead? So, when we reached Prādha village I claimed I'd forgotten the tinder box from my supplies and doubled back down the mountain to fetch it from our camp. The day and hour were so tightly planned there was no way we could stall. The other four left me to do what we'd been ordered to do.

I made sure by the time I started back up to the village the damage had been done. The screams had been silenced; there were only masses of black remains left. Only one of us four made it back down." Here he shuddered, squeezing his eyes shut for a moment as if this could rescue him from the memory. "It was the dead of night; the sky was pure gold from the flames. I heard a cry coming from the forest; terrifying but small. I wanted to run, but when I looked up, I saw the moons crowding each other in the sky, dropping low over the mountains with their curious eyes fixed on the forest, not on the flames. I felt strangely drawn to them and found myself going into the forest towards the spot their light descended on.

I pushed back layers of trees to come out to a smooth clearing where the moons' attention seemed to be focused. Imagine my surprise… there you were, lying in that clearing not one day old just wrapped in a blanket waiting to be found. You were the very last of your tribe; left behind to survive. Your blanket was embroidered with your tribe's true name: *Íshenii*.

Now, the moons only come down to see the birth of Guardians, so I knew from that moment someday you would awaken and know your true self. At the time I lived in the temple at Grālin, no place for a dhana. So, I took you with me to the Harūd mountains, to the darna village there at Nandhacot. I put you in the crook of a tree and I waited until someone came by and found you. When I was certain you would be cared for, I crept back down the mountain and was picked up inside the border of Adanandū by the Palace Guards. When they questioned why I hadn't come back with the others I said I'd gotten lost on the mountain. Whether they believed me or not didn't matter; they could see I was rattled enough not to speak and sent me back to the temple.

The other remaining assassin vouched for me and I was out of favour with the Elders for a time but when the next appointing came up my name was put in the chalice much like yours with no one to claim responsibility. So, you see, though I wasn't young like you when I became an Elder, I still understand what it's like to have no choice but to come here."

"You didn't do it though," I said to comfort myself more than to defend him. "I didn't stop it," he pointed out. "A hero by default is hardly a hero. I ran away so the only choice I had left to make was to not choose. It was still a choice."

I looked away; afraid I would cry. Elder Anan had looked after me when I came to the Halls of Learning those years ago before I even became an Elder; he had been a father to me. I didn't want that picture of him in my mind to change. Why did it all have to change?

"My parents didn't want me to come here when I was a dhana," I began.

Anan held up his hand to stop me. "I sent the summons, it was me. As I said, I knew who you were from the day you were born, and I knew that if you were left up in those mountains you'd never come to awaken. That couldn't be risked, Rā-alta. Who we are is something we must all accept with all the joys and sorrows and privileges and risks that come along the way. You are too important to this world." He took both my hands in his. "Too important to me. The only dhana I ever had."

"Did you give me my name?" I asked, feeling it was time I knew about that too. Unlike any other análong who would take their second name when they left their parents to go out into the world as an adult, I was renamed when I entered the Halls of Learning as if I'd never been that dhana called Cicūrī by darna up in the mountains. I hadn't disliked my new name exactly, but it felt strange in my ears, strange to think I was surrounded by other students who only knew me as Rā-alta. I wondered sometimes what that she-dog named Cicūrī had done that she must disappear behind this new little stranger.

"The marks on your face, you've always wondered about those," he said, ignoring my question but raising my curiosity. I tilted my head to listen; it was true the star-shaped scars had marked me out somewhat in my youth. "It was where the moonlight touched you the night you were born; the mark of a Guardian. Rā-alta; heir of the stars."

"From *rē'all:* star," I murmured. "Perhaps you were trying to get me used to thinking of myself that way… a shanár name for a shanár dhana."

"I didn't know you would end up here anymore than I knew *I* would, but," He shrugged, "It is always by sorrow that the heroes of Ebūda are made." He bent over stiffly and picked up the fallen amulets and twisted them back over his head, dropping them safely underneath the folds of his robe.

I wanted to be angry and in some distant way I was; angry that I'd been lied to, angry that my darna name had been erased so early in my life, angry that I'd been held all my life to análong standards only to find out I wasn't even an análong. I wanted to be angrier, but there was so much to swallow, instead of running away from Anan I only wanted him to make it all better as he'd always done since my life began in Bri'ën back all those years ago when I came here to begin as a student.

With a defeated sigh, I asked for Anan's earnest advice on how to proceed, my head buried in my hands, for this may be the last moment my life belonged to me as I chose to accept the truth of my identity…but nothing more. Tsōl, nothing more just yet.

"You must find someone trustworthy; whom you would trust with more than your life to take care of the Guardian of Hope and raise her as an análong far away from Bri'ën until she has passed her trials so that she has a chance of escaping the NaÓma. Be careful that no-one finds out who you are too, for Guardians have always hidden among us." Anan said faintly as his eyes glazed over in the way they did when he received one of his premonitions. "And be careful, Rā-alta, be careful that the one you trust will raise her as their own dhana so she may pass her trials genuinely, for the heavens always know deception before we even think it. Find her a *dl'ah'sha.*"

I nodded silently but wondered aloud, "How did you even get the necklace, Anan?"

He grinned and his wrinkles settled into a joyful pattern about his eyes. "I, of course, am the descendent of Rï'íd."

Rā–alta
5

Sā'úū

As I trudged back to my chambers to stay the night, a thousand thoughts coursed through my mind beginning with: *Couldn't the last Guardian stay with us in the Palace?* There wasn't a safer place in all Ebūda and never had been. But even I knew the beautiful city we called our home had numbered days, for every evening as I gazed out over the veranda, I could see the once- bright rooftops fading and could smell the stale air devoid of the great crackling feasts and festivals so commonplace even two years ago. I had been taught all my life that all things end, and *must* end, for all things to begin. And besides, who would be her dl'ah'sha? Certainly not me. I was bound to the Palace as an Elder and I must remain one as a Guardian. And I…I had my own faults.

For many months now, I'd asked for action to be taken and now I was given not only a direction but a means hand-delivered to me to take that action myself. Would my path be altered severely or simply just long enough? And would the same happen to me as would Lān? While it was most certainly true I would never see him again, was it also true Lān was now sentenced to die? He'd said it wasn't an *exact* science. And when I found the dl'ah'sha for the new Guardian, would I have that same sentence as he said? Would it be immediate? If I were a Guardian (and I had to let myself think it if I were ever going to be ready to accept this quest), it meant my life in Ebūda was a punishment from a life before, as it was for every Guardian, from their lives before amongst the stars. And then I thought perhaps I was no better than the dhana I grew up with who made fun of the curses of the Guardians, the heroes put over our world to protect it; magical but pitiful creatures reborn to Ebūda in punishment to serve out their life sentences from a far-off world we weren't even sure was out there. We thought of them as irrelevant, not noble. Now I was the victim of my own young tongue and I wondered with an awed terror what my own punishment was for.

But more importantly, it also meant I was one of twelve; that all the stories I'd learned as a student had really been of myself and my true family all this time. I wanted to laugh and cry and go find those eleven others and tell everyone in Ebūda I had a real family out there waiting to be found; that I had always felt false amongst everyone and now for the first time I felt achingly real! For all throughout my youth as I watched the others play, I wondered if I had siblings in that life before; if somehow they had passed into that place the old ones go before us without my even knowing.

In a way I could feel a tiny vindication that I didn't belong. I'd carried that secret inside for three hundred and twelve years, knowing in my heart I was the only one left from the tribe blamed for its own demise. I was surrounded by those who said of us that we had eaten until we starved to death; that we had stolen until we had nothing left. Somehow, knowing the terrible truth that someone else had decided my tribe's fate was a strange relief. I didn't think that they had, but it was still a weight lifted from me that I now knew absolutely that my parents hadn't chosen to leave me alone in the world. Now this disconnection was the truth of others as well; of other Guardians out there like Lān who may have grown up much the same; taking that burden from me alone.

If I were to take my own advice, I'd stop wondering about it and arguing with myself and do something about it. *Shē'a*, do! I would do what I had been born to do. Guardian or not, I should at least strive to be who I'd claimed to be to all of Ebūda: one of compassion. And action.

What a gift and a curse.

And after I'd eaten lightly in solitude, I laid under the embroidered coverlets on my bed and tossed. The more I pondered the choice, the more I appreciated that Lān had done the same long before me. If he had listened to his head and not his heart, I'd have never been born. I wondered about this Guardian of Hope, this new *sister*, and if I had the power to stop her birth if I simply went about my business as an Elder and ignored her not-yet-here presence. But isn't that what Lān must have wondered of me? Did he know how long it would be before my coming, before his end?

Ra-alta, didn't you just decide to do what you've said?

And as I thought of this my feelings suddenly turned downwards into a shallow resentment. Why did I have to be the one to decide? Anan was right, an Elder was completely removed from society; a gilded and imprisoned figure of state. But a Guardian's life was over before it began.

Sitting up, I slouched my head onto my fist and sighed, catching a glimpse of Sā-úū settling down outside the doorway for his night watch. I gazed without thinking, blushing involuntarily as the lines of relationships threaded out before me and whispered of choices already made, wanting to be made, and needing to be made.

Not for the first time I wondered why others couldn't understand. There were so many divisions between us all. Why was it so strange for me to find a g'éalach attractive? Why was I the only one who felt natural about it? I knew what love looked like between the darna I grew up with, those winged cousins of the g'éalach; but I had no reference for shanár love. I'd never felt my shanár parents' hands lifting me up or combing my ears before bed, but I did recall my darna parents' big soft paws covering my cheeks as they checked my temperature and the silky feathers of their wings covering me to sleep. I remembered them flying around the home-tree, chasing each other to tease; nuzzling each others' necks to love. All the faces around me looked the same; *I* was the different one. I suppose the shanár seemed foreign to me in that way.

And perhaps it was because as a dhana I was surrounded by those who looked like each other and walked on all fours and flew while I walked on two feet and could no more fly than turn color that I already knew the secret: we were all slaves to whatever type of love our hearts became attached to.

Before I could allow myself any further ruminating, I pulled on a rich red and gold robe reserved for the most solemn of ceremonies and crossed the room. In one day I'd been handed so many answers to questions I'd asked all my life and instead of being satisfied, I was restless. Now the most important answer I needed was to a question I had no words to ask.

Quietly I opened the door. "Will you come Sā-úū? I think it's time for a walk," I mentioned softly.

He bowed his head quickly and rose. "I will let the Guard know to open the downstairs gates," he said.

"Tsō, not down to the gardens," I interrupted, gathering my shawl around me. "Let's go up to the east veranda."

Sā-úū 's face dropped, embarrassed. "Āsa it is...it wouldn't be *common* to join you so late..." he stuttered.

Oh Rā-alta do you know what you're doing?

"You're right," I agreed, knowing it would be seen as improper. "It wouldn't be common at all...but I think it would be *right*." His looked perplexed but tentatively began to follow me through the long, winding halls upward to the highest floor of the Palace which opened out onto the east veranda. I pulled my skirts close against me with fingers dripping in the ancient jewels of Elders before me, carefully moving over to give Sā-úū room to walk down the hall without brushing up against me. In recent months I'd made it a point to walk with Sā-úū at least once a week through the Hidden Gardens frequented by the Palace servants on their days off, not admitting even to myself entirely why I'd made such a point to it.

But if I was honest I'd admit that normally I changed into an azure-lined robe, soft and golden on the outside not for the season but so that I'd be free to move closer without the chance of the forbidden red of the formal robes repelling him. This evening however, I wore what I felt I looked best in, and when we'd crossed silently through the empty Whispering Tunnels, I dared comment, "*Ha*- Sā-úū, I've known you a hundred years now and I've never asked you how exactly you came to the Palace. You know very well it's considered... *unusual* for you to be my attendant."

"It was not a choice, āsa " he replied immediately without breaking his stride.

I ducked my head to sympathise. "Had your family sold you to work?"

"Tsō, they wished me to do as I wanted. But I am not...you understand," he nodded. He was born into a low class where opportunity outside of service was very scarce indeed and escape was nearly impossible. "So, there are things of course I could never do even if I wanted; things I could never have." I nodded again and he continued.

"You and I are close in age. I was born in the north too and came here as a dhana to work. I saw you once when you were a student out with another dhana from the Palace school. She was speckled all over, I remember. Well, and I used to pull a cart for a rich shanár just over in the Quarter. You were both laughing; you were eating something sticky and it was all over your purple robes..." His face grew red and he admitted, "I probably wasn't doing as much work as I should have been."

I smiled sweetly at the memory of that day seen from my own eyes and he continued. "When I was a little older, I remembered that day and I looked for you when I'd come round that place for work. Sometimes we did cross paths in the market but you wouldn't have noticed me. And then you came here and I came as well, and I've been here ever since on contract. Elder Anan has always looked after me. He told me once that you'd be a great lady some day."

I looked away as we'd come to the end of the tunnel, passing the corridor leading off into Elder Corin's game room where several Elders and teachers sat engaged in their nightly game of *úitstics*. I could hear the echoes of the smooth tiles clinking together happily along the hall's arched ceiling. We passed then through the Room of Mirrors, its tiny glass fragments reflecting back fractured portraits of the gold and scarlet gilding on my skirts and the cerulean wisps of Sā-úū 's heavy headdress.

Rā-alta, slow down....

I knew what the contract involved. Attendants were servants or slaves with permission to sell themselves for blocks of time to the Palace, body and soul. For most, their service equaled room and board but for some who had been exceptional in their previous post could be given a sum of nendē to purchase things in the city to send back to their families. Nothing but death could release them from the contract so most came from terrible places and could be counted on for complete loyalty as there was little or nothing they wanted to go back to. Perhaps I shouldn't have asked any more, and yet, I needed to know that something I wasn't even sure of.

Be careful Rā-alta, do you want to know the answer?

The stairs up to the roof were very tricky and Sā-úū kept as close as he could without touching in case I should fall in my ridiculous costume. Inexplicably, as if I hadn't seen him every day of my life for the past hundred years, I found myself turning away shyly so he could not see those star-shaped scars around my eye and nose I felt burning into my skin with embarrassment. I noticed for what seemed the first time how much taller I stood over him, how crooked my shoulders slumped, how I felt decidedly preoccupied with the ungainly shape of my fingers. Why hadn't I worn my silver robe? Didn't I look better in that? And just as suddenly I scolded myself for being so concerned.

We stood gazing at the elaborate green, blue and gold painted cornice above us framing the veranda. The moon's skirts were pulled back to reveal the bruised evening-sky and as we stood on the dormered east side of the palace overlooking its back, listening to the whir of the na'bōman faintly catching the thickening evening air below us. We both shivered, then looked away in embarrassment.

When we spoke, our voices broke into tiny bits in the frost, making the words seem to suspend in that dry cold which comes at the end of a winter without snow.

"Do you think…?"

"You look …"

We both stopped and looked away, each regrouping to try again. "You first, of course āsa," Sā-úū said.

"Tsō, you. I insist," I breathed.

His eyes shone bright, but he didn't finish his thought. "There's talk amongst the upper servants about what's going on in the north. Will the Elders be able to protect the Palace when they reach us?"

"Oh Sā-úū, Sā-úū, I just don't know," I murmured honestly.

I looked down over the city, counting the dim lights of the fires of those working into the night and those too lazy to put them out. Sā-úū was right, I'd asked him to do something awkward, something that could get us into great trouble, even separate us if someone found out. But it was me who'd invited, and I was now ever more aware that time was winding down. Turning my eyes back on him, I carefully arranged my skirts around me down to sit on the stair and motioned for him to come sit near me. Suddenly the business of everything in this world seemed flat beneath the heaviness of Guardians and quests and living and dying. Forbidden red was the emblem of blood and holiness; yet how could we lowly creatures reduce these things of the universe to mere color? Though I would never abandon my world, if I were a Guardian I must not allow myself to be distracted by inconsequential things.

I returned to my original question.

"What made you sign the contract though?"

Sā-úū suddenly stood and turned his back on me in frustration and I could only sit in surprised silence as he began to pace back and forth. I'd never seen him agitated before and an unbidden knot of fear tightened across my stomach, making me feel even colder in the night air. "Sā-úū, what's wrong?" I managed to whisper, fearing I'd done the wrong thing by coming up here, asking him to come nearer than what was allowed. Maybe I felt separate from such things now but nobody else around me did. Though it felt as if I'd been given some sort of sight beyond the known world, nothing in that same world had actually *changed*.

"I don't know how to make you *understand*, āsa."

I reached out my hand, unsure of what I meant to do but pulled it back quickly when he turned back around to face me. "*Try*," I encouraged.

Taking a breath, he sat down a few feet away, looking out over the railing to the night sky. "The day they came to bring you to the Palace, I was there by the carriage outside your hut. I heard the shouts and I left my cart behind in the alley. A dhana ran after carriage crying and I've always wondered… was she yours?"

I closed my eyes for a moment. This wasn't at all how I thought the conversation would turn, but if I'd learned anything that day it was that one never knew what was coming. "Tsō, she wasn't mine. I was her dl'ah'sha; I lived with the family and I cared for her. After that day I wasn't allowed to see her again. Any of them."

Sā-úū nodded. "I heard you crying when they forced you into the carriage. And I… I followed because…it may sound silly, but I didn't want you to ever cry again. All these years I wanted to make sure nothing ever made you cry again. And I've failed, you see. Over and over."

Just like that, tears came unbidden to my eyes and I blinked hard to keep them back. All those years, all those tears. I thought I'd been utterly alone looking down from my window high in the Palace. And now to know I'd never been alone after all… He looked down and studied his own feet, murmuring, "I wanted to…so badly."

"And I wanted you to," I heard myself saying before I even knew what I was talking about.

What have you just done Ra-alta?

So I quickly moved on, cleared my throat and asked, "But you said there wasn't a choice. What did you mean?"

He looked away sharply as if he'd been caught at something. "Tsō, not for me, tsōl. I mean, it didn't need to be. Some análong see service as a punishment for our class because we can never own property. The only home we have is our master's; the only things we own are cast offs. But I say as long as the thing you most desire is near you, it's a happy life even if you can never…well, it's how you look at your choices. Is that what you were asking āsa?"

Rā-alta, don't…don't you know you can never have this?

But it was the end of the world after all, and I was down to the thing I had to know. I wondered, what good were the rules and laws if they forbid the best intentions of our hearts? Weren't they supposed to protect the very best of what we could be and do? Now it seemed they were nothing but limits I'd outgrown. The question finally became clear in my heart.

"And is it a happy life Sā-úū? Are *you* happy?" I leaned over to whisper, my heart thudding in my ears.

He looked up finally to me and his face softened as he whispered in return, "Near you, always."

The wind continued to whisper on the veranda, telling the city of all its secrets, all its lost dreams. Confident our privacy was still ours, we returned in silence to my chambers and said goodnight, with my attendant taking his place outside the heavy blue door. I changed into my nightdress, the only time of the day I was able to dress myself in privacy and I lay down to think. Now that I had the answer to a question it had taken me years to figure out how to ask, I knew with a strange certainty that this would be my last night as an Elder. In the morning I would wake as a Guardian. And as this certainty washed over me, my hands flew to my chest as if they could catch my beating heart. Somehow, I didn't hear the sobs as they escaped me.

But the gentle knock at the door told me someone did, and when I opened the door to him, he said sincerely, "I don't know what to do, but I'm here." And I opened the door wider, no longer afraid he would be taken away from me. For wasn't I a Guardian?

Later, in the small hours of the morning, I gazed over the foot of the bed at the glowing embers in the fire grate. It bothered me that before Sā-úū mentioned her, I hadn't thought of the dhana in a very long time. It had been my first and only job outside of school before coming to the Palace and

I was badly suited for it. A dl'ah'sha had complete charge of the education of only the brightest of análong. Usually the dhana was sent to live with their ah'sha near a temple to learn to read and write but some families paid for the dl'ah'sha to live with them and this was the situation I found myself in. But I was terrible at it. It was the first time in my life I'd lived in a shanár family and in my heart, I felt myself a darna. I could teach the dhana to read but a dl'ah'sha was also responsible for teaching the dhana to *live*, and the everyday details of living in the same space with análong of my own kind escaped me. And while dhana will overlook a great deal, I knew I should have done better.

In those hundred years I could have looked for her. I didn't. I'd committed the worst of sins; I'd forgotten. This was how I knew that Elder or not, I would have to find someone else for the Guardian of Hope.

Lighting a candle, I sat by the window and sorted through every análong I had ever known but found myself returning over and over to my dearest friend from my days in the Halls of Learning. She was a southern shanár living in the very southernmost province of Dridū along Sé Elamangúō. She'd been barred from entry into the Halls of Learning three times by Elder Anan himself because of a vision he'd had that she would eventually lose her innocence and walk away from this secluded life of sāama and porāma we led in the Palace, becoming a threat to that way of life. I didn't learn of this until after I became an Elder and was shocked then that somehow she managed to be admitted regardless. Somehow, I felt a new understanding towards her...

When I met her I was dazzled by the multitude of dark freckles covering her light blue skin, so vast they seemed to almost join together. I wasn't the only one who noticed; she was teased mercilessly by the others for them. Her ears were short and stuck right up at an angle unlike the rest of us with ours smoothed back with ribbons. I thought they made her look like nothing but mischief that I so wanted her to befriend me. I don't think it would have ever happened if the others hadn't tripped her on the stairs and I, not brave in the least, found myself screaming at them to leave her alone. I'm not sure who was more stunned but when I helped her up she followed me and eventually we were put to room together until we finished school.

F'ala...

How could she even be described? Fierce, clever, the closest thing to a sister I knew. My best friend. The one who left me behind, promised to return, and never came back. And before Anan had left me earlier in the day he'd said something curious about choosing the new Guardian's dl'ah'sha. He'd said that I must not listen to what others might fear, but to what I knew. What I knew was that from one outcast to another, it seemed our lives were destined to intertwine once more.

"F'ala," I said aloud in the dark. "I could have found you... I wanted to. But I never even tried because *you* broke your promise." And now I knew that I had to find her, because as certain as I was that my heart belonged to Sā-úū and my past as a Guardian was true, so I also knew without doubt that F'ala was the only one in all Ebūda who could care for the Guardian of Hope. F'ala was a good many things, but what she had was the only thing truly required of a dl'ah'sha: the purest of hearts.

F'ala? Please be out there... please. Don't you know the world needs you?

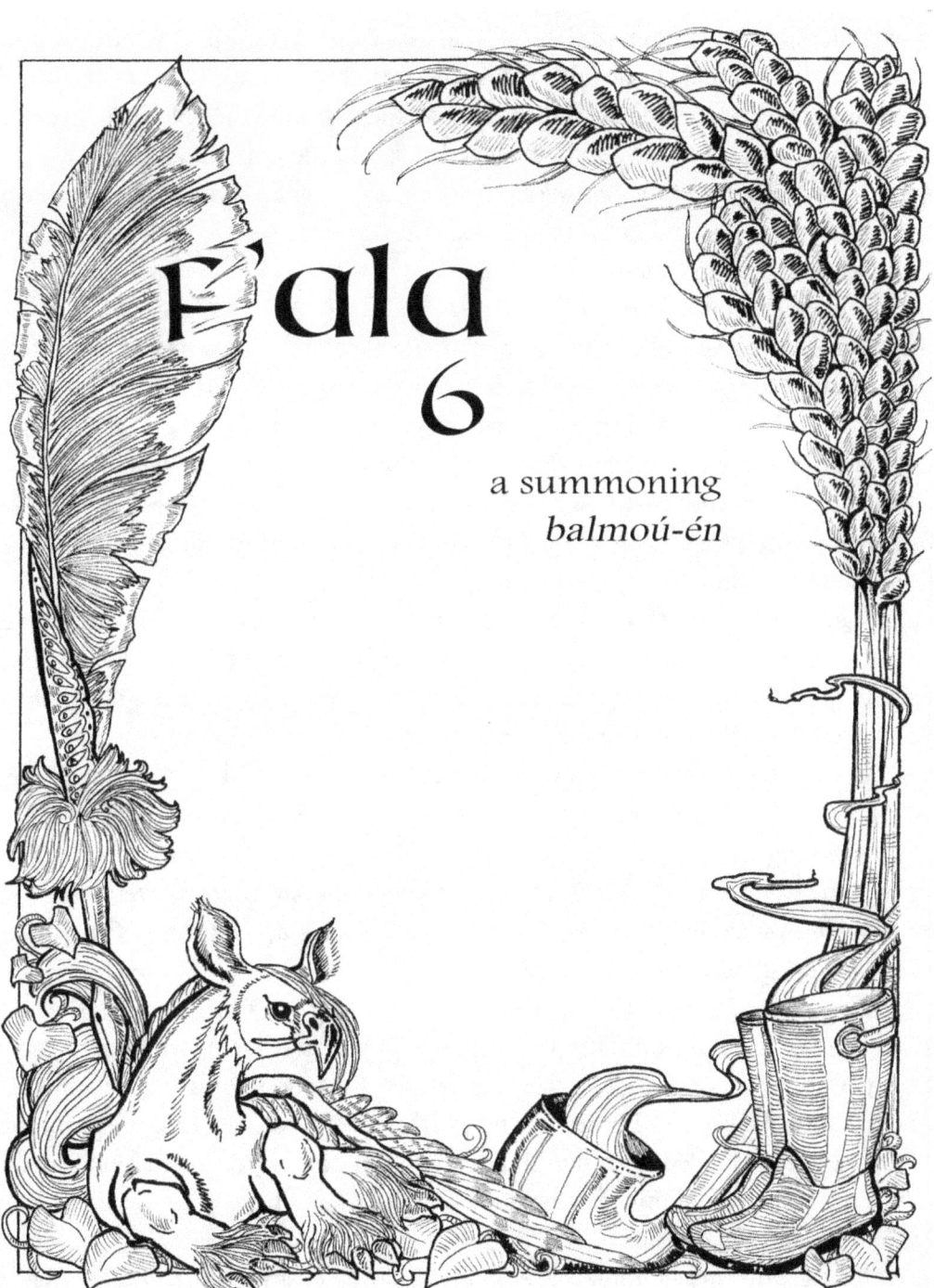

F'ala

6

a summoning
balmoú-én

"S *DORĪĪ*: blessings in the name of Elder Rā-alta, the Wise and Gentle!"
   Early…it is much too early on a day off to be blessed for anything.

I rolled over on the bed and realized the last time I'd seen the yellow jug by the hearth it had been full. The knocking that wrenched me out of oblivion started up again, its beat piercing me from ear to ear. "Must stop that wretched noise," I hissed aloud and regretted the volume of my own voice.

My legs weren't especially steady, but I managed to get to the door. Looking down through the small spyhole of my most *heavy and unwelcoming* door I saw a g'ealach messenger with a mishmash of ribbons and charms tied round his neck and spied the elaborate scroll-case slung tightly across his back with my name carved in Dala-oúam.

Great, he's from the bloody Palace.

The thing about the Palace, besides being palatial, was that its inhabitants had absolutely no common respect for anyone else's schedules. Sending out a messenger to my hut in the deepest south of the southern prefecture meant only a summons that expected me to drop everything and come immediately to Bri'én. I'd spent the last three days camping out in the far fields to cut down lāāca stalks. It was exhausting work that had to be done not once but three times a year and today my ambitions only included sleep, sleep, a break to sleep, a short nap, and possibly some tea. Besides that, I had more than a slight aversion to going into the city.

It was also thanks to those twits in the Palace and their unending laws that anyone even dared step foot on my land. Once they realized the river flows through the west of my fields they gave everyone "walker's rights" to come walking right in to use that water. And I've made it quite clear that's as far as they go! But messengers go wherever they please.

I dropped down to my knees out of sight behind the door and called out, "I bought one last week so get lost!" There was no reply. The silence ensued long enough that I straightened my legs to rise when a faint scratching sent me right back down to a crouch. From the far window in my hut I could see the fellow jump against the storehouse door and stand, his paws spread evenly across its frame, calling out to my unconcerned pantry while I watched from inside. "But this is an official message from the Palace! I must deliver it to Ta-F'ala!!"

"Wrong address," I yelled, thinking only that his claws would scuff my newly-washed door.

The voice came back closer, sounding very official. "The Ta's sister swore to me this is the right hut! I have travelled across Adanandū and consulted with the folk of Pōcarū. You will not fool me!"

"Don't be silly, not everyone in Pōcarū is trustworthy. Surely you've heard the grandmothers tell not to trust just anyone," I called over my shoulder, idly spinning my bracelets as I waited him out.

There was a pause that could only be described as irritable and I knew he was considering. Then, "There are no other huts *on this side of Pōcarū!*"

"Well then it's a shame I'm not home." I sunk onto a sitting cushion by the hearth, determined to wait him out.

"I shall not leave! I am bound to deliver this message by order of Elder Rā-alta! I am her personal attendant!"

I hauled myself up from the soft cushion with a heavy groan. "Well I'm not bedding anyone's personal attendant for the night so give me it already and you can be right on your way." Opening the door quickly, I stepped back with a snap as the messenger came crashing down onto my floor, his silver bells rolling across the neatly swept sod. Helping him back onto all fours, I pried the scroll case out of its harness and opened the all-important message. He scrambled up onto his hind legs and covered his eyes respectfully with his paws.

"You are summoned to Bri'ën." he stated matter-of-factly. I rolled up the scroll and whacked him across the head with it, and then regretted it just a little. But not much, as it made the most satisfying *thrrrrrrrrrrrrrip*. Glancing at the message I saw that my presence was requested immediately. Well, I called it.

"Message delivered. *Dhá*." The messenger nodded gravely in agreement but didn't move. "By law you must come back with *me* or I must send the Palace Guard for *you*," he politely informed me.

I rolled the scroll up and thwacked him again. *Thrrrrrrrrrrrrrrrip*. "And if I don't go with you, are you going to run back, get the Guard and send them back for me? It's a six-week trip to Bri'ën one way in a cart with no stops! By then I could be dead or in hiding!" I scowled at him, realizing there was no way out of it. "You don't need to remind me; I do know the law, inconvenient as it always manages to be."

It was the first harvest; the lāāca needed to be burned off, cut, stacked, drained, processed and separated. It was a tremendous job for my sister and I and there was too much I'd rather be doing, too much I needed to be doing here than to walk for weeks for an hour or two of awkwardness in front of an Elder answering for something I wasn't even aware I'd done. An Elder, it happened, I'd spent most of my youth with.

Rā -alta...

"If I'm gone, I could lose my entire harvest," I said scornfully. The messenger made no remark. "I haven't broken any laws," I stated for his benefit as I quickly packed a bag with absolutely nothing practical. He sat down to wait, murmuring, "Then you have nothing to worry about besides being late." He fixed me with a stare that looked like concern for my mental state with a side of sarcasm.

Get yourself together F'ala, it's not like you've never seen her before.

I sighed and removed the fruit bowl, hammer and inkpot from the pack to be replaced with clothes and such things one might actually need for a journey on foot. Locking the door and taking a quick glance back over my garden, I lit my pipe and set off grimly beside the messenger; everything slung tightly across my back with a roll of nendē wedged in a little packet at the bottom of my left boot. My toes gave a little cry at the thought of being cramped up and already I couldn't wait to make camp and let them go free.

We started off around the east of Sé Elemangúō just out of sight of the village busybodies doing their weekly laundry and the old gē on the other side bathing. The dried-up waterfall where my sister made her home was our first stop. I rarely went out to my sister's when Ādō saw us in the distance she came running to see what was wrong. She stopped cold when she saw the messenger and her eyes became huge. "What have you…?"

"Done? Nothing, *dhindhē*," I thanked her. "I've just got to go into the city for some things. I'll be back as soon as I can."

"But the harvest, I-"

"You can't do it alone. Try to get Madhal or someone from the village to help but if you can't then just… just make sure the onandals are fed," I instructed.

Ādō looked doubtful. "But I don't know how to talk to them. They'll only listen to you."

"You don't need to, just leave their straw in the trough under the *inlen* trees. I've told them before if I ever have to leave, you're next in charge." I turned to go but she flung herself at me and awkwardly hugged me around the middle. "Don't be too long," she managed.

Rolling my eyes, I gave her a quick squeeze back and pulled her arms off, motioning to the messenger to follow. As it was, the detour had cost us half a day and I wanted to get back as soon as possible. Though I'd never been in trouble with the law, after all these years there couldn't be any good reason I was being summoned back to the holy city. Why would she call me back now? And how was I going to face her after I'd broken my promise?

I didn't mean to make you cry…

But more importantly, how was I going to pretend it didn't matter; that *she* didn't matter? That I was the same análong who left all those years ago? Somehow, I felt I was shouting so loud in my thoughts I could be overheard, so at the crossing into the evergreen forest, I settled into a quick walk just ahead of the messenger. As I watched the last bits of smoke curl around my fingers, I put out the pipe, deciding I might as well begin quitting now. After all, a lecture from the Elder on what was proper for a lady to do would be both humiliating and a painful echo of the past I'd fought long to outrun. In fact, it would be dancing on an unclosed circle, and I wasn't one to admit out loud that I had any. And how did I know I wasn't going to be put in prison? There aren't any creature comforts in dungeons, that's well known.

I slipped my pipe into the knot of my headscarf. Smoking was a gē's pastime anyway; one I overheard a good deal of opinion on through the walls of my shop in the village. Too many análong thought I was not only too coarse for a she-dog and unsuited for marriage but also a heretic, a recluse and otherwise unintentionally offensive to their way of life. So far, I hadn't managed to spread this the entire way to Peridūr but I seemed to be working on it at a steady crawl. And if it hadn't been for the actual current troubles in the north, I might have liked to spend a holiday after this excursion, taking some time to drop in on the old gē of the mountain tribes in their gaudy, smoky rooms sipping *am-as* and smoking the long, curled pipes curled around tree-limbs like lazy snakes.

As it were, the first two weeks went slowly and silently through the Náasaa Forest up to Mdalē, with the only spoken words between the messenger and I being the nightly agreement of where to sleep (I in the tree branches and he at the roots). He found wild dūūcerfrūt and berries to chew on while I cooked mine over a fire in the small copper pot I had packed in my sack. The nights had become very dark now that many of the softly glowing *tacashe'l* flowers had dried up into little hard knots upon the ground, the early evidence of drought hung everywhere. But still we both found enough to manage comfortably on until we came upon a town or village.

Outside the Laughing Dog Tavern in Daú Dsindhar I stopped, bending down to wedge my fingers between the thick wraps around my feet to ease the blisters working their way up and down under my boots. We had walked now for the better part of five weeks, making our way across the wide grainy fields of western Adanandū tinged a dry ochre and through the thick, dark forests interspersed before coming to Madharit where we stopped and found the shopkeep to buy provisions from. I insisted we stay only as long as it took to gather up enough to last us another week because talk started up immediately among the eavesdropping villagers over my traveling with a Palace messenger.

A few days after leaving Madharit the messenger and I came upon low slopes where the ancient bashō trees and their soft white floss and the thin, canopied inlen trees stood guard to the proud swell of land on which sat the holy city: Bri'ën.

Such a long, long time.

Finally the whirring white blades of the na'bōmen crested lazily in the distance. The slopes were steeped in a low purple tint; it was too late to finish the journey so I built a fire easily from brush but sent the messenger out to collect wood to feed the flames. As soon as he was out of sight I allowed my mind to finally wander to what lay ahead of me.

Would anyone recognize my face anymore? Perhaps I should have gone with my first instinct and just refused to come. Goodness knew I hated the trips to the lower centerlands I took every year to gather bashō floss and buy spices.

Tsō, even I could admit now that refusing to come would have been much worse. A scene at my hut door was even less appealing if the Palace Guard showed up to collect me. There were still things I didn't yet have a reputation for and flagrant law-breaking was one I'd rather keep out of the mouths of the village gossips when they recounted my litany of wrongs around the wall during their midday gossip. I aspired to wear anonymity like a cloak whether anyone cooperated with me or not. One had to wonder how I even kept up such a fascination for the locals when I certainly didn't have the time to go on such colorful adventures I heard I was going on!

I suppose on that count it was true there were things about me no-one knew of here; that one could say I was the daughter of *if* or *someday*. Despite my outward nonchalance, inside I wanted to always be ready for the someday and prepared for the if, even if I didn't know what that could be. The problem was that when *if* turned into *when* (and who could ever know the moment it did?), I missed it entirely because I was too busy getting ready. And then, everything was over as if in a breath, as if I were looking so hard to grow up I opened up my eyes to find myself long grown. Maybe it was a natural part of being an análong I'd never been told about in all that schooling. Or perhaps it was just my own defect. But sometimes I thought that more likely it was only that my innocence was gone and there was no more place for someone like me in that magical realm of someday much more suited for those who hadn't lost their class. Someone had to be best and someone had to be last. I had already been best.

I thought about how different my upbringing must have been from the messenger's for me to have ended up as a miserable village Ta- and he to have come out the happy servant to an Elder. For in our own ways, we were just as bound from freedom in our respective corners of Ebūda.

But as for me, I was born in the village of Orambūsū, just east of Pōcarū. My parents were very faithful análong who spent a good deal of time at the local temple petitioning for a dhana. They promised Mī'á the Creator that if they could have this wish, they would take the dhana to Brī'én to be schooled in the Halls of Learning, to know the forbidden knowledge of sāama and porāma and the like and rise to a class well above them. They hoped for a he-dog who would have a life in the temple.

And after many years, they were given their wish; only, they had me. Nonetheless, after I had finished my studies in the village with the other dhana, my *a'ma* took me on the long ride by cart to Brī'én as she had wished, and haggled with the Elders to test me. But we were sent away and she was told that "*Students are chosen by the Elders, not brought to them.*"

She persisted. As I'd already learned all I could from the village teacher, she took me to the Ta- of Pōcarū (who refused to teach me anything further as my parents were below his class) and then to any learned análong she could find in the surrounding villages until she thought I was ready to prove worthy to the Elders to study at Brī'én. Again, they sent us home. They said it was not their choice; that one of the Elders had personally rejected me and there was no way around this. The Elders' vote must be absolute. I was simply outvoted.

It seemed my a'ér agreed with the decision, saying that after all, Mī'á had given me to them and A'ma should have known better than to bother the Elders over it. Fate had decided me, and we should all be content by it.

Yet, on the fourth try I was admitted to the Halls of Learning to study. I didn't know how I got there and I didn't ask; it seemed enough to simply exist happily surrounded by all the knowledge

of the seen and unseen world. And though I often wondered if I should be there, I was given the purple robes and quill of a student and a little cell to sleep in near the Circle Garden and its fanciful, crawling plants and sculptures. A'ma came to see me on holidays and A'da sent me letters written through the Ta- of Pōcarū.

And soon enough I met a friend who also came to Bri'én against her own odds. Rā-alta, my eventual roommate, was the other misfit because of her pureness. Where I lacked focus, she excelled in answers. Where I surpassed in awkwardness, Rā-alta sailed through calmly. The only thing I seemed to be sure of as I got older was to defend her (so often with my fists) when the others assumed her gentleness to be weakness. And as for her, she shared her words and her past with me so that I would never be alone.

Rā-alta revealed to me that she had wished to be a student since the time she had been the one shanár standing in the streets of her village in the mountains of Peridūr looking up to the trees, watching her darna cousins spread their wings in flying lessons that she could never be a part of. But her family forbade her to leave Peridūr for the many years it took to train at the Palace. When she was summoned by the very Elder who turned me away from those halls, her family had as much choice to keep her back as I did now to appear before her. Why her? This very question haunted me all the days we spent together and still again sometimes in the fields when my mind worked over the mysteries of my life during threshing and plowing. Why did análong walk the paths they did, or was it truly all down to destiny and Fate as Rā-alta and A'da believed?

I wasn't thought of as terribly clever but A'da believed I was the very center of Ebūda. Back before I became a student, he would take me all the way to Bomtsala village on the other side of Sé Élamangúō to have new dresses, caps and smocks made and then parade me about on his shoulders in my lovely new things all the way home. I remember a thousand and one sneaked sweets by the river while A'ma did the wash and I should have been doing the mending or reciting lessons. A'da always had time after his work in the fields to tell me shadow stories by the evening fire and when A'ma brought in sacks of dūūcerfrūt to bake, he would sneak one behind to dry so I could have a seed-rattle. And it was my a'da who walked all the way behind the cart every time we traveled to Bri'én to ask for me to be examined just once more to enter the Halls of Learning, and then he who followed us all the way home the same when I had been refused and gave me sweet lāāca pips to chew on in consolation.

But of course I was admitted and in my ninety fourth year in Bri'én, A'da sent word to me that there was a g'ada coming to our family. I counted the days til Dhandōdhaī festival when we would all be going back to our homes and worked on sewing a little doll for what I hoped was going to be a sister. When my *ēdandha* Ā'dō was born thirteen days before Dhandōdhaī, I couldn't wait to shed my robes and ride on the special aircart, a luxury A'da had somehow arranged so I could ride on the back of a darna and get home in a quarter of the time it took by foot. But on the eleventh day, the night I should have been leaving to go home, I received an urgent message from the Ta- of Pōcarū:

Your a'ma is become late. She is gone on to wait for caémba. As she could not stay in this world, I am caring for your sister A'dō. Please wait in the city for your a'ér to send for you.

This was the letter sent to me by the old análong in the neighbouring hut, Nanē Chēso, and I was shocked that A'da had not asked for the Ta- to send it directly from himself to me. The Elders allowed me to stay on as they did for Rā-alta during holidays; the realization that A'ma was gone hadn't sunk in to me until a few months later. I was too wrapped up in waiting for A'da to send for me to come home, standing by the window every evening in the little room looking into the Circle Gardens. Why hadn't he sent for me? When would he?

Then the years rolled by, skipping from one class to another in the Palace, winding through the others' news and happiness and tears, for life is not kind enough to stop only for the grief of one. Rā-alta's parents never got over their anger at her acceptance into the Palace so she stayed with me during holidays, the only other one who was never sent for. And though we shared a sadness, it wasn't of the same kind.

Finally, one morning when I had finished my studies and was preparing to leave the Halls of Learning forever, a sliver of light fell on my face through the window, and I realized that youth had pushed me away like the wind rolls autumn leaves along into winter. Now it was foolish to wait and hope for a message from A'da I knew was never coming.

When I walked away from the Halls of Learning I left everything behind: my graduate scroll, my robes, my trinkets, and *her*. Long since being a dhana and still not yet an adult, I promised Rā-alta I was only going home to find A'da, to find out what caused his silence. I'd come back soon and we'd go on to our apprenticeships together so I didn't even need to take my things. I told her she'd hardly miss me.

As she stood on the steps and cried, I didn't tell her that I was afraid my a'ér wouldn't *want* to see me, that I wouldn't *like* my sister, that I'd get lost on the way. I didn't tell her that as she stood there with her arms around me, it was me who didn't want to let go. It was she I feared to become lost from.

And I didn't tell her that I was saying goodbye to the only análong in the world I wanted to be with, that I'd noticed some years before that I'd begun to notice the curve of her cheek, the blush at her collarbone, the sweetness of her gaze. Instead, I put my cheek to hers tightly so she couldn't tell my tears mingled with hers and then took my leave through the gates outside the Hidden Gardens where only the servants would silently notice my going.

I kept to the alleys so no one could see me cry and before I even made it to the Bantrū road, I stumbled on a stone and landed face-first in the dust in a small clearing of trees. Somehow all the strength leached out of me and my body flattened out as I was unable to pick myself up or make myself care. What did I think I was doing? Or more importantly, what did the Creator think *They* were doing?

As I thought of that I found the inspiration to get up and raise up my head to the sky. I was, by análong tradition, old enough to question the law, yet young and bold enough to do it aloud. I'd been raised as a faithful análong, taken to the temples and taught all the rituals. Now I wanted answers from Mī'á direct.

"Are you there?" I howled up to the sky. "Do you even exist? Then answer me and fight me face to face instead of listening silently like a coward! What kind of bully are you to take someone's a'ma away! *Why her?*"

It was the first time I'd questioned it aloud and no answer returned. The sky looked back serenely, unconcernedly. I sunk back down to the ground and deeply slept for two days in that same spot, gazing up to the Palace above me now and then but unnoticed or uncared for by anyone passing by. No-one knew who I was; as students we rarely left the Palace so I was indistinguishable from any other rat in the street.

I thought of Rā-alta, and with a sting in my heart realized I wasn't going back because I wasn't actually leaving. In those two all-important days I discovered how small I was in the world; how angry and alone and cowardly. Now, finally, I knew A'ma had gone from us. A'ma was not coming back. My little sister had been kept behind in a life I didn't belong in anymore; a world that had lived on without me, just as the one I'd lived in didn't include her. And my a'ér had forgotten me. There was no reason to go back.

Not knowing what to do with myself but feeling somehow propelled forward as if there were no road back anywhere at all, I began to walk aimlessly down through the alleys and soon enough an older shanár approached me and asked if I was looking for work. When I backed away to go without reply he reached out and grabbed me, turned me around and covered my head with a hood as he bound my hands roughly behind me. I was pushed forward and led along until I felt a kick to the back of my knees and was picked up and tossed clumsily into a soft pile I quickly determined to be someone else, or rather, a *few* someone elses by the sound of things.

It was a rough ride. We dare not even whisper to each other as we jostled around in what had to be a freight cart. After what seemed days, the cart stopped and there were more voices; arguing and yelling out prices and then more hands, grabbing us and handing us each to other, rougher hands.

When the hood was finally removed and I got my bearings I could see I was somewhere I never thought I'd see, somewhere I'd hoped never to. It was so dark, yet I could make out the faint outlines of many other dhana even younger than me huddled nearby. This was the *Cāilon*; the wretched undercity. Suddenly all bets were off; I wasn't too proud to call out to Mī'á to save me.

This would become my home for the years I lost count of, this place where I learned that there were much darker things in the world to be angry at the Creator for than my young concerns. This place where my secret was born, where my scars were made, where I fell and where I failed. And when I left that place, I had changed again, yet again.

My dreams of someday returning to the Palace died when I left the undercity. I had lost my class; I had no right to enter that place as anything more than a servant now and in that light, how could I ever be near Rā-alta again? It was impossible. She would be so ashamed of me now. I hadn't chosen to go there, but the world rarely gave us fair marks for our deeds. It certainly didn't issue out its labels based on our *intentions*.

Then, having nowhere else to go, I stayed in Bri'én and sold myself into a household as an attendant for a contract of some years. This was a good arrangement, though I had little freedom other than running through the lower streets to the markets and back. Because three families lived together in the longhouse of my new masters, I was given the storehouse behind it to live in and it was here I learned how to make it on my own. I was grateful; at least this was the story I told myself all those years until I very nearly believed it enough to forget the thing I had done *before*, the ones I had left behind me.

And sometimes, only very rarely, I would hear of Rā-alta from the old grandmothers in the marketplace selling fruit. I committed everything fast to memory: that they saw her toting a dhana along, that she was wearing the bright colors of a dl'ah'sha, and then, the scarlet robes of an Elder. I tried to be glad, but the gulf now between us was insurmountably wide.

The spectacle that went along with the discovery of the name of a young she-dog in the ancient chalice at election time was one no-one in Bri'én could escape. We all knew there was nothing honorable in the way the Council of Nine Elders was chosen and hadn't been since the days of the Kings of Ebūda. The names drawn out of the chalice on election day were always male descendants of the Elders seated in the Palace at the time. But it seemed that day the system had betrayed itself, for however the name of Rā-alta was submitted, it was forbidden to remove it. In a landslide victory Rā-alta won the vote after weeks of deliberation and investigation. In the end, no-one would admit to the shameful act of submitting the name or of voting her in.

And though I was never far away and heard all the daily news of the whole process, I never saw her during those later years and she never saw me, and I was sadly glad she hadn't. I learned to be content to be that close and only that close as long as she was well.

Don't ever look at me Rā-alta, lest you see me.

By then even my name had changed; now I was called *F'ala*, and after my time as an attendant was up, the master of the house asked where I had been born. It seemed that the master was the cousin of the Ta- of Pōcarū, the village closest to my home village of Orambūsū. In truth, I missed Drīdū terribly and its heavy heat that everyone complained of as being suffocating. To me, the thin dry air of Adanandū stole the breath from my throat. Its punishing cool made the body shiver and worry for warmth, while back in Drīdū one's limbs were comforted in the constant heat; swaddled in the happy sunlight. Here the legs stiffened against their will and after all this time, I wanted to go home.

At the end of my contract I got up before daybreak and put the dhanas' clothes out on the ends of their beds. I emptied the chamber pots, brought in water for washing and built the morning fire. Then I walked out into the chill air with my clothes bound up on my head and some food on my back. The youngest dhana, Mēsh'hl, had been my favorite and I, hers. Small and serious, her funny little laugh brightened those long years and for her sake, I was given two bags of seed and a pair of shoes. I never wore the shoes and never lost them; but I used one bag of seed to hire a cart to take me to Pōcarū. The master had arranged for me to become an apprentice to the Ta-.

As I journeyed through the centerlands down and through the north of Drīdū I reflected on my strange fate. I came into the world just above the class of servants, was pulled into the world of the Elders by fate, fell into slavery and servitude and was now rising again to the place of a low scholar. When I was done with my studies I would be above everyone in the village, even the elders. And while that wasn't a great deal in light of the whole of the world, what did the rest of the world's titles and statuses matter in a small village?

When I arrived, I moved into the tiny storehouse behind the hut of the Ta- hlRūū. He was not one to appreciate humor of any sort but for the time of my training, which was twelve years, he taught me to paint the long script of official letters I would someday be responsible for writing out for the entirely illiterate common class my own family belonged to. In that time, I paid close attention to him and stayed very close to the hut, working in the fields to help plant and tend and harvest. When I did not study or till, I cleaned his hut and cooked his meals and pretended to be interested in the life I had no interest in but had no right to refuse.

When the Ta- became late, I was obligated to take over his business. In that whole twelve years in Pōcarū and for another thirty-eight after, I hadn't once seen my family whom I was told still lived nearby. I didn't intend to return there; I merely kept the former hut in the village inner circle of Pōcarū and converted it to my own shop I expanded to include sign and furniture painting. But with some hired help, I built a hut and storehouse of my own on the western side of my family's lands away from the borders of Pōcarū and Orambūsū. I didn't even know if A'da was still alive, but as the oldest dhana the lands were mine if I would front the upkeep. So I took the west side to live, and kept up the fields between the Náasaa Forest and the salt hills to plant.

By the time I became Ta- I had come to see A'da as an old enemy, and my sister Ādō, then a dhana of seventy-four, as a stranger for whom a future living near might be possible as long as I didn't think of her as related to me. As soon as I'd earned enough as the new Ta-, I sent the price of the land in nendē with a property note to A'da's hut. I never received a reply, making the land mine by default.

And now I was on my way back to the city, back to a world I'd never belonged in and had since become so distant from. Over the weeks I'd been walking in silence with the messenger, my mind argued with me over whether or not I should tell Rā-alta what I was too cowardly to tell her that day on the stairs, what I had hidden in my heart all these longyears.

On one hand, what right did I have? I couldn't let her know how far beneath her I had become, how little I had to offer.

On the other hand, why *shouldn't* I? She was an Elder, a little bird trapped in a big, opulent cage who could never fly away to her own life anyway. Why not just say it? It wasn't a case of changing the future; I would sort things out in Bri'én and come home anyway to live out the rest of my life in my hut and she'd stay in the Palace and live out hers, it was simply the way of fate. Nothing would change if I told her.

Ironically, I wished I could have asked Rā-alta what do to. But somehow, I knew she would have said simply: "*Try.*"

Fala
7

what was left behind
in Bri'én

*ban'á cī'sa la-base daas
an Bri'én*

THE sacred city of Bri'én sits on a large mound of land just smaller than the Hendū mountains and is perfectly round with the city itself being circular in design around it. Just in the northeast of Adanandū, Bri'én is ringed with a large gate guarded by keepers perched atop the ends of long poles extending off the top of the great outer gate. The keepers live in apartments built high on the opposite sides of the wall and constantly relieve each other throughout the day and night. But the thing about the them is their continual singing back and forth to keep themselves awake.

I was never much of a singer myself (that is to say, I can't.). This has never endeared me to my neighbors.

But everyone sings or plays about something it would seem, as if the whole of Ebūda survived on its own spicy, mournful song. Truly, I couldn't think of a time that I was ever bathed in true silence, not even in the tiny rooms and cells and sheds I had lived in; not in my own hut in the dark night or alone on the plains for the year's gathering of bashō pods to open and weave into cloth. Even alone, with my mouth shut tight, there was still some sort of melody always around me; pushing its movement through me that I could never quite pin the origin of.

The Palace, home of the Council of Nine Elders, sits at the very crest of the city's hill and is surrounded by circles of tall, white na'bōmen. These harness the wind from the top of the upper Dhang'r and power the mechanical chambers and pipes of gold inside the lower Cāilon underneath the city proper. All those pipes move water through vast networks to water homes, move waste through ducts and turn great wheels to grind meal. This immense system powered by the servants and slaves of Adanandū marks Bri'én as the most advanced city in Ebūda. Huts, temples, and streets are built around the Chi'chúang marketplace down the hill towards the main gate and out from the wide Bantrū road into the crowded, stinking Cāilon-da wedged between the inner and outer gates to the city.

These inner walls surrounding the Cāilon-da are smooth with maze-like dips and bends into which never ending stairs have been carved for those who live in the rooms at street level to travel up and down without ever entering the city itself. And in the southernmost side just inside the great main gate is the Serdaga Quarter, where all the noise and color and bartering of the common class go on.

As it was, we were approaching the Southern Gate when the messenger halted abruptly and bowed in the middle of the faint road scratched out in the dust. When he did not rise up immediately, I took my pack off my shoulders and sat down for a rest. But the midday was upon us and the air had already warmed considerably, leaving me nervous to get our errand over with. "What are you doing?" I asked, harder than I'd intended. He looked over at me and said simply. "I am thanking Mī'á we have come safely back home."

Rā-alta would have done the same, I thought, and softened towards him despite myself. "*An-an*, it's no matter. We've been walking all this time and you've never even told me your name," I said, positive I would be embarrassed by this fellow once we arrived at the Palace but somehow reluctant to insult him. He did belong to *her*, after all. "If you're going to present me to *Elder Rā-alta* I ought to at least know who you are."

"Kind of you to ask," the messenger bowed low to the ground.

"Just your name, please."

He nodded with satisfaction and answered, "G'éalach saō Sā-úū, servant of Elder Rā-alta. My home is west Peridūr, Dladha village."

"Good enough Sā-úū. And you know who I am so let's get on," I said as I pulled myself up from the ground. Sā-úū rose up and followed me quietly, shaking his head, which I took to be his disdain for my lack of decorum. But I spied a faint smile and knew he appreciated being known by name, as did we all.

Soon enough we heard an old familiar voice belting out something absolutely ridiculous over our heads which could only come from a gatekeeper.

I cringed just under the great, sparkling orbs hanging on silver chains across the main gate. When I was young, I loved to jump up and swing on these with Rā-alta on our sneaky outings from the Palace. The chains themselves looped around a labyrinthine metal arch, woven into Dala-ang letters which twisted into the words of musical notes. Notes, which played in the correct order were said to compose the most important magical charm protecting the city and only those from the Elder class could read them in the correct order. But today I didn't care as I once did to try and harness such magic; it was my mission to avoid the customary theatrics that went with trying to enter the sacred city.

Too late. Above me, balancing impossibly on one foot atop his pole was the keeper, eyeing me slyly. He hadn't aged a bit since the day I'd left Bri'én, and he knew me at a glance no thanks to my cursed spots and the time I'd spent as a servant near that gate. His name was A'ffarsa and he sang out so loud and wantonly that every passerby going about their own business suddenly knew I was there; and the curious looks they gave me told that not much had changed in the last one hundred twenty-eight years.

"Who is this speckled stranger? Shall I let her *in, in, in*?"

Those who'd been passing by stopped and turned to answer him in sport, some shouting "Let her in!" and others, "Don't do it!" A'ffarsa pulled himself up to flip around the top of his pole theatrically, making a grand sweep with his arm to usher us into the claps and shouts of his sudden audience.

Picking up a stone, I hurled it up at him, shouting, "I'll let you in, you *pinūpi*!" But Sā-úū grabbed my skirt in his teeth and dragged me off into a patch of brush before I could settle things. I grumbled to myself, "I'm a Ta- for bless' sake, I don't need his permission!"

"Oh, but you *do*!" A'ffarsa sang after me as he contorted his body this way and that around the pole's end like one of the city acrobats. "Don't they ever fall?" I muttered under my breath.

Sā-úū abruptly hollered back, "I order you to end this mockery of Elder Ra-alta's guest and allow us to pass!" Then he shoved me off through the gate with his head and into the Serdaga before I could hear A'ffarsa's retort.

"That was unwise saō," Sā-úū murmured as he loped along at my left on the stone street, nails clicking along beside my softer, shoed steps. "I hope you remember to respect the Elders."

I whistled rudely, observing, "You're the most talkative servant I've ever met!" Wickedly, I grinned and bent down a little to eye him, commenting that it seemed he must *like* my childhood friend. But I should have kept my mouth shut when I suddenly found myself picking up all the pots from a cookware stall I walked right into, unable to balance my own fool self on my own two feet once I felt the tiny fear that I might actually be right.

Swift, F'ala. Really good. You know what would be an even better idea? Shut up.

Now, according to legend, the Palace had been built sometime in the fifth generation of análong and surely was just as magnificent then as it was the morning Rā-alta and I first arrived at the gate, looking up through the warm fog as new students waiting with arms out straight to be draped in purple cloth by our teachers. "Saō?" Sā-úū checked. "A moment," I murmured. The servant nodded and wandered gently into the courtyard apart from me. In an instant I'd walked into a wall of memory without moving a foot; images and voices twisting like feathers drifting in a sea around me. Shaking my head to clear my eyes of the sparkles of time blooming at the edges of my vision, I picked up my feet with great effort and moved forward in watery steps under the great jeweled arch and into the first courtyard of the Palace; my once-world.

In my nostalgia, I forgot Sā-úū; I did not linger, but walked quickly into the main hall leading into the Halls of Learning, where I once joined my peers for long lessons, fearsome debates and idyllic hours of study. The air here was somehow lighter than any other place in Ebūda even weighted under those unending spires and cornices and cupolas of the Palace. Around me I saw the smooth marble floor where rows of students once stood and recited the principles of enlightenment back to the teacher; the wide shelves built into the walls where we'd bunched up together to kip in-between classes. In the next Hall still stood the low, heavy tables where we sat hunched over our Dala lessons, copying our letters over and over to learn the essence of the words, the life of the language. My mind heard a clear voice as if its owner stood next to me: *"The ideas and voices of a thousand beings have made this word; this is why our language is so precious. It has been brought to us by the Guardian Anō through the gates of Ebūda from the mouths of all the beings of Creation. We speak a tongue of many …and of none."*

On the upper floors where Rā-alta and I once snuck in the late evenings to talk and dream were airy lofts filled with heavy, dark furniture and long silky tapestries far away from that cold, yet cozy cell she and I kept home in over the Circle Garden. Well beneath us, even below the garden levels, servants were quartered in simple rooms and complexes opposite the Palace baths. And to the left I looked into my favorite place in the Palace, the Way of Shadows, tiled in mosaics of jade and amber, its cutwork lanterns casting lacy shadows across their late afternoon glow.

I was too busy tracing the shadows with my eyes to notice the two young servants standing in the eaves staring at me. When I looked up and caught them, they allowed their gazes to roam over my face shamelessly before giggling and running off. I whistled and looked down to Sā-úū, who'd followed me silently. "Does no-one have anything better to do than stare at my spots?" I demanded.

He didn't blink when he said flatly, "I'm sure I hadn't noticed, saō."

It was such a polite, measured reply I couldn't help myself but to grin knowingly at him. "You did."

He lowered his eyes. "I did."

Suddenly, Sā-úū dropped to the ground and bowed, covering his eyes with one front paw and balancing on the other. Following his gaze, I shook the sweet dust of memory from my thoughts. There, under a low arch robed in gold and adorned with rings stood Rā-alta looking slightly taken aback to see me as if she had not quite expected me, or perhaps had expected to be disappointed. My throat squeezed shut, refusing to let any breath pass in awe of her. Fear rose in me as I saw in her the years that had gone past, realizing how different I must look to her as well, hoping I looked half as good to her.

"F'ala!"

I knew that voice; it held the same reserved laughter unchanged through time. I stepped back at the sight of her. Every doubt, every misgiving, every fear I'd had all those years past screamed at fever pitch in my ears for me to run as I tried to see her all at once; the robes, the jewels, the splendor of an Elder's raiment. The curves and shape of beauty I'd only seen in dreams. And here was I, in my hunting kit and boots, plain and filthy after such a long journey. She was air; I was earth. Whatever awkwardness we'd had before as dhana was gone; this was *us*, finished and grown.

Walking as fast as must be possible under so many clothes, she stopped still a few feet in front of me, her shy smile brightening the whole corridor. "It's you, F'ala, it's really you. You're so…"

My heart caught suspensefully in my throat and then dropped as she finished, "*Tall*. You're much taller than I thought you'd be."

"Oh, sure. And you! You're so…" *Beautiful.* "Tall," I finished lamely. "You're really tall too."

Did I just say that? You are blowing it, F'ala!

But Rā-alta didn't notice. She laughed, leaning forward to slip her arm under mine to guide me down a narrow hall to her chambers. "We're the same height," she observed and tapped her finger on my shoulder. "And I see you've grown into your freckles."

* * *

Idly, I picked up a jar from the windowsill of Rā-alta's quarters. She said nothing but studied me, her brown eyes holding the softness of the memory of a shared past when we sat side-by-side dreaming of future days. I continued to walk around the room, surveying the quarters of a real Elder, trying not to appear aware of her eyes following me, trying not to meet her gaze. A sliver of light reflected near the window snapped me back to why I was there to begin with: I was in trouble. This wasn't an invitation for a chat. In all these years she had never sent for me, though she had all of Ebūda at her beck and call to find me if she'd wanted to.

You could've looked for me.

Stopping to sit by the window I felt peevish and obstinate, the high ceiling of the chamber making me feel small, but I said diplomatically, "How did you know where to find me?"

Rā-alta's mouth twitched into a tiny, regretful smile. "About fifty years ago a messenger was on his way to the north of Bri'én and stayed here in the Palace for a night. He knew Elder Talishin somehow and I overheard him say he'd come from Pocarū. I knew that village was near Orambūsū so I asked him if he knew your family. He said he didn't but when I described you to him, he said he realized who you were and that you'd become the village Ta-. We had an understanding then; anytime he came this way he would have a place to stay on his travels and he'd bring me any interesting news from Pocarū." She looked at me from the side of her downcast eyes like one who was rightfully above me rather than someone from the distant, rural mountains of Peridūr.

"Freckles are good for something, I guess. You *spied* on me," I accused.

She shook her head with a slight smile. "An Elder can always ask for information they think will be… useful."

My resolve to reveal myself died behind my quick temper, and under a sudden outbreak of angry gooseflesh along my neck, I stood to disperse the excess energy. I hadn't rehearsed what I was going to say in all the weeks we'd been walking. Usually my strength was in winging it but now I couldn't find the words I needed and fell back on my failsafe: anger. If I was angry I could do just about anything. "Then you've known where I was *all these years*! Why didn't you write? Why didn't you send for me sooner?" I demanded, terrified both of what she might say and what she might actually know of me.

Her head rose sharply and she volleyed, "Why didn't you just come back as you promised, F'ala? You're the one who *promised*!"

Hearing it now for the second time, my name sounded odd coming from her; the syllables flat in her northern dialect. Strange, all the times I'd thought of her through the years I never seemed to recall the difference in pronunciations between our home prefectures. Names mattered. Rā-alta had lived up to her name, "*star*." She was as worthy to be an Elder as she had been worthy to be a student. And I also grew into my adult name F'ala; my life personifying its meaning of "*without*."

Without you...

Now it seemed as if I'd always been *Adīī'á F'ala*, that my birth name Adīī'á Rī had never existed. Yet try as I might, I couldn't make that dhana disappear from memory. And sometimes when I looked into the old family album hidden under my bed and caught snatches of my young face peering out from its pages, that little stranger named Rī accused me of forgetting something important I could never name.

I hadn't realized how hard I was breathing until I heard the little puffs of air in the silence between us. I waited for Rā-alta to speak, to release me from so many years of the shame of being accepted on pity into the Halls of Learning, the secrecy of why I'd returned to Drīdū so many years later and the thing my heart longed for her to hear. I needed her to somehow lead me.

"I'm not who I was," I said lamely by way of explanation, which wasn't a lie.

Rā-alta leaned forward, her eyes sharp. "But what happened to you? You disappeared, F'ala. Even when I did get any word of you, there was so much time gone between school and when you became Ta-, it didn't make any sense. Where did you get lost to? Why did you... how could you forget me?"

I never forgot you, not for one day. I knew before I even said goodbye that day that I... There was my lead, yet my mouth remained shut, too weak and stubborn to answer.

Rā-alta slid her eyes closed for a moment, a faint look of what? Pain? Flitted across her face but she would not be enticed. She spoke, her voice was just above a whisper, "You became a Ta-."

"You became an Elder."

"You have your own shop and lands."

"You have your own quarter of a *Palace and servants*. Let's not even get into what your closet must look like."

She eyed me concededly and then nodded. "*Ācū-ācū*, you win." But then her face thinned, and she said sadly, "You're not my Rī anymore, you're F'ala. Who named you that?"

My face grew hot. It had been many years since I'd been called by my first name at all, and I longed for her to call me by it again. But my path had already been laid out forever as F'ala. Most análong took their adult names when they took on a trade or married, but some of us were given unlucky names according to what the world saw of us. In the underground I had no name. It was only in coming back above that I was given any name at all. She didn't need to know why, *couldn't* know why. I wouldn't subject her tender heart to the unkindness of this life. "I chose it," I lied.

"That's unusual, and I suppose, lucky to be given a choice. But why would you choose a name that means "without"?"

I answered with a question. "Rā-alta, how is it you never got a second name? Is that some sort of Elder thing?"

She sighed and let me off the hook. "My name was changed long before yours. It *is* my second name. I didn't want to be called Rā-alta, it's a shanár name and it just doesn't... sound right I guess.

My darna parents named me Cicūrīi. But when I came to the Palace before we met, Elder Anan gave me this name and that's who I've been ever since. I guess you could say I've been grown for most of my life."

Kih-KOOR-EE. I considered this delicate name, so foreign to me but at the same time, befitting of her. "Well I don't know about you," I admitted, "But I think I was happier when I was Rī." And maybe that's what Rī thought I'd forgotten.

Rā-alta pulled open a long drawer from her table and extracted a tattered scroll. Carefully unrolling it to spread out before us, she stood back pleased and waited for me to say something. "Where did you get this?" I wondered aloud, unable to keep my fingers from tracing the worn lines of a dhana's drawing. I remembered it well; it was shortly after Rā-alta and I were assigned the room over the Circle Garden. She was terribly homesick, and I often heard her crying in the night for her own tribe. For a while I pretended I couldn't hear it at all, that I didn't know.

But then one night on impulse I crawled into the tiny bunk with her and she quickly fell into a calm sleep beside me. The next day she told me of her village on the mountain, of the darna-styled round hut built high around the trunk of a *dhubdhub* tree that she lived in with her darna family, of its wood-paneled roof that could be pulled open in the morning and closed during storms, of the long vine rope she used to swing down while the others flew to the ground. We never slept apart until the day I left.

And so, I took all these memories and tried my best to put them on that scroll and together we hung it over the bed so she would always go to sleep at home in a sense. I wrinkled my nose; it was a rather crude drawing. I'd scrawled a figure of little Rā-alta standing on the railing of the house and there beside her was another little figure I didn't quite recall. Squinting, I realized it was me, Rī, standing beside her, holding her hand. "It's not good but," she shrugged bashfully.

I felt myself blush furiously and I shrugged back. "It… it's fine. I can't believe you still have it."

"I could never get rid of this! It's all I had left of you." She lowered herself down awkwardly to the floor to sit at the table. "F'ala, I've learned something about myself, something I wasn't sure I should believe in. And if I don't believe in it, I can hardly ask you to have any faith in me when I ask this great favor of you." She paused, as if ready to reveal that something to me, but then shook her head and smiling faintly, motioned for me to sit by her. "I think it must be a truth somewhere coming up from deep within me, something that my spirit has surely always known and it's only my mind meeting it for the first time."

She reached over to the center of the table to pass the small bowl of sugared nuts to me and I was distracted by the light scent of her skin as her cheek passed near. "It seems I'm not who I was either, F'ala. But it doesn't matter. Here you are with me again, and I need your help. In fact, the whole world needs your help very much."

"It figures." I moved to stand from the table, unsure if I was offended or pleased that after all these years of silence she brought me back because she needed my help. But she reached out and grabbed my forearm, knocking me off-balance. I felt my arm slide out of her grasp, feeling her warm skin as her hand brushed against mine and unthinking, I grasped her fingers in mine, allowing her to pull me back down to sit and we sat at eye-level staring at each other, each waiting for the other to start. My fingers weaved through hers of their own mind, as if my heart reached out through them. When I didn't let go, Rā-alta's eyes widened but she smiled shyly in return and my gaze couldn't help but lower to where our fingers entwined.

"I can never leave here," she began.

I know, but I still have to tell you…

"I can't have a life like you can…"

Just tell her! This is Rā-alta, the same Rā-alta you've always known. She's not going to laugh.

"But there are things I must take care of even from inside this Palace that I cannot do myself. You see, there is a Guardian waiting to be born, the Guardian who will save this world and bring about caémba so the análong can be given souls. This Guardian of Hope, this dhana, will be tested by the will of the Creator and I must find someone to care for her, someone to be her dl'ah'sha. And it cannot be me. It must be you."

I heard her words, but I found it impossible to listen to anything but the fragile beat of my own heart, impossible to look away from where my skin met hers until a shadow passed over us and I realized with horror that the door to her chamber was standing open. Sā'úū stood benignly in the doorway, hailing us that another Elder was calling for Rā-alta. I dropped her hand immediately, feeling its warm life tear away from me as I hid mine under my legs.

"Tell him I'll be down in an hour please," Rā-alta instructed her attendant and he left, but not before I saw her face soften towards him and color just so slightly that immediately I felt thin inside like a dhana who had seen too much. The look that passed between them was the sweet gaze of a secret shared, and at that moment I realized with a cold knot in my throat that I would leave there in silence, never speaking that thing inside me that had begged for years to be heard. So, it was settled. By that momentary glance, life had verified what I'd already known, that I had no business thinking I'd had any chance to begin with.

When she turned back to me, she continued as if she hadn't heard the metallic shredding my insides so deafening in my own ears, "What we learned of the Guardians as dhana was true, but there was much more we were never told, that not even the Elders knew. And out of all Ebūda, I had to choose a dl'ah'sha. You were the only choice; maybe the worst choice."

"Well flattery won't get you anywhere with me," I said smartly and regretted it. Though it had been such a long time between us, I could tell that she had indeed missed me. And part of me was elated and still all the angrier because of it. Rā-alta turned slightly and part of her face fell into the shadow beyond the light coming in through her broad window. "I don't have much time to make you understand so you have to *trust* me," she said wistfully.

When she told me that she was the Guardian of Wisdom, my heart was so bruised by what I'd seen in that moment between she and Sā'úū that I didn't have the strength to question it. *Why not?* I thought morosely; *She's always belonged to the stars, to some place above me far, far more foreign. Just one more reason I was so beneath her.*

And as she explained prophecies and dreams and Guardians and the end of the world I watched her and thought only of myself, nodding and agreeing when it seemed I ought to, wondering how long everything in the world around me would seem to have been shattered and badly put back together.

"How could a Guardian be a dhana? That doesn't even make sense," I heard myself ask half-heartedly.

"Because we've been told all our lives the Guardians will come and save us and now we're too old and comfortable waiting for someone else to do it to work for it ourselves. We question everything happening around us so quickly instead of trying to fix it. Dhana question to learn the truth, but adults question to comfort their own fear. We should wonder, why couldn't a dhana do this?" Rā-alta explained.

"*Cīama,*" I found myself agreeing though I hadn't believed in any of the dangerous truths we'd been taught in the Palace for so many years, those ideals of enlightenment so guarded from the common class. Wait, what was it again? Ah shě'á, that all of reality could hinge on the lowest of beings, that no living thing was unimportant. I sighed. It was a pleasant thought but outside these Palace walls very little was important in the end and those who could out muscle each other got the best. Yet, I was too weary to argue and instead nodded and rose to take my leave. Rā-alta stood too and put her hand softly on my cheek to say goodbye. Without thinking, I leaned into it, half-closing my eyes so not to betray unshed tears.

"I have chosen you and done as I was bound to do and now I bind you by my power as an Elder. Be careful, there is so much out there I don't even know. But what I have told you, you cannot speak to anyone else. Above all, you must keep the dhana safe from the world's eyes until she has passed her tests and awakened as a Guardian. You must protect her with your life and with your spirit. I chose you, F'ala, because I knew whether you believed me or not you would still do as I asked. I knew you had the heart to be a dl'ah'sha." Then she leaned forward and kissed my forehead. "I know you. I know you, Rī," she whispered and stepped away to allow me through the door.

"If you come back this way, next year...to gather in the fields maybe...don't pass by without stopping," she said awkwardly, that veneer of old hurt coating her words. I returned a watery nod, looking past her as I left the same way I had *before*, parting in a lie.

Now, I was a decent runner; I could hold my own climbing the hills, mending fences, chopping wood, but in that moment my legs were too weak to propel me forward and I stumbled out into the empty hallway weaving back and forth so that Sā'úū standing at his post probably thought I was drunk. I eyed him angrily, wondering what she saw in a servant when the truth hit me right in the back of the head: the lowliest can be the most important.

How quickly you forget who you are, F'ala. Or rather, who you aren't anymore.

But my pride didn't let me go without hissing at him once the door had closed, "You'd better *deserve* her."

Suddenly I was in no such hurry to get home and I reasoned I had time to go the long way to Drīdū. Fleetingly, I thought of my sister and all the work she'd been left with and considered cutting out any detours but then thought against it. Ā'dō could be counted on; she was much more responsible than most teenagers. While she lived by herself in a cave behind a dried-up waterfall on the Orambūsū side of my land, her friends were in Pōcarū and for the last few years she often spent the evenings with me on the warm doorstone in the evening sun and helped me keep up with the land.

Ā'dō loved anything fantastic. In fact, if Rā-alta had any smarts at all she would have called on Ā'dō to begin with and left me quite out of it. Gambling on faith in the end was a fool's game Rā-alta seemed intent to play. But Ā'dō was quietly whispering through adolescence, carrying the wisdom of the young within her, and there was a blush around her that belied her class and made everyone stop to admire. If anyone had a natural aptitude to be a dl'ah'sha, it was my ēdandha.

And sometimes I envied the natural ease with which she glided into village life and just as easily walked back out, as if she were but part of nature's seasons and would return on the wind's next pass. Class didn't matter to Ā'dō and I thought it could only be because she had never had it to lose. There was a sparkle in her words, in the manner in which she spent so much of her time thinking of ways to make others comfortable and happy. Sometimes I could have gotten lost in my curiosity of her ease if not for the reminder that simply being my sister brought its own punishment.

Like myself and Rā-alta, Ā'dō and I were complete opposites. Where I naturally went out to work and accomplish, Ā'dō spent her time dreaming about how to improve. When she ran into me one afternoon in the village those thirty-eight years after I'd become Ta- and recognized me by the spots I could never hide from, she began following me around at a respectful distance. I neither encouraged nor discouraged her visiting, finding the idea of her crossing into my life amusing but certainly unnecessary, and when she quietly showed up at my hut's door I allowed her to sit by me on the doorstone as if she had always been there.

The walk back seemed somehow hollow without Sā-úū's silent presence that had filled the air with the hum of companionship and kept me from getting too far lost in my own thoughts going into the city. On the way out of the Palace I was presented with a small drawstring bag containing a sealed

scroll with my instructions and a signet-ring with Rā-alta's seal that would get me anything I asked for along the way home just by showing it. The bag also contained a generous roll of nendē to make up for the wages I'd lost while traveling.

She said she was one of the Guardians...

Though you couldn't go anywhere in Ebūda without running into paintings and carvings and sculptures of such creatures, I couldn't remember when I'd last thought of the stories we'd been told years ago. At one time I'd believed of course, but I'd long grown out of that. We were taught that anyone could be a Guardian, so be kind because you just never knew. But even so, it didn't make any sense for Rā-alta to be.

The story of the Guardians went as such: at the beginning of time when Mǐ'á the Creator formed all the worlds and the Law of Orders to govern over Creation, the stars were placed in the skies over the faraway world of the gelim to guard it. Every morning when the sun arose and took its place in the sky, all the stars went into the Celestial Courts to make their nightly report as they were made to do, and all were happy enough to do it. All, that is, except a family of twelve stars who had heard from passing comets that there were other worlds beyond that of the gelim and they wanted to be free themselves to explore the heavens. It was their curiosity that cursed them; they talked each other into abandoning their post and off into Creation they went to the outer worlds.

It is well-known that the gelim, or *hū-man-cīnd* as they call themselves, are the beloved of Mǐ'á, all the things of their world were created for their care. For abandoning the purpose they were created for in the gelim world, those twelve stars were called into the court of the Third Heaven and sentenced to be extinguished as if they had never been; their names erased from the records of the heavens. But the stars pleaded to be spared, for in their travels they had come to the edge of Time and found a small, wild world outside the Law of Orders where the remnants of imperfection, the mistakes made throughout the Creation had been strewn and forgotten. They told the story of a race of creatures not quite *hūman* and not quite *aanēmal*, a strange and defenseless tribe that were tormented day and night by the evil things of that world.

"Let us live and remain with these poor creatures," the stars pleaded, "for we know we are banished from the gelim world forever and it is well known Mǐ'á is a benevolent Creator who does not punish without reason. Allow us to end their torment and become their guardians instead. For are they not almost *hūman*?"

Still, the Creator was known to have a facetious sense of justice and made this deal with the stars: they would be spared to become the Guardians of the world called An'dan, but they would be reborn as análong, the very creatures they had begged to protect. They would never truly be accepted as análong and their lives would befit the sins they'd committed as stars. No longer would they have the power to move about freely in the skies. And if they could live as análong with all of the limitations of mortality and prove to the Court of the Third Heaven that the análong possessed the qualities of their higher cousins inside the boundaries of Time, the Creator would absorb their world into the Law of Orders and confer on them souls so that they would be equal with the gelim.

Of course, it happened so long ago before anyone living was born that no-one truly knew anymore if the story was true or how exactly the stars were to prove anything or for that matter, if gelim even existed. So many stories had been told over the years of how the Guardian A'nō sealed off the country we call Ebūda from neighboring An'dan, how our world and the gelim world was connected through gateways scattered across the land, how someday far in the future the Guardians would do as they bargained to and Ebūda would become immortal.

To those who work the land, it is well-known that walking a good distance by oneself is the truest way to work anything out, Now that I'd been on my feet alone for three weeks going home I'd had time to think with a clear head. I knew that what was certain was that in the stories a Guardian was a runaway star reborn as an análong in punishment and if I knew Rā-alta, it wasn't possible she'd done something so terrible to deserve such fate. Tsō, she may believe it, but it couldn't be so. And if it couldn't be so, there was no other Guardian out there waiting to be born to save Ebūda. Most likely she'd just been holed up with those old buzzards in government so long she couldn't help but believe them. Well, at least I was off the hook from having my life turned upside down by some little stranger and I could go home and forget I'd made the trip I'd waited too long to make.

As I was nearing the little trade village of H'rel, I recalled how much smaller everything seemed along the way; how the dark brown spots of decay had begun to imprint themselves on the once gaily-colored huts and roofs and banners of only last year; how the análong there seemed to walk a bit slower and the music leaned more to the mournful and less towards the spice. I wondered if this was really so, or if it was only that the despair inside me had somehow cast a pall over my eyes.

I stopped to rest, dropping my pack against the root of a tree and slid down to the soft grass beside it, resting my head against the tree's broad trunk. I took a deep breath of the cooler forest air and with such force it scared me, the reality of what had happened in Bri'én struck me right through the throat like a dagger of ice and I choked out aloud, "How can you miss something you never even had?"

An answer came from somewhere behind me and I jumped straight up off the ground to face the direction of a voice who said, "It is because the heart never gives up; it keeps on loving after we've said our goodbyes." And before I could call out, a round little g'ealach not much bigger than a pup came out of the brush, his mouth full of yellow-weed and his face stained with its pollen. He sat down beside me and finished chewing. "I do love yellow-weed," he said, and I now noticed the long, identical scars on his ears.

Swallowing loudly, he continued, "Speaking of love, isn't it a funny thing? I once heard a story about two darna who fell in love, but their parents forbid them to marry. Of course, this happens

all the time up in the north where those tribes come from and usually they marry whomever their parents approve of and go on. Such is life."

Surprised at the utter randomness of this encounter and his blithe tone, my curiosity won and I asked, "So they just gave up? Didn't they ever think of each other again?"

He smiled, his eyes crinkling up into merry little slits. "I said *usually*. Usually those darna just marry off and live their lives. These two did not. They didn't marry according to their parents' wishes, that's true. In fact, neither ever married at all, preferring to go their separate ways and love each other from afar, but they never stopped thinking of each other. You can't just stop loving."

I felt my insides soften and still as if my very spirit were quieting to listen and I sat down beside him. "Then...how does one love someone from afar exactly?"

He tilted his head and studied me. "Love is so simple it can never be mastered; it is inside everyone, yet beyond all. Some, no matter how hard it is to be apart, choose to stay away to avoid being a burden on their loved one's heart. But others choose to take care of their beloved from afar, paving the way for their happiness no matter how it hurts to be distant from it."

I sat and thought about this stranger's words that made little sense but somehow rang purely true. I had no power to pave anyone's way; no special connections to provide anyone with happiness. "But what if they have everything they could ever want? What if they don't need to be made happy?" I asked. "What if their happiness comes from...elsewhere?"

He considered this. "What is something they cannot do for themselves?" he asked.

I chose you...because I knew whether you believed me or not you would still do as I asked.

"I'm not special," I pondered aloud. "Even if it were true, there's no reason someone else couldn't do it. She wouldn't have known why I was the worst choice, I'm the only one who knows."

"Maybe you're not special and maybe you are the worst choice," he agreed. "But you are the one who was chosen."

"It isn't fair," I muttered. There was no pain-free option here for anyone involved, and yet it was true that when I started out to Bri'én I knew I would come home alone and life would continue unchanged. That happened. But I also knew that above all, by her very nature, Ra-alta *should* be loved, and wasn't that was the most important thing? The little g'éalach nodded as if agreeing with my unspoken thoughts. "As do you," he smiled. "And you will be, I swear it."

Puzzled, I didn't answer but stood and grabbed my pack, ready to spend the night in H'rel before making the last leg home. "If this thing happens... I mean if she's right... I'll do it. I'll do my best so she doesn't have to worry about it. Because she can't do it for herself. Well, dhindhē and all for the..." But when I turned, I found myself quite alone in the clearing. My eyes searched the brush frantically, but he was gone and I hollered into the trees, "Nā! You didn't tell me your name!" Echoing back from somewhere high above me came the reply "They call me *Horẽ!*"

My steps now became lighter as I cleared the forest and entered into the village through the outer wall, relieved and resigned somehow to the dedication of a plan that promised vaguely to fill the great hole in my heart with the intentions of love.

But as soon as I reached H'rel I let out a room behind the public house and sat in the darkness looking out onto a starless night through its tiny window. I lay in the straw with my cheek cradled in my palm, hoping in dreams I could fool myself into thinking it was hers. The hot tears fell and dampened the straw beneath me, and for the first time in my life, I cried the plaintive and justified cry of a broken heart.

ā'dō̠g̠

moons and curiosity

na'g'éalach 's m'gūrna

"WHEN is she coming?" I asked, unable to contain my excitement as I wriggled around the shovel in a sort of frenzied dance. The late afternoon air was thick and bitterly sweet from burning off lāāca past its season and now we worked hard to cut it and stack it. Hauling it back to the storehouse was never my idea of a great time but now the entire first harvest was overlapping into the second crop with F'ala having been gone so long to Bri'én and no-one in the village willing to help me get it done in time. If anyone else had been my dandhō...

My dandhō stuck her own shovel firmly into the ground and lit her pipe lazily, drawling as if bored by the thought, "On the remote chance this is in any way real... I have no idea. I've *only* told you because I'd have a tough time getting rid of you to keep it a secret. No-one else knows, understand?"

I wiggled my shoulders up to hers. "Because deep-down you're afraid it really is going to happen and you want some help." I grinned and pointed at her. "Because you're scared there really are Guardians watching you!"

"The only thing I want help with is getting this lāāca done so we don't lose it altogether," she snuffed.

I returned to transferring the burnt stalks to smaller piles we would tie into bundles and take back to dry from the ceiling of the storehouse. But first, when we returned to the hut, we'd sit out all night on the doorstone and cut the tops off to drain out the sweet, thickened syrup into buckets. Under the stalks, F'ala would also cut the roots off and it was my job to pull the big seed pods off to separate and pull the seeds out. "Well," I mused, "When she does come I can take care of her. It'll be good practice for when I marry someday."

She didn't answer as usual. I smiled to myself uneasily that day, wondering if we would always hold each other at a distance; if I would ever be able to tell when my dandhō was teasing or not with the familiarity of other siblings I watched from a distance in the village. F'ala could not be bothered with an indulgent smile or a genial joke to assure me that the future was indeed on its way and we'd face it together as sisters. Her customary silence told me that all the normal things I wanted at my age I'd have to work for, and enjoy, alone.

And not that she made it easy! It's true I was much more skilled and independent than almost all of my friends who spent their days learning to keep house and prepare for marriage. Their older sisters and mothers and aunties were teaching them to make lace for their wedding veils while I was out getting filthy in the lāāca fields with my dandhō. They sat in the late afternoon sun by the village wall talking of future husbands under the indulgent smiles of the grandmothers while I herded the big, lumbering onandals from one field to another, hollering to F'ala until I turned hoarse to head them off in the north field before they destroyed saō Dōnan's fence. Again.

True, I could run a homestead all by myself and I didn't regret that. But heavens help me if I even mentioned a he-dog! Why couldn't my dandhō just *try* to be normal? How could she ignore all the village talk, just allow them to think whatever they wanted to? And why did she think just because she wanted to live out in the middle of nowhere by herself that I wanted that too?

"Why do you call yourself *saō*?" I asked her shortly after we'd met and she explained that she went by a he-dog's title so her customers in the other prefectures wouldn't know she was a female and pay her more for her work. "Why not just charge them the same?" I wondered but she dismissed the idea outright. "You've never been outside Drīdū so you have no idea how the world works. I don't just want the nendē, I want the *respect*. Somebody maybe this will change; and in the meantime I intend to collect what I deserve. Some análong want their own title; I want the *same* title." But I thought it was just a little dishonest and when we fought with each other I usually went back to this failsafe fact as proof she was ruining my life: "Why can't you just be normal? How am I ever going to be accepted if my own dandhō is a *liar*!"

I dove my shovel harder into my work as my frustrated thoughts grew louder replaying years of old arguments, but she didn't notice. Now my thoughts turned inward to pity and everything seemed morose: *Nobody likes me anyway. No wonder, they barely know me. If I had a normal sister...I guess it doesn't matter, I'm not even pretty. Nobody thinks scars are pretty! Then again at least I'm not spotted like-*

I put down my shovel to rest and scolded myself. *Oh Ā'dō, that's not like you, and not at all kind!* It was natural to have something about your appearance you didn't like and for me it was the broad scar across my forehead I'd been born with. Like so many other things no-one would ever speak of, the origin of that scar was unknown to me. But F'ala's spots, *well*. There were many spotted análong in the world of every race and color in Ebūda but the millions of freckles dotting my sister that made her look as if someone had thrown paint on her were her own biggest shame.

In fact, they were what brought us together in their own way.

I knew that in the present F'ala still thought I had had our a'ér all to myself in the years she was gone in Bri'én but it wasn't true. The truth was, I was named for our mother, Adōsha, and as soon as he saw I looked just like her, A'ér sent me to the neighboring hut a mile or so away of old Nanē Chēsō to be raised by she and her husband. They were kind to me and I had everything I needed, but wherever I went others knew I had been taken in. They knew my a'ma had died, my a'ér had sent me away and my dandhō had never come back. There were no other families like ours. And though I was liked well enough in the village, I was never included in the ways the other she-dogs were. I was like a familiar visitor; never a native.

The only thing I knew of my dandhō was that she had gone through the Halls of Learning and that she looked, as Nanē Chēsō described her, as if a bucket of paint had been thrown at her. She was never spoken of as anything but my dandhō, so that I never even knew her first name. So, when I saw a strange, short-eared shanár in the village sitting outside the Ta-'s shop smoking a pipe with an impossible amount of speckles crossing her face and arms and legs, I wondered if this could be my sister. I should have been going right home after school, but I lingered outside. When she left, I followed her to the village wall.

"Who is that?" I asked one of the old gē gossiping on top of the wall. "That is the new Ta-. She's from over in Orambūsū, daughter of Adīi'á. She was gone off to Bri'én for years. They call her *F'ala* now."

My ears stood on end. Adīi'á was my Aér's name! Both my dandhō and I were born in Orambūsū! And her name was Adīi'á F'ala.

After that day I started watching the hut of the Ta-, trying to get a glimpse of her to confirm what I already knew was true. Relieved, I noted that she had Aér's eyes and ears and one afternoon as I slid down the outside of the wall I'd been surreptitiously watching from, a thoroughly unimpressed voice overhead made me jump when it announced, "You must be Adīi'á Ā'dō. My *ēdandha*."

With no more ceremony than that I realized F'ala had moved on from all of us in her heart and had not come back from Bri'én to mend our family as I'd grown up thinking she would. I knew then that as I grew, my dreams must someday come second in order to the care of our Aér in his old age, that my wishes of us all somehow beginning all over as a real family were only that: wishes. She said nothing else, not *It's good to meet you*, or *I missed you so*, or *Here, let me show you where I live*, just gathered her things from her shop and began walking home. I half-heartedly followed, trying to memorize the way but as the sun drew close to the trees I fell back and cut through the forest to get back to Nanē's hut.

Slowly it became a routine: after school I would go to visit F'ala at her shop and tell her about all the little episodes of the day whether she wanted to know or not. And though something in me was overjoyed I finally had some family to speak of, I could never quite tell if it mattered to her. A few grunts in response was all I ever got from her for several years, but as she never told me to stop, I continued to come.

"Why don't you come with me to see Aér?" I timidly suggested one day as I sucked on a sweet out on the shop doorstone. Behind me my dandhō stood in the doorway studying a scroll but dropped it clumsily on my head. Picking it up, she seemed flustered and said I could come anytime I liked now provided I never spoke of him again. And I was furious at her for making me trade him for her, but still I came.

"Why won't you come?" I asked only that one time. She looked right through me and said only, "I'm not the same anymore. He's not the same. There's just no need to."

I wanted to say, *Of course he's not the same; none of us are the same, none of us remain the picture we all keep in our hearts of each other. We're only a family, after all.*

But since neither of them knew the truth of the other, it hung upon me like a silver web, making the air crackle between F'ala and I with the anticipation of revealing that truth every time we spoke. How many times did I silently wash the bowls or pull up water from the well or burn lāāca in the fields alongside her, hoping that my presence would say without speaking, *I was as alone as you were*?

How heavy did the air become around us just begging for me to tell her what really happened; that we were so different we'd become the same? Was it that I believed she had to discover it on her own to believe it or worse, that she already understood but didn't care?

You left and I was sent away. Don't you know neither of us ever saw our parents again?

And when I then turned one hundred thirty, Nanē Chēsō and her husband packed my things up in their cart and took me to the shop with the dowry they had saved all of my life and handed me over to her. As was shanár tradition, since we had no a'ma and our a'ér had all but given us both up, I was now the property of my dandhō until I married. She was not about to share her hut with a stranger, so she helped me set up my own place in the cave behind a dried-up waterfall on her land and there I stayed. So grown up. So alone. And like it or not, this was our family. Just the two of us.

"Nā! Ā'dō! Let it go!"

Snapping out of my thoughts, I shifted my weight to find I'd begun to put soft grooves in my hands from the shovel handle. "*Óōnōúa*," I apologized and began lifting the long stalks by hand to tie up. We worked on without any particular conversation for another hour in the mild heat when she finally pronounced the work done and we stood back, resting on the shovels once again and looking over our bounty. Large piles of the thick, ugly stalks lay in crisscrossed heaps here and there in neatly tied clusters. We loaded these onto each others' backs to begin the walk back to her hut through the dense trees.

"Don't forget your pail," she reminded me, stooping down to pick up the little bucket I had brought our tea in. "Dhindhē," I thanked her and turned carefully to start on the path, balancing my load across the bumps of my spine gingerly. F'ala called ahead, "Go straight, I'm right behind you. And hurry up, the sun is...setting?"

Carefully picking my way through the short stretch of forest bordering the fields, I stubbed my toe on a rock and held my tongue between my teeth, feeling my cheeks burn smartly in the oncoming darkness. There was a comfortable feel about the air, but I struggled to adjust my eyes to the dimming light. It *seemed* as if night was descending much faster than normal, but then again, we'd been working diligently without checking the time. "Maybe we've been gone longer than we think?"

"Just walk faster," she barked, but I could tell in her voice that she sensed it too. Then a whiff of something oddly sweet floated past my nose, like burnt lāāca. "Dandhō, someone's burning something. Can you smell that? It's hot! But I saw you put the fire out back there."

"They'll be sorry! They've only got right to come onto this land up to the river only!" F'ala grabbed my bundle and yanked it off my back. "Here, help me get this off. We'll leave them here and come back at sunup. Never mind about the smell for now, it smells too damp to go on long." I struggled with the stiff ties across her back, listening for any foreign sound around us that might mean trouble, but this only slowed my fingers. "But what if someone steals the lāāca?"

"They wouldn't be stupid enough to steal food these days. Not yet." My dandhō clenched her fists in resignation. Pulling frantically on a knot I could no longer see in the sudden and total darkness, I asked again tentatively, "Dandhō, when do you think the Guardian will come to us? Did Elder Rā-alta say it would be soon?"

"She didn't know," F'ala said without pause. "And we're not going to worry about something that probably won't happen. *Ahn, īlaúa!* It's so dark." I knew by her tone this was the last she'd say on the subject, but I also knew for all her words my dandhō didn't discount the possibility of Guardians so lightly as she'd tried to make me think earlier that day.

F'ala pulled me along clumsily. I didn't know where we were running to but a few deep scrapes and a sprained wrist later, she pulled me out into the familiar clearing behind her hut where we could see each other outlined clearly in the moonlight, our features made grey and harsh. We ran around to the front of the hut, then stood staring at the sky over it. F'ala swore impressively at the incredible sight of the twelve moons of Ebūda crowded into view, hanging impossibly low as if they would fall and smother us.

But their faces were full of curiosity and their eyes bright with wonder. Just like my dandhō could somehow understand the low speech of the onandals, I was the only one I knew who could see the faces of the moons. I didn't understand how others couldn't see the mischievous grin of Māndolf or the broad smile of Tsāi'ín or the crying eyes of Clāiron, but tonight their faces were all intently focused on one thing: my dandhō's hut.

"What does it mean, Dandhō?" I whispered.

"It's a sign, a sign I saw only one other time in my life and that was long ago in the city..." She refused to finish the thought, as she always did when those years in the city crept into the present. She turned to me, eyes shining from the flat light. Then she narrowed her eyes and growled loudly. I followed her gaze past me to the doorstone where a small, thin, white creature lay, practically glowing in the dim light.

It was a dhana, a young análong she-dog curled up on her side, naked as the morning light is pale. Aside from the shallow, open sores on her cheeks and forehead she was completely colorless, as if her color had never been given. And as strange as that was, I knew only one being in the world was without color: Āe'rū, the Guardian of Death.

Everyone said that only dhana could see the Guardian of Death because it was in her nature to lure them away to *Hala-Asal*, the place of unborn spirits where they would be reborn again, over and over as revenge for her own rebirth from her life before as a star. But grown análong could not enter Hala-Asal, nor could they see the Guardian of Death. When they became late their spirits simply slept, waiting for the Guardians to bring caémba. Or if they were righteous, they returned to the forests to become the grandfather trees. "Is that...Āe'rū?" I dared to ask.

F'ala stood for some time without answering me, so long that I began to wonder if we were some-how already late, if we had indeed been crushed by the moons and didn't even feel it. After all, how did anyone know for sure the moment when they left this life?

"It's not Āe'rū," she murmured, mesmerized. And that's how I knew everything Elder Rā-alta had told her was true, that our lives were about to change in a way so much bigger than the little village we lived near, so much bigger than the cycles of planting and harvesting, the festivals and holy days. F'ala wasted no time on emotions, and ever since she'd come back from Bri'én I saw deep sorrow in her face. Sorrow she seemed to think she was hiding much better than she was. It was the same heaviness I'd seen more and more around the village as news from above us kept coming about far-away cousins disappearing in the war with the NaÓma.

I wasn't sure what had happened on her trip, but I knew my dandhō was changed somehow from those three months she'd been away and she was no more likely to tell me why than she was to tell me why she'd turned the painting of herself and Elder Rā-alta kept in a frame by her bed around to face the wall. That mystery was one I could be sure I'd never know the truth of.

Even so, as F'ala's face fell into a mix of disappointment, resignation, and wonder, she held herself stiffly, studying the strange little creature. Beside her, my heart caught in my throat in little terrified, joyful bubbles that pushed the fear out of my mind and I ran forward to the doorstone. "It's not Āe'rū," F'ala said again but louder, more confident. "Tsōl, it's something else entirely. Something not of us, something *new*. But we'll call it análong." Then she snapped back to herself. "Well get it inside of course! I have to go back and get the lāāca!"

Pointing to the sky, F'ala led my eyes to the lightening evening. Purple and gold clouds rolled in against the dark blue sky. The moons had completely disappeared as if the darkness had never come. She pushed past me and the dhana and knocked the door open, ignoring my protest that "it" was in fact a "she" and we were going to leave the lāāca until morning. Maybe it was just too much for her to be wrong about something. Sighing, I bent over and gingerly picked the naked dhana up from the cold stone. She was about the age I would have been when F'ala left Bri'én; maybe around seventy years, but much lighter than I'd been then.

Once inside I laid her on the low table in the common room and went to grab a blanket from the chest of clothes. "You didn't think to prepare at all, did you?" I asked, aloud, bemused. It was quite unlike my dandhō, who was ever-practical and often the first to take a thing seriously. I dreamed, she planned.

"I told you I didn't give it a second thought," she said, as if that made it so. I draped the colorful blanket around the little one's shoulders, unable to take my eyes off the strangely beautiful contrast of stripes against such a blank canvas. She suddenly looked up at me with great, glittering eyes; black as night.

F'ala and I both gasped. For as I knew instinctively that there had never been an análong born without a color, so had there never been born an análong with those same lifeless eyes. This was why Elder Rā-alta had been so earnest in warning my dandhō to keep the little thing away from the eyes of outsiders. She could only be a Guardian.

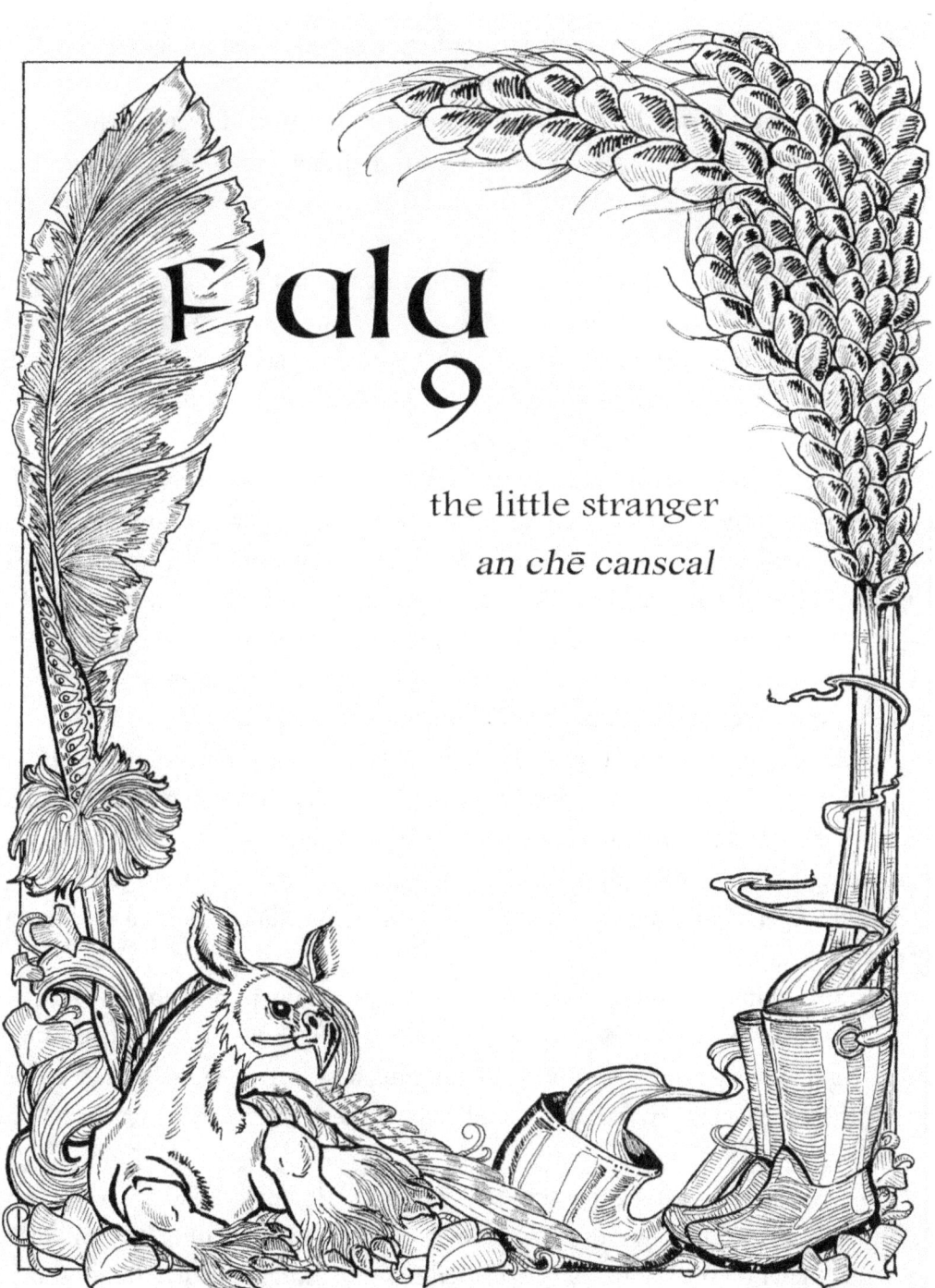

Fala

9

the little stranger

an chē canscal

IT was nearer to dawn than I'd have liked when I returned with the last pile of thick stalks to dry in the storehouse and I sat down inside the door on the old bench. I picked up my pipe and unrolled the tiny herb pouch. Tapping the pipe full and striking a spark on the tinder box I kept under the window, I leaned back and breathed in the savory smoke as slender chills began to run up my spine, admitting to myself that this was the end of my trying to quit. The cold drew out its fingers to grasp my shoulders; that familiar feeling when one has done something wrong or is about to. I would have to go back into my hut and accept my fate. Luckily, I'd gotten all my tears out in the forest where I couldn't be seen hours ago.

Ā́dō was right and wrong. I hadn't thought of preparing. Not in the way she thought I should with blankets and clothes and things a dhana would need. My heart had been so sore on the way home that though I'd accepted my assignment, I wasn't able to believe it tangibly yet. Now here it was right on my doorstone and I found myself wanting to go back and do it all over. I'd tried my best to prepare myself; a task so huge it crowded out the practical.

Tsō, F'ala. This is the thing she cannot do herself. It's the only way. You cannot turn back.

Through the door's thin, old cracks I could see the usual three visible moons shining against the other side from high up above where they should be. I finished my pipe and smacked the door with my hand in frustration, licking the resulting scrape to my knuckle. My heart was in two minds: peaceful, as it knew this was the way I would go on, and mournful, because somehow it felt that once I stepped back into my hut, it would be a last goodbye to a dream. And surely, the loss of dreams was the sharpest loss, for it meant the death of the future.

I picked myself up with resolve and came through the front door to find Ā́dō quietly stirring a pot of tea over the hearth. The little white creature slept in the next room on a pile of blankets on the floor. "You may as well sleep here, sun-up is soon. We'll figure out what to do about this situation later." I reasoned. Ā́dō looked over and nodded, resting the finished pot on the low table with a faintly smug look. *Actually*, I thought to myself, *You were right, Ā́dō. I knew you'd know what to do with her if it came to it.*

It was an uncomfortable first night. Every time I fell successfully into sleep, I awoke to the dhana staring at me from her blankets on the floor with those strange, endless eyes. When I then fell back into a fitful, dreamless sleep I awoke again to her standing beside my head with that awful repulsive stare. On my other side facing the wall, Ā́dō climbed over me to put her back on the blankets where she belonged.

"Go back to sleep, she won't disappear and she's not bothering me," I lied bravely, aching to turn onto my side but too disturbed by the prospect of those dark eyes burning into my back to do it. Ā́dō laid down with her on the floor and this seemed to settle things. Finally, the late-bird began his song outside the window to call awake the lazy and I forced myself up to tiptoe over the dhana and slip outside stiffly to draw water out of the stone well to boil for morning tea. Nothing like a terrible night's sleep to make the joints refuse to wake up. Busying myself with building the fire and the usual chores, I caught the first bath and went out to get some flour from the storehouse for Ādō to mix up our *banbhala* and jam. On return I found myself in the middle of a silent and awkward tea, stared at from all angles.

"She needs clothes," Ādō complained as she loaded up the table, observing the dhana trying to puzzle out what to do with the spoon placed in front of her. "I could trade for some cloth in the village and hire the tailor," Ādō began.

"I have an old dress you can cut down for her," I said around a mouthful of the porridge. "We don't need to make extra trips to the village to get someone poking around out here."

Ādō pursed her lips. Sewing was not one of her talents, and though she always complained this was because I wouldn't teach her and do my sisterly duties, the fact was that I was even worse at it. I reached across the table to take away the dhana's spoon, taking some banbhala on my fingers and swiping it inside her cheek with some sloppy success. "I guess I could," she conceded. "She looks about school-age, doesn't she?"

"She will not go to school," I said immediately. "We'll teach her what we know; every day our lives will teach her right under this roof, right in these fields. Everything we do she'll learn to do as well."

My sister looked at me sideways, unconvinced this was enough.

"I'll keep the shop closed for a week I think, no-one's going to notice another week after my trip. Let's get as much done in the fields as we can to catch up and I'll help a little with the sewing *if* I can." I stopped, glancing at the little stranger but turning away from the hard weight of her glare. Still, she made no indication of hearing or understanding or even knowing we were present other than the faint chewing motions her mouth seemed to be working out on its own. "In the meantime, just tie a sheet around her and bring her along to the field. We can't leave her here by herself. I guess we'll just have to start as if she were a baby and go from there."

* * *

"I need to have some sort of plan," I said, swinging the mallet steadily to pound *shore'l* seeds into flour. "Food and clothes and chores are all very good, but they don't fill all the hours of the day. I can't leave her here while I do my work in Pōcarū so you'll just have to come and stay with her in the daytime. I'll give her lessons in the evening I suppose." Somehow speaking these things aloud made them a bit more manageable.

Ādō stood watching me for a while, hand smartly on one hip, the dhana tied up in a sheet around the shoulders with thick tar spread over the strange wounds on her face to speed their scarring. She stared ahead, unblinking. "Something the seeds did to offend you?" my sister suddenly asked. I stopped and realized I'd been pounding so hard the seeds were whittled down to a fine dust kicking up into the air. I dropped the mallet from my sweaty hand. Embarrassed, I intoned seriously, "She'a, stupid...seeds." But at her knowing smirk I broke into an unintended giggle and we both laughed loudly.

I wasn't blind to the look Ādō then gave me when the laughter died down and I tried to head her off. "On the instructions of Elder Rā-alta I have to teach her as we were taught, to read and to write and such," I informed her.

"But if you had taught *me* in all these years, I could help!" my sister protested. This old fight was one she was not going to win or let go.

"You know that can never be. The only way I could do that is if you had been sent to…"

"The stupid Halls of Learning, I know, I know. I'm not *chosen*, I'm not *special*, I'm not the same *class*. But I can't believe you out of anyone are fine with that stupid old rule!" she stamped her foot in frustration.

Now it happened that I wasn't fine with that old rule at all when it came down to it, but moreover because I knew I was a fraud upholding it when I had fallen out of the class given to me. Class divided families, it was a problem that divided Ebūda and upheld it. But now I had a task to do, and I was going to do it with all my heart as well as I could. I had no time to break rules and start revolutions; Ādō would have to shoulder that herself.

"But I still need your help to stay with her," I allowed. "We need to work together. We could be a team… like sisters."

Her face brightened immediately. "*Na'dandha!*"

I nodded and watched her and the dhana sit down in the straw. They made a sweet picture and a distant word flashed across my mind as I turned away to finish my chores: *asama*. Family.

* * *

They had gone back to the hut hours before when I went out to feed the onandals. These large, gentle beasts lived in the thickets around the hills and grazed along the northern edge of my fields. They spoke a simple language made up mostly of calls and whistles that many birds can speak, and as I found out when I was very small and got lost wandering, so could I. And since I was able to understand them and speak to them, I knew that despite their thick claws and sharp beaks, the onandals prized peace and had magical abilities the análong knew nothing of. And so, when I filled the trough I kept under the trees to feed from, I asked them to use their powers to seal off a border around my land this side of the river so no strangers could pass onto it.

The onandals nodded their lumbering heads in agreement but wanted to know why I asked for this. Whether they knew of Guardians or not was beyond the language they used but they understood one word as well as any other living thing and I whistled to them: *dhana*. Child.

Without another sound they left their food and spread out evenly, lowing and calling to the ground in great concentration. The soil below me began to vibrate and I stumbled back as an immense golden cloud of fireflies rose and spread out into the sky in a swirling pattern, connecting out to other glowing clouds of the same until I saw what appeared to be a sort of net over the sky flash brightly and then vanish.

"*Shāe ē nē-da*," they whistled, "It is done."

"Dhindhē," I lowed my thanks in return, "Dhindhē *a'mōr*."

When I returned home that evening I stopped at the storehouse to bring in more flour and as I balanced the bowl of this on one hip and used the other to bump open the door, I dropped it squarely upside down at the ruckus which greeted me. Water had gushed all over my common room and in the middle of this stood my soaked sister wrestling the little white stranger into a spare basin.

Grabbing the two white hands and pinning them behind her back, I held the dhana's head down as Ādō quickly scrubbed her and tossed another bowl of water over her to rinse. "Get her dried off," I hissed, tossing Ādō a towel and grabbing the broom to start on my once-dry floor.

The flour and mud had made a thick paste of the pressed sod floor that crept languidly towards the sleeping-room, and this took so much of my attention I didn't even notice two pairs of eyes fixed on me until I heard a frustrated little cry. The dhana was stuck fast inside the basin we'd washed her in, her tail wedged right up between her back and its smooth sides. I tried my best but couldn't keep from snickering, then giggling, then turning my back to laugh aloud while at the same time snapping, "Don't you know enough to tuck your tail down when you sit? You'll break it!"

Together my sister and I pulled and jiggled and jimmied until the little stranger popped out of the basin with an audible *thwack*. She herself made no sound, however, and I asked again a little louder, "I asked you a question, dhana. Don't you know what to do with your own tail?"

Those endless black eyes stared at me, waiting, but not mindlessly. I wasn't sure she could hear me, but I knew she was listening to something. "Can you hear me, dhana?"

Ādō moved closer and put her hand on my shoulder. "Shouldn't we give her a name? We've got to call her something."

I considered but didn't answer. Did we just give her a name and hope she knew it wasn't hers or did we have to wait until she told us? That was the first test, to know her own name. *You should have been specific about this!* I shouted at Rā-alta in my head. And as I thought this, it was almost imperceptible but I definitely heard a small, light voice say, "*Mi'halē*."

Ādō's eyes widened. "She said something!"

Surely she didn't say...

And I don't think I imagined until that very moment that she was a real, living being with intelligence and individuality and not just the symbol of a belief. I certainly didn't believe until that moment in the possibility of this little creature having a whisper of a chance of truly being a Guardian of Ebūda.

"Say it again, dhana," I coaxed.

The little stranger's face screwed up as she stared ahead distantly, the tar spots softening into her forehead and cheeks and her mouth opened clumsily. "Mi'hal̃ē. *Ta ah…I am Mi'hal̃ē*."

Ā'dō wrung her hands together in exuberance. "Her name is Mi'hal̃ē! Don't you think that's a pretty name, F'ala?"

Pretty had nothing to do with it. In Rā-alta's instructions she was clear that the name itself was important; not only would this Guardian, *an lhéoran ihn indūsa*, know their name, but we would also know them *by* it.

Mi'hal̃ē. How would a dhana of her age know such a word from a time before, a time from an earlier Ebūda which had gone into dust generations before we were even born? In the Dala tongue, the modern word for hope is *indūsa* which comes from the root *inū: bright future*. But in ancient Dala, that word was *mi'hal̃ē*, which meant *hope from despair*.

We had been taught by the Elders that words change depending on what is happening in the world at a certain time. Elder Rī-íd, the original Ta- and prophet of Ebūda, formed our written language from the tongues of the beings of other realms; the remnants of the voices of gelim and nelim and hadim (who call themselves in their own tongues *hūman* and *angéll* and *aanēmal*) as heard through the gates of Ebūda. He made the change in words after Ebūda was separated from Andan into its own country and the análong were rescued from the darkness of that place. In essence, when the análong were given a future, the word mi'hal̃ē was replaced with the written indūsa, and forgotten in Dala altogether.

Because the análong at the time were hasty to forget any reference to their past suffering, they accepted the new word quickly and mi'hal̃ē was only spoken by Elders who believed the dangerous truth that we should never forget where we came from.

As Elder Talishin said, "*This word means the true, sustaining hope only attained after one has walked through despair and survived. It is the pure hope of those who refuse to give away their innocence, the hope that utter loss brings in its wake that it should never happen again.*"

Hashāma; the concept of innocence. These were the things Ā'dō would never know; they were not given to the common análong but only to those whom the Elders felt could retain their true nature despite being shaken by knowledge or experience. That was what innocence was to the Elders. Not the purity of a heart but its capacity to remain unchanged by the evil of the world. My sister, like the others, would never know words like mi'hal̃ē had existed in our language and were no worse off for it. It was nothing more than a pretty name. Innocence was something that would only exist for them before their eyes were opened.

But Rā-alta and I were accepted as those that were blessed with the capacity to know, kissed with the desire to reach up, and cursed with the knowledge of what they must do. This was what made Ebūda a land of so many secrets and meanings, what kept us locked and hidden away from the rest of Creation, what blessed and cursed us with our place outside of the Law of Orders. This dhana had began as we did, with eyes wide open.

"Well then, Mi'halĕ. You've had a bath and if you've already had your tea then it's time for bed," I motioned towards the sleeping-room and Ădō quickly steered her towards it, chattering on directly at her as if they had years of catching up to do. But I retired to the loft above and lit the candle on my writing desk, smoothing out a short piece of scroll to write a progress report to Rā-alta.

What should I say? What did I want to say? Or rather, what must I *not* say? I sighed and looked over at the scroll I'd been sent back from the Palace with, willing my hand to end my indecision. Test number one, she must know her name. Well, she knew it, so I'd stick with that and that alone:

Mi'halĕ ē namen dhana úō: Her name is Mi'halĕ.

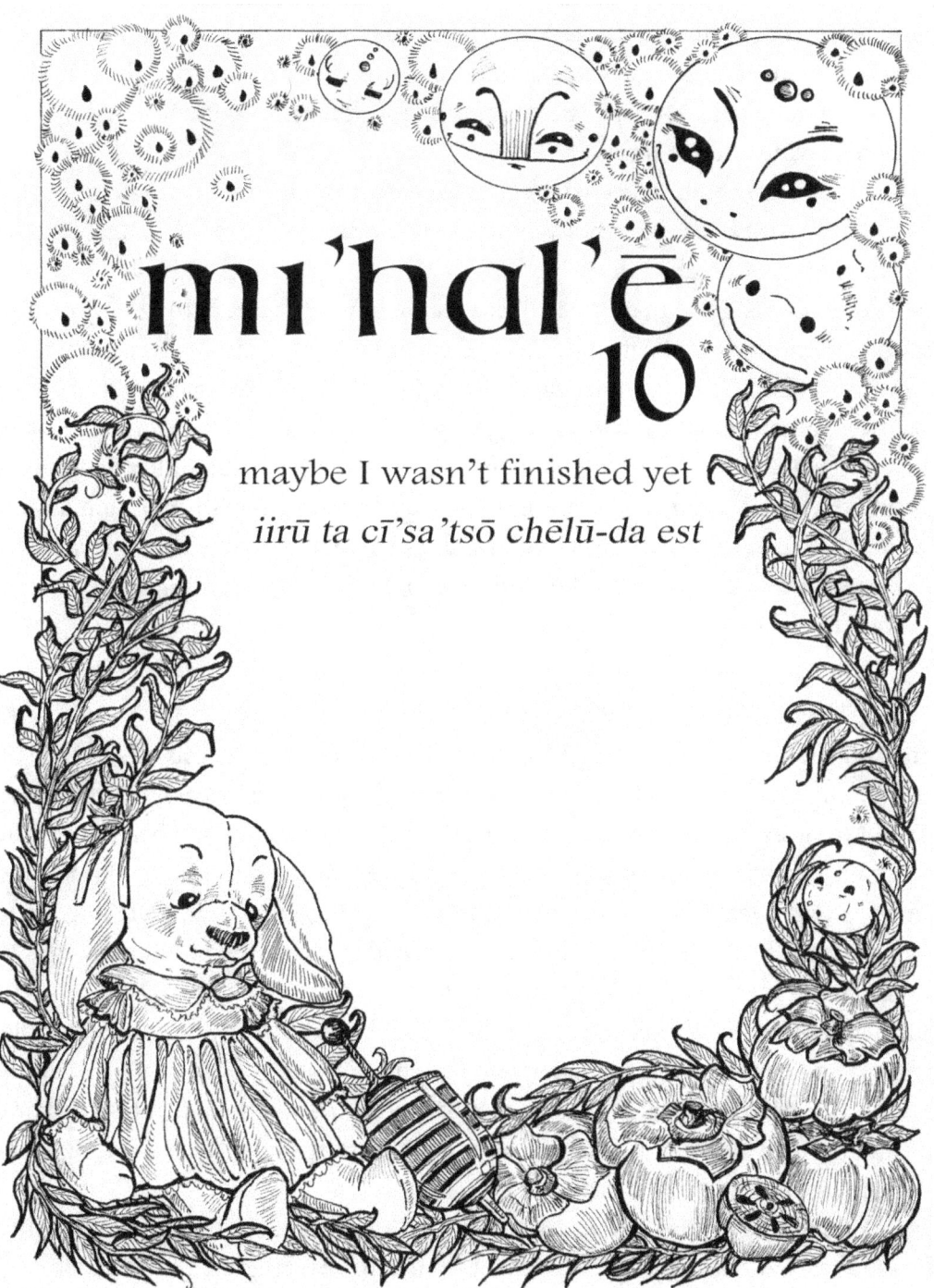

miʻhalʻē
10

maybe I wasn't finished yet

iirū ta cī'sa'tsō chēlū-da est

bRIGHT - *dark - loud - pain - color - burning - burning - here - now - fire - drowning - hurt - hurt - hurt...*

And then, this is what I know that I can say: I had awakened.

Images became words and pain became sound, filling me, swirling and twirling until one bright word shone before my eyes: Mi'hal̆ē. Shining, brilliant, lonely, forgotten, joy, despair, starlight, darkness, fleeing, loving, asama: family.

My eyes opened and my body began where it had not been before, in tiny tinglings here and there; sparkling and heavy all at once. Somehow, I knew that I wasn't, yet here I was, unable to say when I had begun, when Mi'hal̆ē became *me*.

Light came into my vision so that I knew I was seeing. Sounds came through my ears and smells through my nostrils; little dots of patchy sound and watery odors swimming by that my mind caught and named with words. Mi'hal̆ē ...it sounded right in my mind but stumbled out of my mouth.

And there were others about me as well, bigger than me, but somehow *with* me. And just as my name sounded foreign, the words of these others outside of me seemed familiar yet tasted strange.

In those first days everything was so bright it hurt, and my mind was full of so many words that had no meanings, sounds whose disembodied syllables made no speech. The sun was too loud; the water, too sharp. The air, so deep. And their voices, scorching.

Maybe I wasn't finished yet.

* * *

This was the languid time of youth when I learned how to be an análong, this other name they called me that had the sharp aftertaste of loneliness about it. There were a great many things to learn about this word and I regarded the others with confusion and a little resentment when they pushed things upon me to learn because there was such a sense of urgency behind them I could not understand. In my own good time I learned to pay attention to the burning in my middle telling me to eat and the dry pull inside my throat telling me to drink. I learned that the weight upon my eyes told me to sleep and the crawl along my skin told me to scratch.

The calm, gentle hands of Ā'dō showed me all the things in the hut, this round, wooden place where we ate and slept, so I could learn their names and remember that a cup was not a bed and a window was not a ladder. The strong, impatient hands of F'ala guided me where to sit and stand and lay down and sit up. And my own little hands reached out and glided over every surface, feeling, memorizing, seeking something I didn't know I'd lost.

There were other things I didn't so much have trouble with as simply didn't agree with. For instance, it was much too hot to bother with this business of covering up and I know I caused F'ala much grief when I stripped and watered the floor. She impressed upon me as deeply as she could that in the case of my itchy, ill-fitting clothes, dry was the only policy and the *toi-ō* was the only place I should go for such things. Harder to understand but reliable nonetheless was the concentrated look on Ādō 's face that meant she was about to explain something and the irritated twinge of F'ala's voice to tell me it was time to go to bed and lay down immediately *because she said so.*

Learning where things were in the hut came in its own time as well. On the ground floor, a hearth was dug into the floor and was covered with a square, handled board when not being used, and everything seemed to revolve around it throughout the day because we cooked over it and kept warm by it and suffered from it all the same.

Above us, the loft was built halfway under the thatch where F'ala wrote her letters by its tiny window. But the festival mask with staring yellow eyes and a pink, crooked leer hanging at the top of the ladder kept me from climbing up by myself. Though small, the loft was neat and tidy and held a shelf of F'ala's collection of little figures shaped like *pūra*. Pūra, F'ala said, were once eaten at nearly every meal because they crowded the Silver Sea. I had never seen or eaten a pūra, but she missed them greatly and the sea even more. When F'ala was too busy writing to notice me, I quietly took each of the figures off of their stand behind her and examined them, giving them names like Hēla and Éūsha and Dōl. I whispered to them where they'd go and what they'd do once they escaped the loft. But I was always, always careful to return them to their exact spot because F'ala seemed to always know if even the dust in her loft had moved!

Behind the loft ladder, a wall divided a small space away from the hearth and in the doorway of it hung a short indigo curtain to section off the sleeping-room. In the night when I couldn't sleep, I would find myself inching closer and closer to F'ala's bed, for the heavy shadows of the common room blackened across the doorway frightened me, though I could never say why. I didn't have a bed to sleep in like F'ala but I liked my place on the floor above the striped blankets and straw mattress just the same. When it was too warm, I could slide underneath F'ala's bed to keep cool and when it was cold I could do the same to stay warm; cocooning myself up in stripes. The sleeping room had a large round window above F'ala's bed that faced the sun and in the morning, I found it impossible to sleep any longer once it had peeked in at us. Still, I liked to lay in bed as long as I could to listen to the little brown birds that hopped and chirped outside the window.

But I fought sleep all through the night, for my mind was so full of words scattered about that I felt I must find the meanings of each and put them into some sort of whole, as if the life around me was just too slow for all the things inside that needed to grow and be and I must solve this puzzle of why I was here *right now.* The daily cycles around me quietly made room for my presence as if I had been there longer than perhaps I thought I had, and I began to wonder what happened to F'ala and Ādō before me, before the time they said they'd found me. Yet soon enough I had memorized the hut and all the things within it as if it had also always been where I laid my head to rest.

There was an order to every day, a pattern the three of us followed so that it wasn't such a surprise every morning when I woke under the not-so-strange roof on the not-so-strange floor. It was less a shock when that spotted face belonging to F'ala frowned at me as I opened my eyes, and scarcely even startling when Ãdõ's cheerful whistle at the door announced there was something waiting to be eaten at the table.

I was taught new words with which to measure the days of the week: they were called *donchin*, *norsa*, *eredin*, *da'sin*, *shoúlin*, *ninchan* and *amiti*. Then I discovered the months and that they were numbered twelve. I saw that in Dhūlii and Ts'irind, the longest months, there was a time just around the seventh hour in the morning when the sun rose high enough to heat the air around us to its usual thickness. But until that very moment I would shiver with cold under my blanket as long as I could. Then suddenly I rose, the quiver of gooseflesh turned to the itchy prickle of instant sweat; indistinguishable from the moist sheen that hung about on everything from the air.

I would come to hate that time of the year, much preferring the dry heat of Gōl, hLon, and Dhoisa which at least could be escaped from underneath the hut's domed roof and didn't soak my clothes.

Clāiron and Sherin were those punishing months when it seemed even our thoughts slowed a bit to keep cool. Māndolf, Dō-ang and Pendin were the months when F'ala covered me with strong, sticky *trian* juice against the sunlight to sit even by the window. Dandōdh was the best month by far, the month of festivals. And when Tsāi'ín came, the dark blue of the evening sky seemed to freeze us just to gaze at it, and even Ãdõ wrapped her bare feet in long clothes against the sharp, bitter ground.

No matter the month, F'ala made certain the hours of my day could be accounted for by giving me chores of which it seemed she put a lot of thought into. The daily drudgery of rolling and tying up my bed, beating the dust from the floor rugs and clumsily singing the work-songs that F'ala belted out confidently made up the most of the mornings. In the afternoons I helped Ãdõ pull the shutters open from the windows to air the hut out and keep mold out of the sod floor and wood-covered walls. In the evenings we sat comfortably on the doorstone to painstakingly braid straw fibers into the rope which held the hut's thatch together on the roof. Then Ãdõ left, and F'ala had her evening pipe and scooped the ashes out of the hearth before we went to sleep.

In the mid-week, Ãdõ allowed me to help with her own chores after we finished mine. She used F'ala's wheel and loom to spin and weave cloth of bashō floss. If she was weaving, she would explain to me the movements of the loom and let me run my fingers along the soft pattern of the cloth as it unfurled. I was allowed to help pull the bashō floss into long strands to be spun and then wound through the loom. Sometimes she dyed the floss first and this was the greatest fun of all to make happy colors of boiled water and plants in large shallow pots as wide as I was tall to dunk the floss in. Every bit of cloth was always saved to be cut into strips and folded over to sew into squares to replace rugs or cushions when they became too thin.

But the chore I looked forward to, my own special job, was to set out the bowls at each meal from the dish-box and wash the pale, shallow dishes, cups and fat little sauce jars. I liked to carry the jars around until I was told to put them away because F'ala's strong sauces left a deep, thin stain all around their smooth insides so that they always looked full of something rich and lovely to me. It made me feel taken care of somehow to think of our dishes full of good things when I saw those stains that no amount of scrubbing ever faded away, to know those stains had been *before* me.

And all the while, I learned where I was to go and not to go, because where to go was as important as where not to, just as what to do was as important as what not to. I was to come to the table when called to eat. I was to go to sit in the corner when I argued. I was to sit on the short orange stool to be taught and the flat striped cushion to rest. I should know when I was dirty and not need to be told because as F'ala said often, *I was big enough now.* But that only made me wonder, when had I been smaller than big enough?

Past the hut's door was the Outside, where the air was heavy and light shone in ribbons through splits in the thatching over the sleeping-room. Something in me desperately wanted to find the light at the end of those ribbons but F'ala and Ā'dō told me I must not think about it. And something must be terribly wrong with me inside, I thought, because it bothered me night and day. When they finally took me out to sit on the doorstone for that first time, it was with F'ala's hand clamped firmly on my shoulder so I wouldn't go any further than allowed.

I didn't remember being taken to the fields in those first days I came into the world; there was too much of a jumble within me to sort out what was Inside and what was Outside. But now I was terribly aware of the piercing brightness, the flat, hot smell of the air and the searing dryness of the ground underneath my feet. Ā'dō took me on her lap to sit next to F'ala on the doorstone that first time but I immediately tried to get away, wondering why I'd ever wanted to go there to begin with.

Only the passing of days softened Outside to me and made it a curious place once more as I slowly became aware that this was the wide space F'ala and Ā'dō both disappeared into every day that was beyond the strict border of where I was allowed to go. For at first, I thought that when F'ala opened the front door, she ceased to be and it was only by some strange magic she appeared again hours later and this made me afraid every day that perhaps she wouldn't.

Early in the morning F'ala rose and ate with me and did chores before putting on her boots to disappear down the thin dirt road from the hut across the field into the forest until sometime before sunset. When she arrived, she came in for tea before going back out into the near field to gather or plant or til. As for me, I stayed at the window watching the saddest part of the day pass; the end of another day in a world beyond which I was no part of and the beginning of night when we were together again.

From up that same road F'ala disappeared from in the morning, Ā'dō came from some unknown place to stay with me until F'ala's return. I liked to stand in the doorway of the hut for this happiest part of the day to watch for her head bob up in the distance growing larger and larger as she came closer and closer up through the tall grass along the road. And how could I imagine anything past that very spot?

Then after tea in the evening and F'ala's return from the fields, Ãdō left us to walk down the long dirt road and disappear into the twilight, into the forbidden Outside. This was the other reason why I disliked the twilight, for Ãdō left us and it was only F'ala and I who sat by the open hut door and watched the sun go down, arguing occasionally about the smell of her pipe and then silently laying down in our own beds to listen to the sounds of little unseen night-things outside the open window.

Eventually when I had remembered all of the Inside things without any more help, I was allowed to come with Ãdō to the small garden right outside the east window to pull up groundnuts and to the storehouse connected to the hut to fetch dry foods and spices. And here, where the air beyond the garden was hazy and light dotted the ground through the tree canopies was another part of Outside I was told firmly I was never to enter by myself, ever.

For a time, I thought perhaps I would be swallowed up if I ever dared venture into it for F'ala was very serious about that one most important thing. I knew how serious she was because when I argued about that particular rule I spent more time in the corner than from any other disagreement we had, and there were many. And because she was so firm, I was all the more curious about that side of Outside, for I never saw she or Ãdō go into it either.

The one particular time of day I would eventually be allowed to go out by myself in the small space where the storehouse and hut connected under the thatch was to bathe as quickly as possible three times a week, for F'ala sent me out early in the morning when she cooked and sometimes even before the purple dawn. And no matter the oncoming heat of the day, I always came back clutching at my bottom to pinch some warmth back in. F'ala herself bathed every day after coming back in from the fields either outside in the evening sun or in the morning cool in a covered wooden tub by the hearth that was used by me when I was very small. Or when I was *new*, as I never seemed to grow at all.

Yet there were still chores I would have volunteered to do, such as anything requiring a trip to the mysterious river. When F'ala came back from the river with the clean linens she hung them over ropes tied from the hut's thatch to the roof of the storehouse. From the window in our sleeping room I watched the floating forms of blankets, petticoats and aprons whispering up and down on the breeze's soft voice. I thought that surely these were *samanē* watching us and as the wind lifted their gauzy skirts, I dropped to my knees beneath the window's ledge, hoping not to be seen.

Still, it was the possibility of seeing the river that kept me such a nuisance to F'ala with my begging and arguing. But I was bright enough to sense that the anger that surrounded any conversation about my ever going into the Outside was actually a dim fear of something far bigger than me and I never tried to get there on my own.

And this was how our days and nights passed for the first year I knew of my life, that time in which I became an análong.

mi'hal'ē
11

the ambiguous nature of
words

m'mūd'hē m'sunchē ihn
na'nalar

THEN when I had been alive for one year that I knew, I learned about death, a lesson which started with my favorite food.

Every day of the week Ādō and I worked together at some sort of job. Dōnchan and norsa were for threshing, churning, plucking and processing the grains and fruits and vegetables for the week. Eredin was the day to bake and preserve. Shoúlin and ninchan were days devoted to sewing, quilting, knitting and patching up. The endless task of making cloth was only outdone by the equally tedious sewing and mending of shoes but Ādō did all the hard parts.

But my favorite was the first day, amiti, which trailed on from the last day of the week, ninchan. On the morning of ninchan, F'ala got up even earlier than usual and left the hut with her bow and arrows to hunt. It was the only time I was left alone, as F'ala said I was now big enough to mind myself and not set anything on fire.

Minding myself was the easy bit; my chores didn't vary from any other day and there were plenty of them. Fighting off boredom by myself was another matter. When F'ala returned in the afternoon on ninchan she would disappear into the storehouse for hours doing what I didn't know, while I practiced writing on the low table in the common room. Not my first choice of amusements.

F'ala was always writing letters, it was part of the things she did when she wasn't away in the Outside or working in the garden or going off to do things in the field or washing at the river. I could imagine what might go on in these places as I knew the meanings of their words, but I didn't understand the purpose of letters. Letters, as I could picture, were a bit of parchment from someone to someone else. There were only three of us, so what was the use of letters? I never saw where they went, and I was too timid of the mask at the top of the ladder to sneak a look at what they said.

For several months F'ala had been teaching me to write on parchment. I couldn't imagine what I needed to do this for and often didn't work very hard at it on my own, but she persisted, leaving me long bits of writing to copy so I'd learn the horizontal swirls of Dala-ang and the vertical slashes of Dala-oúam. "See here?" she'd say, painting a stroke upward and dotting it deftly on the side in one long motion. "This side is thick like the side of a tree. Your strokes are much too thin, they hold nothing but water!"

So, I'd try a few lines, then scowl and lay my head on them to nap.

I didn't like to copy but I desperately hated to *write*. "Open your mind and put down your thoughts," F'ala would command. My thoughts had nothing to say to my hand they couldn't say to my mouth. "Why can't I work on it when Ādō comes?" I whined one afternoon, thinking I could talk Ādō into letting me off the hook to practice. "Because you're the one who needs to practice, not Ādō," I was told, and that was that.

Before my first year was over, every week on the morning of amiti Ādō would come down the narrow path from the woods and stop by the hut to invite F'ala to come with her to the shrine. It was a strange exchange: Ā'dō standing at the door in a long golden apron over her dress and silver ribbons tied on her ears and F'ala in her plain short dress and boots shaking her head, saying she wasn't dressed, go on ahead. If I asked why we couldn't come along I was told the same: *we weren't dressed.* When I once mentioned we weren't short on cloth I ended up in my space in the corner, now well- marked by the end of my nose.

But one evening as we sat on the doorstone watching Ā'dō disappear into the forest, F'ala said these magic words: "I guess it's time I took you to the shrine." I remember there were two moons in the sky when she said this, one smiling, one leering, and I stood up so fast their faces blurred in front of me. "Really? Are we going to get dressed?" I said hopefully.

"It's time you learned about Mī'á. We'll go with Ā'dō this week," she thought out loud without really answering.

"Outside?" I heard my voice sound small, thrilled but scared all the same.

F'ala's reply was swift. "With the two of us and never, *ever-ever* on your own! That hasn't changed and it never will."

I nodded carelessly and went inside to put myself to bed, suddenly eager to lay alone so I could think of what the shrine might be like. I knew the word Mī'á had many meanings: *creator, beginning, source, root, origin.* But just like my practice script, the words I spent the next afternoon printing out were so small and constricting. Even so, the next morning my excitement couldn't be dimmed when Ā'dō came knocking at the door in her golden apron.

"We're coming!" I shouted and threw open the door to Ā'dō's wide-eyed surprise. "You are? You are! Where's F'ala?" she looked around me in the doorway. Turning, I saw F'ala in a deep blue dress I'd never seen, covered with a golden apron just like Ā'dō's. With F'ala's head uncovered and her ears tied up in silver ribbon, I wouldn't have known her at all if not for her spots. "Close your mouth, you look stupid," F'ala swatted my cheek as I gaped and pulled me along outside the door to the back of the hut and past the garden.

The walk seemed to take forever and with both Ā'dō and F'ala pulling me by my hands I had no time to let my eyes explore the sights of new trees and grasses, or to enjoy the cool, green breeze that seemed to live only under the tree canopy. How unlike the flat, dry brown patch of ground the hut stood on with only a few small trees to block the angry sun! I remember thinking that this must be the holy place where Mī'á lived, somewhere in these magical trees immune to the heat.

From that day on I was taken to the shrine every week in order to "visit Mī'á." There were many things I didn't quite understand about Mī'á but they all started here, at a small clearing underneath the low tree branches where a tiny little house stood atop a pole; the shrine. The shrine's roof was wooden, curved and pointed at the ends, which was nothing like our hut's circular roof of hairy thatch. I wished I could run my fingers along the red shiny paint and trace the ornaments carved into the ends of it but if F'ala wasn't a fan of misbehavior during the week, she doubly hated it on amiti so I kept my hands to myself.

Under the shrine lay a shallow tray filled with yellow and green-colored sand where we lit sticks of dark brown incense that smelled both spicy and sweet and said prayers to Mī'á. Ā'dō told me that Mī'á was the Great Spirit who created us and gave us our food and shelter. We prayed to ask for our needs and show our gratitude. I didn't understand why we had to go to a little shrine in the trees to visit Mī'á if the Creator was everywhere as F'ala countered, but I certainly wasn't going to argue and go back to sitting at home again on amiti.

The shrine was the only place I saw F'ala pray; the very suggestion of her having to ask someone else for something was unthinkable, yet she did silently along with the rest of us. As for me, praying was like writing. My heart wasn't as interested in gratitude as it was in what could possibly lay beyond the shrine, and since no-one else could hear my thoughts to check up on me, my prayers were more often questions about the Outside *past* the Outside.

At the shrine Ā'dō taught me about *mbúana*. This meant the things we did over and over and over again because we had to and after a while, we began to like doing them and then it became hard to remember ever not doing them. Mbúana meant approaching the shrine with our eyes covered and then bowing to it (but trying not to trip and fall onto it). Lighting the incense sticks and pouring water on the ground underneath the shrine was called *lalōmō*; making our shrine pure so Mī'á could come close to us (but remembering that the Spirit was still everywhere all at once).

The prayers and songs we said while walking to the shrine and back were called *dorāma*; the ones we said by ourselves when we touched our head, nose and chest were called *urcūrū*. *Tsúana* were the little stones and beads Ā'dō and F'ala turned over and over in their hands as they kneeled and repeated names I could never quite hear with their foreheads touched to the bottom of the shrine. They said this helped them focus on what they wanted to ask the Creator. I had plenty of questions to ask and I knew I could do it without all the stones, but I managed to stand and watch; learning and keeping my mouth shut.

The shrine was also the only place F'ala ever really spoke to me about anything important in particular. It was strange because she never had any trouble snipping at me any other time. Amiti was the only day F'ala didn't go to the fields at all, and in the early evening she sat with me on the hot doorstone, allowing me to look at her picture-scrolls of plants and animals so I could memorize their names.

But I thought we should always talk in all those quiet spaces in those evenings on the doorstone or on the way to the shrine. After all, there were only three of us and my only other prayers were to ask for some more of us análong to talk to and keep away the sadness of that silence. "You could make more like me, after all I'm a very convenient size I think. I never hit my head on the doorframe," I helpfully suggested to the Creator.

Ā'dō said I could talk to Mī'á anytime I wanted to, anywhere I wanted to, and this made much more sense to me. For, like the words on parchment that seemed so static, the motions we went through at the shrine were disconnected from what I would come to be aware of as a continual movement beyond what I could see, and that I understood was what we called by the name Mī'á. So I would walk about the hut speaking aloud to the Creator often, and F'ala put a quick stop to that, saying that shrines were the place we had a long talk with Mī'á with our heads down (which was called *ararō*), and by the twelfth moon, *didn't I pay attention to anything?*

And after that first year when I learned all of these important and menial things, I also learned that things end. We woke, we slept, we ate, we belonged, we lived, we prayed, and we died. It wasn't just that I learned this lesson and put it away inside my mind to mull over later, but that I encountered it over and over in different forms and from many teachers over time.

Besides the shrine visit, on amiti we also ate stew, a thick, salty soup with chunks of meat poured over rice. I had other favorite foods of course; steamed tea buns and lāāca cakes with their sugary crust or milk nuts and rice porridge. But amiti stew was by far the thing I asked for most and over time F'ala became more and more irritated that I asked. She explained that amiti was about resting from the week's work and enjoying the good things the Creator provided for us, the best that we had, and as such she worked hard to make sure we had the stew. But I never saw this work or what went into it, and in my self-centeredness I asked for it more often, complaining that I would like to eat the salty stew every day.

My memory held brightly a certain day at the temple when I first became aware of the end of things; a day in autumn when I held the brown incense sticks and breathed in their fragrance. On that certain day only F'ala and I went to the shrine because Ā'dō had not come down the road that day. Ā'dō, who was sweet and kind, seemed to be weak in one way: illness often followed her and as time went on I became annoyed at the days I spent only with F'ala, for her words were so few.

"You are *spoiled*," F'ala answered me in a sour voice. "We don't eat this on any other day because it is against the Law." The Law was something F'ala had not yet described to me and I was unusually outspoken in that instant for law was a word I had no concept of yet. It seemed to me she was only making this up and I blurted, "The Law is stupid. I want to eat stew every day!"

F'ala took me hard by the shoulder and wrenched me around to look her in the face. More amused than frightened because I'd never been punished by her own hand, I looked back at her deep in the eyes which only angered her the more. She gave me a look I'd seen more than once on her face towards me, a look that said I was wrong; that I myself was wrong somehow. This must be something else I didn't know about myself. In that moment I felt the world flow around me, circling as it did when I looked past the shrine into that movement I knew as Mī'á, threatening to drown me in knowledge.

"On nanchin I go out into the forest to bring back a hadim to prepare for the stew. We eat the meat of a living creature on amiti to remind us that we also will stop one day and die. Like the hadim, we are connected, fragile and mortal. From now on, you must remember that we do not go on and on. Everything you see in this world will die in its time. I will die someday, you will, Ādō will, just as we were all born."

I hadn't been particularly aware of the hadim until then other than a stray snake that might run across my foot on the way to the shrine or the flat, painted pictures on F'ala's scroll of creatures I'd never seen in real life. And so, I hadn't cared so much about the true reason we kept customs. But that day I realized going to the shrine must mean something more than just looking at the pretty carvings, smelling incense and saying all those prayers; it must have something to do with living and now my favorite part of all this was something that had to do with dying. That day I realized from her scolding that when F'ala left our hut with her bow and arrows, she was going to steal the life of some hadim.

When we ate meat, it had once been as living as each of us; waking and walking and lying back down. That meant there were other, smaller beings out beyond us that I knew nothing of, and they knew nothing of me. And perhaps there were other, bigger beings as well. In an instant my world became far larger and stranger, and at the same time so tiny and constricted by the prospect of such a thing as death.

As I walked in front of F'ala back to the hut that day, my head became fuzzy with questions that came back over and over to wonder why was it fact for F'ala and curiosity for me? Why did I want to see so badly to know?

"I know you're thinking it," F'ala said suddenly as we neared the clearing leading into the garden. "You're thinking I'm a shar'dhūa."

I wasn't thinking it, but I didn't look up as I became instantly aware that my walking had become stiff and disjointed. That word, shar'dhūa, something about it niggled me coldly.

"I've told you never to go into the forest and you've been careful to listen to me. But you are learning more about the world and you may be tempted to go there in a way you weren't before. Listen to me very carefully now: you are never to follow me into the forest on ninchan, never. Óngman; when something dies, is hard to understand. It steals the breath of our life and we cannot wake again. And when I hunt, I mean to kill." I could see her glancing at me from the side, but I was trying to put the feelings of fear from the words together with what I knew of F'ala, for though we rubbed each other the wrong way often, I'd never truly feared her. Now I was struck by what power she must have to steal life itself. But I was also struck by my own wonderment of what might happen if I saw her do this, and the surprising desire to in order to believe in it.

"You're big enough to mind yourself when I go hunting and you're big enough to understand you must never follow and distract me and cause me to need more than one shot," she lectured, but softly.

It frightened me in a way I couldn't explain. The word óngman had only meant an end to me, a boundary of sorts. The end of my arm, the end of a meal, the end of a dress's hem. The end of something living was beyond what I could understand. I remembered birth quite well and assumed everyone else did too. But when F'ala explained death, it uncovered the possibility of loss I'd never had to think about before. I didn't understand how we fit together in the little hut, only that we did and if F'ala and Ādō died, I would be utterly alone. So, I didn't answer. Rather, I stood making little circles in the dirt with my thin shoe, taking more notice of the grime on it than her words because I didn't want to talk about them not being there one day.

F'ala sighed heavily and pulled up her skirts and apron over her ankles before entering the garden.

"Death is the end of our time *here*. The thing is, you and I and Ādō are of one kind, and the most important thing to our kind is that we do all that we can for the dying. We cannot keep from being born, and we cannot stop from dying. In these things we are each equal," F'ala said. "That's all we need to talk about today."

But just as I didn't know where I'd *been* before I went through the confusion of birth, I didn't know where I would go after my death. And though I took some comfort that F'ala claimed the three of us were the same kind, I couldn't shake that feeling of wrongness under her eyes that suggested I may be of the same kind as she and Ādō, I still wasn't *of* them. I understood enough never to follow her.

I'd learned an important lesson that day, but my mind immediately skipped forward to latch onto F'ala's words about being of one kind and I felt a sort of expansion of my own concept of myself which crowded out my other thoughts of the day. I was determined to uncover the truth, to catch up with F'ala and Ādō now that I'd been allowed to see a tiny piece of the world around me.

It was about a month later when F'ala decided I should also be dressed to go to the shrine and set Ādō to sewing an small apron and ribbons for me. I was quite excited to be given an opportunity, no matter how small, to fit in. On the big day I was to finally be dressed, F'ala went to her trunk to fetch both her apron and mine while I sat on the bed kicking my legs in my enthusiasm.

Many of F'ala's things were hidden in the trunk she kept at the end of her bed that, like every other interesting thing it seemed, I wasn't allowed to touch. I was to learn this was where she also kept her small looking-glass.

She picked up the shiny round glass and held it up facing her, fussing with her ribbons and moving the glass this way and that as her eyes followed it. "I want to see!" I whined and when she was finished, she leaned down next to me and held it up before our faces.

I fell straight backward into her, knocking the glass out of her hand but luckily just onto the bed where it was unharmed. "Someone's *in* there!" I stammered, scuttling backward to the wall. "Get up!" F'ala tutted. "It's a looking-glass. That's us, you and I. It's just our reflections." She pulled me to my feet and stood behind me, leaning over to keep a better hold on me as she lifted the glass again. "Look again and don't *touch* it. It's only a picture of us," she reminded, and I peered in at the two faces looking back at me.

Now up until that moment I'd been dimly aware that my arms and legs didn't look like those of F'ala and Ādō's. That is, while being much smaller, mine were so much lighter as to have no color at all where theirs were varying shades of spring-sky blue. I'd noticed that F'ala was covered in clouds of fine brown speckles but Ādō wasn't. I'd noticed that F'ala's ears were short and thin, Ādō's were long and rounded. F'ala was taller, Ādō was shorter. I'd noticed the large pink mark across Ādō's forehead and the cuff of bracelets F'ala never took off of her upper arm. But for me, well I'd never given much thought to what I really looked like as I'd never seen myself reflected back.

Looking at the glass now, I saw that I was much smaller than F'ala, my face rounder and my ears somewhat pointed like F'ala's but longer like Ādō's. My eyes were not incense-brown like theirs but black and colorless like a night without stars. My face wasn't speckled at all like F'ala's but above my eyes and on my cheeks were small, pink patches I touched with my finger to find were the rough bits of my face I often picked at but never knew how they appeared. But most noticeable was the color of my face, or rather, the lack of it. The word that came to mind was samanē; a spirit.

"What's wrong with me?" I whispered, staring hard at F'ala and this stranger in the looking glass. "Nothing is wrong with you," F'ala said sharply but I thought maybe she didn't understand what I was asking. "Why don't I look like you?" I asked. Now she looked uncomfortable as she hadn't even the day she explained death to me and put the glass back in her trunk, not answering me right away. I followed her around the room as she dawdled until she turned to me in irritation. "You can't look like me because you look like you. I don't look like you, do I? We all look like ourselves."

"But you and Ādō …?"

F'ala interrupted impatiently. "Do you have arms? Do you have legs?" I nodded. "And eyes? A nose? A mouth? Ears?" I nodded. "And a tail? Have you got a tail?" I nodded grimly. My tail, that bit of unnecessary and undisciplined end of my rear flicked in agreement of its own accord. "Then you look like an análong and that's all you need to worry about." I sensed this wasn't the real answer I was looking for but that there was also truth in it, so I nodded and followed her out into the common room.

And I did worry. In the coming weeks when I gazed from F'ala to Ādō and back again as we ate together, did chores together and visited the shrine together, a word kept coming to my mind, warm and lonely and welcoming and excluding all at once. *Asama*. It had to be the connection between them, the thing which separated me. But asama spun out and touched so many other solitary words that equally made no sense to me: *mother, father, brother, sister, aunt, uncle, cousin, grandparent, child*, and perplexingly, *dl'ah'sha*. How could there be all of these other words for things that didn't exist? And what was I, what word belonged only to me?

The only word that came to me was samanē. Spirit. Invisible. One who had no place in the world.

* * *

I learned to call them Dandhō and Little Dandhō in my head, but never in front of them. Though confusing, these seemed the most sensible terms I could think of to describe who they were to me. As for them, they most often called me *dhana*, another disembodied word with more meaning than I could understand.

Now, it didn't seem to matter to me that both Dandhō and Little Dandhō had kept the truth of death from me because I was only truly angry with F'ala. Or perhaps only my heart was broken over the matter that because she felt withholding things was good for me when I knew better; that F'ala was so very sure of herself and her own opinion that nobody else's ever mattered. She thought I was too stupid to wonder about the world beyond us and too small to handle the truth that we weren't alone. And I suppose, too weak to accept I wasn't wanted in that world I'd been told over and over was too dangerous for me, but clearly wasn't so for my sisters.

I lay in bed all that week thinking of what I knew, telling Dandhō I was too sick to do my chores and I was lucky enough to be left alone. Little Dandhō came every day as usual but also left me alone. Now as I thought back to the day Dandhō had told me about death and venturing out into the world, I wondered if there was something more I wasn't being told. Laying on the floor one night I spied something hidden up underneath F'ala's bed and had only had time to look at it in snatches but now I knew what it was. The word was *asama-loúr*.

I pulled it out and carefully flipped through its pages, studying the painted faces of *other* análong I'd never seen before. Perhaps they were in the Outside somewhere, but perhaps they were dead. I was confused. There were pictures of she-dogs like me but they looked like Dandhō. And yet, her eyes were wider, her face rounder, her spots lighter and fewer. Her limbs, shorter. Then I recognized Little Dandhō. I could tell they were much smaller than me at the beginning of the book and much bigger by the end. Somehow, she had grown, somehow Little Dandhō had grown; they'd changed from the pictures. Would I? *Had* I? And though Dandhō said I was part of her asama, did I have my own in the Outside? Wasn't anyone looking for me? Who were the others who had the same eyes as Dandhō and the same nose as Little Dandhō? Where had they gone?

Had they been killed by even other análong like Dandhō killed with her bow? Was that why the world was so dangerous beyond the little hut?

Others…

But Dandhō didn't know of my newfound knowledge, so I decided to wait her out. That amiti it was only Dandhō and I at the shrine again, and when we returned I set the table for tea and she mixed the leaves carefully in the stout little pot and told me I could fetch the day before's leftover cakes. As we sat across from each other she cleared her throat. "Feeling better then?"

I wiped my face with one hand and took a rudely enormous bite of cake. "Tsō." It was a lie. If I felt anything, it was the attraction of being difficult on purpose because I *knew*.

Dandhō's eyes narrowed. "I think better enough to eat cake today and do some chores tomorrow. Ādō will come late tomorrow and bring her wash. You can rest in the morning but then I want you to help her pin it up." I nodded obediently and said nothing more, thinking maybe I shouldn't be so bratty since Dandhō was actually being easy on me after the talk about death.

The next morning I dawdled around the hut after she left, sketching the little birds outside my window on my copysheets and rolling around in the bedclothes far longer than I should have when I heard a happy voice outside calling "*Chūba*! Hurry and put your overskirt on. We're going out!"

I didn't need to be told again. Grabbing the stiff overskirt from the wall-peg, my fingers flew over the door latch and I stumbled to keep up with Little Dandhō as she hurried up the path.

"Where are we going? What are we going to tell...?" I huffed behind her.

"We're not going to tell her anything. We'll be back by before she is. Don't you trust me? I'll make sure nothing happens to you," Little Dandhō assured me. "I'm never going to be as clever as F'ala and I don't have the answers for you, but there's lots I can show you. We're going to Sé Elamangúō."

The river! In my mouth my tongue rolled over the name and I trotted along happily, my curiosity far outweighing any danger that might await me. It was easy to trust Little Dandhō; it felt as if we'd known each other for far longer than my memories allowed because she seemed to understand me easily.

I dragged my little linen basket behind me lazily, but ahead of me, Little Dandhō walked with hers balanced perfectly on her head. Her shadow, long and elegant curled along behind on the worn path through the short dry grass.

"Quietly, come here," she called against the soft wind as she kneeled down in a patch of tall grass and sat the basket beside her on the ground carefully. Dumping mine over with a huff, I thrust my face into the grass and saw we'd come to a little pond of water ringed by thick, high fronds. We were perched on top of a small overlook and below us ran Sé Elamangúō itself, a wide, shallow bed of sparkling water to rival the glisten of the stars themselves.

"Others!" I exclaimed, but the wind carried my word away beyond hearing. Below us, a breath-taking scene of dozens and dozens of análong had come to wash themselves and their clothing.

As I gawked open-mouthed, Little Dandhō explained that the world Outside the hut stretched so far and so wide it was full of análong. She told me how to tell what part of the world each group had come from by how they pulled their ears back on their heads, what coverings they wore or how they washed. There were blue análong like Dandhō and Little Dandhō; brown and tan ones; and grey as well. They were speckled and spotted, striped and patched, dappled and plain. Some stood upright just like us and others ran along on all fours and some even flew! Others veiled in elegant robes while some stood naked and sweaty under the beating sun. But all moved in a waving rhythm as they pulled and beat and worked their cloth in the river's shallow foam, chanting soft but strong music I could catch snatches of in the breeze. I wished I could look at them forever, contemplating the different-colored folds of skin, the speckles and marks and feathers and shapes of eyes.

Little Dandhō pointed to a winged análong rolling about happily in the dust; beating up a happy cloud around him. "That's a darna, an análong of the air."

"And those?" I raised my nose in the direction of several squat-legged análong crouched in the grass with blankets fastened to their strong backs. They were rooting plants from the ground with their claws, snipping off the knobs by their teeth and transferring them into baskets.

"Na'g'ealach. Análong of the moons."

"But what are we?"

"Na'shanár. Análong who wear shoes." Little Dandhō smiled happily. "All of us are análong, just different sorts."

Like I'm different? I wanted to ask but could plainly see that this wasn't the case, because wings or shoes or not, all had a color. And whatever Dandhō had said about arms and legs and tails went silent inside me for I could only see what I was lacking amongst all those análong. Little Dandhō sighed softly, her brow crinkling. Her smile faded just a little as if she realized she didn't have the answer to the question I wasn't asking.

Because she must have also thought what I suspected: that whoever had made me had forgotten to give me my color.

Sighing all of the air out of my lungs, I flopped onto my back and watched the flat white-streaked sky, squinting my eyes against its brightness, listening to the song from below in full with my hands clasped behind my head. I let the sun's flat warmth stroke my face back and forth in between the stretches of pale cloud wisps in a lull in time to the song's pulse as the washers from one side of the river chanted to those on the other side who answered back in rounds.

(gamahl lalāi gamahl lalāi)	(wash away, wash away)
shāe éh pala nō mahhaba	it is the custom of the house
(gamahl lalāi gamahl lalāi)	(wash away, wash away)
gamahl lalāi gamahl lalāi	wash away, wash away
na'dhēr céan gamahl sōtala tī	those who wash misfortune out
(gamahl lalāi gamahl lalāi)	(wash away, wash away)
cī'úa cūr-se dhāmā dōpa	will have a happy village
(gamahl lalāi gamahl lalāi)	(wash away, wash away)

Eventually I must have fallen asleep to its rhythm and a sudden shaking woke me. I looked up at the laughing face of Little Dandhō who'd taken the clean linens all the way home and come back for me. I was filled with the strong-colored smell of grass as I rolled over and rubbed my hands of the prickles it left on me. "I shouldn't have left but we're still on F'ala's land and no one is allowed past the river to bother you anyway." She helped me up and we snuck off quietly as I mused over the scent of clean all over her hands.

We came to a shallow field and stopped to sit on a log in the withering shade of the trees. Feeling bold, I asked, "Where does F'ala go every day?" Little Dandhō hesitated but then pointed to the right where in the afternoon haze I could faintly see the tops of huts and treetops poking up here and there. "There's a village over there. It's called Pōcarū. We can't go over there," she sighed. "We'd be in real trouble if we were seen."

I thought about this and blurted out, "If *I* was seen."

She gave me a guilty look and then looked away.

"You've been there," I accused without malice. "You and F'ala leave every day and come back but I never can. It's just me that's the trouble, isn't it? It's just me that isn't supposed to even think of Outside. I don't understand. They don't look so dangerous."

Little Dandhō signed and looked down at her hands in defeat. "They don't like things that are different. Believe me, I'm different too. And so is F'ala. We just want to protect you from things that have happened to us."

"Is that why *we're* asama? Because we're different?" I asked.

"I think it must be," she answered, reaching around to give me a hug. "And because we are, if you ever want to, you can call us your sisters. Your na'dandhō. Only if you want to."

I smiled and pointed out, "That's confusing. How would you know who I'm talking to? I'll just call you Dandhō and Little Dandhō because F'ala is my big sister and you're my little-big-sister." And she smiled back, impressed with how clever I was.

We sat a moment more and I gathered up enough courage to say what I'd been thinking when I lay in bed pretending to be sick. "But sometimes, I think I just don't belong here, like maybe… maybe I came from somewhere Outside. It seems like there's something in me that's being pulled up all the time, trying to escape out of me." I paused, waving my hands as though trying to catch the substance I was describing. "But I guess my body's so heavy it can't escape. I'm lost in here. I'm trapped."

"I know that exact feeling," she exhaled and smiled, and I could tell that she really did so. Which was why I so dearly loved Little Dandhō, for she was sometimes almost like me. I still liked my days with her over my evenings with Dandhō even though the evenings had become cozy with the three of us each at our own separate doings in the hut while the kettle whistled over the hearth for evening tea.

I smiled gratefully in return, wondering if it could possibly be happier day after seeing all the wonders I'd seen when a small, colorful creature fluttered near me and took off again. It flittered as if teasing me, and after several tries, I caught it and gingerly sandwiched it in between my hands, feeling it tickle me between the folds of my fingers. Little Dandhō laughed. "Be still and he'll sit on your hand. That's a *lhēsha*. They don't come near the hut because we grow grain in the fields. Na'lhēsha eat from flowers."

"*Lyeee-shaaaa*," I repeated, memorizing the delicate feel of the word in my mouth. The creature peeked out at me from the little hole my palms made around it and my brow, furrowed in the concentration of studying the pattern on its wings, unwrinkled when it fanned them delicately. I smiled. It rested for a second more before flying off and leaving me. "*Hembarē!*" I cried and immediately stood to follow after it in the grass. "Don't go!" Little Dandhō called, "Mi'hal'ē! Let the lhēsha go to die in peace."

I stopped immediately, poised on one foot and turned my head stiffly towards her. "Óngma?" Her face softened, and I sensed she was going to tell me something else about death. Something true but cruel to spoil the sweet of this already bittersweet day.

"Lhēsha only live a very short time; it's said only long enough to make another living thing smile. Then they can die happy knowing that they lived their purpose," she explained. "Try not to be too sad."

I stared at her, utterly horrified. My fleeting happiness had cost something its life. I had killed, *just like Dandhō*. But I hadn't meant to. I didn't know! It must be true then, that death was so close to life even I had such power to bring it about. But something inside me snapped back with the certainty that I had *no right* to use it. Without thought, my legs moved, hoisting me up and carrying me through the tall, thick grass far beyond Little Dandhō's sight. I had to escape.

I had to escape *myself*.

"Mi'hal'ē!" she gasped behind me, her shouts blending into the field's dry shuffle underneath my feet. Faster I ran without looking up, leaves and branches scratching painfully against my bare legs as I went on until I could no longer hear Little Dandhō's panicked voice and when I turned my head to see how far I'd gone, the ground came up fast to meet my face. Stiffly pulling myself up to my knees, I picked bits of skin off of my palms from the fall and came face to face with the feet of someone else; a real análong right there in front of me. It was a brown dhana just a little taller than I with short folded ears, bright blue eyes and thin, long legs. He wore a long blue smock and short trousers.

"*S'bonála?*" he said and backed away from me, eyes wide. "You're a samanē!" He pointed right at my chest, his hand trembling. "You *are* a samanē, aren't you? Are you *she*? Are you Āe'rū?"

"I'm Mi'hal'ē," I squeaked, as terrified of him as he was of me.

"But you must be a samanē! Look at you, you haven't any color. What are you doing here? Where did you come from? What *happened* to you?"

I brushed myself off, feeling my face puff up hotly. "I'm an análong just like you. I live with my dandhō in our hut way over there," pointing in the direction Little Dandhō and I had come from, hoping now I'd remember how to get back there. I demanded back, "Where do you come from?"

"I come from Pōcarū of course. Who's your dandhō? "

"F'ala," I started but was stopped by his stare.

"F'ala the Ta-? She doesn't have any asama except her sister Ādō. Everybody knows she left for the city when she was little like us and never married. Who are you really?"

I sat down with a defeated little sigh. "You're the first *other* I've ever met. I don't know where I came from, or how old I am, or who I belong to. I just know I woke up and I live with F'ala and Ādō and I'm not actually allowed to be out here." I rested my head on my hand with another sigh and rolled my eyes after pulling up a sleeve to my shoulder to show him that my skin was truly colorless everywhere.

"I'm not the *other*, you are," he murmured, looking me over closely. "But if you don't know anything about yourself, you *could* be a samanē."

I am, I thought. I must be. Is it so different than being an análong? But I wasn't going to admit that aloud.

"I'm Anshē," the dhana said, waving his hand. "I don't really have many *na'dasha* so you can be mine I guess."

Dasha. *Friend.* I wondered if this was the answer to my prayers for more análong like me. I was starting to think Mī'á might be back paying me today for all those days at the shrine. "Why don't you have many?" I asked, figuring I couldn't lose now so I may as well ask.

Anshē blushed. "Well, my ēdandha and I are, well, we're just…"

"Different?" I guessed. He nodded. As I'd run away from Little Dandhō just moments before I'd felt like I never wanted to smile again; that my smile was the whole problem when it came to the lhēsha. Now I couldn't help myself. How could life not be wonderful from now on? *I had a dasha.* Someone to come back to. Someone who connected me to the Outside. "Let's be different together," I grinned, holding out my hand to him.

He looked at my hand keenly for a moment and then said, "I don't think I should tell my ēdandha about you. She can't possibly keep a secret."

But it was too late. Something crashed wildly through the waving grasses behind Anshē and out tumbled a little brown dhana much smaller than I. Cute, brown and blue-eyed like him, she pulled herself up and brushed off her yellow sundress.

"I found you *shinō*! What kind of brother leaves his ēdandha behind?" she exclaimed but stopped in mid-breath when she noticed me.

Anshē rolled his eyes. "This is Rāca."

Rāca crouched before me and studied my face silently in great concentration, reaching her hand out only to be slapped by her shinō. "Don't touch," he hissed. Then, just as quickly as she'd dropped silent, Rāca jumped up and down, patting her cheeks in excitement. "Shinō! You caught us our own samanē. I can make wishes!"

"She *might* be," Anshē corrected her. Rāca leaned over, putting her face right in mine to inspect me better and I returned the favor, not pleased at the scrutiny. Her face was lightly freckled, her long ears were both wrapped and tied at the ends with yellow ribbon to match her dress. She was chubbier than her brother, a head shorter than me and she had a pale patch over both her eyes. In a way she reminded me of the early pages in the asama-loúr of chubby little Dandhō. "If you're not a samanē, what are you?" she demanded.

Anshē stepped in to my rescue. "*An dasha ta óō, 's an dasha nūl úō.* My friend and *your* friend."

Rāca looked uncertain. She touched her cheek and then pointed to my face. "But something's wrong with you. Análong are brown or grey or blue of course. Brown for loyalty!" She threw her right hand up in the air as if signaling something.

"Blue for prosperity!" Anshē punched the air with equal enthusiasm.

"Grey for peace," Rāca nodded and crossed her heart with her other hand.

Anshē quieted. "But white means death." I squirmed under his gaze. It couldn't be. Even Dandhō wouldn't keep that from me…surely.

"But don't worry. You're our dasha and we'll keep your secret. We won't tell anyone we saw you," he pointedly looked at Rāca to make sure she was listening. She rolled her eyes but then suddenly looked very pleased with herself, turned around and marched off through the grass, singing, "I found a samanē! I found a samanē! Wishes for me!" Anshē laughed. "She does that and nobody listens to her anyway. So, will you come back and play? We come here after school every day."

Play. School. Words I knew precious little about and wanted to know more of! "I might come again," I said vaguely.

"*Ēdeshan!* I'll look for you," he said and then disappeared into the grass behind Rāca.

Standing for a few moments in his wake, I allowed the soft breeze to ruffle my ears as I thought about my good fortune. There were other análong my own size who liked my company, not evil análong as I had been warned of. Then again, these dhana also knew something bad would happen if others saw me. Why was I the only one who didn't know?

I ran all the way back to find Little Dandhō at the log where I had left her. The sun shone flat and hot on my head and a little breeze pricked its way across my nose to cool me. I had found a dasha, and I recalled with a strange, warm flush that he liked me despite my color, or lack of it. After all, though I didn't know how so, he was also different just like me. I slipped my hand in Little Dandhō's as we slowly walked back towards the hut.

"Why didn't you come to find me?" I asked. "I knew you couldn't get very far. I should know, you won't make friends locked up in the hut all day." I smiled shyly, again thinking how much I loved Little Dandhō and now how angry I was with Dandhō that she hadn't told me the meanings of colors. Was there no end to what was kept from me?

"I know Anshē from the village school. Next week if we're very careful we could come back. I'm pretty sure he won't tell anyone," she smiled down at me. "Are you still upset about the lhēsha?" she asked.

"A little," I admitted, though I'd forgotten about it in the excitement of finding a friend.

"They're small and their lives are fleeting. But they know their purpose and their contentment with it is what makes them beautiful. Their purpose is what keeps them from being too sad to fly. It's a different sort of life than ours, but it's not less."

"Does everyone have a purpose?" I asked.

"Shě'á," she said, reaching over to smooth down my left ear. "Everything that was ever born. And it makes all the difference in the world to know it."

"How do you know what it is?" I asked eagerly. Maybe this was the answer I was looking for, the reason I had to be kept a secret. Maybe my purpose was something really secret.

Little Dandhō slowed, thinking. "You have to discover it. F'ala says it like this: everything that ever lived must take three journeys. Two of them, the journey to be born and the journey to die, must be taken alone. But the other journey is the one to find your purpose. No-one can tell you when it begins and no-one can tell you when it ends, or even where you will go."

"And I have to go all alone too?" my voice sounded smaller than I liked.

"Tsō," she smiled. "You'll never be alone on that journey. Everyone you meet, even for just a second, is part of that journey. So remember never be unkind to others; you need them. And be good to yourself, because everyone you meet needs you to finish theirs."

"Am I part of yours?" I asked incredulously.

"A very important part," she assured me.

"And do you know what your purpose is, Dandhō?" I asked.

"I don't know what it is. But I think it has to do with you."

"Then, "I mustered up my words to please her, "I'll try."

That night I laid down in the dark and congratulated myself on fooling Dandhō, but my thoughts kept coming back to a question I'd forgotten to ask that afternoon. What if I never found my purpose? Or worse, what if I didn't like it? But as I lay silently listening to Dandhō's shallow breaths, I felt a tugging at the edge of my consciousness which so frightened me that I pushed it away at once lest the very size of that knowledge should swallow me whole and I would be lost forever in understanding. I was only a dhana after all, and though I wanted to know my purpose, I still only wished to know the things of the young.

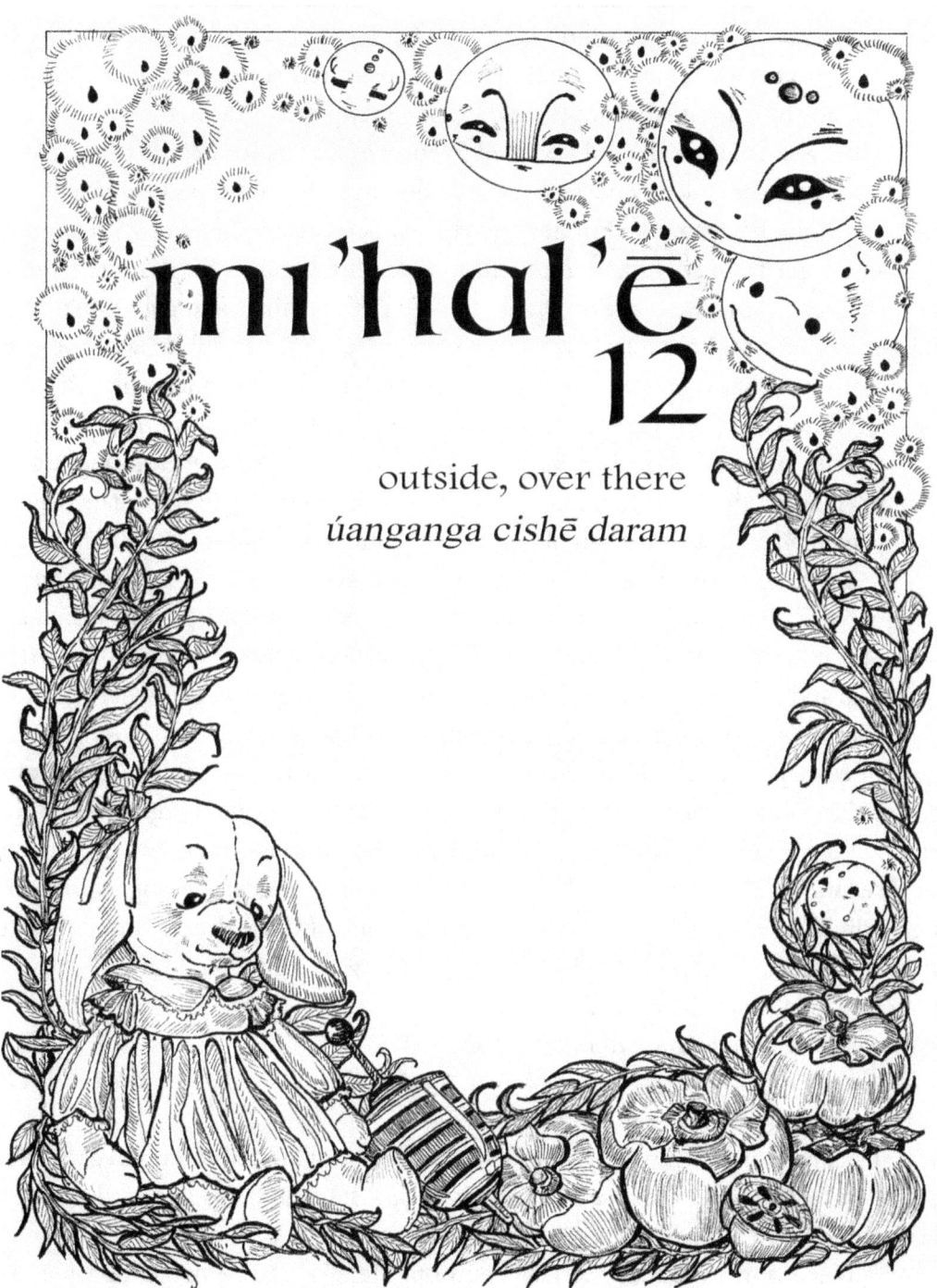

mi'hal'ē
12

outside, over there

úanganga cishē daram

ODANDHŌ had no idea where I had been that day at the river and true to her word, Little Dandhō took me back the following week to the field and every week after for a long time as I waited to see just how long it would take Dandhō to tell me what I already knew. They were beautiful days, wonderful, exciting times when I learned that there was an entirely separate world existing alongside the one I knew made only for dhana and I could catch a glimpse of it through the game called play, a world of laughter and color and sound I wanted to enter every chance I could get.

Rāca had a little doll she called De'úa'tē. This little doll in its yellow dress kept us entertained for many hours as we took her in and out of her gourd-shell bed and covered her with a scrap of cloth and made food for her from sticks and grass. Rāca made little houses for the doll from mud and grass and every week I came, we made up stories of De'úa'tē 's comings and goings in and out of the little mud huts. Sometimes Rāca allowed me to wrap up De'úa'tē 's ears like hers, and she showed me how to pull them up like other dhana she knew. *Of course,* I thought once when I'd known them long enough to know a bit more about their household, *this is why my ears hang loose and lopsided. It's because I don't have an a'ma like they do to put them up.* Once Rāca even brought a tiny set of cups painted purple and green which we used to have imaginary teas, and this pushed away my sad thoughts. How wonderful it was to be small! I'd never thought of it before, for all of my belongings were things of my Dandhō's that had been cut down to my size, not made directly for me.

Anshē and I played ball games in the hot, bright sun as Rāca found new and wonderful things in the grasses to play with. Anshē had several stretchy bright balls on string we batted back and forth, running up and down the dry field, cleverly avoiding any stagnant areas where mud seeped up through so I didn't bring back signs any signs I'd been Outside.

And sometimes we played school, my favorite game of play because I could see a little of what else I should know that I didn't learn at home. Anshē played the teacher and taught us from his school book which had pictures on its large pages. Rāca sat closest to him on the ground but I had to sit behind because I wasn't dressed for school. She-dogs wore yellow dresses, he-dogs wore blue smocks. And though I didn't like the yellow color, I soon wanted one of those dresses more than anything. But at our little play-school, Anshē taught us songs and how to salute the Ebūdean flag, and hit us across the scalp with a stick when we talked over him.

Rāca taught us how to remember numbers in a poem:
One little gēsa smiling at ten golden gifts under the temple eaves. One hundred red rolling balls bouncing over one thousand midnight forest shrines.

But it was the afternoon that Anshē gave us a writing lesson that he and Rāca began to look at me with the fear they'd had of me when we first met. It began when he sat us in a circle and passed out sticks to write in the dust with.

"We're going to learn to write today so pay attention. Here is how we make the Dala-ang for my name. Here is the beginning of it: *Ahn...*" He made some squiggles on the ground in our little circle.

"And the last bit, *SHEE!*" With a flourish he dotted the squiggles and sat down pointing to me. "There, it's easy. You try, Mi'hal'ē."

I'd been casually laying on my back with my knees up but I rolled over and quickly scratched out all three of our names at my feet without thinking. "Anshē: *a-n-s-h- -e*. Rāca: *r-a-c-a*. Mi'hal'ē: *m-i-lat-ha-lat-e*. You don't know how to write, do you? Is that why your book has only pictures in it?" It was too irresistible not to point out his error, not for the sake of being right but for the sake of sharing what I knew with someone other than Dandhō.

Quickly I could see I'd said the wrong thing.

"Hembarē," Anshē said quietly. "Stop doing that, you're just a dhana like us. you can't write."

Scrambling to my feet, I dropped my stick and gaped at him. "It's just writing," I stammered, terror flooding me over in icy washes at the thought I might have just trampled over an ever-moving line of acceptance between us.

"Then who taught you?" Rāca demanded, putting her hands to her hips and facing me.

"No-one! I just know!" I defended myself, picking up the stick again and hastily writing *Anshē ē dasha ta óō*. "Anshē is my friend! Look!"

"F'ala must have taught you, she's the Ta-!" he said scornfully.

"No-one taught me!" I shouted back at him, fists clenching. How dare he call me a liar!

"If you're so smart you'd know that's impossible. You're lower class just like us and you're younger than me!" he argued.

"Then bring me something from your school and I'll read it! I'll show you!" I shouted as Rāca snatched her doll up from its place in our play-school as if to protect her from something. "I sure will, you *liar!*" Anshē shouted back and grabbed his ēdandha's arm, marching her off into the grass and out of my sight, leaving me bewildered and hurt in the dust.

The next week they indeed brought back something, a little scrap of decorated scroll Anshē triumphantly held high in the air above the whispering grass, shouting out to me before we met, "And A'ma told me what it says too, so we'll just see when you try making it all up!"

Laying the scrap flat on the ground and sitting behind it, Anshē gave me a smug grin as Rāca stood at his shoulder, arms crossed. It was me against them and I was ready to win. I picked the scrap up and examined the beautiful marks on it, recognizing it as my own Dandhō's fine script. Well that made sense. I'd discovered this was what Dandhō did in the village all day. Everything in the village was written by her; signs and scrolls and letters alike. Turning it over in my hand, I saw the signature and looked up at Anshē, feeling not a little conceited. "Dandhō made this!"

Rāca glanced to Anshē but he waved his hand. "She lives with the Ta-. Of course, she can recognise the writing!" he said, as if I could do nothing myself.

Now entirely irritated, I said slowly and clearly, "*For dhana have no blindness but see the world as it is.*" I sat back on my hands in triumph.

Puzzled, four blue eyes stared back at me. "Something really is wrong with you," Anshē crawled back a little on the ground away from me. I shrugged nonchalantly, wishing I could unlearn it somehow. "But don't you think," I said, "Don't you just think some an'álong are a bit *more* different? Maybe they can just do other things and you didn't know it yet? Maybe they were always different?"

Anshē sat in the dust with his smock-sleeves rolled up and carelessly whipped a string attached to a small ball he had brought from home. As the string whipped around his head, a thin *wah! wah! wah!* rang through the air. He looked off vacantly over the field for some time as Rāca played with the edge of her yellow dress skirt also waiting for his reply. "I think maybe you ought to go to school with us, so you learn right," he said finally, lowering the toy to the ground.

I felt my face twisting in disbelief. I thought he understood about me! "But I'm not allowed to!"

Rāca put her hands on her head, pushing her belly out in thought. "Everyone would stare at you anyway. They'd run away or push you or trip you. I know all about it." Anshē gave her a swat on her ear. He said thoughtfully, "It's no good a dhana telling a dhana anything. You have to learn real things from grown-ups. You have to learn what you shouldn't know. Besides, you'd have us to sit with you. The other dhana do all that stuff to us too but we still have to go."

I looked down at myself, never feeling so separate before in my life and my hand twitched suddenly, making me wish to grab onto someone else's. It was a curious feeling and before I could stop myself, the words came out of me: "But Anshē, aren't we... dasha?"

Anshē glanced over his shoulder nervously, eyes widening a little. He nodded with no enthusiasm.

And since he agreed, I decided it was right to let my hand reach out. But he stepped back just slightly, so quickly out of my reach I nearly missed it. His eyes never left mine as Rāca hissed, "Don't touch her!"

Now this thing had bothered me for some time. I'd watched how Anshē and Rāca held hands, smacked each other playfully back and forth and knocked each other down in the dust, dirty and laughing. I'd also seen how they never came quite close enough to me to touch even when we played together. At first, I thought perhaps this was only because they were siblings, something I knew so little about anyway.

But as I thought more about it, I recalled that Dandhō and Little Dandhō were siblings and the three of us touched each other all the time. Little Dandhō helped me to dress, Dandhō sat near me to sleep. Rāca, however, was always careful to lay her doll on the ground or in its bed so I could pick it up. Anshē never handed his ball to me as he did to Rāca; he kicked or threw it over to me to catch.

It dawned on me that they'd never entirely stopped being afraid of me despite knowing I wasn't this Āe'rū they feared. One more mystery I couldn't ask Dandhō about lest I blow my cover.

"So why should I even ask Dandhō if I can come to school if everyone would run from me anyway?'" I asked bitterly, unsure if I was angry at them or at the truth.

Anshē scuffed his wrapped feet into the dust. "Because really we haven't got anyone besides our A'ma," he looked back down at the ground quickly when he saw me beginning to anger again. What sort of answer was that? "And you ought to learn properly don't you think? I mean it isn't your fault that you know things, but you don't know what you ought to. You don't know how much trouble you can get into if you know things you shouldn't. Well, I wish you would come anyway. I mean, we like you, you know?"

For this I was grateful and glad, for I knew then that I had truly been seen by someone else and I smiled bittersweetly to myself, letting the sadness seep in to comfort me. The next week Little Dandhō didn't bring me to the field to play with Anshē and Rāca and it was probably just as well.

* * *

That morning I considered my shoes; their heavy curve and worn buckles and thought of the woes of being a dhana and being told that I didn't need what I wanted and knowing I didn't want what I needed. Spending time with my friends had made me aware of how much nicer my things were even if second-hand and how guilty I felt for wishing for even better. Red shoes. I was desperate for red shoes and I knew from my friends that while the color red was forbidden to anyone except *holy* an'álong, I also knew if such could be gotten anywhere it would be in the village.

I could tell Little Dandhō had been to the village already before she came to the hut to stay with me that day because she wasn't wearing her plain day-dress. Dandhō had nothing to say when Little Dandhō lined her eyes with black paste and came home with her head uncovered, her pale pink dress changed to a dark brown and her wrists clinking with sparkly little bracelets. I knew better than to ask to wear such things; I was only a dhana. There was no say in this sort of business for me.

Two weeks before the fight over Anshē's book, I had noticed two thin silver rings at the end of Rāca's left ear and I instantly felt the heat of jealousy prick me. "My a'ma gave them to me," she purred, pulling gingerly at them for I could see the flesh around the thin metal was puckered and angry. Then her voice swelled extravagantly as she gloated, "They're silver cos I'm little but as soon as I'm big enough A'ma said she would get me a big gold ring for my nose like the she-dogs in Pōcarū wear." Anshē pulled at her tail to shush her but I silently cursed her and her rings, all the more because if I asked Dandhō to get me one she would know I had been talking to other dhana. Then again, if I was clever about it… Well, perhaps.

"I want a ring for my ear," I blurted at the table that evening, spitting out rice grains in between my words. Dandhō gave me an even look over her mug and continued drinking. She put the mug down quietly and then folded her arms and leaned back on her cushion beneath the table. She made a deep noise in her throat as if thinking it over and said, "Whatever would you do with a ring in your ear?" But I had already cleverly thought this out and said, "I want it because you have one. I think it's pretty." There, nothing to be suspicious about. *Very clever. Flatter her.*

She sat back up to the table and picked up her spoon. "You're too little to have such things. Even Ā'dō only got hers last year." I looked immediately to Little Dandhō who steadily picked at her rice and shot me a look from the corner of her eye. There was nothing to be said about it, no argument to be made. When Dandhō said things in *that* way, it was better to be silent. All the same, Little Dandhō could have helped me out and I sat pouting through the rest of the evening.

Determined not to be outdone, the next day when Little Dandhō took me to see my friends, I marched right up to Rāca and put my head up in the air. "Guess what Dandhō got for me?" Unimpressed, she continued playing with her doll. "Not silver rings in your ear," she answered. I smiled. "Tsō, something much better and it's in both of my ears." Rāca shot to her feet and stood on her toes to see. "Stand still, let me see!" she demanded. I stood stock still and waited for her to inspect me. "There's nothing at all in your ears, Mi'hal'e!" she accused and sat back down with a thud.

"Well you didn't look hard enough. Dandhō bought me diamonds for my ears and they're so fine you can only see them when I turn my head just so and they sparkle in the light." Rāca sat trying not to look interested but her curiosity got the better of her. "Turn your head! I want to see!" But I wouldn't do it, not for ten silver rings. And I didn't feel a bit sorry.

It was then the week after the fight that Little Dandhō decided to take me along to the village so she could visit her friend. I was happy to follow her for the chance to see where Dandhō spent her days away from us and somehow the story about my diamonds stuck in my head and made me feel somehow brave enough to go to think my ears shined as if they had some power, even if it was a lie. Little Dandhō made me to swear by the twelve moons that I would stay in the trees in the outer wall and not be seen, and while my intent wasn't to be seen, it wasn't to stay in the trees.

The village of Pōcarū was built up as a large circle of sprawling huts. A short stone wall surrounded the edge of it and pale, soft-flowered trees ringed this wall on one side. Little Dandhō explained it was even more risky to go into the village because Dandhō's shop sat outside the east edge of the wall of Pōcarū, so we should not be seen as long as we kept to the west gate and she didn't leave the shop; though we couldn't count on it. I could see for myself the small brown hut covered with long streamers blowing from the thatch roof with writings on them in her scrolled script. The doorstone was so high and wide it made a sort of porch to sit on. Unlike our own hut's thick but plain windows, trinkets and baubles clinked in the breeze from the windows and door.

Little Dandhō pulled me along quickly, reminding me of the time. As we approached, I was struck by the sudden noise that came to greet us; speaking and singing and reciting in strange accents and from all directions, foreign sounds and smells of foods frying and simmering here and there in the air. Little Dandhō stopped and hid me behind her as she sniffed. "We're almost there. Go to the right and follow the treeline. Whatever you do, stay below the windows so no-one sees you. I'll come find you when I'm done." I nodded and split off from her as she continued straight ahead.

Within a few paces the treeline became thicker to my left and thinner to my right along the low stone wall just to my shoulder and I suddenly came upon a blur of bright blue. A hut! I was so close I could touch it. In fact, I could hear voices coming from inside and I reached out to touch the smooth wooden outer walls but then pulled my hand back in case I might be discovered. Something moved above me. A window opened and dirty water splashed down cold atop my head. Dashing back into the tree-cover, my heart nearly burst through my chest as I ran forward sputtering past decorated sheds and large, pan-like metal bowls on low stilts sitting out in the deadened grass. We had these too; Dandhō had recently built a few outside the hut to collect water.

Where the wall dipped and crumbled down low enough to step over, I crouched but couldn't resist looking over just a bit, keeping my ears flat back against my head. I could see a clearing and a lower, carved wall in the middle of the village upon which sat clusters of análong of all ages talking, resting and playing in their own groups. Around this smaller divider, closely built huts crowded between the inner and outer rings and could be walked into by little curved stone gates. Some had signs posted outside with pictures both on their gates as well as somewhere on their roofs with pictures and some were built much like Dandhō's with thick thatch roofs.

Everywhere análong walked and talked; those like I had seen at the river who walked on all fours pulled along carts with food and grains and huge skeins of threads in them. Some even pulled other análong along in gilded green carts! For a time I crouched, fascinated by the performance of a young he-dog singing for some elder análong. As the he struggled to reach his notes, his a'ér signaled to him with his hands and tail; gestures that seemed to mean he was proud of him and to keep up his song.

When the he-dog scratched out the very last note he bowed and the elders all nodded but his a'ér smiled only for him and clapped silently so that his dhana could see him above the others. This display puzzled me and made me ache inside to realize that those who cared for me did not do such simple things as this and it puzzled me further as I understood that I felt lonely toward *them* after seeing how other dhana were treated.

But how could I be sad for long while gazing at the tall shanár with their heads wrapped in long gold-specked cloths and the short g'éalach with their cheeks painted in bright dots and the winged darna whose wings were sprinkled with powdered colors? I watched the dhana trotting along behind their a'mas, tugging plump, naked babies onto their skirted hips and dragging sacks of nuts and dūūcerfrūts along in the dust.

The he-dogs wore only short trousers covered in dust and the she-dogs wore thin dresses or skirts with their ears tied back with a single ribbon rather than the smart blue and yellow clothes of the school dhana. And there in the center several grandmothers stood chatting around a large, raised hearth set with blue-patterned tiles. The colored smoke coming out from its tall stack and the bundles of bright herbs by their respective pots told me this was festival cooking.

But as I gazed at this strange, moving mass, thinking on and on, something somewhat familiar caught my eye at the inner wall.

There were gathered a group of dhana, some wearing the familiar flat blue smocks like Anshē's and some wearing the yellow short dresses like Rāca's. *This must be the school,* I thought. *Where are they?* The dhana sat below the wall on the ground and atop the same wall stood a tall shanár teacher in a robe holding up a small pictured sign. She was speaking and waving her arm wildly and the students were all paying close attention. What was she so intent on saying? If only I could get closer…

Beside her in another small area a few dhana were singing back and forth to each other. One stood and clapped, chanting to the seated dhana, who clapped in rhythm back and chanted in answer.

I watched this for a time, happy to listen to the noise made by their voices until the tall análong with her sign caught my attention again. She asked one of the students to do something; a he-dog. He wasn't very happy about it, I could see. Just a bit taller than Anshē, he suddenly got up and ran around the circle, wagging his hands behind his ears, pulling at them and shouting "*Sābaba! Sābaba!*" to the teacher. Some of the dhana around him covered their mouths and laughed and some looked on in horror. Shocked at this display of mischief, I was thrilled to understand it. Because just like asama, I knew the sound and shape of *mischief* but not its nature and it was sure to get a reaction from my Dandhō not unlike what I'd just seen. It would come in handy someday, I thought.

A hand rested on my shoulder and caused me to squeal in fright. I spun around and came face to face with Little Dandhō. "Mi'halě," she warned. "You're awfully lucky no-one saw you!" Then she looked over my shoulder at the scene. "That's Sindrē, he's always causing trouble."

"What will happen to him?" I asked, eyes fixed on the silent, still teacher sitting very calmly in the middle of it. "He should get a nice smacking," she said carelessly and as she said this, the teacher arose with such abruptness that she caught him about the middle, folded him over her knee and gave him one sound smack across his bottom. His look was one of bewilderment; he had not thought she would react. Releasing him, she sat down calmly again and all the dhana roared with laughter. But Sindrē sat down and sobbed. "Not so mouthy now," Little Dandhō said.

On the way home I couldn't stop thinking about what I had seen and how I'd have done it better. It was thrilling, new, and… free. The possibility of not doing what I was told seemed the ultimate freedom until I tried this out in my own hut and found suddenly that instead of being freed of rules, I lost my freedom entirely.

I'd waited until Dandhō told me to bring out the dishes and instead of rising to pull the dishbox out of its cabinet, shouted gleefully, "Tsōl, *sābaba!*' Shocked, Dandhō's mouth dropped open and in that one amazing moment I thought would feel something like flying, her face betrayed a strange emotion foreign to me. She stopped what she was doing and hauled me outside roughly by the collar of my dress.

"I don't know where you could have heard that but you can stay out here until you feel like apologizing!" she shouted and she slammed the storehouse door so hard the drying cords of vegetables shook from the ceiling and sloughed off their parched skins around my ears. I sat down against the wall and peered out the small window, fingering a length of hanging herbs and wondering about my dinner. *Should have thought of that before*, I thought in my best impression of Dandhō. Still, a small, private excitement grew within me and I said the word over and over to myself in the darkness now that I couldn't be heard just to make it really worth it.

My very first punishment! I couldn't wait to tell Anshē and Rāca. They probably knew Sindrē! And now that I was like them, everything could go back to the way it was before the fight. I was too proud to let my moment fade into an apology, even if it was the right thing to do. So, I sat a while longer hoping maybe Dandhō would come back out to get me and hear me all over again.

But eventually as I began to shiver and wonder if it really was all that fun, a light knock sounded on the door. "She's much too proud to come out here and get you herself," Little Dandhō said thoughtfully as she opened the door. "I think she's more shocked than really tipped off about it. And she *knows*."

As Dandhō would have said, *Oh by the moons!* "What's going to happen to us?" I whispered, the thrill draining right out of me.

"Probably won't talk to us for a while. Might give you extra chores. Will definitely give me extra chores." Little Dandhō shook her head. "What's done is done."

"Do I *have* to apologize?" I tried to hide the disappointment in my voice.

"You don't want to?"

"I got in trouble and I got a punishment! I'm like Anshē and Rāca," I whispered, hoping she'd understand. To my relief, she nodded with a small grin. "Well, sometimes it's better to pretend for the sake of others. But you don't have to be sorry to apologize."

"But it will be lying if I say I'm sorry."

"True. But now I'm in trouble because I took you to the village. Are you sorry about that?" she asked.

"I am! I didn't mean to get you in trouble, Little Dandhō!" I cried.

"Well you could say you were sorry for that part only then." She held up a finger. "In your head that is, and it wouldn't lying," she whispered. "Besides, it's getting cold out here and if we don't think of something quick, we'll both be sleeping here for more than just tonight."

I thought it over and nodded. "*Tse.*"

And Little Dandhō was right. Dandhō stopped speaking to her for two months and after that night we didn't see Anshē and Rāca for what seemed like forever. Now Dandhō knew that I knew what I wasn't supposed to know. In the meantime, she didn't apologize for lying to me but rather moved forward as if it hadn't happened to give me as much knowledge as she could cram into me in endless lessons about everything as if we couldn't possibly catch up fast enough. And of course, there were new chores, chores for older dhana because I'd used words only grown-ups should use. I didn't know if I welcomed Dandhŏ's silence outside of lessons, but the chores I didn't mind as they required me to leave the hut.

Life took on an endless, droll taste for the next few months after Little Dandhō quietly returned to us because Dandhō needed the help. To keep my mind off of my woes, I was allowed to come with them to the sparkly brown salt mounds at the bottom of the Dhūdahara hills outside of Dandhō's fields. They gave me a little silver hammer to break off a chunk of the salt for my pocket to hold. I was more interested in crumbling the sparkly grains in my hands than actually to helping gather anything of substance; imagining that it was some sort of rare and precious stuff I could somehow seep into myself. This wasn't altogether untrue. As Dandhō said, the key to análong cooking was spice and lots of it. "Análong food should be experienced entirely; from the lips and nose and throat all the way down the gullet. Nothing should escape the heat and taste of it," she said. And once, after I'd taken too big a helping of *cordarash* pudding, I could agree that real análong cooking could be felt *everywhere*. But so could Dandhō's silence.

I consoled myself over the whole thing by learning about the wonderful Ebūdean festivals and holy days that flew by as I stood in observance of the activity flurrying about me, for sadness did not stop the year from slipping away through the door drafts; tugging on one's tail as it passed by.

During Dhūlii, Dandhō scolded Little Dandhō and I to hurry and dip four hundred candles by the end of the month; two-hundred long and two-hundred squat. One hundred of these we wrapped in cloth and set in a dry corner of the storehouse to use for hĒladdon. I particularly enjoyed hĒladdon, the day of everlasting light when we lit every corner of every room in golden candleglow and rang special little bells Dandhō kept in a deep blue lacquer box in the loft. On hĒladdon Little Dandhō made a special light tea with oiled *banúa,* steamed pale flour buns and yellow rice pudding dotted with dried dūūcerfrūt bits and golden roasted lāāca seeds; all light, yellow foods. This was the day when I trailed Dandhō all through the hut with my hands folded behind my back, carefully observing her light each and every candle and lamp, each one from the others' flame to remind us that we all came from the same source of light and creation. I was allowed to sit up all night the eve of hĒladdon to help watch that the light never died.

Likewise, Dhandōdāi was the high point of the year. Dandhō put up the shiny gold and silver garlands around the huts' eaves and carefully placed paper flowers of indigo and spangles in bowls on every surface. The colors of Dhandōdāi were bright. The savory, spiced pudding colored with herb dyes was boiled down into a tight little ball of sponge and doused in fiery hot sauce, then served up on a special platter ringed with fat dūūcerfrūt halves and shiny ribbons. Dandhō stayed home from the village and cooked for days with Little Dandhō, then surreptitiously disappeared for an afternoon and came back to drop little brown candies and green or purple ribbons into my outstretched hands. Little Dandhō brought me even better presents such as soft, striped stockings or twirling sticks I liked to rub together to see their shining colors fan in a mesmerizing arc; things one would find in the village shops.

The Sanga-da was a similar festival. Of course, I wasn't allowed to go to the village to celebrate, but Little Dandhō made sure we had a little of it at home. The painted masks and lanterns fascinated me, and I was lucky enough that she brought me some of the steamed rice buns and sweets to fill my fat, grinning lantern I made to house them. But the hut was always strangely silent on this day, because Dandhō didn't want me to know about all the pranks played on the villagers by the dhana.

The next year, Dandhō looked at me in consternation over her nose and said, "When you dip the candles this year with Ā'dō, you will be responsible for all the hĒladdon candles. Every one of them must be finished on time." On that hĒladdon Dandhō lit the very first candle from the hearth and then passed it to me, pushing me towards the mounds of candles which sat upon looking glasses scattered about our hut. "Be careful; light each from the last slowly." And so, this became my part in the holy day.

Though I realized in dismay that preparing the pudding for Dhandōdāi would never be trusted to me, that same year I was given the responsibility of putting up the trimmings in the sleeping room as I wished, and I'd never felt so grown! Little Dandhō showed me how to fold the deep blue bits of paper and pin them into pretty flowers of my own and these I wore in a crown on my head during tea. And all those days my smile held a crack in it, for I wondered and wondered what these wonderful days would have been like if Anshē and Rāca had been there and I realized that while my sisters had kept all of this from me, they had also kept themselves from *it*.

I had moved from tolerated observer to junior participant, and I could not help but think that the next time I saw my friends, they would no longer know me.

F'ala
13

the day she saw my heart
ashē balla-da amúa ta óō

was still furious beyond words with my sister all these months later. Not only had she betrayed my instructions, she'd lied to me and started the dhana on a path I now had to correct. True, as my letters to Br'ién had gone unanswered, I'd been wondering night and day how I'd bridge the gap between life-learning and book-learning without betraying anything, but it was *my* problem to work out.

I lay in the heavy dark trying to see patterns in the stars through the window and admitted to myself that the truth hadn't come out a moment too soon. Mi'hal̆e was much too curious to contain for much longer. After all, we only hear with our ears and see with our eyes, but we learn by experience. Now that she'd mastered the basics of análong life it was time to begin to teach her the dangerous truths in the hopes she'd discover her purpose as a Guardian.

"Today we learn something new," I announced the next morning. Across the table Mi'hal̆e sat on bent knees, black eyes intent on my hands as I picked up a smooth yellow mug and lifted it to my mouth. My own eyes observed the liquid circling its bottom. "Go find me a roll of parchment from the loft."

Her steps were silent and when she returned, I smoothed out the roll she offered across the table, pulling my brush and ink from their place by the dish-box. "I'm going to tell you a story and you must pay attention, because this is the story of all análong, everywhere. In the beginning of all things, there was Mĭ'á, the Creator."

As I spoke, I drew the circles representing the early worlds of time, the twelve stars and their path across the sky. I told her of the arrogance of the Guardians, of their punishment and rebirth, of the hope we had that they would one-day save our world from death and win us souls to join the rest of Creation within the Law of Orders. With my brush I mapped out Ebūda and the forbidden land neighboring us; An'dan. I showed her the mythical field with no name we análong believed our spirits rested in after death to await caémba. And I stressed that the only way they could live again was through the Guardians fulfilling their agreement with the heavens.

But Mi'hal̆e only stared hard at the page from the corner of her eye without moving her head to look.

I waited. Then I ran out of patience. "Did you hear what I said?"

She nodded as if somehow bored. "Stars reborn as análong. Need souls to live again. Ebūda not part of the Law of Orders. Guardians have to fix it. Why do I need to know this? If they have to do it, what does it matter to me?"

"Because Guardians must live their lives as análong just like us," I nearly stuttered in my irritation. "They're part of the journey of everyone they meet. The point is there's no way to know who a Guardian is, so you could meet one and not know it."

Mi'hal̆e scratched the table lightly with her nail. "So, you could be, I could be…"

I gagged. "*Theoretically*," I stressed. "But they need our help to achieve caémba."

Her bottomless eyes made me uncomfortable. "But will they? Achieve it, I mean?"

"No-one can know the future," I said carefully, trying not to voice my own doubts and influence her perceptions. "The Guardians are more than stories; they're part of our culture, part of our belief in the universe beyond us. Belief is hoping for something you can't see. It grows into faith," I spread my hands out. "And faith grows into certainty. But we have to start off with hope. We hope the Guardians are successful."

She looked away towards the window and contemplated the world beyond. "What will they do if they see me?"

I sighed. Wasn't that the question we all wondered? "I told you that the sea disappeared. But far from here the rivers have also dried up and for years there has been fighting over water and food. Análong are desperate, desperate enough to kill each other for it. We're very lucky we still have enough water from the rivers but if they dry up too…well. I've heard of unspeakable things. And they blame the drought on those who are different in any way."

"They'd kill me," she said flatly.

I nodded and pressed on. *Think of Rā-alta…*

"White means death and mourning. They would see you and think you were bringing death like Āe'rū." I admitted. "They would strike first. You see, fear isn't evil in itself. But evil can form from it."

She looked down at her little hands and her eyes slid shut. "You didn't tell me what the colors meant."

"Tsōl."

"But Anshē and Rāca!"

"You can't see them again. I can't trust that they wouldn't tell others about you, even if just by accident," I interrupted.

"But they wouldn't! That's not fair!" she quickly stood from the table and clenched her fists.

"Tsō, it's not. Take it from me, there's very little in life that is."

As she set her jaw against tears, I thought of the day before in Pōcarū; passing by the market heavy with the heady scent of sweet spice used in skin oils that brought my old auntie to mind. Glancing at the various shapes of the shopkeeps sitting in the dust by their wares, I could just picture her strong figure clothed in bright skirts so wide a dhana could hide under; her generous rolls spilling over. I thought that this was all that was right with Ebūda; all of its plenty and all of its generosity, so much to love. And when I looked at little Mi'hal̃e and her hollow eyes and pale arms and legs, I could only think of all the worst that had become of Ebūda; its famine and its death. Its want.

"Mī'á just forgot to give me my color," she whispered. "That's all."

I nodded. "Shĕ'á. That's all. Nevertheless, you can't go out again."

"Dandhō?" she asked, calling me by the name of an older sister for the first time, "If there are so many análong out there, how do you know you're supposed to take care of me? How do you know I don't belong to someone else?"

I rolled up the parchment, eager to escape and go meet Ādō to begin hay-making. "Because I'm the one who promised to."

"But what if you go to wait for caémba? Then who will take care of me?" she asked, looking at me intently.

"The one I promised," I whispered, not confident at all this would be the case.

"But, why aren't you afraid of me if everyone else is?"

Oh, but I am. I'm terrified of what you could be...

"Because I have hope. That's all."

"Tse," she agreed in defeat and left me to go cry in the sleeping-room. Quietly I tidied up the table and left her to her own tears.

* * *

"But they accept her Dandhō, they *like* her. What's it going to hurt if she has some friends? She's just a dhana," Ādō argued as we slipped young green leaves under our headscarves to keep cool and took up our pitchforks.

"Because if she's a Guardian she doesn't get to be a dhana!" I humphed in frustration.

"But you could let her, you could give her that before she has to...."

"You don't understand. If I let her run around with Anshē and Rāca and she makes all these friends, what do you think will happen someday when she has to go? What happens when she realizes who she is and what she has to do? It's too much to take away from her, just trust me on this."

"Because that's what happened to you? You had to say goodbye to someone? Is that, is that what happened in Bri'én when I was a baby?" Ādō's face was still, waiting.

Shĕ'á. I was a dhana until the day you were born, and then it all ended.

But even I knew I didn't mean it in the way it sounded in my head. It was simply a fact of the order of events, not anyone's fault. At least I thought I was grown enough to see that now. She'd run out of patience for me to answer.

"Well at least can't you try not to ruin it for her like..."

"Like I ruined it for you? I see you looking after your friends in the village." I snorted, "I'm not blind."

She looked down, her delicate eyes reminded me of Rā-alta's just then and I felt myself soften. "Aren't you lonely by yourself?" she asked timidly. "Like, do you have to be so different from everyone else? I don't even have a chance to be myself with everyone talking about you all the time. Don't you even want to get married, Dandhō?"

"I am who I am, and I don't resent who others are, I'm just not them. You can't be anyone else either, it's impossible not to be yourself. And what would I need to be married for? I'm not alone, I've got you," I tried to gloss over but then stopped. Perhaps she was old enough now to be trusted with despair. I rested my pitchfork against a tree and fiddled with the end of my tail. I took a deep breath. "There was someone, there *is* someone. But it just can't be the way I'd like."

Her eyes widened, and I could see her entire vision of me broadened in a way I wasn't sure I liked if it made me have to say any more. "Were they, are they *lower class*?"

For the first time in months laughter rolled up through my belly but I clamped my throat over it. Class was always the number one reason to keep anyone apart. Was it possible to be crushed to death by the weight of irony? Rather, I turned it back to her. "Tse, how about you? Is there anyone?"

Ādō's face deepened to a bright shade of pink but to my *great* relief she admitted there wasn't. "Ah, but you wish there was," I said knowingly. She nodded. "It's just…hard to get to know anyone being so far from the village and having so much to do," she spread her arm towards the fields. I nodded. Most análong met their betrothed through their parents' connections. In our asama, I was sister, mother and father to Ādō and completely awful at all three.

"Mi'hal'ē is old enough to be let alone a little more, I think. I don't trust her any more now that she knows everything but at least the onandals' charm is still keeping strangers out of here. And, after we're done with hay baling, perhaps you could go spend some time with Pūdha in the evening instead of coming to work the fields. I think I could handle the work myself once or twice a week."

"Really?"

"I don't mean for you to end up like me. You'll have everything you need when the time comes," I assured her. "I've never told you but, under the window in the storehouse; the blue box sat under there? It's full of nendē. That box is yours, for someday."

"But where, I mean how did you get it?" she stammered. I frowned. "I earned it of course! You forget, most of the work I do at the shop is for análong outside Pōcarū and they don't pay in bags of rice and seed, they pay in coin. And when the time comes, we'll hire a cart and go to Bri'én for your dress and dowry. You'll be the best-dressed bride in Drīdū, I promise. You'll look so high-class they'll be falling all over themselves to lead the way for you."

Her brow stayed furrowed though, untrusting. "I didn't think you wanted that for me. I didn't think it mattered to you," she said quietly. I threw up a hand in frustration. "Of course, I do! What made you think I didn't?" When she looked away, I grabbed her hand and said truthfully, "I don't say things. I don't know how is all. That's all."

"Maybe just try *I want you to have the things you want because I'm your sister and I love you.*" she said with a hopeful look.

"I thought I just did but yeah, I'll try to remember. And you know, I had a much different beginning than you, but I do know this: things just disappear if you let them. So, if someone comes along, well you just let me know. But if you have questions, you know, *those* kinds of questions? Ask your friends."

"I won't," she laughed. "Have questions, I mean. And Mi'hal̃e?"

I sighed. "That's not the same. I do want her to have friends, of course I do. But what I want doesn't have anything to do with anything. You have to trust me on this because you've got as much choice in the matter as I do." And in the end, my sister deferred to me and we worked the day out in a companionable silence we'd not managed since the dhana had first come.

The next morning, I sat across the table from Mi'hal̃e waiting for the outburst that never came, the accusation she had never voiced, and I found myself feeling guilty. Mi'hal̃e had been with us for nearly four years and at that moment I noticed that no longer was her face foreign to me; no longer did I think of her as an abomination. In fact, I couldn't remember when I'd last seen the village dhana through the windows of my shop and not compared them to her; realizing that she was indeed a flesh and blood análong. When I began to think of all those things I'd kept from her, the color of her skin faded into the background behind the gentler things she didn't know. I'd taught her how to survive, but as with my sister, I hadn't taught her how to live.

This is why you told Ā'dō to begin with, remember? Because you knew she'd know what to do. She ought to have a birthday, I decided. *And we'll go to Ā'dō's to celebrate.*

I told my ēdandha the plan when we returned to haymaking later in the week and she set about sewing Mi'hal̃e a brand new dress while I began my own project. Three weeks later on the eve of Clāiron I mentioned it after the evening-meal.

"This is a special day," I told Mi'hal̃e as I waited for her to put on her night-dress. I pulled her ears back awkwardly with a tie and she eyed me warily, wondering why I wasn't after her to go right to bed. Fishing about, I pulled out a little wooden comb from my painted jewel-box and slowly ran it over her ears, smoothing the fine hairs as I'd remembered A'ma doing for me before I slept. It struck me in a way it never had before how long the years had been in Bri'én and how long A'ma had been gone and the melancholic peace of a circle closing washed over me, bridging what was gained to what had been lost.

"We're going to see Ā'dō right now, so I want you to put your shoes on" I said, picking up a small basket by the door in which I'd hidden a surprise. The dhana said nothing but I could see her eyes widen and she allowed me to lead her by the hand in the dimming light over the field and through the forest until we reached the dried old waterfall halfway to Orambūsū. As we climbed up the stone steps into the alcove I'd built Ā'dō years before, I could smell something sweet and my sister's voice called out for us to sit where we wished.

All around the main room unspun bashō puffs hung illuminated by clusters of candles that gave the effect of a snowy night. The flat stone formation that protruded out on the left wall was used as both a table and bed and it was draped in a soft cloth above the bedroll and piled with little gifts. Something seemed to glitter all around us; some good feeling had taken on its own presence and shone with joy.

I was overcome suddenly with bittersweet wonder as I remembered too that A'ma had died on a beautiful snowy night and Ă'dō came into a white-covered world as well. My last good memory of Rā-alta those years later was framed in that same living whiteness after we became graduates in the ceremony amidst ten thousand flakes of white in the Palace courtyard. I watched quietly as Mi'hal'ē's eyes darted everywhere, her fingers reaching out to every surface to explore.

"S'bonála? What is it?" she asked.

"*Orū.* When I was small, there was still snow in Ebūda. It looked like this," Ă'dō said of the soft balls.

"Orū," Mi'hal'ē murmured, her fingertips exploring their softness.

"Snow was the most beautiful part of Ebūda," I agreed, my voice belying the sorrow I thought every análong felt for having lost it. "You remind me of it," I murmured. Orū. Snow which had not touched the land in at least fifteen years, snow made up of tiny crystal jewels as many and unique as each of us ever born. Snow, which lay like white mounds of melted sweets over the hills and frosted thin black tree limbs; snow which froze and yet warmed the thin winter air in twilight. Precious to us because it only fell during the month of Tsāi'ín and our festivals of light were held while the land slept.

"Orū … orū," Mi'hal'ē repeated. "It's the same color as me. Does it mean death too?"

"Oh of course not," Ă'dō clucked but I held up my hand to silence her. "It came every year during Tsāi'ín when the land sleeps and the crops die. So, in a way, it was associated with the death of one year and the start of another. But then as you know, the land wakes and everything comes alive again. When the rains stopped and the sea disappeared, there was no more snow."

"Enough of that," my sister interrupted. "Let's all have some cake to celebrate Mi'hal'ē's... uh...her …" she looked at me for help, realizing a birthday indicated we knew when the dhana was born. I stepped in and guided her to the table. "Birthday. It's your birthday. We don't know exactly when you were born but this is the day you came to live with us."

Then all explanations were forgotten as the dhana discovered her presents and made short work of pulling off the wrappings and lining up her new dress, ribbons and shoes before coming to my basket. Her reaction was less than joyful. "It's a doll," she said flatly. I nodded, picking it up and showing it to her. Admittedly, it wasn't the most beautiful thing but it had black, embroidered eyes like her own, a simple shift and a yarn tail. She was reluctant to take it.

"Rāca has a doll," she said sullenly, looking down at something interesting on her shoes. "Rāca, my *dasha*," the dhana noted. She stared coldly at the doll I had sat up nights sewing in the storehouse with Rā-alta's picture from the bedside to keep me company after she'd gone to sleep. "Rāca let me play with hers. *Before*."

"So now you've one of your own to play with!" I pointed out sorely.

"Dandhō worked a long time to make her for you. Don't you like her?" Ā'dō soothed from across the table. Mi'hal̆e said nothing but glared at the doll, her arms crossed stubbornly.

And so I left her there to spend the night with my sister, taking the upper road home by moonlight to put together the other gift I'd been working on by morning, not that she deserved it.

When I returned to the hut mid-morning after an early visit to the onandals, Ā'dō and Mi'hal̆e were coming up the path swinging presents at their sides and singing happily. I sat in the sleeping room, waiting.

"Dandhō? Are you here?" Ā'dō called out and pushed aside the sleeping-room curtain. In bounded Mi'hal̆e in her new clothes to find me sitting on my bed underneath the new surprise. Her eyes lit up with joy and Ā'dō dropped everything on the floor. "F'ala, when did you make *this*?"

Scrambling up the ladder beside me to the bunk bed now connected to mine, Mi'hal̆e flopped herself onto the coverlet with a satisfied sigh and ran her fingers curiously over the twelve painted figures on the headboard. "Guardians," she murmured.

"When did you manage this?" my sister asked, inspecting the joints. I grinned unabashedly, pleased with my work. "I've been working on it for a while now in the trees behind the storehouse but I brought the pieces in last night and put it together. And don't think because you've got a nice new bed you're going to lay in it all day and skip your chores!" I hollered up to the dhana. Her foot flipped over the end and wagged at me in answer.

Just as I'd thought, they'd stayed up the night talking and I walked Ā'dō out as far as the treeline so she could go home and get some rest before our next round of haymaking.

"So, the little figures on her bed, you painted those?" Ā'dō asked when we'd made it out to the middle of the field. "I had a similar bed before you were born, before I left for the city. A'da made it for me," I replied.

"What are they?" she asked, grinning softly.

"They're meant to be the Guardians. Well, what I used to imagine them to look like. But that's not what I came out here to talk about. I've heard some news in the village," I said quietly, rubbing my nose. "The river levels have finally fallen all the way into northern Drīdū. You know what this means. Our main water supply is beginning to die."

Ā'dō's grin slid from her face. "What can we do?"

"Stick together and defend what we have for now. Two villages in southern Adanandū were burned to the ground last month and the NaÓma have spared only the youngest to send out ahead of them

to scout for water and food." I swallowed and looked her hard in the eyes. "They're coming." My ēdandha closed her eyes. "But what happens if there isn't anything for them to take?"

"They kill. You must understand that the NaÓma live on fear. The fear of dying keeps them going, keeps them hungry and angry enough to kill anyone in their way. The illness that started taking out the darna those years ago isn't something anyone has been able to control so they're trying to outsmart the drought and outrun the plague. If they're not stopped they'll kill everyone right down to the southern coast of Ebūda either by their swords or by their germs."

"Then…?"

"Then, the end. Only the Guardians can close the book on this world."

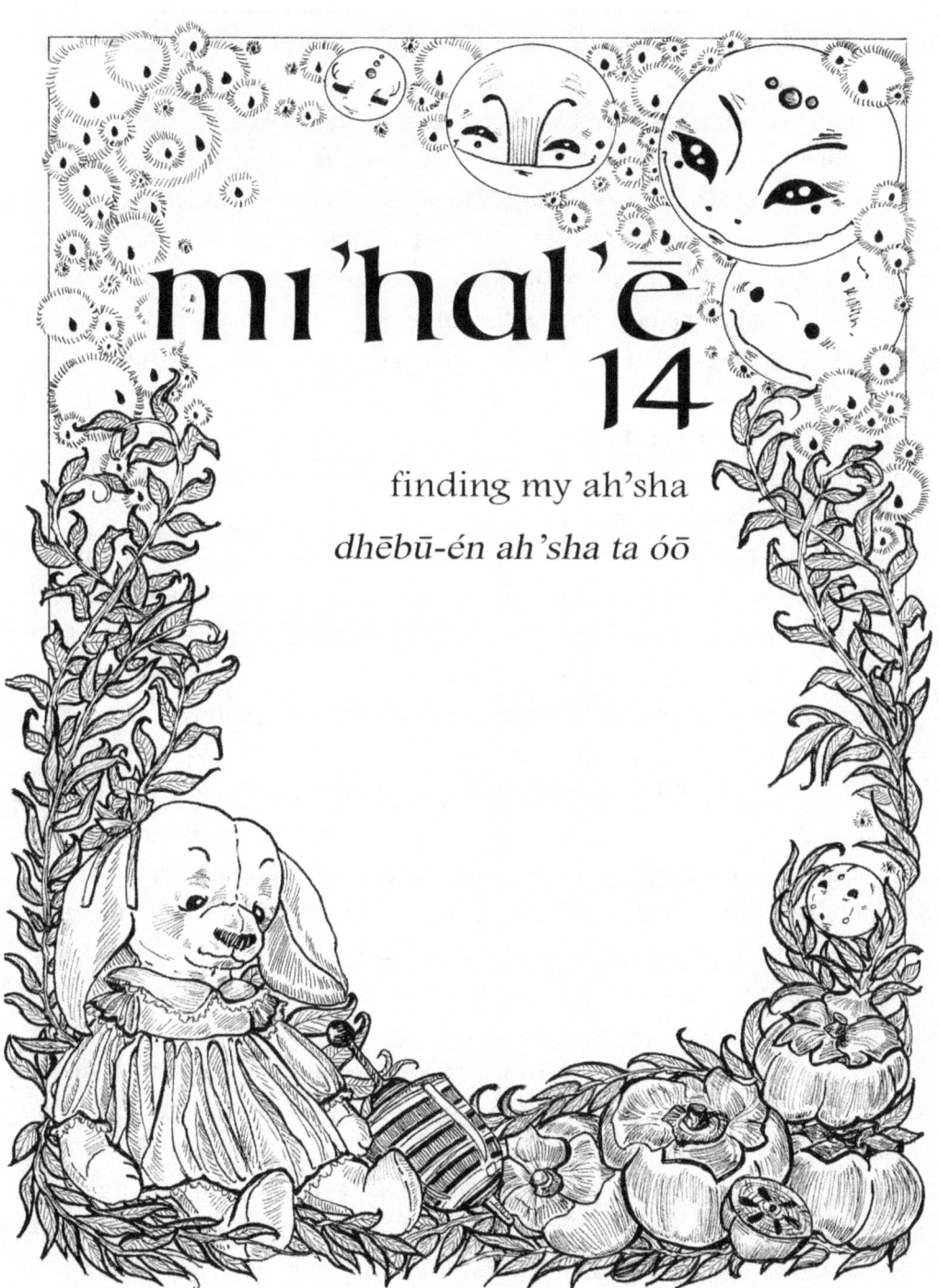

mi'hal'ē

14

finding my ah'sha

dhēbū-én ah'sha ta óō

WHEN I was alone I explored our hut; this tiny little world I had come to love and feel safe inside, yet longed to leave. I was not as naughty as Dandhō would have thought me to be, but I did like to look and feel and hear and taste a little more than she would have ever liked as well.

I discovered early on that knowledge calmed loneliness; that though it didn't guard against it, learning filled up the emptiness. I must have been very alone, I think, for I wanted to know everything, just everything. And since I wanted to know so much so quickly, I bored easily if settled on any one thing for very long. This irritated Dandhō to no end. But even so, there was some knowledge so bright, so large and ever moving that even I dreaded to think on it.

Dandhō insisted on teaching me more intellectual things when I would rather hear about her *memories*. I learned from her memories about the shining Silver Sea that surrounded the three sides of Ebūda. I learned that the evening mist would roll in atop the water to blot out the twelve moons and the dhana would run out into the waves and meet the shallow boats coming in with the day's catch of pūra and bring them back to be steamed in dumplings. But then the rains dried, and the waters shrank until the sea was no more and the land simply vanished into the nothingness where the shore had ended, never to be seen again.

Dandhō said that the sea had swallowed all the sorrows of the análong; any who came to its shores left drops of their sadness that only added to its waves. But now that the sea was dead, the análong must swallow their own sorrow. This is why Ebūda had her troubles. It was because the análong didn't know what to do with all their worries Such things ate away at their hearts until their minds became drowned with despair and fear. This was why dhana were no longer allowed to walk near the shores, lest they disappear into the nothing too.

Dandhō told me of beauty, which had to do with prosperity. An análong with a thin asama could be accused of neglect by a village magistrate, but one whose wife had curves and a generous figure gained respect. Round and roly dhana showed abundance in a village and laughing eyes proved a happy tribe. Spots, stripes and marks on the skin were prized for their rareness and rarity had more worth. Dandhō said that an análong would never alter his spots.

But it seemed to me that the análong, who loved their stripes and spots loved their colors even more, and even Dandhō didn't like mention of her spots. It was the fact that I didn't look like Dhandhō and Little Dandhō or Anshē and Rāca that bothered me more than my actual color, which meant nothing extraordinary to me at all but that it was mine. It was the fact that we never spoke about it that made it ugly; the fact that I was considered to be without color at all, as if I were missing the very thing that made me alive. My color had gotten lost; stolen from me or forgotten to be given in the first place, leaving behind an invisible bit of space no one saw, yet everyone objected to.

So, it was natural that one evening when no-one was paying attention, I snuck into the storehouse and dug into the heavy jar of *hlin-hlin* berries used for dying cloth. Pulling off my dress, I carefully smashed the cooled purple-ish berries into my skin and shivered as the juice ran down my arms and legs in the twilight air. I stood shaking until I'd completely dried to a light indigo hue, then pulled my dress back on and slipped across the garden quietly back into the darkened hut, creeping sweetly across the floor and up the ladder to my bed. Thinking in the morning Dhandhō would wake up to a true and proper análong under her roof, I was terribly pleased with myself and couldn't stop stroking the delicious new weight of my own hands imagining how pretty I must look.

But in the morning, I felt anything but pretty when Dhandhō yanked me up from my covers and dragged me out angrily to the washtub. My yelps from the harsh scrubbing she gave me were only interrupted by an occasional expletive from her about my foolishness and the silence thereafter that spelled out I'd clearly messed up. This didn't deter me from one more try, however. Like anyone else, I bruised when bumped and so took it into my head that if I couldn't dye myself to look like my asama, I would do it some other way. It took several days to pinch myself enough along the arms to get a satisfactory shade but when I had, I ran in to show Dhandhō and Little Dhandhō during tea. This time Dhandhō took me out into the garden and struck me across the bottom angrily without a word before then promising, "Do that again and I'll give you a bruise you won't get rid of."

"I just wanted to be like you! I wanted to be the right color, like an análong!" I wailed, struggling against her. Dhandhō stopped and lowered her hand, crinkling her eyes in either anger or laughter and I didn't want to know which. She picked me up under the arms and held me up at length away from her, looking me over entirely. "That's ridiculous. I've told you before, we all look like ourselves. We're not supposed to look exactly alike. And you are an análong; what else would you be? You think and you feel and that's what we are. All we are and all we are. And if you'd pay attention once in a while in your lessons, you'd know that."

And for the time that satisfied me.

* * *

But when I thought of Dhandhō's words, the sparkle rose in me again, that glimmer of movement which would, if I let it, drown me in light. I pushed my hands against my ears as if to keep my very self from leaking out of them. "Hembarē!" I whispered against the terrible knowing, "Please!"

Dhandhō knew somehow that something more than my color obsession wasn't right with me and watched me for a few days before taking me up to the loft one afternoon. I was no longer afraid of the mask that guarded its ladder and the loft had changed some over those years since I'd last stolen her little figures to play with.

Dhandhō pulled a scroll down from the little shelf above her study table. I pulled out a stool from under the table and sat down, boredom already sitting in. I'd rather look at the scroll myself and try to figure it out but Dhandhō insisted on teaching me. She liked to speak about circles opening and closing and I could never quite catch what this meant. "What's a circle and how can it close?" I asked, idly playing with the end of the scroll's place-ribbon.

Dhandhō sat back and put her hands behind her head, looking at the ceiling to gather her thoughts. "All of the things we learn and experience form a circle around us. This is what I mean: living is like eating food without spice. The mouth tastes the food and the body absorbs it, but only the mouth experiences and understands the wholeness of it. The body can only take parts of it at a time and break them down to use. Food can be eaten again and again and the mouth remembers the shape of it and the texture and the feel.

But when food is eaten with spice, it's felt by all of the body. The nose smells it, the back of the mouth is heated by it, the belly is warmed by it and even the hands and feet and head are touched by its circulation as if one's spirit itself inhales and understands the care put into its preparation.

This is what learning is like; eating food that is properly spiced. When I tell you or show you something, your mind gathers it and thinks about it, putting images to the words you hear. Your mind will remember what I have said," Dhandhō rapped me gently on the head and smirked. "If you pay attention, that is. But until you experience the idea I've given you, your spirit won't understand it. It remains an incomplete circle around you. Sometimes you must experience things over and over as you grow or as you travel or as you meet others in the same situation until, like spice, it fills your understanding; until it becomes whole. This is when experience becomes memory and the circle closes like a gold ring. Then nothing can break that understanding or take it from you."

I slid down on one arm, tracing little circles with my other hand on the table. My fingers tightened as I clamped down that little bright spot in my mind, stopping it before it had time to canvas across behind my eyes and sweep me away, for the more I learned, the more I was afraid of getting lost inside it. I looked up in curiosity. "Why doesn't Little Dhandhō ever teach me this stuff?"

Dhandhō didn't look up. "You know very well she can't read these scrolls. That's why she shows you some things and I show you others"

I stretched and yawned. "But why? Why don't you just teach her too?"

She sighed as if she'd been explaining this for so many years she was exhausted and carefully stretched the scroll out across the table to reveal the intricate penwork across it. Dhandhō always seemed so much more delicate on paper; like perhaps that side of her could only escape through her quill. "It's decided when we're dhana who we'll become, and that's not who she is."

Alarmed, I sat right up and demanded, "How is it decided? Who decides it?"

Calmly Dhandhō answered me, "Those who bear us into this world and those who play amongst the stars."

"But what about us? Don't we have any say?"

"Of course. Who can make us into anything if we refuse?"

And I thought hard upon this but couldn't understand, for if I had a purpose as Little Dhandhō said, and what I would become was already decided for me, then who was I after all? But Dhandhō never spared any time for such wonderings. She tapped the table and folded her arms across her chest. "Recite."

It was in these later hours after evening meal that Dhandhō's character came out in the open. Little Dhandhō laughed all the time, the sound of it cheerful and light. But Dhandhō rarely laughed and when she did, it was dazzling and abrupt as if her whole self held still until those moments to burst out of her. In fact, she could laugh for great lengths of time, churning out new giggles long past the rest of us when we wondered what could possibly still be funny. If I watched her long enough, I could catch her soft, shy smile as she worked on the other side of the table, immersed in some thought I could never guess at.

There was no laughter, however, when recitation was involved. She had me to recite the tenants of mbúana over and over again as I scratched out little pictures underneath the table with my nails.

"I said, recite! Porāma!" her voice interrupted my artwork.

I sighed with great effect and plopped both my arms onto the table as she opened up another scroll to check me. Bored to tears, I began. "*The principle of porāma states that all things are related; all things of the air, land, sea and imagination are linked through cause and all owe their continuing existence and state to all others within or without the Order because of their supreme origin.*"

"And andama?"

"*Andama: all the things that cannot be said. In the space between beings where experience is shared, the need to express feeling in words falls away and such things can be said without sound. It is the feeling between us that passes in a look, a touch, and the silence of being. Also, the speech of the heart that supercedes mortal language.*"

"Well done," she said over her nose. "Now the principle of sāama."

"Why do we have to do this every day?" I complained, scrunching up my face.

Dhandhō reached out and flipped the ends of the pages swiftly over my fingers. "We can stop when you understand. And you'll understand when you start asking questions that aren't *why do we have to do this every day*?"

"But why can't I learn something fun?" I wheedled.

"Quite simply because you must know everything you must know. While spinning and sewing and pulling roots will help you survive, they won't help you gain caémba. And let me say this to you: we may know everything about ourselves and we may know nothing. It doesn't matter. What matters is how we conduct ourselves in the scope of our knowledge."

I slumped down in my seat, muttering "*in the scope of our knowledge*" smartly to myself.

* * *

Dhandhō slumped down on one hand across her table one afternoon. "Dhana, can you not sit still?"

I made a face in return and huffed atop the little stool opposite her and dropped my hands carelessly in my lap. "I know all this already," I whined.

"Not well enough or you'd know you must repeat the dangerous truths to yourself over and over until they become part of you," she flicked her quill at me in a scolding manner.

I couldn't help but roll my eyes, taking up the parchment once more to read aloud. A sudden, crisp sound above us on the thatch caused us both to start and Dhandhō rose from her chair and crossed the little loft swiftly to climb down the ladder.

Listening as hard as I could, I jumped up as I heard my name called and slid down the ladder, pulling my skirt up over my back as I did. "Get the buckets," Dhandhō shouted and ran outside. Buckets only meant one thing. Rain!

It wasn't that the rain never, ever came but rather only very rarely and not at all as the rain had once come to Ebūda in great drenching droves called *ushatala*, filling up the lakes and rivers. In those times there were even houses which rested on the water atop long poles. But like the snow had faded into memory, so too did the great ushatala and now the rain came once a month, if less, and when it did there was a great scurry about the hut to collect all of the barrels and buckets and bowls and jars from the shed to put out in the garden. If for chance one of these filled to the brim, it was my job to run and get another to switch. When the rains stopped, the water we collected was kept in the shed to supplement the water drawn at the well near the storehouse, which had become something we must never waste.

Because I was a dhana, I was allowed to run outside naked and sneak an extra bath in the garden where I stood. But both my sisters took off their clothes down to the underskirts and sat soaking up the cool downfall atop the garden stones, the cloth clinging and revealing their figures in a way to show a picture of someday what I might grow to be.

Rain made everything happy, even the hut seemed to smile through its windows at having its thatch bathed. My limbs felt sweetly sleepy after a warm rain, like they'd just been stretched to pure bliss and all I wanted to do was nap once I'd dried off. The only thing I didn't like was the way rain made everything stink for a day or so, but this was a small price to pay for the good humor everyone found themselves in because of it.

I couldn't have known this would be the last hard rain I would ever see, and as I lay naked and happy that night in my own bed, tracing the figures of the Guardians on the headboard, my last thoughts were not of the poor análong outside of Drīdū who were suffering with no rain at all, but of my own self-centered wishes for more rain-days for us.

Then late in the night I was awakened by a sudden urge and tried to lay still as long as I could, hoping to fall back asleep. When the urge didn't go away after a few moments I rolled over to the ladder. Carefully toeing my way down, I held my breath and glanced at Dhandhō's shadow-darkened form in the bottom bed. Satisfied I hadn't awakened her, I tiptoed through the door curtain and quietly out of the hut to the toi-ō. But as I came back through the front of the hut taking ginger care not to whack my legs on the table, I heard a soft, grown-up noise coming from the other side of the sleeping-room curtain.

I immediately stilled into place and my ears pricked up over the beating of my own frightened heart to catch the rising and falling of the sound. Listening carefully, I realized that it was crying I could hear. And I swallowed down fear with a gulp as it became plain to me that it was Dhandhō's voice hitched with such sadness.

I couldn't move at all for whole minutes, standing in the cool darkness unsure of what I felt. My legs twitched, wishing to run out of the door and into the forest as far away as I could get from that unfamiliar sound. But I stayed where I was. Dhandhō might not know I was gone from the bed above her and something within wouldn't allow me to enter the room again. So I pulled together the sitting cushions stored under the table and arranged these into a square, curling myself up into a ball atop them. I fell asleep with my hands on my ears to blot out that awful sound that wouldn't stop.

In the morning I woke late to the sound of Dhandhō laying out the dishes when I should have been. I could feel her watching me and I wondered that she allowed me to sleep so long that I missed my early morning chores. As I pulled myself up stiffly from the floor, a blanket she'd tucked around me slipped from my shoulders to the floor and Dhandhō and I stood looking at each other. She gazed at me evenly and I was suddenly afraid she knew that I knew. She looked away first, turning to pick up the kettle from the hearth to pour the tea silently.

In that very instant, watching the way she unevenly divided the tea and banúa between the cups, giving me the better share, I suspected that Dhandhō had been crying over me. That she *loved* me. And in that same instant that I understood it, I hated her for allowing me to know it.

Dread, a dread which confirmed not only that she loved me, but I also loved her in return washed coldly over me. I wasn't sure I wanted to know it, for there had become a fond tolerance between us after all our distrust and conflict and I thought perhaps this was as comfortable as it could and should be.

Dl'ah'sha…

The word that was never said, yet seemed to connect us, tickled the back of my mind. The word my quill could never quite catch to imprison on paper. Then the feeling of anticipation filled me; the awkward premature knowing that someday a circle would close and it would be me crying those misplaced tears of an adult and experiencing things only a dhana could wonder about.

When Little Dhandhō came that morning, Dhandhō quietly left without her usual litany of reminders, telling us that she was going to go tend the onandals for the day. I watched as her figure disappeared from the path into the lower field and out of sight and I sprang on Little Dhandhō with every bit of charm I could muster, begging her to take me one last time to the village.

"If F'ala finds out…"

"I don't care!" I interrupted. "She can tie me up in the storeroom forever if she wants!"

"Well," she gave in, "I guess it's a good enough day to go."

And it certainly seemed to be. The sun was hot and a celebration of the end of the summer market was well underway when we reached the treeline around Pōcarū.

There were tented stalls where análong stood in bright, patterned dresses and short-trousers calling out things to sell such as glittery windbells and decorations. Beside these sat even more with great flat bowls of petals thickening the air with their heavy, colored scents. Boxes of food were being traded back and forth; the hands reaching out and crossing in a moving sea of exchange. And even further down were low tables of other beautiful things; silver bowls filled with radiant spices being sold in little brown sachets and neat rows of blue-wrapped sweets lay tied with thin ribbons. Sticks of bright incense dotted every sill and table, their smoke hanging stagnant and heady in the air.

Happily, I needn't have told Little Dhandhō how I longed for one of the little sweets and she left me in the trees and took a little cloth bag out of her pocket to the seller, opening it to reveal seeds. The seller ran his finger through the bag and nodded. Then Little Dhandhō smiled and took four of the sweets from his table, wrapping them in her headscarf.

When she returned, I stuffed the candy right into my mouth and sunk my teeth down into the sweet, creamy gum finding it was too large for my mouth. Teeth stuck together, the gooey candy oozed back into my throat and I opened my jaw with my fingers and pulled out long, sticky strings all over my dress; sucking them back up as I chewed and coughed. Little Dhandhō took a sweet out from her headscarf and pulled a little bit off from the top, poking it into her mouth lightly to suck on. "Just a little at a time," she smiled.

I followed her along the outer wall behind a row of huts I knew to be near Dhandhō's shop and found an overturned rain barrel to climb upon for a better look at it.

The outside of the shop was painted dark brown but the trims on the windows and underneath the slanted roof were of a bright blue. Through the rounded back window, I could see rows of glass jars of paint and ribbons, long-handled brushes and all manner of paper and scrolls scattered everywhere. A large jar of golden dust shimmered in the corner on a low lacquered stool and from the ceiling, feathers and sparkling baubles and silvered streamers were strung and wavered in tandem in the light breeze. The shop contained everything Dhandhō would never admit to, while the hut showed everything she wished me to know.

But my real interest was inside the inner wall where I remembered the village school to be and I was determined to see my friends one more time, even if only from afar. From the place where I'd spied on the little school yard before, I sat again gazing at the dhana in their smocks and dresses; a waving river of yellow and blue. Not seeing Anshē or Rāca, I strained my neck over the small wall, flattening my ears out to their full width to hear the chatter.

On the right some tall he-dogs in blue were tossing around a brightly colored string-ball like Anshē had; slapping it back and forth to each other as it floated up and down. Their laughter brought a little smile to my face and it was only when I heard a sharp cry to the left that I took my eyes away from them.

Sitting along the inner wall in a circle were a group of she-dogs grasping at a bit of parchment. Rāca stood to the side of them, shouting and reaching up for the parchment they held high over her head. "Give it back!" I heard her little voice rise, tears cracking it strangely. One of the others snatched it away from her and ran with it to the he-dogs who unrolled it, shouting "Āe'rū!" The game immediately stopped, and they crowded around Rāca, shoving at her. "Get the teacher, she's seen the Guardian of Death!" someone called.

"I haven't, I haven't!" Rāca pushed back, nipping at the hands trying to contain her. "It's my dasha, I swear!"

The yellow dresses closed around her, questioning and pointing. "Someone's going to die tonight," someone said in a threatening tone. "Rāca saw the Guardian of Death!"

A tall, familiar face stepped up, towering over Rāca and said menacingly, "Do you think you can just call up death when you please? How do we know you don't *want* her to come? Maybe you want someone to die!" It was Sindrē!

Rāca said nothing and I pushed myself farther up atop the wall, flattening against it to stay hidden when a sudden flurry caught my attention at the edge of the crowd. I held my breath as Anshē pushed through the circle, reaching Rāca and pushing her behind him.

Sindrē looked pleased with himself and shoved Anshē in the chest. "Your sister is trying to bring death on us. What are you going to do about it?"

Anshē looked down at the ground, face reddening. "That's just a superstition, my a'ma told me so. Rāca didn't do anything wrong, it's just a picture of her dasha. Her name is *Mi'halē*." Sindrē shoved him again, hard enough to knock Anshē down. "I think you're a liar and you're up to something."

"She just drew a picture of her dasha so why don't you just leave us alone!" he looked up and his face was full of anticipation. I pulled back into a shadow, willing myself to look away but finding it impossible. My whole body winced when the blow came and my eyes squinted as Anshē's bloodied nose gushed across his smock. Rāca crouched down and wiped his face with her skirt, her face wet and puffed with tears.

Sindrē took the drawing and threw it up into the air where it was caught and thrown from one dhana to another, their shouts of "*sēoula!*" "*samanē!*" and "*tsoú'úa!*" mixing sharply with Rāca's crushed sobs. Sindrē looked down at Anshē in disgust as he said over his shoulder, "Let the teacher deal with them. Their aér brought the sickness to Pōcarū anyway. It's all their fault." And as he said this, everyone edged away from them and they sat in the dust alone, holding on to each other.

I reached my hand out over the wall, wishing beyond anything that I could touch them; that I could push Sindrē right back but I was pulled back from behind so sharply I grazed my knees on the stone and saw flashes of little stars before my vision cleared. "We have to go," Little Dandhō said sharply and I nodded numbly, understanding that to disobey her now would mean a worse fate than Anshē's if I was seen.

She didn't need to explain the words to me or tell me I would never see my friends again. Perhaps the great fears of Dandhō would not come to kill me, but I knew that I would never be welcome there and I knew that I would never call Dandhō any names again, even in my mind. As Little Dandhō dropped me off back at our own hut, it looked small and dark to me and somewhat menacing, and I felt poisoned by the things I'd seen.

But while I had left that morning with nothing but bravery and audacity, it all drained out onto the floor when I realized Dandhō had already returned and was sitting in the sleeping-room waiting for me. Heavily I walked into the room and sat down on the floor, waiting for my punishment. When it didn't come, I looked up and realized Dandhō had been quietly staring at me.

"I wanted to see my dasha, just one more time," I began but she cut me off.

"Do you know why Anshē and Rāca are bullied?" she murmured. I didn't answer, realizing with horror she must have stopped by the village on the way back from the fields. I shook my head.

"Their aér had gone to Adanandū for the bashō harvest by himself because their a'ma was busy with the twins. Shê'á, there were twins younger than Rāca. But he came back with sickness, the sickness that's been picking off análong left and right for years now. Then the twins came down with it. They all died and when they did, the village condemned their hut. Análong fear them and they treat them badly. And you," she squinted her eyes at me, "you defied me. You showed absolutely no concern for the rules or your elders. It's not just análong out there to get you, it's the unseen as well. But what would I know?" she shrugged her shoulders, suddenly standing from the bed. I was confused and began to follow her, but she turned around and angrily ordered me to the loft.

"You will take out every single scroll and copy them all, twice! I don't care how long it takes!"

But the knowing began to creep over the back of my skull, the suspicion that the punishment had more to do with keeping me too busy to try and escape into the world than to punish me for actually having done so. "I won't," I said evenly, crossing my arms.

"You will!" her voice raised and mine matched, "I won't!"

Then she said the words that changed everything between us: "You will because I'm your dl'ah'sha and I told you to!"

I clenched my fists and hollered back, "That's not how it works! You can't just decide to be my dl'ah'sha, I have to choose you!" Then, running past my Dandhō I vaulted up the ladder into the loft anyway, kicking it out behind me and hunching over to bury my head in my lap as it crashed into the hearth. Minutes that seemed like days passed and when I heard nothing, I scooted myself to the ledge to see if she was still in the hut.

She was. Sitting on her knees gazing out the window, Dandhō's hands worked into the hem of her dress and I could see her strong, speckled shoulders tremble. The hearth-ash had been scattered across the floor and wall in a black messy spatter and the ladder lay askew over it. My only way down was to jump so I pushed myself away and rolled onto my back to gaze at the ceiling. As I lay there telling myself I didn't care if I had to live up in the loft forever, I didn't notice I'd drifted off into sleep until I pried my crusted eyes open and saw how dark it had become.

The popping of a fire pricked up my ears and I stood, realizing the ladder had been returned to its rightful place. Carefully I made my way down, ignoring my empty stomach, and went straight to the sleeping-room, climbed into my bunk and pulled the covers up over my dress.

Dl'ah'sha. It was that one word that refused explanation, touched so many other words and existed only between those who gave it life. A dl'ah'sha couldn't appoint themselves, that I knew. But the truth was neither could they be chosen. We were both wrong; it was a relationship that simply happened between análong. It could never be forced.

The warm glow of evening from the common room had gone cold when I opened my eyes again and was replaced by that chilly early morning warmth that bloomed over my skin like yawning flowers. I sat straight up when an enormous crash rocked the hut, forcing my voice out against my will: "Dl'ah'sha!" But my cry was met only with the far-off reply of dry thunder over the fields. I knew it wasn't fair of me now to call her but at the next bed-shaking bolt of lightning I pitched to the edge of the bunk and called out "Ah'sha, I'm scared!"

Listening hard I could hear the stretching of fabric and Dandhō's strong, thin hand snaked up to catch me by the arm and yank me down onto her bed. She silently pulled the covers back and turned on her side to face the wall. Curling up with my back to hers but not touching, I made myself as small as possible and pulled the blanket over me.

Up until then I had always been the little stranger, the dhana belonging to no-one, existing within the sphere of my asama, but never really touching them. Aói. Love. It baffled me; its size and shape so beyond me, so intertwined with a multitude of tiny meanings intending to make it less. I understood the love of sisters, the love of friends. Now this new word lay beyond my reach that would follow me forever, the sort of love that filled in the holes of what was missing. Ah'sha; something precious.

And in that moment without celebration it had happened. I had called my ah'sha, and she had answered.

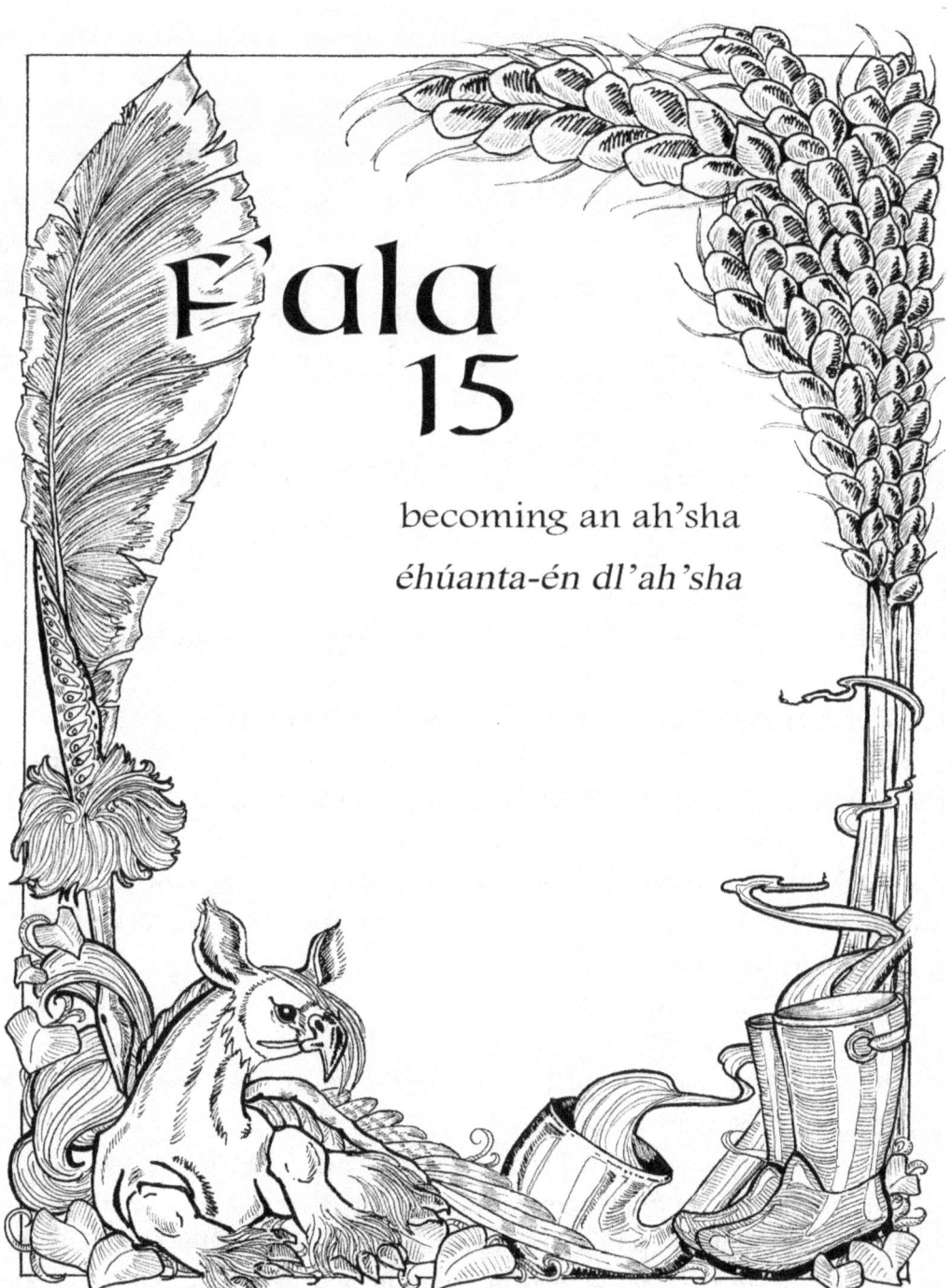

F'ala
15

becoming an ah'sha

éhúanta-én dl'ah'sha

T HE onandals were ill.

The flock that shared my land numbered somewhere around five hundred, one of the largest in Ebūda, and of the fifty or so I had seen, many had dull, dry manes and missing claws. Their leader assured me it was only these of the group who had been feverish and lethargic, but I had my doubts as he admitted even he'd not seen such symptoms before.

Omnivores by nature, the onandals hunted for small game in the northwest of my land while I hunted to the south, but I hadn't seen any sick game outside of their flock that might have passed something on. They grazed a wide part of my fields for the tough, high grass but nothing seemed amiss there either. Nevertheless, they asked about the dhana and I knew it was more out of concern for their ability to keep up the charm they had laid around my property than curiosity of her.

At home, the tension had soared as I discovered the dhana had defied me again and somehow, it was amidst this that she called me by the name ah'sha.

Was this how you thought it would happen, Rā-alta? Is this what destiny is?

And even so, while such a relationship could never be undone, I still felt somehow fake. How was I supposed to know what else to teach her? How much longer until Rā-alta sent for her? What if the onandals were a sign of worse to come?

Remember the most important thing.

That's what they told us every day in the Halls of Learning. Base your whole life around it, put every question to it as a test, make every decision based on it. It wasn't as easy as it sounded. Too many other responsibilities piled up on top of the most important thing it seemed.

The night after Mi'hal'ē snuck out for what would be the last time, she called down from her bunk just as I'd begun to drift off. Exhausted, I covered my head with my pillow until she kicked the ladder. "Alright already, I'm awake!" I heard her roll over to the edge of the bunk, waiting for her to climb down but she only lay there in silence. I lay quietly impatient, waiting for her to speak but after a while filled with her gently breathing in tandem to me, I heard the tentative question. "Ah'sha, what am I? Why didn't you tell me I wasn't real?"

"What's put that into your head?" I asked, irritated not that I had to lie to her but that I truly didn't have an answer for her no matter how she rephrased this tired old question.

"I know what all the colors mean now. I know what the words mean now. Everyone is afraid of me," she replied simply. "Samanē, sē'oúla..."

Spirit, foreigner. "Then you understand why I keep you here." And I felt her somehow nod in the night against her blanket. I knew from my own experience that this was to be one of those times when one grew into one's own timeline; and it was impossible to tell whether the one doing the growing was she or I or both. But like so many of these moments in our lives it would go by unnoticed, silent until one looked back and wondered if anyone above us catalogued our little actions, for who could ever know the moment of *change*? Supposedly the Guardians did, But who kept an account of the milestones of the Guardians?

"Does it matter that I didn't tell you? About the colors? You know anyway," I pointed out in defense.

"Shĕ'á!" she answered back immediately. "It matters! Aren't you my ah'sha? *You* should have told me!"

I nodded to myself, but said to her, "This is the last time I'm going to speak to you about it so listen. This is how you will always be able to say you are análong: because I am your dl'ah'sha, and you are part of this asama, and those who live as análong are called análong and die as análong." And this was the truth as much as it needed to be.

But soft words couldn't heal the hurt between us over that last excursion for some time.

And soon enough, I had bigger things to worry about. One afternoon while closing the shop I turned and found myself I front of a suspicious young análong tattooed across the face in the style of the NaÓma.

"Ta-F'ala, I've come to warn you that the grave illness from the north has broken the southern border into Mandaca village. My *friends* have heard that you are a lady of *independence* here in Pōcarū. If you would need any assistance in the future, come to me and I can give you an arrangement to allow you to escape before it should spread to your village. Because one never knows these days. One never knows."

"Your friends aren't my friends and independence means needing no assistance," I reminded him through gritted teeth. He looked at me through measured, squinted eyes and put his head down close to mine. "I've heard you own a large piece of land that has been quite fertile through these times of misfortune. I know that you're also not stupid. You wouldn't want anything unfortunate to happen to your loved ones, would one? I come prepared to make an offer for your land and of course allow you a small plot on it in gratitude for your support. What is your price?"

"I have no price. It will not be sold." I turned and walked out past the village wall without a glance back. But all the way back to the hut I checked carefully to see if I was being followed and once I'd returned, I sat Ā'dō down at the table to give her a serious talk after the dhana had gone to bed. "As long as the river flows even one drop, we won't leave this land. I'll send word to Rā-alta tomorrow and maybe that will get her moving to send for the dhana. I can't possibly believe the city isn't safer than here now. The NaÓma may be tearing up the rest of Ebūda but they can't get past the magic of Bri'én. It's much too old."

Ā'dō's eyes narrowed as she thought. "I was told by someone in the village that the illness can be prevented by some of the NaÓma healers and that's what's keeping them strong. Nanē Indarū bought a bag of their spice and they told her if she and her dhana drink it three times daily for a month, they won't get the sickness."

Angrily I slapped the table and shook my head. "How stupid can you be? I've heard that story too and it's nothing but a lie. Nanē Indarū has sold her whole house to death itself and you should know better, Ǎ'dō! As I live and breathe don't you dare take anything from a stranger!"

My ēdhandha's eyes widened and she backed away from the table. If I'd frightened her, it was all the better because she must understand that while she was the more loving of the two of us, she was also the more naive.

Straight off the next morning I wrote out a long scroll to Rā-alta, telling her of Mi'hal'ē's progress, her mischief, and the situation in Pōcarū with the sudden presence of NaÓma spies and asked her what was to be done next if the illness indeed spread as far as us. In my mind I knew it was coming soon by the onandals, because nature always proclaims fate ahead of itself if we are observant enough to hear. Now I was anxious with the nervous anticipation of something evil and almost hopeful that the word would come so it could be over with.

Once the scroll had been sent by messenger from the village, Ǎ'dō moved into my hut temporarily so that she and I could take shifts watching things during the night and I quietly cut down my shop hours. If Mi'hal'ē was bothered by our new schedule, she never showed it but sometimes sat up in the evening on the doorstone beside me quietly watching out over the treeless field outside to the end of the path while I puffed on my pipe, letting the long smoke curls hang lazily in the thick evening air.

Two months passed. It was a flat, unusually warm afternoon when Mi'hal'ē and I readied the hut for the cold season. So, with Mi'hal'ē reaching as high as she could to balance out the weight of the large wooden shutters, I pulled to loosen them from the outside and quickly untied the fasteners so we could gently walk them one at a time out and across the windows and retie them to block the winter wind.

When this was done we tied the inside fasteners as well and Ǎ'dō pulled out the stiff winter covers from the storehouse and hooked these to the wall hooks across the windows on the inside, leaving only a small window in the sleeping room and the loft window uncovered, which made the hut considerably darker but also much more airtight. "Good, that's done." I said, surveying our work. Mi'hal'ē walked over and fingered the bright stripes on the winter covers. "It's too hot," she stated.

"We can manage. Soon it will be too cold," I answered and gazed out the front door which I'd opened for some air because she was exactly right. "How do you know?" she asked suddenly. Rolling my eyes, I replied, "Because I'm a million years older than you and I have a million other winters to go by."

She giggled. "You're not that old!"

"Oh? How old am I then?"

"A million-and-five," and she collapsed into a fit of giggles as I conceded, "Probably. One loses count after a few thousand."

I stepped out into the cool dirt and took off my foot-wraps to rub my feet and watch the colors soften in the distance over the blackening trees whose tops could been seen peeping over the very edge of the deadened wheat in the distance. As my eyes began to drift into a sleepy haze, I imagined one of the treetops was swaying a little, towards me.

Then swaying a bit closer.

Then swaying until I sat up with a start and realized it was no tree!

"Hurry; go hide under my bed and don't make any noise," I called inside the hut, picking up my staff from its hook above the door and walking quickly out to the end of the path to stave off the trespasser. As I approached, shielding my eyes from the orange evening light, I could now make out the the swaying top of the trespasser's staff. As it came into view I saw the figure, a dhana, was actually not much taller than Mi'hal̆e. She wore a thin short dress and high wrappings on her legs and feet but looked to be a bit older than that in the face. Her skin was of a dark pinkish hue and her and her thin eyes were lighter brown like mine and Ădo̅'s so they almost looked to float in her face, as did the faint speckles across her face and shoulders.

"This land is protected, how did you get through?" I called out before we met.

"I didn't go through it, I went over it," the figure answered back, not stopping but walking right past me easily. "I've come for her." I turned in my tracks and demanded, "Exactly who do you mean?"

"Mi'hal̆e is who I mean. Or are you hiding another Guardian under your roof?" she said matter-of-factly and struck her staff into the dust to stop a few feet from me.

Wait, what? Rā-alta said nothing about another one!

"Then who are you?"

She leaned over to pull on my dress. "I'm called Éĕshī; Guardian of Creation. I will be her new caretaker on the journey."

"Back up," I felt a sudden headache coming on. "Rā-alta said nothing about another Guardian or a journey."

"Well she *has* lived all her life as an análong. Bound to mess some things up."

"Are you trying to insult me?"

"I don't need to try. At any rate, you were told of the tests the Guardian must pass. Be certain, you can only teach her so much yourself. Really, so little, and she has much more work to do. I will take her to do that work." Éĕshī eyed me and began again towards the hut. Bewildered by this new development, I dumbly followed but picked up my staff firmly in defense. "I'm doing the best I can," I mumbled.

But I swiped my hand out to grab at her staff, shouting, "Wait! How do I know you're who you say you are? Rā-alta wouldn't have *purposely* left anything out."

Éĕshī slid her staff slowly out of my grasp, searching my eyes with hers with a mirthless smile. "You know who I am, Ta-F'ala, What I am. Look at me, look at my eyes."

But I looked away; her eyes were so like mine yet thin and twisted like a locust's smile. Her skin, like the dhana's but yet not. My mind could see her as neither one or the other and it unsettled me.

She couldn't help but laugh. "Only análong have such a need to sort things into little boxes rather than see them for what they are. Such authority you lot think you have in Creation when you're not even a part of it!" Éĕ'shī leaned carelessly against the staff and sniffed the air in contemplation. "I'll prove it to you then if you must be so stubborn.

Before I came into this world, I saw a dhana once in the city of Bri'én, a graduate who left the path of enlightenment and ran through the holy city in despair. I saw a dhana who was taken far down into the undercity and smoked in the *dondatra* dens like an old gē until all her robes and ear-rings were gone, even her shoes; only her bare neck was unmarked."

I stiffened, remembering the smoky, sultry dens of my past where slaves were taken to entertain and be made complacent, a thing I'd managed to put so far out of my mind it had slipped into non-existence. But I wouldn't give in so easily. "You know nothing. Speak if you want to but you could be a street artist for all I know. Even they dye their skin for display."

She sat down then on the ground and crossed her legs, settling her head easily in her hands to recount. "*An-an*, I shall continue. And then I saw this dhana had been taken into the den of one particular he-dog, a large one who would only take young she-dogs in, the younger the better."

"Enough," I snapped. "It's a common story; the story of many a slave."

But Éĕ'shī went on, unwavering. "She escaped that place, someone saw her and reached down through the grates to bring her up into the light. She was cleaned up and signed into a contract to serve this one's household. But she was injured somehow, the cut so deep it nearly took that arm off. And then it became infected and the dhana wasn't expected to live."

I froze, unsure if I should breathe as the pages of my life were being read out before me. Somehow, someone knew of my falling. Someone knew who I was, what I'd done. And here she stood before me.

"It was fortunate the master lived near a surgery, wasn't it? The arm was saved and the infection treated. It was quite a scar, so deep. From that day on it was covered with a cloth band and bracelets." She pointed to but didn't touch the band on my arm. "A scar that lies witness to the crime that made it. And no-one has ever seen that scar outside that surgery because you never take that band off.

And frankly, that's gross."

"I wash it!" I protested.

"Whatever." She pulled herself up and dusted off her dress. "But, how quickly one falls," she observed. "You didn't stop speaking with your a'ér just because he stopped speaking to you. You *fell*. If your ēdandha knew, if your patrons knew, you wouldn't be so independent. Rā-alta doesn't know and neither does Mi'halĕ and you're so afraid..."

I growled. "And you'll never tell them if you think I'm going to tolerate another mouth to feed under my roof!"

"Of course not. It's not my story to tell. My existence in your world is only a punishment, I don't have anything to do with your affairs. When I'm done, I can leave."

"I've heard enough. How long then until you two go on your way?" I snapped.

"How would I know? I'm only a chaperone," Éē'shī said vaguely. "You're the dl'ah'sha. It's your decision."

I threw up my hands. "And you just told me I'm awful at it!"

"It can't be helped, you're only an análong. But a dl'ah'sha is a rare thing, indeed. You did right there at least."

"If you're not going to help then shut up," I grumbled but she got up and looked me over studiously.

"I will, actually. Consider this: you don't *see* Mi'halē. You've got to see her to be able to love her. You think you do, or maybe you don't, but you *can't* until you see her. A Guardian is born into this life as a punishment and you must acknowledge that. Stop worshipping us as your saviors, stop putting all your hope in us. Mi'halē, Rā-alta, myself, we were cursed with our brothers and sisters in this way: *to know, to live, to forget, to be forgotten, to lose, to see, to hear, to endure, to forsake, to guard, to give, and to remain.*"

I shook my head. "I know she's not perfect. But she's a dhana. Smart-mouthed, defiant. I can't even imagine what she'll be like when she gets older."

"That's not what I'm talking about. I mean, you cannot see the good she will do until you see the evil she has already done. And that's doubly true for Rā-alta," she nodded knowingly. "Open your heart so you can see. Then you can truly say you love her. And you want to so badly." Éē'shī looked out into the distance. "Then you will truly be doing this for her too. I think you can love in that way, because that's the sort of love you've wanted all your life."

"Then how could I if I've never had it?" I demanded, feeling like this undertaking with Guardians and such was weighing ever heavier the longer this day dragged on.

"That's the thing about you análong, isn't it? If you can't, then Mi'halē *must*, or your world will crumble to dust. So, let's get cracking then, shall we?" she said the last bit cheerfully and continued up the path to the hut, leaving me scrambling behind her feeling suddenly old and slow.

Éē'shī walked through my door and took up her place much in the way Mi'halē had, as if she'd always been with us. Before the day was through, she had a place in Mi'halē's bunk, a bowl and cup at the table and a cushion on the floor. Her coming of course put the final strain on my carefully constructed household, but it was a help that she didn't eat or drink as much as the rest of us. "Guardians of the land are dependent on the land to live," she explained to me. "Guardians of the air can draw on unseen things to survive."

As Éē'shī's time with us grew longer with no immediate sign of how long this would be, I stopped hunting for our amiti stew, for as I had long feared, the hadim began to grow thinner and the small game moved upward towards the onandals' territory. I felt it was a right sacrifice to keep them well, and though Mi'hal̆e had never seen them, she knew of them and agreed we could manage without. After all, there were reminders of our time left everywhere these days it seemed.

Now that the threat of the drought had made itself known to us and the awareness of the NaÓma hung in the air like a flag, the days stretched out into an impossible length that chores just couldn't fill. The evenings were spent in the loft going over the lessons which Éĕ'shī sat through patiently but never added a word.

"Small and less are places on the wheel of life; the Order in which all things lie in creation. It is right to acknowledge one's place in this order because at each place on the wheel there is something higher protecting something lower. So that in truth, as this wheel turns nothing is ever the smallest or highest. As such, smallness and insignificance can never define importance because the wheel is always spinning. The highest moves to be lowest, the lowest moves to be highest. This is the principle of cīama. Though we as análong are not included in the Law of Orders that governs Creation, all things in reality are within the wheel of life," I read one particularly steamy afternoon.

Mi'hal̆e wiped the sweat from her cheeks and murmured, "Cīama. The smallest can be the most important, the largest can be the least." Éĕ'shī nodded and laid her head daintily on her arm, seemingly untouched by the stagnant air. Tsō, it was boredom which plagued her. And it was only too soon before I began to forget the days when only two eyes gazed at me from across the table instead of four; when there was one head sleeping above me in the doubled-bed instead of two.

And this was in no way odd to Mi'hal̆e; this complete stranger that I had brought into the hut to live with us without introduction or question and I suspected that Mi'hal̆e felt I owed her a dasha for the ones I'd taken away. This I could forgive, and it made a silent peace between us; an understanding that neither of us would ever speak the names of those who weren't there anymore. Rather, those who lived under my roof split the chores amongst themselves with Éĕ'shī coming with me to the field and Mi'hal̆e staying in with Ā'dō.

Just as Mi'hal̆e accepted this happily though, Ā'dō said nothing about the arrangement and I knew it made her nervous to realize the hazy thought of the dhana leaving us someday was now dazzlingly real. I found myself having less and less to question about the company I kept as my fields became drier and drier through the warmest winter I'd ever known. Éĕ'shī could look after herself and so was no burden to me.

But she and I began to come back to the hut with less and less in hand those days and when I looked at her across the table I found her eyes to be the waiting eyes of one much older, glazed with the expectancy of one who is always waiting for an end only they can see. Waiting for me to do something so obscure I couldn't even fathom it.

Outside our own small world, tales running around the village of atrocities to the north of us became wilder and wilder until finally someone took sick in Orambūsū and was quarantined to the east of that village and this caused tremendous panic in Pōcarū. Through this, I still heard nothing from Bri'én. Though Pōcarū correspondence was often slow, we hadn't received any messengers since Éė'shī had come and it was apparent from the strangers in the village making themselves visible near my shop that the question of my selling the land wasn't settled.

"Ādō, I have to do something soon if I don't hear from Rā-alta. It's been too long since I sent that scroll," I worried one evening as we chopped wood.

"Everyone's talking, Dandhō. Everyone is saying most of the north is already dead and the land is burned away. Can you believe it? Do you think they're making it up to scare us?" her eyes were wide.

"Tsōl. Orambūsū is quarantined with the illness," I said, picturing the ominous white sheeting over the huts and the black streamers across the doorways. "It takes a few weeks but then it ends so fast there's no time to bury. The bodies have to be burned. But if they keep to themselves over there, we've got a chance of escaping it. Even so, it's so close. That's why Mi'halė can't stay here much longer," I said resolutely.

"But where in Ebūda will she go? And how will we get her there?" Ādō demanded, putting her axe down.

"I've decided that Éė'shī must take her."

Ādō's hands rested on her hips and she glared at me. "Have you lost your mind? Éė'shī's no bigger than Mi'halė! Haven't you heard what they're doing out there? When there's no more food the dhana are left behind on the roads. And some, some eat their own to stay alive. What if someone finds them?" Her last words came out in a choked sob as she looked away and accused, "What kind of dl'ah'sha are you to send them away into that?"

My fists clenched to keep my temper in check. "How dare you lecture me! What else would you have me do? Let her starve to death right here? Slit her throat and keep her from the NaÓma's hands? You forget I could have always taken her to the Cāilon-da and sold her. That's the fate of foundlings in some places! I'm giving her the best chance at staying alive I can think of!"

Ādō's eyes grew wide and frightened and her voice softened pitifully. "Would you really? Could you have sold her like that?

It wasn't her fault she knew nothing of me; nothing of my heart and the things it looked at and away from. It wasn't her fault she didn't know I went to bed every night asking Mī'á how I could possibly go on for one more day of this uncertainty. And it wasn't her fault she didn't know I woke up every morning with the words "*for her*" on my lips and dragged myself on.

If she was asking me could I do such a thing now, I couldn't. Instead, I said nothing and let her try and understand all of me whether she could forgive it or not, for when I was younger, I couldn't have answered so quickly in a world that taught it was natural to do such things. She gave up and asked, "But what if someone else catches them and sells them?"

I sighed. "Look at them. No one's going to come close enough to them to catch them and I'm counting on it. It was a different world when she first came to us. When análong have what they need, they also have the time to persecute in order to keep it. But when nothing is left for them to have, neither do they have time to worry about their old stigmas. I'm not even so worried about the NaÓma anymore; their numbers are dwindling the closer they get. It's the sickness that's finishing off this world. For all their swords and bows and cunning, the NaÓma have no power over sickness.

But if it's true that the little one is a Guardian, I think they can make it. You've never known Mi'hal̃e to be sick, have you? I don't mean all her stomach aches; those are just her excuses to get out of chores. I mean she's never caught anything and neither has Éẽ'shī. Maybe they're just immune. So I'll send them to Bri'ẽn. There is no safer place than the sacred city, no place more protected by magic.

And they're small enough to keep out of sight wherever they go. I'll draw up a map through the rural places, the illness can only survive as long as there are análong to carry it. When they get to the city, they can use the ring Rā-alta gave me if they absolutely must to be taken directly to her, but I don't think they'll have a problem finding her once they reach the city. There's just nowhere further south for us to go even if I thought we could take them and flee."

Nothing was simple here, nothing obvious. At least not to me. I wished desperately we did live in the world of Rā-alta's beliefs and dreams, of Ã'dō's simple absolutes. I looked away. If the world truly had turned this vile, and for us there was no way to know for sure being so far away, only a Guardian could save Mi'hal̃e anyway, no matter where I sent her. It was now that I recalled a question I had asked of the Elders in the Halls of Learning so long ago. Why couldn't an análong bring us to caémba? Why did we need Guardians to do it for us anyway? But now I understood the Elders' answer in what Rā-alta had said to me in her chambers. The análong had forgotten how to be análong. Truly, we had no idea how to save ourselves, just as I'd had no idea how to be an ah'sha.

I spoke softly. "I think...that while Mi'hal̃e has been with us it wasn't my own belief that I acted on but the faith of Rā-alta. I can't say when it became my truth, but it did. Now I know that if the two of them are Guardians, they will finish what Rā-alta thinks they are here to do. I see a short future for myself, and I wish to honor the promise I made."

Then nothing more was said as we finished chopping and stacked the wood but Ã'dō put her hand on my shoulder and I knew she had hesitantly agreed it was the right thing to do. Now, I would write to Rā-alta and wait for the right moment to say goodbye.

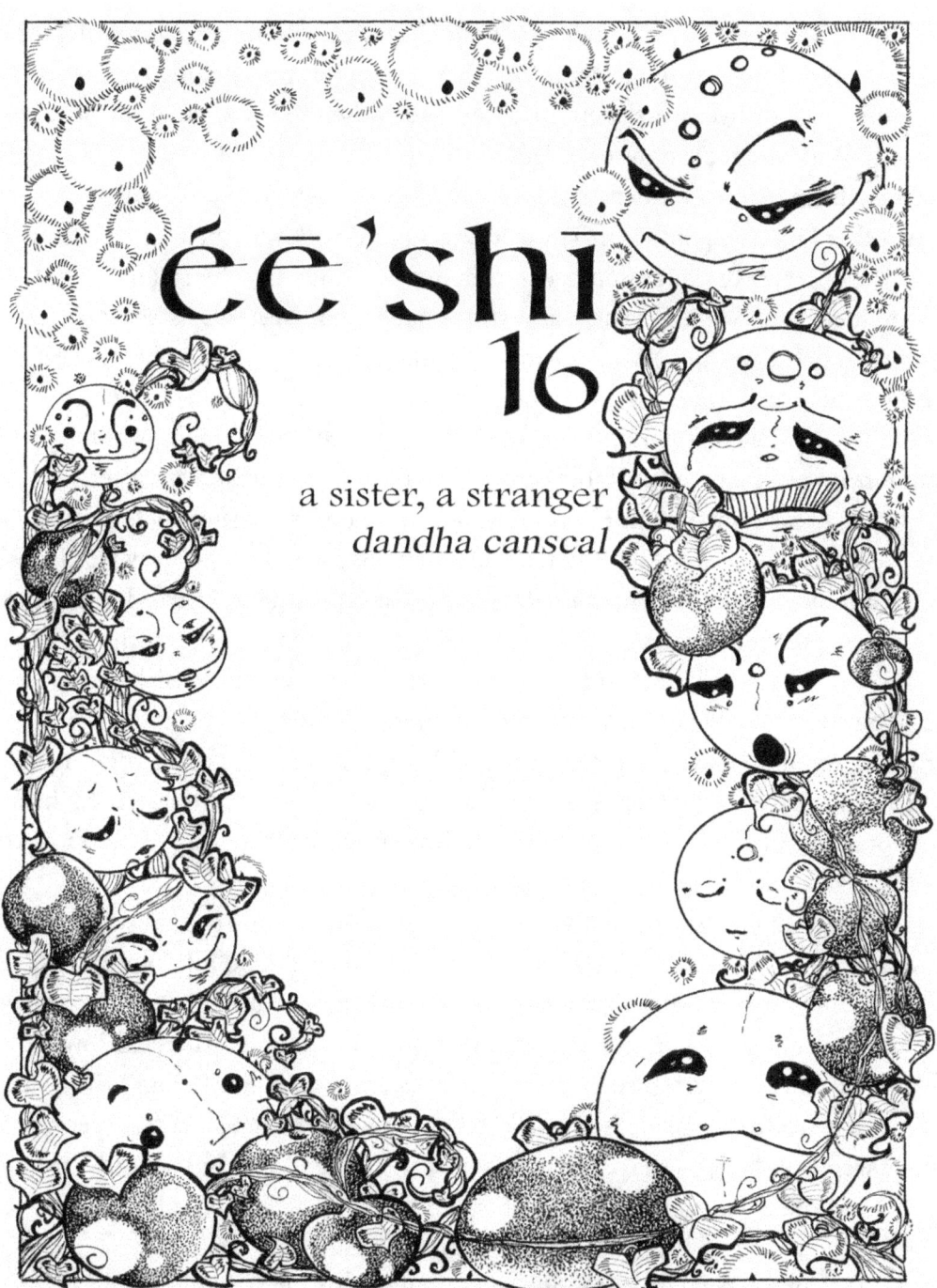

éē'shī

16

a sister, a stranger
dandha canscal

$\mathcal{T}$HAT summer passed, stagnant in its brevity, pushing the cold season further back into that lazy year.

I knew I'd upset F'ala by recounting her past to her, yet it was the only way to convince her of my identity. There was nothing for me to criticize her on. Why did the análong elevate the Guardians so? Couldn't they see our lives were spent in observance; when they only had the business of living to worry about? What did it profit us to judge?

My own curse lie in being forgotten.

Unlike my other kin, I was the Guardian who was graced with memory far before my birth into Ebūda. I was the observer of Ebūda's progress from its beginning, the Guardian who called an'álong into Ebūda by their names from Hala-Asal. And though I had seen all its early secrets, I was no scribe like my brothers Sada and Nārū, nor was I a witness of its sins like my brother Hor'ō-cō. And neither was I meant to walk among the análong as my sister Ā'dō, who had her memory, like the other Guardians of the land, taken as part of her curse. Tsō, when the last análong was born and it came time to manifest myself, I closed the doors on Hala-Asal, and none were born after.

When I awoke, I knew my time in F'ala's household would be very short before the journey. It is a stone one must carry around the neck when you are the one who knows every word is the last, yet they do not. Even the análong are acquainted with this concept and have a word for it I kept close to my heart: *andama*, the things which can never be said. And all that summer, I think I counted even our steps, they were so few. I knew that before the journey was over (that which the análong call the last journey), one of us would lay dead and it could not be Mi'hal'e.

Could I move amongst these strangers as one of them, knowing that Ā'dō would never find true love, that Sā-úū and Rā-alta could never be, that Mi'hal'e and Anshē may indeed meet in another existence, but not in this one? Moreover, would I last through the days waiting to die without knowing the hour?

With every passing night I wondered these things as I took note how the rain skipped a season and the buckets came up from the well a little less full. As F'ala pushed food into our bowls, I wondered. As we began to reuse the bathwater over and over until the three of us bathed together, I wondered. And as I counted every blade of grass fade from green to pale yellow and then to brown, I wondered.

Mi'hal'e looked at me with greedy eyes as if I had answers I could give her and she asked over and over where I had come from, breaking my heart a little every time that she no longer knew me.

"But where were you born?" she asked slowly as if I simply didn't understand her words. "The field," I'd say. "That one?" she pointed to the wheat and ryegrass field divided by the path to Pōcarū, as nondescript as a field could be. "That one right there?"

I'd nod and she'd look away in disappointment. "But you don't look like the others," she muttered one morning after the usual questioning. I smirked. "I don't, you say? Says *you*."

"But at least you *have* a color, it's just a different color."

"How about you pay attention to what you do have rather than go on about what you don't?" I snapped impatiently, and she left me alone for a week.

"The moons didn't come to look when you were born," she observed suspiciously on the eighth day after her silence. "They don't come down to look at everyone," I said.

"How old are you?"

"Older than you."

Another week went by with no more questions.

"Are you here to be my dasha?" she asked finally, her hands clenched on her hips.

I looked her over. "Sort of. Let's call it that."

And from then on, she was so glad to not be alone any longer that she talked nonstop it seemed.

Then the cold snap finally came and F'ala was only too glad to remind us all how clever she was to ignore our protests and keep the windows covered during the extra warm months. We huddled together at night under many blankets in our bunks, but suddenly, just as quickly the skies became blistering again, announcing another change.

F'ala's moods were precarious at the best of times and as the weather changed yet again, she said fleetingly one evening on the doorstone that the important thing was to know the most important thing. "No matter what happens," she said cryptically as we lay panting on the ground beside her. "No matter what happens, think of the most important thing. Ask yourself this over and over until it becomes clear and then nothing will be too hard for you."

When neither of us commented she leaned back against the hut and lit her pipe, observing, "They say there is no greater pleasure for an análong than to walk on his own fields and inspect his gardens. Or to count his dhana. Or to walk beside the seas. Or to sit on his doorstone in the heat and take tea. Or to sit by his hearth in the cold and breath in his pipe. Or to listen to the windbells and the cicadas in twilight." She drew on her pipe and sighed out the smoke in little puffs.

"Anything else?" I snickered and was shot a sour look. But it was measured, I knew, by sadness.

"Would you like to go to Bri'én someday?" F'ala asked Mi'hal̆e suddenly. The dhana looked at her strangely, tense hope tugging at her lip. "I'm not allowed, you said. Never ever," she finally answered with caution.

"Well, life's much too long to say *never* to anything," F'ala countered, looking off into the shimmery distance over the grass.

"You're trying to trick me and it's cruel!" Mi'hal̆e shouted at her, leaping to her feet and clenching her hands. "You've never told Éĕ'shī she can't leave the hut, just *me*."

F'ala leaned back on her elbows against the door and smiled approvingly. "Tse, tse. I was only asking if you'd ever thought of it? I think Éĕ'shī has traveled before. Maybe she can take you. You certainly couldn't go *alone*."

I watched closely as Mi'hal̆e held her pose then quickly turned her back to us, but not before I saw the frustrated sparkle in her eyes. "Of course I want to go."

F'ala's voice was low and lost in memory as she murmured. "It is called the shining city; the holy place of all Ebūda. Here in the south we speak one way; they in the north speak another way but in Bri'ěn everyone speaks as they do all at once.

Once every four years there's a march all around the country that ends in Bri'ěn. It's called the *shēgū'in-srala*, the March of Kingdoms. Análong of the three prefectures dress in their finest and march on foot to the sacred city for a festival. During the festival the Elders read the new laws and if common análong want, they can protest them then."

F'ala took another long draw from her pipe and let the smoke curl around her nose before continuing. "Underneath the city is another city of little domed houses and high above everything sits the Palace and its many rooms and gardens. Don't you wish to go?"

"I said I did," Mi'hal̆e said resentfully, playing with a stick in the dirt around her feet without looking up. F'ala shrugged and pulled herself up with a long sigh to walk back into the hut and begin the evening tea.

I stayed for some time, watching Mi'hal̆e push the stick back and forth, licking her lips on occasion and shielding her eyes from the sun with her other hand. "I've been there," I said softly. "It's just as she says."

"Everyone must have," she said sulkily. "Except me."

"Well perhaps you'll go one day," I said flatly, becoming annoyed with her even though I knew what F'ala was up to.

"Sure," she grunted and followed F'ala back into the hut.

No matter how F'ala protested, I could see her love for Mi'hal̆e and the struggle she waged against sending her away. I had no advantage in this. When I left Hala-Asal, Bri'ěn still stood tall and the rivers were fat and there was no way for me to know how much time had elapsed during my journey. When I told F'ala it was up to her to decide when the journey for Mi'hal̆e and I would begin, it was not to flatter her, but the stark truth.

Then came the day when F'ala and Ǎdō no longer ate two scoops of rice in their bowls but smiled softly at us and told us to finish our own bowls. And it was not so long after that that we were also given one scoop. And then the little cakes Mi'hal̆e so loved for tea became smaller and smaller until they disappeared, and we drank the tea with less and less leaves. When the morning meal vanished, Mi'hal̆e began to worry and asked F'ala if we would ever have it back. "Not today," was all that she would say.

Now F'ala would save up all her water to make her one cup of weak tea in the evening, going without drinking anything else for this cause if she had to. When then three months passed without any rain, putting Drīdū officially in drought, she took the tea leaves and packed them away in a little golden tin, keeping this underneath her bed with her other secret things we weren't supposed to know about. Once in a while she would sit in the evening outside the hut and chew on the leaves but the rest of us couldn't stand the bitterness enough to ask for her to share.

Shortly after came the day the storehouse ran out of grain and Mi'hal'e bawled of a genuine sore stomach, confiding in me because she didn't want to worry F'ala. "You're making it worse checking the storehouse looking for something that isn't there," I pointed out. "Close the door and find something to do to take your mind off it." But sometimes I would find her sitting on the floor out there imagining the long strings of onions and bags of flour that once crowded the room.

The day Ādō became ill was the first time I saw F'ala visibly afraid. She'd come to stay with us in the morning but by the afternoon her eyes were dull, her face blushed and what little she'd eaten was thrown up outside the window. F'ala had come home early from Pōcarū with a pale face and I knew from the fatigue in her eyes as she stepped into the hut that she'd seen death. She wasted no time examining her sister's underarms and neck but sighed in relief when she didn't find the deep red blisters of the northern illness she'd been dreading for months.

Laying her sister out on the floor by the hearth, F'ala wrapped her in blankets and stoked the fire until she cried from heat exhaustion but sweated out the desired amount of liquid as was the practice of análong healers. Completely unconscious for ten days, Ādō was blissfully unaware as F'ala spoon-fed her bitter tea and washed her naked body by the hearth twice a day with clean water we all volunteered from our bath. She didn't hear Mi'hal'e cry over her, nor did she see how thin F'ala was becoming. It seemed we had passed some unseen mark in time and were now speeding towards some sort of end.

"If the illness comes to the village, Ādō won't last. She's always been weak," F'ala observed from the table late one evening as her sister slept. I nodded, knowing this to be true and raised my head when I saw movement over by the hearth. "I think she's awake."

F'ala leaned down and took Ādō's hand. "You've slept more in the last ten days than I have in the last ten years," she chided. "So lazy."

Ādō attempted a smile that didn't make it past her lips. "Dhindhē for taking care of me. Wish I could... don't want to say goodbye."

"Nā, you're not going anywhere," F'ala interrupted. "You're going to get married someday remember? We're going to Bri'én to spend all my nendē and then dhana for auntie F'ala to put to work in the fields, alright?"

Ādō closed her eyes. "Maybe."

"You will. One day you will have a dhana and every time you look at that dhana, you will say, *I will give them this and that because I didn't have that when I was a dhana.* And you will not give them too much or too little, but just enough so that when *they* have a dhana, they will also look at that dhana and say, *I will give this dhana this and that because I had enough.*" F'ala said softly and patted her sister's hand briskly. She looked over to me and her face brightened. "I think she'll be alright this time; she just needs a lot of rest."

I agreed and went outside to take my place on the doorstone to watch the sun descend underneath the sparse treeline across F'ala's field as we did every evening. "I haven't written to Rā-alta yet," F'ala sat down beside me to confess. I said nothing and after a few minutes she continued. "I just thought, if the sickness stayed north of us," she shrugged sheepishly. "Well maybe I wouldn't have to send her."

"Are you going to?"

"Do you think she's been happy here? There's so much she wants that we can't give her," F'ala asked.

"Want isn't the culprit of unhappiness, dissatisfaction is," I said clearly.

When she didn't respond I explained this way: "Are you happy, Ta-F'ala?"

She snorted. "What kind of question is that? I have everything I need."

"Exactly. That's not what I asked," I crossed my arms and no more was said as she worked out my words and went to bed.

* * *

I would always remember the last night in the hut before our leaving.

Āʹdō was sleeping in the common room near the window. That evening I remember Mi'haĺe and I slept in the top bed until F'ala suddenly complained it was so hot she worried we might come down with something as well and laid the blankets out for us to sleep on the floor where the air was cooler.

For Mi'haĺe it was exciting to sleep-over on her old bed. We settled down together and watched the sky out of the window for a while before the giggles overtook us and trailed across the floor, scurrying into the corners.

"Īla'úa! There has to be two of you doesn't there!" complained F'ala from above us. "Twice the noise."

I covered Mi'haĺe's mouth with my hand and buried my face in the blanket to keep from laughing aloud. It had no effect.

"Settle down," F'ala snipped a few moments later. I rolled over close to Mi'haĺe's ear and spoke softly. "Let's play a game. It's called undala. It means, *I wish.*"

She murmured back in agreement.

"I say something I wish for and then you do the same. So, I'll go first: *undala, undala,* I wish I could fly!" Mi'haĺe giggled into my other ear. "*Undala, undala,* I wish I were taller!"

"I wish I had lots of jewels." I laughed a bit too loud.

"What would you do with them?"

"Eat them for morning tea," I said, pretending in that fleeting moment to be a dhana; to have this last moment of frivolity. Mi'halē laughed and then clapped her hand over her mouth. "Your teeth would sparkle! My turn. *Undala, undala,* I wish I had an a'ér."

"I wish I had an a'ma," I returned.

"You're just like me, you have no parents," Mi'halē's eyes crinkled and she touched my face gingerly. When I didn't move away or answer she flopped on her back and nestled her hands beneath her head.

"*Undala, undala,* I wish every night were just like this," Mi'halē whispered. I could hear F'ala moving a little in her bed and I said gently, "No night can ever be the same. Every morning the world is born again."

"It certainly won't be the same if I don't get some sleep soon because you two will be sleeping in the storehouse!" a voice above us snapped.

Mi'halē rolled over and buried her head in my shoulder silently but I could feel her grinning all the way into sleep, nearly missing the exhausted whisper that dropped in the air just before I followed her: "*Undala, undala,* I *do* want to go to Bri'én. Let's all go to the city, all of us."

"Let's," I said carefully. "Someday let's do that."

But she'd already nodded off, not hearing my reply.

Sometime later I awoke to a flat, wan song piercing through the window screen. I lay in bed listening to it, thinking its wide shrill sound must encompass the entire world and I could only recall it from golden afternoons in a much younger Ebūda. As I looked over I saw the silhouette of Mi'halē sitting straight up in the moonlight at the other end of the bedroll, watching. "Lay down dhana, it's only the locusts," F'ala murmured above us.

Shē'á, that song came from the sound of thousands of tiny creatures becoming one voice, and someday it would mean a strange comfort to us; a memory of F'ala's voice calling against fear in the last night when fear was vague and somehow, larger.

When I woke, Mi'halē sat staring at the table where there was no morning tea in her bowl and F'ala called me outside the hut door to speak.

"There's no time for me to explain it to her," she said nervously. "I want you to take Mi'halē away to Bri'én. I've packed you some supplies and a map and I want you to follow it exactly. It's the longer way to Adanandū but you're much less likely to meet anyone along the way. When you reach Bri'én try to get to the Palace unseen but if you meet any trouble at all, use the ring I've packed. It belongs to Rā-alta, the Elder. Ask to be taken right to her but only if absolutely necessary."

"Then I'll take her now if you tell me why you're sending her," I agreed, almost excited to face this danger in my deep desire to end the waiting of it.

"What will happen to her here if I keep her?" F'ala said in exasperation.

"Answering a question with a question is the strategy of liars. I'm asking you, Ta-F'ala, what you mean by sending this dhana off into a war? How do you know I won't sell her off to save my own life when things become too great?"

She looked off into the distance and took off her headscarf, a gesture I didn't miss the significance of. "Look at me, I'm only an análong. When I was only a dhana I walked away from the world of the enlightened ones. See my life now? You've seen my past. I walked away with the skills I had to make a living and did as I could to preserve what hadn't been destroyed in me by my bitterness towards my fate. But the truth is none of us knows our own fate. And I put my faith in Rā-alta, and my intent on raising the dhana as best I could. I didn't do the greatest job, but..."

"You didn't accept her as a Guardian, or Rā-alta," I pointed out.

"That's true. I carried out my loyalty to her regardless of my beliefs. I was to care for Mi'hal̃e without giving up her identity, to regard her as the Guardian Rā-alta deemed her to be, and that's what I did. And that's what I'm doing by sending her away from here because I know she won't survive the danger here once that war reaches our village. But if you are what you claim to be, then I know with you she has a chance out there to make it back to Rā-alta."

I smiled. "You were so convinced you weren't worthy to become a student. Elder Anan saw you as one who would struggle with innocence and enlightenment. But struggle doesn't mean defeat."

She swallowed hard, taking in my words. "But I did lose my innocence after A'ma died. I lost it in the Cāilon."

"No-one loses their innocence, F'ala. They drown it in bitterness or leave it behind because of what has happened to them, thinking that it's a weakness and a hindrance. It is up to every análong to remember who they are, fears and all, or then they will lose enlightenment. If you are created as an análong, you do not become something else because something evil has happened to you. Nor do you become something else if you have done evil."

Smiling gently to her, I continued. "I don't think you've lost your innocence or walked away from enlightenment at all, F'ala. I think you wrestle with it every day, which is the only thing a mortal can do, and *must* do. You've allowed heartache to pass through you so that you could rise to your purpose. You've seen yourself as you are rather than who you wish you were, and those who are able to do this will gain caémba in the end for they will allow themselves to become their destined selves."

She nodded thoughtfully and turned to leave but stopped in the doorway.

"*Dēma, dēma ta aói an hē,*" her words were faint and said only partially to me, and then she left, for words had run out between us.

I turned to fetch Mi'hal̃e, thinking to myself, *Ah F'ala, I know you love her.*

ā'dō
17

hello, goodbye

a'dhā 'a dhá

ISTAKENLY, because I'd survived through the ten days of fever, I assumed my life would return to its cycle of work and hope, dreams and disappointments as soon as I could freely move about again. Little did I know within the epic surrounding Mi'hal̄e, my own part in it was coming to its end.

I was one hundred and forty-four when I died.

It was only a few days after I'd been able to get up and sit outside in the sun that my dandhō came to sit at the other end of the doorstone to stare out to the end of the path past the fields into the browning forest. I wanted to tell her how frightened I was on waking in her hut and not my own cave, and also how happy. But as I saw my proud, strong dandhō's thin shoulders slump, I said nothing. What F'ala didn't say in words, she shouted in silence.

"It's time," she murmured, her voice scratchy and low. "It's time that she went back to Rā-alta. I'll speak to Éḗshī in the morning."

And as before, I sat quietly stunned at my own stupidity in being seduced by time into thinking Mi'hal̄e would always be with us, that we'd somehow become one new asama. We'd discussed it; I knew the day was coming. But now I sat perfectly still, screaming in my own head at my dandhō beside me.

We were almost normal, almost real and now you're going to ruin everything. How could you send her away? How could you send away our ēdandha? How can you call yourself an ah'sha and send her away? Don't you love us?

I knew she would tell me it wasn't safe here any longer, that we didn't have a choice and I wondered if this sister I'd always thought was so much stronger than me was really only just calloused. How could I have known all along we would lose Mi'hal̄e and somehow still be surprised?

My eyes felt heavy with sadness, fatigued with holding back tears I wasn't sure I'd earned over the thought that with Mi'hal̄e and Éḗshī gone, F'ala and I would return to our familiar but distant understanding. I hadn't trusted Éḗshī at first, it was true, but she'd made up for the loss of Anshē and Rāca for Mi'hal̄e in a way no-one else could. There were times I felt like she replaced me in that space between Mi'hal̄e and F'ala, but Éḗshī seemed closer to me in age somehow and for that I was thankful. While Mi'hal̄e rarely came to me for advice anymore, Éḗshī stayed around to chat after chores.

Now all this would change, and I would again be the youngest sister, the forgotten sister. In those six years that had gone by now like a whisper, F'ala had become not only my Dandhō but also my friend, yet still so much of her remained hidden. When Éḗshī came I began to notice F'ala drawing into herself, her face closing to me as she went away back to where she had come from when we first met. Now she would disappear again, and I would never know her story.

Damn you. How can you call yourself an ah'sha?

I wouldn't allow myself to think of the whispers in the village or the white-draped quarantine huts or the thick, dark smoke over the distant trees. No, I preferred to think of the coming loneliness as if that were some kind of relief, a space of safety where I could be free to think wistfully of a future I knew wasn't coming. I became so consumed by the weight of such thoughts I didn't even notice I was already alone on the doorstone. F'ala was nowhere to be seen.

* * *

That night, the dhana both went to bed and I lay on my blankets in the common room which had been moved closer to the window for air, watching my dandhō up in the loft as she packed a rucksack for them to take on the journey. On her table at the top of the stairs she'd laid everything out in little piles, so organized.

I'd rarely ever seen her so still, her hands so deliberate other than when she was working to write and paint the beautiful scrolls filling her shop. The bottom of the bag was already stuffed with rice balls and dried duccerfruit pips, a flask and a tinderbox and striker. Did Éē'shī know how to build a fire? I knew Mi'halē didn't. Idly I wondered where my dandhō had squirreled away so much food but came back to attention when she began packing the clothing.

One by one she pulled Mi'halē's little dresses and stockings out of a pile and folded these with the utmost care to stash away in the sack. Laundry was F'ala's least favorite chore; she would much rather be out in the fields and her hands showed it. They weren't large but they'd become calloused and red. Now I watched as her hands tenderly smoothed the fabrics into neat creases, lingering over the simple lace and tiny buttons as if she were imprinting all of the embraces she never gave the dhana into the very fibers so that every time she dressed she would clothe herself in love.

It was a strange thought to have of my practical dandhō, a strange sight to see her pour herself out all over the table with no reserve, thinking I couldn't see her from below. But then again, since the day she'd told me she had once been in love, my mind was always trying to fill in the gaps of what she hadn't said. My face reddened as I admitted to myself how many times I'd tried to pull back and see her anew. Now she was doing it for me. How many times had I wondered about that nameless análong, about whether my sister had held them, kissed them. Was that still another part of her no-one could ever see? It made me all the sadder that after that night it would be the two of us in silence again. If Mi'halē had done nothing else as a Guardian, she'd given me the sister I already had.

Then, F'ala pulled out two scrolls to put away in the bag. One I recognized from the back room of her shop, our grandparent tree. Though I couldn't read it, I knew the names of our asama for generations back nestled in its painted branches. This was re-rolled tightly and bound with ribbon, then the next, smaller scroll was pulled out and examined. This one was of great interest to me as F'ala lingered over it, a crease forming in her brow, then smoothed it to her chest for a moment with eyes closed. It too was tied and tucked into a pocket hidden inside the bag and she sat for a moment at the table, gazing out the window silently. The bones in her shoulders poked out weakly and they shuddered as she looked down and wiped her cheek with the back of her hand.

Suddenly I felt terrible for my earlier thoughts, realizing that she had outdone us all in love. When she came down the ladder I was too ashamed to look up, so I buried my head in the blankets and pretended not to hear when she said she would put more blankets on the floor so Mi'haľe and Éếshī could sleep. And after a while I fell asleep to the sound of cicadas and the giggles of little dhana in the next room.

* * *

Before us, Mi'haľe and Éếshī scuttled up over the thick forest roots leading up the path towards the sunlight as F'ala and I followed separately behind. I was a bit hurt she walked so far from me but thought perhaps she just wanted to be by herself after the night before. As they climbed up to the top of the bluff looking over the last few miles of her land, she stopped a few feet behind and held out her hand to pass the rucksack to Éếshī. Éếshī took it by the strap gently.

But Mi'haľe caught the movement and her eyes widened in distrust. "Ah'sha, aren't you coming?"

F'ala smiled. "Tsō, you're old enough to go see the city now. Now don't be silly, Éếshī is taking you to see the Elders. Elder Rā-alta is expecting you."

"But!"

"Now, you wanted to go to the city, didn't you? It's a good opportunity, the most wonderful place in all Ebūda! And you can write us and tell us all about your adventures there," F'ala waved her hand carelessly, but the dhana wasn't fooled.

"But it's dangerous, Ah'sha, you've told me!" Mi'haľe struggled to come back but Éếshī' held her tight by the arms. I stood helplessly behind my dandhō, too mixed up inside to be on anyone's side, even when she implored, "Little Dandhō!"

"At some point, we all have to face danger." F'ala's tone had changed, becoming very serious. "Éếshī is older than you so listen to what she tells you. Do what she says, do you understand? Remember everything we've taught you."

I couldn't bear to look at Mi'haľe any longer. Her eyes had closed into little slits of tearful accusation. "But when will we come back?" she cried. My dandhō continued as if she'd heard nothing.

"Remember that whatever happens to you, the most important thing is *the most important thing.* Can you remember that?" my dandhō leaned down on her knees to Mi'haľe's height and softened her voice but came no closer. "Remember it."

"*Tsōl!*" the dhana suddenly screamed and gave one last try to wrench out of Éếshī's grasp. Dandhō mouthed *Go!* to her and in one swift move Éếshī pulled them both over the bluff and slid down into the ravine below so fast we stood for a few moments listening to them wrestling each other across its bottom, unsure of what direction they moved in. Both our ears pricked up when we heard the plaintive cries "*Ah'sha! Ah'sha!*" echo back, becoming smaller and thinner until one last hollow wail of "*I hate you!*" pierced the still before silence fell.

Through my own tears I could see my dandhō's eyes had slid closed, her head dropped onto her chest in defeat. Without looking over she asked, "Did I do the right thing? How can I know?"

"Maybe you just have to have faith?" I suggested, the thought that she might be unsure chilled me.

"I've never had faith like you," she raised her head and eyed me. "It's never been a certainty for me, just a chance. You're so like *Rā-alta*; you've both always known there were Guardians. I just hoped there were. I just… she…"

Elder Rā-alta? Now it made sense. With sudden clarity, in her eyes I saw a glimpse of another story in my dandhō's life which had to do with another kind of love, perhaps one which had stretched across all of Ebūda before me. A warmth flushed over me, a flash of understanding that tied up many questions like fluttering ribbons into a smart little bow as I realized a circle had closed around me. A promise had been kept.

Now as she crouched there I wondered as my dandhō gently rubbed her thumb against the pads of her fingers, gazing off beyond her own hand as if she'd lost something even greater. But I was glad there had been someone. And I envied her with a sweet, satisfying ache I had no words to speak of; that she'd been fortunate enough to suffer for love.

We stood there far too long, both knowing they'd gone out of earshot but unwilling to move away. F'ala's voice broke the still in a whisper, giving the final blessing before we could return:

"*Lī an Ēbōd m'haran m'dōr, 's an Ēal'aass m'dhencē m'dōr*: May the Name cover them, and the Glory surround them."

I came forward and took her hand to help her up off the ground, feeling the warmth of her cheek as she leaned over onto me. "You're weak," I observed. "You're…sick?" She made a face. "Let's just get home."

The walk back seemed to draw out forever; F'ala was actually much weaker than she'd let on and her steps became heavier and slower the closer we drew to the hut. When we made it through the door she stumbled to the table and laid her head down on her arms in exhaustion. There was no water for tea, any extra had been used on me while I was ill and the rest was sent with the two dhana. So, I sat by the window watching the shadows cast by the late sun stretch out over the garden, straining to hear some echo of the laughter which saturated this very space only a day before.

After a while F'ala sat up and murmured, "All things change, don't they? Our days are only a string of changes, a collection of scenes bound together by our own memory. The changing of the seasons." I nodded more in reply than understanding, and pointed out, "You didn't hug her goodbye."

"Tsō," she agreed. Her head dipped again, and her hand rose up to the neckline of her dress, pulling it back slowly to reveal a cluster of angry red blisters outlined in black just below her collarbone. I stepped back, repulsed and afraid. "You're got it," I breathed.

She stood slowly and busied herself putting some things in a sack as I stared. "I want you to get the box in the storehouse, the one I told you about. It's heavy so you'll need the wheelbarrow. Go into Pōcarū and if you meet any trouble, try to buy them off."

I could scarcely believe her words. This was every possible wrong thing happening at once, as if we'd won some celestial competition for disaster. She must have sensed my shock and she turned, looking at me with the saddest of glances for just a moment before she returned to her packing. "Don't argue with your dandhō. You have a chance to live. If the dhana makes it to Rā-alta and passes her tests, Ebūda will be saved. So, it's just a matter of waiting things out, isn't it?"

"Then wait *with* me!" I cried. "If everything is saved, you'll get better won't you? You have to!"

"I'm not going to be here when that happens," she said softly. "I will wait for you, alright? I'll wait with A'ma in the field."

"But I can't!" I bawled.

"You will."

My head felt so heavy it might fall off my shoulders but my dandhō was already at the door, pushing it open with her foot. "Where will you go?" I asked.

"To our a'ér's hut, to do what I can for the dying."

It may have been the next day, or the day after for all I knew before I was able to load the box of nendē on the wheelbarrow and make the trek alone into the village. Somehow I felt freer, the sadness of loss contained under that roof now dissipated into the sunlight. I came upon the lhēsha-spot near the river, and there were two huddled figures sat crying on the log I'd once sat on to wait for Mi'hal'ě to go play. Coming nearer I realized it was Anshē and Rāca.

"What are you doing all the way out here?" I exclaimed, pulling them up to their feet. "The NaŌma are coming! Does your a'ma know where you are?"

"It's on fire! Everything is on fire," Anshē sobbed.

"Where's Mi'hal'ě?" Rāca cried.

I slipped my shawl around them both and pulled them close. "Mi'hal'ě went to the city to be see the Elders," I said, realizing with a sick knot in my stomach that I could see the blazing red welts on both of their necks. They both only cried harder, huddling to me.

"They're here," Anshē said quietly, his tears halting. "A'ma is gone."

Rāca stopped crying as well, looking off into the distance. Then I saw it too: an ominous cloud of thick black smoke rising above the pale treetops. Pōcarū was burning.

We sat and watched this in silence for a time, listening to the loud cracks of tree branches popping in the heat and hut roofs falling in, squashed together under my shawl and its false promise of safety.

Then without warning Anshē clawed at me and shouted, "I tried to stop them, but they burned everything! It's gone! I tried to stop it! Our hut, our shrine, everything!"

"Ē-ō!" I shouted back at him to shut up, clutching his hands before he hurt himself.

"You've got to calm down, Anshē. Nothing is your fault. Ē-ō!" His arms flailed wilder and wilder until I finally slapped him across the face, and he dropped to the ground with a dull thud. I held out my hand to him, suddenly understanding my dandhō in the way only experience could pass on. "Get up. I lost my asama too."

Rāca took her brother's hand and they pulled each other up to face me with difficulty. He tentatively took my hand and for a moment we stood in a circle, becoming a new asama in the way tragedy will form one. Then the two of them broke away from me and we began to walk up through the thicket towards the thick silt of the river. "Don't look back to it," I said quietly. "Remember Pōcarū for what it was, not what it's become."

We put Rāca in the wheelbarrow with the box and took turns pushing it. She began to snuff and hiccup again and we said nothing for quite some time but instead dragged our feet through the dust and pebbles as far as we could. As long as we could go, we would go. "I'm still sad," Rāca piped up eventually.

"That's natural," I said.

"About Mi'hal'ē, I mean."

Anshē agreed. "She never said goodbye."

Rāca wiped her nose with her free hand and looked over at him longingly. "I mean, I never got a wish from that samanē."

Book Two

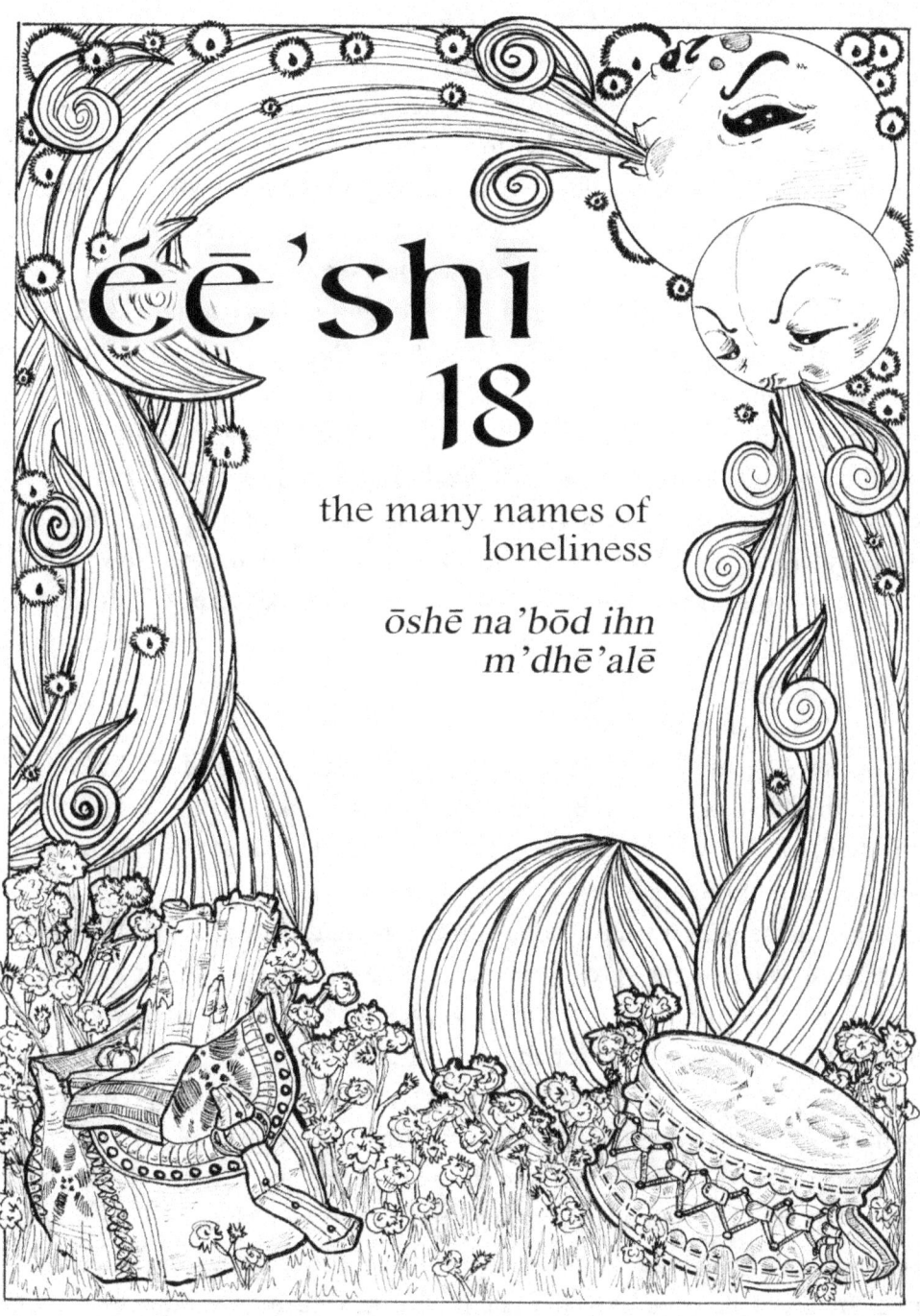

éē'shī

18

the many names of
loneliness

*ōshē na'bōd ihn
m'dhē'alē*

For nearly two years I had lived in that hut, eating the food of the fields, drinking water from the well and gathering, learning, playing, watching. *Waiting.* Then finally my legs stretched out and pounded the ground in the race I'd been born to run.

The morning we left for Bri'ën, I combed Mi'halë's ears silently, knowing her life would change forever but unable to utter the words. When she looked up at me in question, I pulled out her dress and shoes from the clothes chest and told her to cover her head to go out to the garden for a while. I asked her if she wished to bring her doll, but she only stared at me, trying to figure out what was wrong. "You might want her," I murmured but she shook her head hard, saying, "What for?" I pushed her towards the door, muttering that she could do as she liked.

F'ala was in the storehouse. She'd told me to get the dhana and go ahead of her, but something in her words caused my gut to wince as if it knew some danger lurked nearby. This body couldn't cease to amaze me; what I didn't yet have thoughts for, my very skin gave voice to.

F'ala had been teaching me for some time what to do once this journey started. For there were many historical things I knew by watching the análong evolve in my place in Hala-Asal, but the practical things escaped me. She'd shown me how to bury a bowl in the ground and cover it with a bit of leather weighted down with a stone to catch the morning's dew. She showed me how to start a fire with a striking stone and tree needles. She'd told me to make sure Mi'halë kept all her layers on in case the weather should turn cold again and to keep her skin covered in the day lest the sun burn her. But my body would have to recall these instructions when they were needed, for my mind could only think of the running before me.

The instructions were simple. We'd walk through Drīdū and Adanandū to Bri'ën using the rural routes and avoid the Dhang'lara Land Bridge at all costs. I'd stolen glances at the map she'd drawn for us when I could, so I knew we'd need to do a little backtracking to stay off the main roads and on the low ground to pass into Adanandū.

That morning over the bluff my mind concentrated on holding Mi'halë still as F'ala did her best to say goodbye. And when all the words were said and they floated on the air looking for a place to rest, I turned and let my muscles flex into the use they had been made in this world for. I *ran.*

As I pushed past low branches and through thin bushes at top speed, I felt her silent tears splashing on my arm. Mi'halë cried out to her ah'sha in fright at first, but as we moved further down into the ravine with no sign of being followed, those cries turned to anger, and her anger dissolved into exhaustion, ending with one last loud wail into the dust. "*I hate you!*" But while her voice was spent and silent, she still darted her head back and forth trying to bite my hands and pull away.

But not being so worn by mortal constraints, I sprinted without exhaustion or feeling of pain. *Run, run, run!* urged my legs below me, as if they had their own will, and would not be stopped until my feet met with the stone that brought me to my knees and sent Mi'halë crashing down into the dust.

Where the trees had thinned, I pulled myself up to sit against a log to rest, catching my breath so hard it forced out a series of dry coughs.

I sat rubbing at a brush-burn on my elbow, duly noting the tiny bite marks on my hands and the thin scratches on my legs I now felt sharply in the still. Mi'halē lay flat on her back staring at the sky. For a moment I inspected my surroundings, feeling we weren't quite to the point where it would be too far for her to run away in the middle of the night and actually make it back to F'ala if she took it in her mind to. I stood. "Get up."

"*Tsōl.*" She sat up and hugged her knees to her chest willfully but then stood up abruptly and lunged towards me, hitting me across the nose close-fisted before I had a chance to cover. "Why did you take me away?" she demanded. "Why did you steal me?" My right arm instinctively covered my midsection as my left tried to catch her fists. "Hembarē! *Stop!*" I protested, but she reared back and launched all her weight at me. Though we weren't dissimilar in size, the full force of it knocked us both back to roll over each other so that I came out on top and threw myself lengthwise over her to pin her to the ground.

I turned my head and looked at her evenly, repeating "*Why did I steal you?*" so that she could hear what she was asking, and work out herself how she'd come to be so far from home. For what the old análong said was true; by sorrow the heroes of Ebūda are born, and I couldn't spare her from it. "If I'm the one who stole you, why do you hate your ah'sha so much?" I challenged.

Her eyes hardened for a moment, ready to argue, then filled with tears and she looked away, defeated. "They didn't come after me," she murmured. I felt the truth thicken the air around us and I waited. "Ah'sha *sent* me away." Mi'halē looked over at her free hand, absently squeezing it open and closed, then rubbed her eyes with one hard swipe. Her voice plaintive, she asked, "Now who's going to take care of me?"

I picked myself up off of her and put out my hand. "I will," I vowed softly.

"How can you do anything?" she accused me up and down through squinted eyes. "You're just a dhana like me."

"We'll look after each other. Trust me." I waved my fingers again in offering, hoping I appeared more confident than I felt. But she pushed herself up without my help and looked back at the faint treeline over the bluff far behind us.

I knew from my existence in Hala-Asal that the análong lived a life often devoid of words though far from ever silent; sometimes denied of touch but never lacking in meaning, where one must observe to understand and never interrupt the singing which moved all through Ebūda. I knew that Mi'halē, my sister, would ask to seek out the truth and I would have to be terribly careful in my words back to her for she was as much an análong as she believed to be, and listened just as carefully as they.

I put my arms around her shoulders, holding her to me as I realized how small and fragile we were in these little bodies; like flimsy little packages bulging with light too heavy to contain. Mi'hal̃e shrugged me off and asked, "Is this the journey to find my purpose? Is this my second journey?" I nodded. "We're going to Gaú Bri'én, where Elder Rā-alta is waiting for you."

She nodded but muttered, "I'm not going to be kind to you. I don't have to." Ignoring her, I shouldered the sack F'ala had sent with us and continued on to the northeast to Pataprāá village, the first landmark on her map. Mi'hal̃e followed along slowly in silence. Her legs bowed with the gravity of knowing; her shoulders keeled under the weight of understanding that now I knew she would no longer try to escape me. But just the same, now she also knew *I* had known this day would come and kept my silence all those days between us.

And all the little games of ball and chase around the table, the secrets whispered in the night while F'ala softly snored, the unsteady kinship of two vagaries somehow finding joy in ordinary days with each other in the same sense of lost familiarity; all this gone in the moment I'd grabbed her hand to run. Now the silence of betrayal hung over us, or understanding, or freedom. And sometimes a mixture of all three combined to become a blanket of quiet that covered us as we took our first steps into the end of that world.

* * *

It was at least ten days to the edge of F'ala's land, and closer to a fortnight after until we would make it to the wall of Pataprāá if I'd counted right. A field came up to our right, wide and brown and surrounded by a thick line of limp-ish trees where the land sloped into a sort of empty, deep basin. As we came closer it became apparent we weren't alone. Crowded together in perfect slumber, a group of onandals lay in a tight circle near the thickest trees, their huge wings folded peacefully around each other. Their silver beaks were majestic, their eyes filmed and fixed ahead, unafraid.

I stepped carefully in-between their clawed feet and tiptoed to the very middle of the circle where two colts lay sweetly with their heads laid on their front legs as if sleeping. So still were they that only the flies walking lazily up and down their eyelids told us that life had already left them. I backed away out of the circle and took Mi'hal̃e's hand. "The guardians of Guardians are *gone on*," I said, using the common term for death.

"There are guardians of Guardians?" she mused.

"The onandals, the moons; they are the guardians of Guardians in this world," I explained. Mi'hal̃e slipped out of my grasp and circled the great beasts, calmly inspecting them. "Dandhō told me about them. She can talk to them," she murmured. She reached out her hand towards the colts but stopped, looking up when a gentle sound whispered from amidst them. I leaned over to hear it, catching snatches of the onandals' silvery speech faintly and as I did, I could hear many voices come to surround us, chanting as one:

The child! The child! F'ala's child!

"Oh!" exclaimed Mi'hal'ě, stepping back. I looked up sharply to follow her gaze and around her stood the transparent forms of the onandals separated from their cold bodies, eager and curiously peering at her from all sides. "*Ah'dhā*," she greeted them in wonder and they circled her slowly, gently, each giving a last look before they gathered in front of the largest tree trunk and began to fade away from sight, their forms culminating in an assemblage of golden points of light that flashed and then surrounded Mi'hal'ě, seeping into her very skin. Unafraid, she inspected her hands as the light sparkled, then faded away. Echoing beyond us could be heard the onandals' last words:

Fare you well, F'ala's child.

"Why do they call me that?" Mi'hal'ě asked, taking my hand again to allow me to lead her through the trees. "You understood them?" I asked, surprised. She nodded. "Well, aren't you?" I replied. She fixed her gaze on me, brow wrinkling in thought, but said nothing. "Anyway, they've left you their protection."

"Is that what happened?" she asked.

I didn't answer, idly noting that behind us the bodies of the onandals still slumbered, undisturbed. Hurriedly, we broke through the treeline and scurried across the basin's open bottom to the opposite forest and looked for a place to sleep that first night. I caught Mi'hal'ě looking up at the sky through the treetops rather than on the ground for kindling like I'd sent her to do. "What are you doing?" I snapped, pointing to a perfectly dried thicket of underbrush she'd walked right past. "I'm just looking at Pendin. I wonder why he always looks so angry?"

Picking up the brush and snapping it into smaller twigs over my knee, I glanced up at the nearest moon above peering at us in nosy curiosity. "More mischievous than angry," I noted, and she snapped around, eyes wide. "You never told me you can see the moons like me and Little Dandhō!" She said no more but got on to looking for kindling, handing me twigs here and there that didn't make much of a fire in the end. "There isn't a toi-ō!" Mi'hal'ě noted that first night in panic. "Then make sure you pull your skirts up high," I advised, and it was brought up no more.

I was thankful for the quiet that followed in the days to come, so I could focus on finding food and gathering sticks to make a fire large enough to keep us warm yet not so comfortable as to be noticeable by passing Darna that might be above us. For shelter we made do laying branches against tree trunks and sleeping under these little lean-tos until stumbling over a stretch of forest with many conveniently rotted out trunks large enough to rest inside of.

We stayed in these tree-shelters for three days, looking for lāāca pods to carry with us, pulling off sweet moss from under the roots to fill our bellies with after we'd gone through the biscuits and such in the sack. Mi'hal'ě wasn't interested in much but sitting silently so I had her to gather stones to make a fire-ring. This would be her chore every evening as I cleared the ground and set up our shelter and the little pot to collect dew every morning.

On the fourth day I gathered our things inside the sack, and we pressed on until I spotted a flat, yellow light through the trees where we had come to a narrow stretch of meadow. The long grass there whispered in stiff pale yellow and grey waves. In some parts we came upon grain stalks withered and sad but here the ground vines had dried so quickly their thin forms were forever preserved in ill twists and dark curls, entwined like gates of wrought iron but brittle when touched.

Entranced by the shapes of the these, Mi'hal̄ë ran her fingers gingerly along them, tracing their curls before I prodded her to come along. She did, swinging her arms wide to make a loud *shhhh,* *shhhh, shhhh* sound through the grass as we wisped along to the end of the meadow under the pale golden light to the other side where the land leveled into a terrace in the distance. We'd seen no-one along the way since leaving F'ala so I walked on ahead to have a look myself and when I reached the edge of the dropoff, I could see a low, wide valley completely hidden from the view above. Below, it encompassed a cluster of simple huts near the eastern side and these were ringed by a low stone wall. Calling over my shoulder for Mi'hal̄ë, I waited for her to catch up.

There the still, black remains of Pataprãá village sat recently vacated. As we neared it along the outskirts of the valley to avoid the trodden road, pots and blankets and clothes could be seen laying behind deliberately in neat order, dotting the dying grass here and there with brightly colored scraps as if the análong had agreed as one to simply walk away from their home. There was no movement, no fire smoke to be seen nor wagon wheels to be heard. We helped each other over the stone wall, entering the village proper hand in hand to investigate when I saw with a sinking pit in my middle that no-one had left at all.

Black mounds of ash dotted the dirt streets in immense circles. Burial mounds. So, the sickness had swept through here so quickly there was no time to mourn the dead. The air, cold and thin brought the clear stench of old smoke in little wisps. It was fortunate I was a Guardian of the air; the hindrance of sickness wouldn't bother me. But Mi'hal̄ë may not be so immune.

She stood watching the ash and I wondered if she'd ever seen a burial mound. She kicked at a pile of black at her feet, and I pulled her back roughly. I explained, "You must never do that again. It looks like dirt but it's not, it's sacred stuff."

"It's dirt," she said flatly. I conceded she was right, but she was also wrong. "It's an mbúana. There's a power in belief, this exchange between an análong and the universe. No matter what they believe in, an análong humbles themselves in belief to Creation, trusting that it is bigger and older and wiser. It's a thing to be respected. Didn't F'ala teach you that?"

"I don't remember," she lied. I looked over the village and noted a row of sick-huts lined up about ten lengths away from us. Long strips of black and white cloth drifted in the air ominously from the windows and door-posts of each, whispering like spirits. I gave Mi'hal̄ë a little push to move her along.

I allowed her to lie about F'ala without comment because I knew it was the sting of rejection that made her distance herself against her memories. There was a process living creatures went through when they said a last goodbye, and this was its start. But I knew the truth. F'ala had a strong faith and a great respect for such. I heard her pray every day for the dhana on the way to the fields, though she thought I was too far behind to hear and would never admit to it.

As we left Pataprãá, I recalled that throughout time I had seen análong rise and fall and one thing was true about them: from the moment they came into the world, their days were running out. All análong were born with a drop of sadness carried in every glance for they knew they had no souls to survive them and yet, they still believed in law and adhered themselves to it.

But I had seen great joy in the love and care one gave to the other because análong chose to live their days knowing they were numbered with the belief that one day we Guardians would bring them into the rest of Creation. And because they could have just as easily discarded this hope and lived as the rest of An'dan in continual debauchery, their belief in itself was precious, and this was why F'ala valued it so.

But the price of this belief was the Law.

"I'm thirsty," Mi'hal̃e whined suddenly.

I pulled out a spiky shard of *fúasana* bush from our sack, bit it in half and handed part to her. She sucked the moisture out of its middle and then pinched out its short needles before chewing the outside.

I studied our map. "The more we walk, the less hungry we'll feel," I said over my shoulder, tracing the scratchy lines F'ala had made in haste. We weren't particularly off course but a few days behind where I thought we should be, and I thought there was a body of water still before us. It wasn't included on the map, but then again perhaps she hadn't drawn it in. Hopefully. I decided we should settle down as soon as we found a place damp enough to contain a fire for the night so I could sleep through without having to watch it so closely overnight.

When I judged it dark enough to stop, I put the sack down and stood gazing out before us, judging the nearest line of tree shelter to be at least three days away. I took out the knife F'ala had packed along with some string and our other things and tried to break the ground up a bit, but to no avail. The knife only crumbled up the dust even more. I sat back and sighed, irritated that while we were in no way near the lands of drought to the north, the land was already working against me. I looked around for enough stones for Mi'hal̃e to gather for a fire ring. No luck there either. Then again, maybe we should conserve all the needles we'd brought along as kindling for a truly cold night when we'd really need the fire for warmth over visibility. As for now, the air had not tipped much since the sun dropped in the sky. We'd have to tough it out.

"Go put the dew-pot out for tomorrow," I told Mi'hal̃e as I handed her the knife and watched as she struggled to needle a little hollow out beneath her to fit the pot in. Absorbed by her task, Mi'hal̃e dropped the knife suddenly and studied her hands, pink and irritated under its handle. Shrugging, she pushed with all her weight on the pot until it sunk down and then stretched the leather out over its top, weighing it down with its stone.

This was our first night in the open plain and I would have to keep myself awake to stand guard through the entire night for we had nowhere to hide. I felt less worried about freezing when weighing that against being seen out in the open without cover. For a while Mi'hal'ē lay wrapped up in all her clothes beside me, musing on and off. "I used to think about Outside all the time until Little Dandhō took me there and then I didn't very much because I was so busy with things. But I still thought Ebūda was a pretty place, a magic place. Not...this."

"Ebūda was a beautiful land before evil came to it. More beautiful than you'll ever know. You thought it was pretty because you wanted it to be," I suggested.

She continued to look out into the falling darkness, her fingers laced together under her nose. "Is this where you come from Ée'shī, out here? Or is there somewhere even further than here?" When I didn't answer she rolled over. "And, where are all the análong?"

"They're out there, far away. But remember we're moving towards them every day so far away will become nearer and nearer and nearer the longer we walk. Just because you don't see anyone doesn't mean you can be careless. But," I conceded, having been asked so many times by now that I tired of keeping my origins in total obscurity, "I'm from farther than that. A place you've never heard of."

"Well that would be like anywhere," she said sarcastically. "You know what though? So am I, I think. From someplace far away I've never heard of." I didn't answer, trying to spot the first evening star but she spoke up again and I glanced over.

"The first thing I remember is opening my eyes on the doorstone. It was dark and cold. Sometimes I think I was born in the sky and dropped from it because it seems like," her eyes flickered sheepishly away from mine. "Like part of me wants to go back to it. Something is always pulling me up." Then, fishing around lazily in the dirt for something, Mi'hal'ē's hand emerged with a few little pebbles and she sat up on her knees. Putting her hands together, she palmed the pebbles one by one as I saw her lips move ever so slightly in evening prayer, so very like F'ala.

"What's the first thing you remember when you were born?" she asked suddenly, placing the pebbles in a ring before her feet. I smiled to myself. "Opening my eyes in the field. Bright and warm!"

Mi'hal'ē thought about this for a time but said nothing, gazing intensely at me though I didn't return her look. Then she laid down facing me. After a time, she asked, "Ee'shi? In the village we were in...if everyone there was dead, who will remember them? Who will pray their *shonbū*?"

I traced a circle on the ground with my foot and countered, "What if they didn't practice the shonbū prayers? There are so many more análong out there, you can't suppose that every one of them does as the rest do."

She looked up. "Shouldn't someone though? Just because they were alive? Just because we're análong too?" she trailed off. I had nothing to give her. For of all the many things análong did and thought and believed, there were things beyond their sight that were constant all throughout Creation and beyond. How my sister then chose to honor those constants had no influence on their being. "Well I will then," she answered herself and then fell silent.

The night air hung around us, flat and waiting and silent as if we were the last ones alive or the first ones born. A scratchy little voice startled me after quite some time, pulling me out of the doze I'd happily slid into. "Éē'shī, it's so quiet. We always sang every day at home. Why don't you sing anymore?"

I stared up at the sky. "I have no songs here to sing."

"Oh."

* * *

In the morning the dewfall was thick, and we carefully poured this from the dew-pot into a tiny flask I kept in the outermost pocket of the sack. There was enough that I allowed her to have a first lick before storing the precious liquid away.

We pressed on for several days, seemingly walking in one place under the dull sun, passing only one lonely tree house off in the distance to our right and absolutely no tree cover. The days began to blend into each other without landmarks to count from and while I'd assumed we were going in the right general direction, I knew we'd gotten a little off track early on. Yet not so much I couldn't correct for it, surely.

Finally, we reached a line of trees I'd spied what I thought was about a week before. Something was out of place about the trees which were the entrance to a small forest, but I was so thankful to have something other than dead grass to look at and a place to hide I didn't bother slowing down to check the map. Mi'hal'ē was quiet, scuffling over the grass with her feet once in a while in an obstinate sort of way.

As we entered the tree line Mi'hal'ē went in first and pointed out the bark on a short, thick stump which was peeling off in sheets. Working carefully, we pulled off as much as time allowed and stuffed this in the sack. "For emergencies only," I cautioned as Mi'hal'ē stuffed a bit in her mouth. "If we run out of everything, we can chew on this to take off the burn, but you can't *swallow* it or it'll make you sick." She stared at me, chewing slower and slower until she spat out a gummy wad onto the ground realizing why the bark would be a last resort.

Slowly we proceeded on but took in our surroundings in dull wonder. Where F'ala's forest was green and dark, this small patch of trees was caught forever in another season entirely. Brown and brittle, the leaves made a sloped canopy over us so that after looking about and agreeing that we were alone, Mi'hal̃e and I decided it was too early to camp for the night and continued on towards a shaft of light in the distance.

Working together, we pushed back a fallen thicket of branches to emerge into a clearing illuminated with shafts of light passing through the leaf canopy above us. In through this tiny clearing emerged a miniature world completely unlike the rest of the forest preserved in thin, dry tones. Every flower had dried in full on its head, the colors of life slowly drained down to the tips in mottled shades of white. Feeling as if our very breathing would shatter this tiny terrain, we craned our necks to have a look and Mi'hal̃e whispered "Béanda!" before turning around carefully in her spot to face me. "Maybe Guardians live here."

I nodded and we retreated gingerly, pushing aside the branches to make our way around and on through the forest to the other side. By the time we came out hours later into another sort of wide, drying plain, it was very late in the day and I realized with disappointment that I had to confer with the map and face how lost I'd gotten us. I sat down on the dry ground and dug into the sack, spreading out the parchment across my lap as Mi'hal̃e stumbled out of the rustling forest beside me in a flurry of sound.

She stopped, gazing at something small and still on the ground. I reached over to pick it up and found it was the intricate wings of a dead lhēsha. Mi'hal̃e put her hands around mine and I gently dropped it into her palms. She asked, "Do you think what they say about the lhēsha is true?" I smiled gently to myself though she didn't see it from above me and told her this: "Only a lhēsha can tell you that. Which it cannot." Her face fall when I didn't give her the answer she wanted. "But it's not a sin to believe in a pretty story," I added.

"Then I will. I will believe it because I want it to be true," she said decisively.

I got back to the map, taking my attention away from whatever she began to play at on my left side. When I looked up a while later, I saw that she was sucking on her fingers and I pulled them out of her mouth. "You're bleeding," I noted and wrapped them in the hem of my dress. "How did you manage that?"

"I buried him. He found his purpose, so I dug a little hole and buried him. The ground's really hard," she said, pulling her fingers back. I helped her up. It was beyond mentioning she should have asked me to use the knife if she was so intent on digging. But we had a much bigger problem on our hands anyway. While I'd thought we'd been steadily going northwest, I realized that somehow we'd been going in the opposite direction.

Now we were really and truly lost.

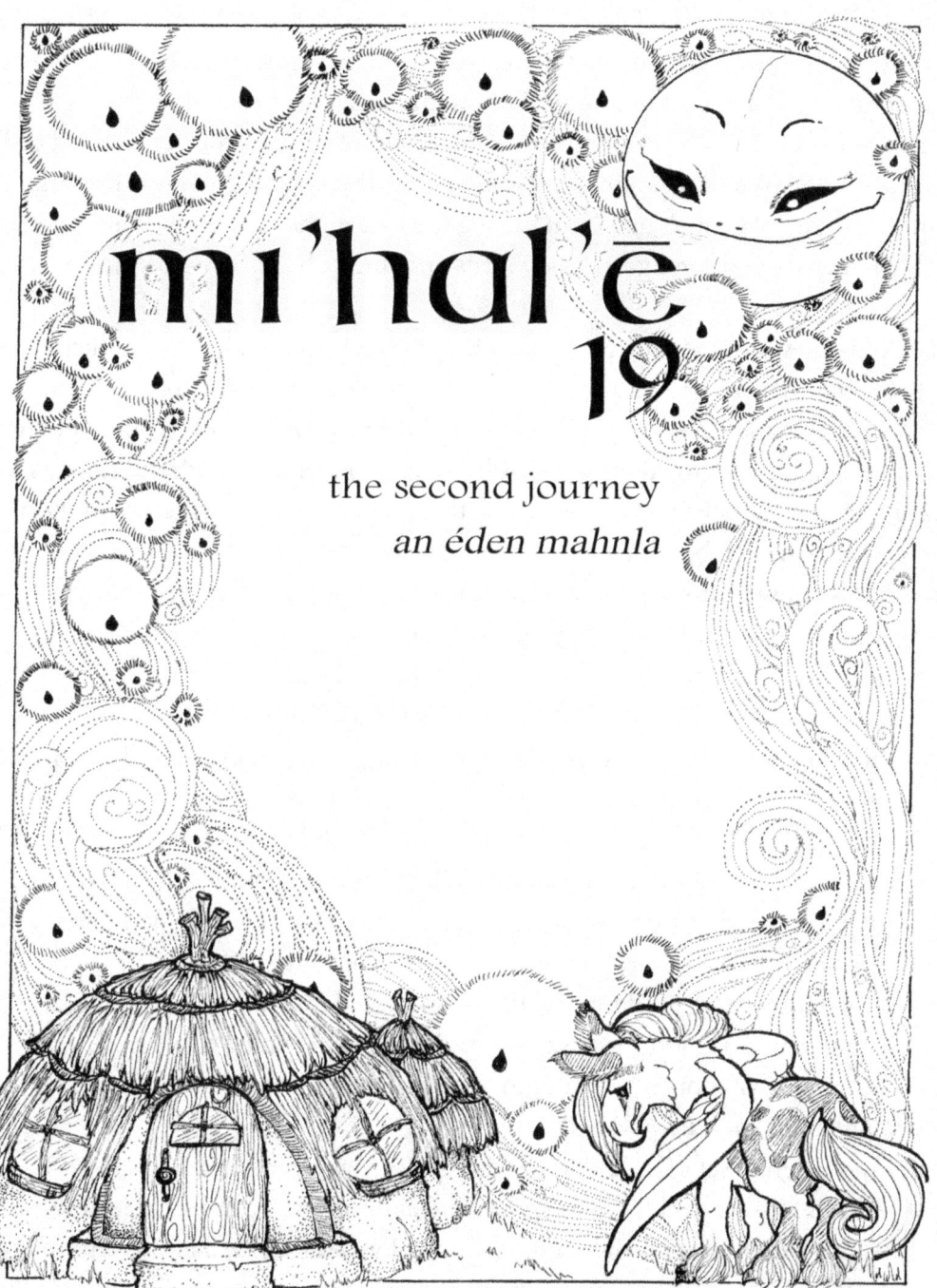

mi'hal'ē
19

the second journey
an éden mahnla

*Y*OU'RE *such an idiot! She lied to you about the Outside twice so what made you think she really loved you? You're a stupid freak and now you're all alone.* Such thoughts went over and over in my mind as I walked along behind Éé'shī, their main worth in being to distract me from the reality of waking up with bugs in my nose and grit in my ears. Somehow it seemed comforting to have some reason, even if only my own fault, for how I'd found myself so far from home.

Sometimes, when I thought I was completely alone, a little voice inside of me could be heard, as if there were a tiny little me sitting on my feet looking up with her own thoughts to speak. Most of the time I heard but didn't pay much heed, but during the first night away from home laying under the trees I couldn't keep from listening to those words about my ah'sha. I couldn't keep from believing them.

At first, I thought every moment about how many hours it would be until we turned around and went back to the hut. At first, I pictured a sort of tomorrow when I would wake up in my own bed and how happy Dandhō would be when I came bursting out through the forest, how sad Little Dandhō must be right this minute on the doorstone without me, how many wonderful things I would have to tell Anshē and Rāca about Ebūda when I saw them again. Because *surely* Dandhō would be so sorry she'd lost me that she'd be a little more allowing from now on. At first, I was too terrified to be without her to busy myself with any anger *at* her.

For all my brain could handle was trying to reconcile the sleepy, familiar web of vines that made up the lands of Ebūda in my mind with the sharp, bright angles of what met my eyes. What had I thought the world would be? I wasn't sure, but I knew it wasn't this.

And even moreso, I thought of food and more food and water and the last time I had any sort of bath. And though it had been so long since we'd had them at home, I found myself thinking of the tea-cakes Dandhō fried over the fire, and these thoughts became so vivid to me I expected to come around a corner and find a plate of them waiting. Little Dandhō's hands pink and dry as she pressed dūūcerfrūt into juice waved in front of me, reminding me of the times we had pressed and cooked dyes for cloth. And Anshē's shy smile dissolved like mist above me, gone.

But then as if my mind were in a loop, my thoughts started over with those ugly words of my little self and continued on with Dandhō and why she had done such a thing to me. A few days later when I was certain Éé'shī was far enough away not to hear, I snapped at the voice aloud, "*If you don't know why she did it either then shut up!*"

Now that my thoughts were free, I tried to guess what we would come up against as we moved forward but realized I hadn't paid much attention to Dandhō's maps during my lessons to even know. Naturally then, I turned toward my own responsibility. I was different, that was true, but what made Éé'shī so much *less* different? I'd been protected from the dangerous place of Ebūda, but now that we walked about it without boundaries, I doubted those who had tried to keep me safe because no such concern was given about Éé'shī. True, she could be mistaken as any of the artists in the village who painted themselves from top to toe and breathed fire from their nostrils or danced or did tricks. But why couldn't I get away with that? And now what did it matter out here by ourselves? There was no one to hide from anyway.

Maybe Éé'shī didn't feel any different inside from anyone else. Was that her secret? Because *I* did. And I wondered if I would have if it had never been pointed out to me.

"If this is the second journey, where are we going?" I asked, speaking for the first time in days.

"Bri'én, like I told you before," Éé'shī answered, looking straight ahead.

"Why there? If this is my journey how can you know where it ends?"

"I don't. That's where Elder Rā-alta is and it's the safest place in all Ebūda. If your journey goes on, you will do just that. *Go on.*"

"That's not true though, is it?" the words tumbled out, surprising even me.

"It *is* true," she looked at me seriously, but didn't stop when I tripped on my own feet and caught myself. "The sacred city is a place protected by holiness."

"Then what's in the *Cāilon*?" I asked immediately, recalling at least one thing Dandhō had told me. There was a city beneath the city that outcasts lived in.

"Evil. It's a place where dhana are sold as long as someone will buy them," Éé'shī answered honestly. "What happens to them?" I stopped a moment, but then picked up the pace when I realized Éé'shī wasn't going to wait. "Whatever the evilness of the world wishes to do to them. They are lost forever, never seen again above the ground."

I put my hands to my hips indignantly as I walked. "Then how can you say the city is protected by holiness!"

"I can say that because it's true. All things holy and evil live side by side; edging each other over for room now and again," she said matter-of-factly. "Everything in an imperfect world must *balance.*"

"*Sāama,*" I murmured, recalling that afternoon I refused to recite the principle back to Dandhō. "But if it's only other análong we have to worry about then let's go home! We haven't seen a single one for weeks!" I complained. Éé'shī said nothing for a while. "I told you," she reminded quietly, "You don't know what's ahead."

"Then why are we going *ahead*?" I asked, a chill coming over the back of my head in little stretching fingers. "Do you know what's ahead?" I asked and was ignored. But the little seed of distrust had already been growing between us now that many days had passed for me to think about all the days *before* when she said nothing of that future time when I was going to be sent away. She *had* to know more than she'd admit to. And though she was only a dhana like me, I still burned with the thought that I'd been made a fool of in front of everyone I cared about.

But what she might know of what lie ahead was more valuable than what she'd kept from me in the past and I had to remind myself that while I'd learned all about facts and figures, I knew nothing of how the world worked. I needed Éēshī too much to run away from her.

Éēshī suddenly broke into my busy thoughts. "Every being in Creation belongs to an asama. Look at the stars. Even they have names and duties and purpose. They're bound to each other, created by the same Creator. The flowers come together to produce more of the same. We all come from someone, somewhere and belong to someone, somewhere. Someday maybe you'll find the ones you belong to."

"I thought I belonged to Dandhō and Little Dandhō," I whispered sullenly, not sure I was going to let her change the topic but then too interested to fight. "You think somewhere out there are others *like* me? And I belong to them?"

"There are many ways to belong, and many asama made up of *unlike* beings. But it's a very big world. Surely, you'll find others even like you."

"And those like you too," I shook my head, willing us to be the same though Éēshī argued we weren't.

Back then, I was much more interested in being like Éēshī for superficial reasons alone. Éēshī's cheeks were high and angled, her skin a pleasant rosy color that fascinated me. But my face was round and chubby and wan unless I'd been running hard and then the folds of my smile blushed the purple color of dawn. My eyes were dull, large, round and pinched at the corners but Éēshī's were so warm and thin it was hard to imagine how she could see. I imagined that the world to her must look bright and pared down to a sliver and it must look *better*, as if the warmth of her eyes colored it so.

Éēshī was tall too. She was angular with wiry, thin arms and legs dusted with short, coarse hair. I was short and roundish, stalky and smooth. Though now I could begin to see the sharp ends of my bones and feel new bumps here and there, my limbs had always been dimpled and soft. Éēshī favored Little Dandhō; they were both spun out of the sunshine while I had the carefully kept air of a doll unplayed with. In my body I was unsure, but Éēshī moved as if she knew the answer before the question was asked and was ready to give it.

I blew my breath out so it tickled my nose. Dandhō would scold me for wanting to be like someone else, I realized with both comfort and distress. Maybe I'd sit and want a little more so I could imagine her scolding again.

Sweat ran down my back, sucking my dress in against my skin and holding it there. Everything around us was becoming drier and drier, more and more flat and empty. Maybe I couldn't trust Éēshī to tell me the truth about anything else but I had to trust her when it came to where we were going because *anyone* knew more than me on that subject. And no matter how loud my little self got about it from my toes, I was too tired not to trust her. As the days wore on it was too much to trace the lines of the past in my mind to uncover where the lies started.

I thought about running away back to Pōcarū time and again. Éē'shī watched far into the night by the fires she built but in the mornings after I'd collected dew, she took a short nap before we started on again. For a long time, I visualized how far I would make it by myself before she woke, convinced that if I just got back to Pōcarū I could find our hut. If I just made it back to the hut, everyone would realize what a mistake it was to send me away and we'd all be together again, no questions asked. It was an impossible, wonderful hope that kept me from digging my heels into the ground and screaming.

And though I thought on occasion of the cozy cushions and blankets and bed, these things weren't so dear to me, they were only the few trappings I could call my own. Though I longed for something softer than the hard ground to lay on, these didn't hold the same affection as the little hut itself. I thought of it standing sentry in that wide land that was my Dandhō's, looking out with sadness dripping from the round, shuttered windows; with longing to the sky. Did it know I was gone?

In the past before Éē'shī came, when Dandhō and Little Dandhō were gone and I was left behind alone in my baby-days, it was the hut's warm, sticky arms that held me against loneliness. When I lay on the bed roll wondering at the night ceiling how long morning would take to journey in on the backs of the dawn clouds' wisps, it was the hut's papery voice that whispered across my cheeks, "*Soon, soon, soon.*"

And now I couldn't bear to think I had left it. What would the hut do without me sweeping its floor of hard packed dirt and washing its walls and shuttering its windows and helping to thatch its roof? How could it be the little hut without *me* inside it? In my mind I heard its cheerful voice rustling through that thick thatch, "*Tse, tse, tse.*"

Except it *wasn't okay.* I wanted to cry; I desperately willed my eyes to weep for the hole I'd left behind but nothing would come. My cheeks burned with the chilled fire of fever, holding my sadness in like a poison. I stood with my back to the moons frowning their sympathy, watching our hut wave forlornly to me in the distance. I reached my arms out and held it, so little now, so empty and thin.

I miss you.

And so, I picked it up after a while and placed it in the pocket of my underskirt, softly and carefully so that I would always have shelter wherever I went.

And then after a few days of this I put it down softly on the ground and followed Éē'shī in silence, the little hut trailing along faithfully by my ankles. Éē'shī looked behind at me now and then, not seeing, not understanding.

Since the rains had stopped, something slow and insidious had been happening to us that we all pretended was invisible. Only Éē'shī would ever speak to me about what was happening to the food around us, the quickly emptying storehouse, the sacrifices being made by Dandhō and Little Dandhō. But still, she was only so practical as to tell me to stop looking in cupboards and start walking more to keep my mind off things. For some reason, I thought perhaps the big wide world was stock-full of the things we seemed to be missing. It made sense in my thoughts at least that it must be.

Now a slow fire crept up inside me and I knew that there was no such thing where we were going, at least not until we reached the city. It was hunger that burned my insides, making my legs twist in sharp cramps when I stopped for very long. Now I only looked at the hours as hurdles to cross to get to the next bit of food and when I reached into the sack to take some bark to chew on, I stopped. It was useless. I was never full anyway but only mildly less famished. Éē'shī was right. We had to keep moving if only to distract us from thoughts of what was missing.

Now and then I shivered under the sweat as it dripped down my legs and I pondered how that could be. Was it possible to be hot and cold at the same time? My mind drifted to the abandoned doll on my bed from my birth-day. I'd never played with it; it's blank face only reminding me that its existence and mine were the same. Neither of us could do anything save watch our own lives go by silently. As Éē'shī held her pace some ways ahead of me, I saw my doll all grown to my own height walking beside me. She had no mouth sewn onto her white face, but I knew she felt happiness to come out and explore so we walked along for some time, my smiling face gazing silly at her crinkled eyes.

Dhindhē for coming. I'm sorry I left you behind.

"We should slow a little," Éē'shī said suddenly. "We're sweating so much. No telling when we'll come onto more water."

I nodded, head spinning. I waved goodbye to the doll and she happily returned to where she came, leaving me behind as was fair. "Hold on" Éē'shī said, putting her hands under my arms to keep me from falling. "Let's just sit down."

She pulled out one of the blankets from our sack and held it up like a sail, dragging it back and forth in the air to make a little breeze across me. Éē'shī stared off into the distance, shading her eyes against the beating sun. "Eat?" I pointed to the bag where I knew some lāāca pods still rattled around deep inside. "We can stand it a little longer," Éē'shī shook her head no.

"How much further?" I said glumly.

"Much," Éē'shī admitted. I laid my head down to rest. "The air is so heavy," I panted. "Can't I take my jacket off?" It seemed ridiculous that we wore so many clothes when the coldest time of the year was still two months away. When we'd left, each of us wore layers and at first my undershirt, dress, jacket, leggings, underskirt, and headscarf couldn't keep me warm enough at night. Ee'shi insisted that we keep our heads covered and jackets on no matter how strong the sun.

"Take it off but keep your undershirt on." Éē'shī allowed.

"But I can't breathe!"

"Lay *still* then. We have to stay covered in the sun. If you think you're thirsty now just wait til you get a good sun-burn!"

"I don't care, it's too hot. I'm gonna be sick," I warned her, swallowing an unbearable taste in my throat. "See? Sick!" I made an unpleasant gagging noise for effect that nearly did the trick. She leaned over me and loosened my clothes, then stood again to make a shade above me with her shadow. "Concentrate more on cooling off and less on being disgusting," Éē'shī's annoyed voice said over her shoulder.

"I wish I could swim in the stars," I said lazily, flopping over on my back now that I felt a bit better. Éē'shī smiled to herself faintly but said nothing.

"I wish I could eat them," I rasped out, trying to get her to really smile and stay still a bit longer.

"You *do*, do you. And what would they taste like?"

"Silver."

Éē'shī laughed flatly. "What does silver taste like?"

I thought a moment, summoning up the taste in my mouth. "Mm. Sparkly. Sweet."

"*Ts'rūndē*, it's time to go," Éē'shī said, pulling me up much too soon. "Can you go on?"

My head still spun gently but the little black dots floating in my eyes while lying down had disappeared. I nodded and took a tentative step. "Slowly," she murmured. We linked arms and putting my weight against her, I walked with Éē'shī until the sun became low in the sky and we found a wide, thickly muddy depression to settle in and build a small fire.

"What sort of a place is this?" I asked and leaned down to scoop some of the damp sod up with my fingers. "Ooh, it's so cool!"

Éē'shī pulled out the map and stood tracing it with a finger, her brow furrowed. "I think it was a river. *Is* a river. *Was* a river?"

"Like Sé Elamangúō?" I asked, proud that I knew at least the name of one river. Mainly because it was the only one I'd ever seen.

"It *is* Sé Elamangúō," Éē'shī realized aloud and looked around her. I let the little clumps of mud fall through my fingers. "But what happened to it?"

"It's drying out. On the map this is a narrow part so we're farther off than I thought we were. It's ok, we'll still get there," she assured me. "Come on, it's what we've got tonight." She pulled up several handfuls of pale green grass nearby and chewed away as she handed me the lāāca pods. "They're not stars, but."

"But tomorrow there might be something better. And we'll be closer," I finished as I laid out the bowl to catch the morning dew and then sat down to suck down the lāāca all in one go, feeling guilty I hadn't split them with Éē'shī. Unbothered, she built a fire after several false starts and motioned for me to sit by her. She pulled out the little wooden comb in the sack to comb out my ears in silence. Her hands were gentler than Dandhō's, yet still I wished I were somewhere else. And then I felt guilty for this. I was the one who wished for us all to go Bri'ēn after all.

"Éẽ'shī?" I started.

"Shẽ'á, Mi'halẽ?" She called me by name and then I knew she was irritated with me.

Don't mention home, I thought to myself. "When we get to Bri'én, can I have a toy?"

The combing stopped. "You want a toy?"

"I... forgot my doll. Back there," I said sheepishly.

"You didn't *forget* your doll. You didn't *want* it," Éẽ'shī called me out as she resumed combing. I couldn't help it as my eyes relaxed back into my forehead. "*Óōnōúa*," my apology sounded weaker than I intended it.

She replied, all worn out, "In Bri'én you can have anything you want."

This then was the thought which carried me through to the next day, for there was nothing better ahead of us. We walked on saying very little except the few times Éẽ'shī reminded me to keep my sleeves rolled down to protect my arms. That day we found nothing to eat. There were no trees in sight, no grass, only sand, pebbles and a few smooth black rocks jutting up from the ground here and there in the distance. With each pebble we passed I busied myself thinking up new things I wanted once we got to the city. I would have a yellow dress like the village she-dogs, a prettier doll, a kite like Anshẽ's and little green teacups like Rāca's. Somehow the possibility of having the same things as them made me feel closer to my lost dasha; it filled me with the thought that someday I would come back, and we would play together with them.

e͞e'shi

20

one is more wrong than
the other

*an ē r'erst'tl gal
an pap'ē*

hAZE hung all around, making shimmery waves in the distance resembling stretches of shiny water to taunt us. Even the sun seemed to emboss itself into the sky so that there was no sun, only a large patch of glow so strong it seared through our eyelids.

How could I have gotten us all the way down to Sé Elamangúō? Had the landscape changed so much since I'd left Hala-Asal that I could no longer recognize it by memory? If nothing else, we were able to fill the dew bowl with cool mud to slather on our faces. Mi'halē couldn't keep from peeling it off as it dried and cracked. I didn't bother reproaching her for making such a mess of herself. After all, we hadn't bathed in who remembered when.

"Keep yourself covered," I warned again as I noticed Mi'halē tugging at her sleeves. She became still.

I bent down and picked up a spiky little bush I'd tripped over and found that it was a lone fúasana bush, its fleshy arms full of deep groundwater it had siphoned up. Handing the larger pieces to Mi'halē, I sat down in the short grass and chewed noisily as I pulled off the fat outer arms to take with us..

"Ts'rūndē." I got up and pulled on her hand to go.

It was a day before we stumbled along upon another long tract of land crowded with stiff grasses nearly as tall as Mi'halē. Pressing through this, I decided we should stay the night right in the middle before moving on because a little shelter was better than no shelter, after all. And with such close insulation around us we'd be completely protected from any wind with no need for a fire. Mi'halē pushed and crashed her way over to me and we grabbed hands and jumped backwards to crush the grass underneath us with our combined weight.

I intended for us to make a sort of depression to sleep in, but when the thick, long strands pushed us right back up, I couldn't help but laugh aloud. "Tse, one-two-three!" I shouted and we leaped again, making little more than a shallow oval-shaped dent. Picking herself up with a grin, Mi'halē cried joyfully, "Again!" and we did so once more. But after a few more unproductive tries the fun wore off and Mi'halē knocked her head on the ground. I gave up, covering the itchy grass with the blanket so we could sleep back to back. Satisfied we were invisible for at least a mile around, I laid down to my first full night of sleep since we'd left F'ala.

In the morning, the soft rise and fall of Mi'halē's voice behind me seemed to thread through a conversation, and I searched frantically for her, terrified we'd been found. But when I blinked away the drops of sleep still clinging to my eyes, I was satisfied to find her engaged in that olden dance of life called play. I laid still for a moment, listening to the careless speech behind me before getting up to tramp down some more of the grass poking up under the blanket.

As I did, I caught Mi'halē's hurried movements to hide the little stones she'd been carrying in her jacket pocket. An embarrassed silence settled over her and it took some convincing to pry her up from the grass bed; simple, but still the softest we'd found yet. But as we moved on, it was soon enough she thrashed a thick stem of grass out before her like a baton, entertaining with a little tune as she marched along with knees high, showing the first signs of herself in weeks.

When we neared the end of this grassy forest, I expected to come out to flat land. And the land was flat, indeed; grey and dry and featureless. But here were masses of thin, blocky wooden poles which stuck up from the ground in neat rows just above my waistline, stained black and some tied with white ribbon hanging limply in the still air. "I know what it is," Mi'hal̃ē's voice was very still, very small. "Ón'gala. A city of the dead."

I nodded in agreement.

She took a few steps in through the tall markers, careful to step around them, and closely inspected their shape and form, though none were marked with any writing to say who lay beneath them and there were no keepsakes strung around them, no beads or incense bowls.

"Under my feet," she waved her arm vaguely.

I nodded again and noticed her for a moment fingering one of the ribbons, pulling it gently, letting it go over and over again as I examined the skyline for signs of where we might be until I saw a very bad sign. The thick black cloud off the to left was too far ahead to yet smell but spoke of a large fire. And where there was fire, there was someone to start it. "Enda'tsorē village," I realized aloud.

"Why don't they all have white ribbons?" Mi'hal̃ē asked, oblivious to the sky's faint blue disappearing before us. She'd made it nearly at the other side of the graveyard already without my notice and I walked quickly to catch up with her, calling out, "Only the graves of the little ones have a white ribbon. White and black are pure colors."

Her ears twitched as she looked at me warily. "Purity," she repeated. "No one ever said that," her voice dropped to a whisper. "They said white is death. White is *without*. White is the color of Āē'rū."

"Aren't the stars white when you look up? So many things mean so many things in this world of análong. They mean this in the north and that in the south, this to the grown and that to the small," I said casually, trying to decide how far west we should go to avoid Daú Gemabanē. If Enda'tsorē was before us, we'd gone too far south, I thought. Now, any further east and we may run right into the sea. Or *not* the sea.

"It matters!" Mi'hal̃ē spat and pulled violently at the heels of her shoes, grunting and spitting until they finally split into long shreds off faded red off her feet into the dust. "We played together every day, and no one would touch me. They thought I didn't see when they wiped off their toys behind my back, like I was sick or something! Didn't anyone think I could *see*?"

Her eyes drew up so wide she didn't see the destroyed shoes and threw her arms around me tightly, burying her head against my collarbone.

"You've ruined your lovely shoes. But then, you felt just a bit equal doing it, didn't you?" I asked gently.

She nodded against me, the tears spreading wet against my smock for a bit before I heard her soft, gummy voice interrupt my thoughts of moving on. "But you know what Éé'shī? You know? I still don't have any color. I haven't turned blue or brown or grey in all this time. I thought maybe someday I would. Maybe I just needed to get bigger. I thought maybe I wasn't *finished*."

"You never will. The meanings of things are just ideas, that's all. Things can have all sort of meanings be equally true. Remember what F'ala says: *all you need to know is the most important thing*." I pushed her away and took her hand, to lead her away. Her expression flattened out into a sort of watery acceptance and she asked, "If that's all I need to know why did I have to learn all that junk up in the loft? I did an awful lot of copying when I could have been playing!" I laughed and pinched her arm. "All that junk is supposed to help you figure out the most important thing."

As we exited the endless rows of graves, I said nothing when Mi'halē silently reached into her pocket and took out her little smooth play-stones. She subtly laid them atop one of the dhana graves and with the same hand, wiped her face clean. "Is it like that in far-away?" she asked suddenly. "I mean *far-away* where you come from, do things have a lot of meanings like you say, equally?"

"I know that things are like that to the Guardians," I didn't quite answer the question.

"Éé'shī, are you a Guardian?" she stopped and pulled on my hand. I turned around to face her and laughed. "Do I look like a Guardian?"

"Tsō, not really. Not like the ones on my bed. At home." She thought about it a moment and continued, "But Dandhō says anyone could be a Guardian."

"So, you should be kind to everyone? She said that too. And you weren't going to be kind to me, remember?" I chided her. Mi'halē's brow furrowed but she stared through me, trying to suss out the truth I refused to give up. I said, "Am I strong like a Guardian?"

"You're stronger than me," she said thoughtfully.

"But still *only a dhana* like you," I smirked. Mi'halē looked down, blushing. "Óōnóúa, I didn't mean it like that," she apologized. I knitted my brow. "You certainly did!"

"Mmm. Yeah, I did," she looked back up shyly, then leaned over to hitch up her stockings with her free hand, now aware of the feel of the hot ground under her shoeless feet.

"It's fine," I said indifferently, but all too aware of my own weaknesses. "To be a Guardian is to walk beside the análong, to carry and shield them but to never belong among them. Only the strongest can carry the burden of their own sins *and* those of Ebūda. That's why the Guardians are called the heroes of Ebūda. That's why Guardians can never belong."

"Well it doesn't sound fun anyway." Mi'halē stood up and followed me again. "Too bad we don't have a Guardian to carry us to the city then," she grumbled.

I stayed silent as we plodded along in the heavy dust, thinking that someday I would have to carry her. Then it struck me as odd that there would be a graveyard so far away from a village but then again, the illness. Perhaps the smoke was a last-ditch attempt by whoever remained to cleanse the village of it. Either way, we weren't going to find out. Leading us to what I believed to be the right direction, I knew if we ran into the inlen woods within the next two weeks, we'd be touching the Tsenairē forest. Wrong way. Well, then I'd know to turn around at least instead of this aimless wandering.

"We're a little off course," I said. "F'ala wanted us to go by way of Dhalit, but that's alright. Besides, Dhalit is a fickle place."

When no reply came, I felt compelled to say something more. "Every year the análong there split into two teams and have a tug of war over the village wall. If the north side wins, the village is called Dhalit for the coming year. If the south wins, the village is called Dhalind'r."

Mi'halē rolled her eyes and I decided vigilant silence would do us better than chatty negligence when it came to going the right direction. It was clear I wasn't as good at reading a map as I'd thought I'd be. *You're getting nervous. Just shut up and walk, Éē'shī.*

And I did, trying my best to clear my mind of my noisy thoughts. For the next five days I said nothing until we came to a small patch of fúasana in the open plain and there we stayed for four days under the wide, flat sky drinking our fill of sticky wet liquid and chewing the stems until our teeth felt fuzzy and weirdly loose. "Now sit down right there on that rock and take your clothes off," I said. Mi'halē lost no time in peeling everything off in a messy pile and sat down on her palms, eyes closed and face up to the sun. "Finally!" she exclaimed.

"It's time you had a bath," I said, breaking up the last little bush and straining its thick insides into the dew bowl. Mi'halē wrinkled her nose. "Do I have to?"

"You stink," I said flatly and smeared a good cold daub of fúasana juice over her back. She leapt to her feet, her skin rippling as the muscles underneath wailed in protest. But I grabbed her bony shoulder and whipped her back down. "Cold!" she yelped. "Oh, now you're cold," I rolled my eyes and continued to work the juice into her skin. "What am I going to wipe off with?" she asked. "You're not. I'm going to clean you up like the ancestors did before they had soap," I explained and got the wooden comb out to drag heavily over her skin. "Ow! Get off me!"

"Stop whining," I murmured and combed briskly until I was sure I'd gotten both the sticky fúasana and all the sweat and grime she'd accumulated off in one disgusting pile on the ground. Mi'halē looked around at herself cautiously, taking note of the pink stripes up and down her from the comb's teeth. She scratched herself all over, wiggling happily. "Felt kind of good," she admitted. "You want me to do it to you?"

I shook my head. "Can't. That's all there was."

"Well you stink too!" she protested, pulling her clothing back on with distaste.

207

"I'm not the one who keeps peeing on their own leg," I said meanly. Then I felt bad for calling her out and teased, "Don't walk so close to me then." I stuck my tongue out and hoisted the sack onto my shoulder.

I set off with Mi'halē still scratching and shimmying along, hoping that we must now be going the right way. I'd given up on the map and put it away for good. F'ala was indeed an excellent artist, but her tiny, spidery writing and linework was so hard to read I decided I must rely on my memory, broken as it was, and my own intellect to get us to Bri'én. In another week, we should be wading through a forest of some sort. Tsenairē bordered the sea. Náasaa touched the Pondasharū mountains. Neither was the right way, but one was more wrong than the other.

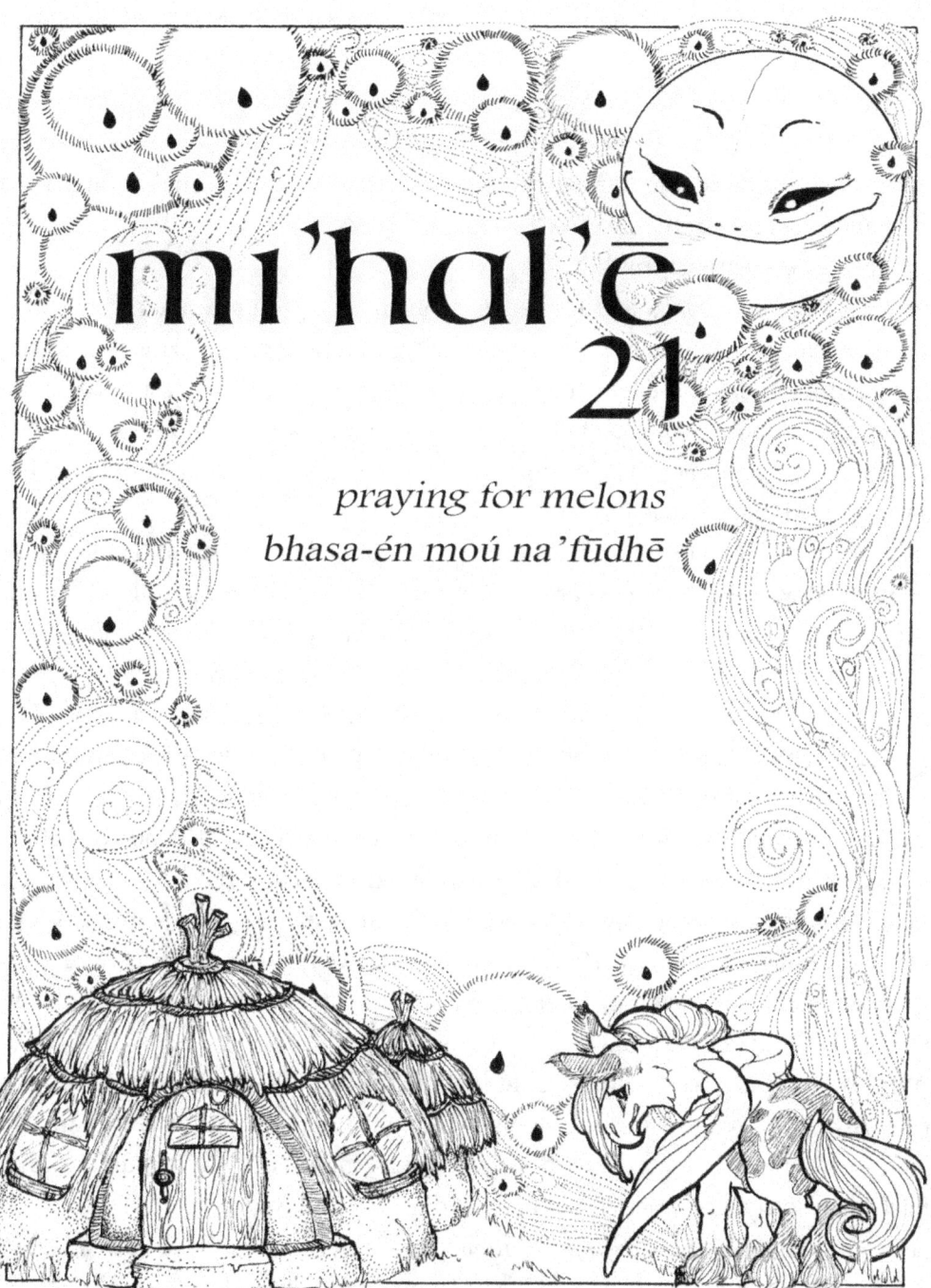

mi'hal'ē
21

praying for melons
bhasa-én moú na'fūdhē

mY tears fell, slipping down my face in finger-waves until they fell to the floor and broke into smiling diamonds. They skittered, sparkling across the corners and up under the bed as Dandhō's voice stilled the air around us. They peeped out at me, safe and smiling, waiting for some other time when I would need them.

"If you'd have gone to sleep when I told you, you wouldn't be waking up with cotton in your mouth now!"

I rolled over on the ground and curled into a ball under the blanket, shaking her voice from my head. Éē'shī glanced over from the fire. "Just wake up?"

I sat up stiffly. "Tsō. I was just thinking."

"Well don't do *that*," she teased and turned away again as I got up to check the dew bowl. "Go ahead," she called over her shoulder and I paused for a moment, not bothering to ask if she was sure but not quite wanting to drink the few drops all at once either. With our feast of fúasana juice just a week ago, I thought it would be a while before I was so thirsty again but somehow it seemed to make the dry seem even drier and I began thinking of every sweet thing I'd ever drank in my life, lining up the bottles in my head to choose from.

"Say your prayers and we'll be off," Éē'shī said as she snubbed out the mild flames with sandy dirt. Prayers. I wondered what Éē'shī prayed about. Mine still anchored around going home but over the last week they'd evolved to ask for tea, juice, lāāca milk, melons. It'd had been at least a year since I'd eaten a melon and now I couldn't stop thinking *melons, melons, melons*.

We had passed the city of Daú Gemabanā the day before. Éē'shī said she was sure of it because of a faded sign she'd seen posted to a rock off in the distance. I could see the rock and the outline of the sign, but it was too worn for me to read. She said now she was sure we would make it to Náasaa Forest in the next week or so and then it wouldn't be long until we could cross the border into Adanandū.

I'd lost count of the weeks and now simply wondered if Dhandōdāi had already gone by or if hĒladdon was coming soon or who was going to make the candles? Or where would we celebrate them… or *if* we would. The only certainty now was the sun in the sky and the moons at night; whatever passed under them from day to day disintegrated into one ceaseless fable of someone else's life I couldn't seem to run away from.

"I thought, I thought maybe Dandhō would be here today," I said unexpectedly and then immediately turned my head in shame of such a stupid thought. But I felt I should explain myself all the same. "When I woke up, I thought I was in my own bed. And then I just…thought a while."

"*Tsōl*," Éē'shī said softly. She reached out her hand for me and we walked on.

Éē'shī had showed me now how to look for *nōma* spider webs on the dead ground and against flat rocks. On the odd chance one was found, Éē'shī siphoned off any water drops desperately clinging to them with a twig she allowed me to suck on. "But won't the nōma die without its home?" I asked the next morning after the air had cooled so much overnight we'd found a frozen web and broke the pieces off to melt in our mouths.

"It's not my concern," Éē'shī said in between licking her fingers. Then absently she murmured, "I'm surprised the nōma have lasted this long. There's always something bigger looking for a meal."

I gulped.

"We might find some *darū* melons out here before we get to the forest," she said hopefully, looking down at the dry soil. "Ground-melons. Look for any dried stalks sticking up in the sand."

Melons! I'd never heard of a darū melon in particular but I was interested! My neck hurt from looking straight down so intently to search. It was my toe that found one, knocking me into an awkward bit of footwork to stay upright as I saw the spot of blood bloom through my stocking. Éē'shī didn't mind me but went over to examine the dried, blackish stump poking out through the sand. She stuck at it with her toe, chipping away bits of the dry earth underneath until she'd made a shallow hole around the vine and loosened up the earth around it.

"Too bad you ruined your shoes," she observed and dropped down to dig with her hands. Working together, we hit upon a hard sphere at the end of the vine and knitted our fingers around it to work it out of its sandy nest. Éē'shī held it crooked in her arm and smiled, very pleased with herself. Her fingers trailed along the lower vine growing from the melon's bottom and she pointed down. "If we're lucky there should be a few more and we'll want to grab them all. Pull really carefully."

I ran my own fingers along it gingerly and pulled upwards. Sure enough, as I worked, the vine came up from the ground and a few feet later stopped, plunging back down. "Ha?" I looked to Éē'shī to confirm. She put her melon down quickly and joined me, digging as fast as she could. Just as the vine lay close to the land's surface, so the second melon lay much less deeply hidden. Smaller, and easier to prize out.

All in all, we dug out four melons with the last being the size of my palm, a dried up shrunken little ball hard as the earth we'd pulled it out of. Éē'shī put it in the sack for keeping. "Just in case," she said. But I could barely be disappointed. It was nothing but sheer joy as we split the others' velvety round rinds with rocks and sat sucking out the juicy green insides which left an even bigger hole in the stomach but quenched the terrible dryness in our throats.

"Ahh," Éē'shī signed happily, resting against the pack with her legs splayed out and dusty. "That was a lovely find. It's gonna hurt later, but still." I nodded in agreement, already feeling the ache under my ribs. "I hope there's more," I said.

"We'll keep looking," Éē'shī assured me.

I had lain down on the ground on my side, lazily rubbing my head against the hard ground to scratch it in the sand. I licked seeds out of my back teeth and closed my eyes in contentment, the cold melon in my belly, the hot sand against my eyes and a playful breeze tickling the back of my neck. I didn't want to move backward or forward, thinking only of gratitude to all of Creation for just that moment, but I knew Éĕ'shī wouldn't let us stop for long, and I was right.

The great fir trees of Náasaa were not unlike the trees in Dandhŏ's forest in that they were tall and fat, but these whispered with soft green needles tipped at the ends with slender bits of brown and they stood on tall roots above the ground that we could pass right under. Running through the trees back home meant getting a face full of stings from the millions of little sharp cones hiding in their fur, but here I felt compelled to caress the lowest branches with my fingertips as we made our way further and further into the woods. Dandhŏ had taught me that forests are the best place to live in a drought because the trees hold in moisture for a long time. Éĕ'shī wasted no time looking for food and we were lucky to find quite a lot of good moss and berries to munch on as well as trees to sleep up underneath in between their enormous roots.

But on the morning of the fourth day under the trees I looked up and saw the sky had turned white and Éĕ'shī hurried me to fill the sack with as much food as we could carry to start off again. It took several days to make it to the opening of Náasaa and as we grew nearer the days grew colder. On the last day we could see ahead a pale light making its way through the trees and the ground below us protested under our feet as we heard our steps crackling in the dry needles. As the trees suddenly pulled back into a tiny clearing lit by the pale sun, I gasped aloud at the beauty before me.

Every tiny thing around us had been dipped in sparkling ice, every pale surface had been kissed by white-lace in patterns so intricate even Dandhŏ's pen couldn't fashion. "Hoarfrost," Éĕ'shī said with satisfaction. She picked off a flower head and licked at it. "Better than nothing," she noted, popping it into her mouth with a loud crunch. I reached out, horrified as I felt the trees around me shrink back in offense as if my clumsy fingers would marr their elegance.

"You don't know when we're going to find water again," she lectured, crunching on a thickly iced leaf. "We're going northward now, and we have to stay away from Sé Elamangúŏ."

"Away from it? But...*water*!" I shivered, realizing soon I'd have to ask her to show me how to wrap my feet properly against the cold ground. *Since I ruined my shoes,* I reminded myself scornfully.

"When we crossed it the first time, we were closer to Pŏcarū and it was nothing but mud. We're much further north now. If we cross it here it'll be dried and out in the open. So, no water. Eat up," she explained and handed me a flower bud. Sighing, I slipped it past my lips and crunched. There was nothing satisfying about it, my gums were sore from constantly eating roughage and then chewing more roughage under Éĕ'shī's watch to clean my teeth. Because teeth, she lectured, can fall out.

As we left the forest the land expanded out into a treeless, strange collection of small hills popping out from the ground. "It looks diseased," I observed. Éĕ'shī smiled. "They're called *nubbins* and you can find them all over Ebūda. Just little hills, but good for hiding behind." As it turned out, they were excellent for hiding behind, and the first other análong we would meet on the way to Bri'én knew this too.

Because we were now on the open plain with nothing to shield us except the nubbins, Éē'shī wouldn't allow a fire to draw any attention. But it was getting so cold at night that after she'd given me her jacket and then her headscarf to wear around my neck, she finally gave in and made a small fire after I whined for a full three days that we hadn't seen a single other análong for weeks. "Months, maybe!"

The nubbins gave somewhat of a block against the limp winds, but the ground was much harder without a soft covering of tree needles and as we walked my body felt as if it had been beaten in the night.

"What's wrong with you?" Éē'shī snapped when I started to fall behind the next day. "Everything hurts," I complained. "I'm so stiff."

"Keep walking, it'll loosen you up," she muttered from behind me.

"That's your answer to everything!" I felt my nose wrinkle as if I were looking for a fight, but I wasn't quite brave enough to pick one so early in the day. My knees, tight and ornery, refused to bend until the sound of panic rang out in the lifeless air.

"*Run!*" Éē'shī shouted, slapping me in the back and jutting forward past me. "What?" I choked out and tried to follow but she was too fast even under the weight of the sack. I could barely run under the weight of my own clothes! "Wait!" I hollered, tripping on my own feet, unable to look back at what I was running from. I kept going blindly against my own thundering heartbeat until Éē'shī disappeared from my view and something reached out and grabbed me.

I was wrestled to the ground, my face covered in cloth and though I pushed back I was too restricted by the two jackets I wore to free myself. "Ē-ō," Éē'shī's familiar voice whispered in my ear and I realized it was she who was cutting off my air. I stilled myself, scrunching up my eyes and making my breath even and shallow against the cloth.

The time stretched out, longer and longer in silence and without any noise I wondered if anyone was out there at all or if Éē'shī was teaching me a lesson. But then I heard a terrible noise; a triumphant screaming, bells, and the hard thud of a g'éalach pounding the ground as it came nearer and nearer to us. "*Úī-úī-úī-úī-úī-úī-úī-úī-úīīīīīī!*"

It had built up from behind us and now miraculously passed right by, the intensity of the screaming waning as it became further and further away. I wasn't great at directions, but I knew it was going in the direction we were trying to go. Éē'shī pulled the cloth off of me and I gasped in fresh air painfully but she held me down for some time before we clumsily pulled each other up and came out around the nubbin. "See, good for hiding," she said in a breathy voice. She didn't need to tell me again that análong may be out there somewhere. We'd finally reached *somewhere*.

"Who was it?" I asked, unsure I wanted to know but too curious not to.

"NaÓma. That's what they sound like," she said, scrutinizing the horizon ahead. I shuddered. That terrifying sound settled into my bones as if drenching so deep as to permeate my blood with something new, yet very old. It didn't sound as foreign as I wished it would, and I felt that old sparkle of knowledge begin to glow inside. I had to get rid of it.

"But, where did they come from?" I wondered.

She pointed behind us where we had come from out of Náasaa. "I don't think they followed us exactly, there were only three of them. But they know someone's out here now."

Our steps became slower now that the ground was turning harder and the knowledge we were not alone weighed over us. That particular day Éḗshī did not allow us to stop to eat at all but pressed on, trying to reach the large black rocks she could see jutting up on the horizon just beyond our reach. Hopeful we'd find the village of Úādha beyond them, our hope turned to sickness when I spied a row of soft shapes on the ground in the late afternoon and we moved as quickly as possible to reach them.

It wasn't something good at all.

I couldn't make myself listen when she screamed at me to stop running and I beat Éḗshī to them, staring at the bodies of five na'dhana curled up beside each other in a row, faces down, their thin arms around each other as if sleeping. Dropping to my knees, I pulled on the ear-ribbon of the middle dhana as if I could wake her up. "Éḗshī?" I asked quietly in disbelief, unsure that they *were* anything but sleeping. But she slapped my hand away from them, hard. "Look at their necks! See those black spots? Don't touch them!" she said severely and pulled me to my feet in a jerk. "They have the illness."

"*Nā*," I hiccuped, my hands flew to my mouth instinctively and I sucked on my smarting fingers. "Nā!" Waves of feeling washed through me. The terror that we weren't alone after all, the lesson that death comes for all living beings regardless of age, the sudden and terrible realization that if the NaÓma were *behind* us, there might not be a way to return home all crowded inside me and pushed upward. I was either going to cry or throw up.

"They've *gone on*," Éḗshī said, wiping her face with her hand. "The illness has killed most of the análong in Peridūr, if not all of them. I know that doesn't mean anything to you and we're not *going* to Peridūr, but I have to be hard on you to *protect* you!"

I barely heard her. The shining little drops no bigger than grains of sand dotted the end of my fingers as I pushed them back into the corners of my eyes, determined not to cry. But they swelled and became such a mass of droplets that they simply rushed over my nails and down my nose, their vibrance so alien against my grimy, itchy skin. I marveled at them so keenly that the pain dulled to a thud in the backs of my eyes and I saw rather than heard their singing little whispers that inside where they had come from, oh *inside* I sparkled. And then as one, the little drops swelled into a kiss against my lips as they bubbled and slid down over my face to stain the front of my jacket. "I don't want you to protect me," I blubbered. "I want to go home!"

Éē'shī walked away and sat down atop the sack with her back turned. I cried louder now out of spite, indignant that she'd leave me to myself, but she shook her head and said not unkindly, "You can't."

Then after a long time Éē'shī picked up our things and came back to me, warning, "It's time to stop this crying. You'll make yourself sick and don't you dare do it on purpose." And somehow I stopped and swallowed, took her hand and got to my feet.

"You can pray the shonbū for them while we walk," she said. I nodded slowly but let go of her hand, blowing a kiss back to the curled little bodies we left behind.

"How did they get here?" I finally asked after they faded away, seeing no sign of life anywhere nearby.

"Their asamas probably left them here and moved on," she said.

My mind couldn't quite comprehend the steps involved in leaving one behind like that and I struggled to form the words to question but Éē'shī broke into my thoughts. "Mi'hal'ē, I don't know why." She squeezed my hand to let me know this was the final question for the day.

But I thought I did, at least I thought that what had happened to those na'dhana was the same thing that had happened to me, in a backwards way. They were connected somehow. I shook my head forcefully, not ready to know it. But I had *one* more question, and after we'd settled down for the night and lay back to back under the fire's low flicker.

"Why did Dandhō send me away? Really, *céan*?"

There was no hesitation when she answered: "Because she loved you."

I frowned. *Aói.* In all my life that word had never passed between my ah'sha and I. We had never hugged or kissed, though sometimes I found myself reaching out aimlessly as if I *would* have. I didn't understand how grownups thought they could contain such things in the flat confines of words and yet… yet I did. For words were never flat or confined. They could set one free when silence became so saturated with meaning it suffocated. Words were the tears of echo, the shouts of secrecy. Why did love have to be so small a word when it felt so immense?

"Then I don't understand," I said resentfully, looked into the endless dark. "Sometimes it's good to have a broken heart," Éē'shī murmured.

"What?"

She continued. "Once it's opened it can hold more. Once it's split, its truth can seep out. Like breaking open an egg and letting the yolk spill out. Yolk's the best part, isn't it?"

"But I don't want to be split open! I don't want to spill out all over. I'll be *lost*," I protested in alarm. If getting broken and lost were consequences of love, then I wanted left out of it!

"Well as long as *you* know where you are, you won't ever be lost," she assured me.

I closed my eyes, defeated by the day and my own thoughts. *But I don't know.* And as I lay there I thought less of home and more of the strange nature of emptiness. For as I idly rubbed my hand over my belly, I was dumbfounded at how huge a hole could have grown in so small a space. How could such an endless emptiness have eaten me inside out? And then I thought perhaps Éḗ'shī had given me the answer: I must be full of cracks.

The next night as we neared the wall of Úādha village, we sat side by side on a flat rock gazing into the fire. It was the first full bonfire Éḗ'shī had struck in several days, saying that because Úādha was a popular spot for travelers to pass through, the smoke of a fire wouldn't arouse any suspicion.

After tearing up her headscarf into strips and wrapping my feet to the ankles because the feet of my stockings were now so thin I had begun to limp, she sniffed at the air around us suddenly. Looking up towards the south, we could see the sky thickened and infused with the dark smell of hot smoke. Gōl stared serenely back at us, behind him the horizon was torn in two; one side black and rolling, the other a flat, flickering crimson. I stood up, the blanket we shared falling carelessly to the ground and cold bumps pricked along my scalp in the air. "Is that Bri'ēn?" I asked tentatively.

"Tsō, we just came from that direction. But it is somewhere," Éē'shī answered, swallowing. "Somewhere that isn't, anymore."

I looked at the red sky crumbling to a burnt golden and cocked my head one way and another. "But it's beautiful," I murmured. "Béanda."

"Andama." Éē'shī agreed.

All things. She allowed me to look quietly at the terrible, beautiful sky for some time. "It's the beginning of the world," I murmured. "The land and the sky are tearing themselves apart and the smoke is so many birds pulling the sky up away from the land." I didn't often share my thoughts like this but for some reason couldn't keep quiet. But as happened in my own head, the words simply came whether I understood them or not. I didn't know what they meant, just that they were *true.*

Éē'shī said nothing, watching me with interest. I sat down. After quite some time watching Gōl sweep the sky just visible through the vapors, she looked over to me huddled beside her under the blanket. "Are you alright?"

My eyes didn't move from their fixed gaze. She must have decided I wouldn't answer so she tucked the cover's edge up better over my shoulders when my own quiet voice interrupted her, seeking some answer but not knowing the question. "Every night I close my eyes, and every morning they open again. No matter what happens to us, my eyes always open in the morning."

Éē'shī nodded in exhaustion, quietly enjoying what was left of our fire's warmth on her face before one of us would have to drag ourselves back out into the chill air and feed the flames a little. " Éē'shī?"

"Mmm?"

"How do you know there's going to be anything when we get to Bri'ēn? Weren't those… weren't they going *away* from there?"

I could tell from the look on her face that she wished badly to tell me the truth, *that she didn't know.* And I wished she would tell me. I wished she would confide to me that she had no better assurance than I had my own curiosity since being dropped on Dandhō's doorstone, hoping to go out and find the wonderful world someday. Éē'shī shook herself out from under the blanket and winced as the air hit her bare thighs. But she wouldn't say that. So, I leaned back on my hands and pretended to believe her when she said, "Every night we close our eyes, and every morning they open again. So then, I know we must be meant to go on."

She poked around the fire-ring, feeding it a bit and leaving me alone to pray in the dim light. I never knew what Éë'shī prayed about but my prayers were beginning to change. *Please let us find more melons.*

ē'shī
22

a hunger, a gift

an m'allor an dl'oc

I could see from our campsite there was some activity in Úādha and I heavily considered sneaking into the village to beg for some food in the early morning. We had completely missed Cúinha and N'debala on F'ala's map and now we were on the wrong side of Sé Elamangúō to reach Calēmantsū. But it wasn't a total loss. Úādha was probably several weeks south on foot from Calēmantsū but it was parallel and if we could continue northwest, we would eventually come to Sé Mōgale river and be able to follow it to the town of Ashetaer straight into Adanandū. But it was still a long way even to that crossing. Well, that decided it, we needed some actual food.

Making sure Mi'hal'ē was dead asleep, I turned the blanket dull-side over and covered her completely. I crept off to the village wall, leaving everything we'd brought with us behind. F'ala had warned me not to speak or give anything away of where I'd come from. Better to let others assume and save myself from tripping on my own lies. It turned out this was excellent advice because I'd come into this world with the same deep accent of the southern análong around me. Úādha sat in the *high south* where there was always a suspicion of northern travelers and artisans trying to settle and bring their foreign ways. My color and accent didn't match, an instant warning.

The wall of Úādha was made of smoother stone than any we'd come to before, painted with intricate patterns ending at the open gate. I took a deep breath and walked straight through, ever-aware of my thin legs, my arms. There was too much for my eyes to take in from side to side and I jumped when I heard a kind voice say, "Dhana, where did you come from?"

An a'ma with a small, dirty dhana in tow waved at me. "So small! T'surundē, come with me." I followed her, vigilant of the empty-looking huts until we came to the village square full of the sick, wounded, drifting, and orphaned. Though none seemed to have the great illness sweeping Ebūda, I could see the few darna left were too weak to fly and certainly the g'ealach were too sick to work. I was surrounded suddenly by this shabby bunch who seemed more curious than threatening as they examined me, pulling my arms out and inspecting my ears.

"*Ha-* do you speak?" someone shouted.

As F'ala had instructed, I said nothing but stared back evenly.

"An artist's dhana."

"Pretty dhana."

"Must be hungry!"

Ah, the words I'd hoped for. I stretched out my palms to receive and found they were willing to part with some fly-speckled dūūcerfrūt and a small bag of grain they tied around my shoulders. Then I turned and ran as fast as I could through the gate and back out to Mi'hal'ē. I'd seen the scrawling across the inner wall as the marks of the NaÓma and knew they'd already taken the strong with them, leaving the village to die on its own. I didn't feel bad for running. These good análong had given me food to move on, not to stay and give them someone else to feed. They hadn't wondered where my tribe was; this was the way of the world now.

I was able to pack up my treasures in the sack before waking Mi'hal̆ē to leave. "We'll go east," I said as we set off, not mentioning my suspicion that NaÓma must be nearby because there was no telling what direction they had gone, and it didn't alter where *we* needed to go. To reach Ashetaer we must cross the ÚadaÚadē basin that flooded every four years. Somehow, I knew no swimming would be involved. Just as well, neither of us knew how to.

"I'm cold," Mi'hal̆ē said on the fourth day as we made our way towards a clutch of bushes grown up in the basin since the last rains. Gōl was low in the sky and over the horizon I could see little hLon peeping. I hadn't even noticed but the frigid month of Tsāi'ín had passed by us in relative warmth and Gōl followed overlooked. But now the days should begin to thaw, the sun become stronger. Now the sun and the moons should begin their annual joust over who shone longer on a crowded horizon. Yet, we could see our words now breaking in the air with substance.

"Ah!" I exclaimed, spying a low hillock rising to the west of us. "Do you see what that is?"

She shook her head. "Is it warm?"

"It might be. Just be very quiet and stay behind me," I said, creeping past the bushes and over to the back of the swell. I listened, motioning to Mi'hal̆ē to stay put as I rounded to the other side and found exactly what I was hoping to: a groundskeeper's hut. "Over here!" I hollered and Mi'hal̆ē scrambled around and up to where I stood surveying the messy, dark little space carved into the bottom of the hillock.

Mi'hal̆ē wrinkled her nose. "Did someone live here?"

"When it used to rain and flood the ÚadaÚadē someone lived here to keep watch for análong or hadim that got lost and might drown. It hasn't rained in so long the groundskeeper must have moved on." Leaving her standing there, I made my way further into the hut to explore, finding several rooms hollowed out underneath the ground barely visible but for light shafts of light shining down through holes punched in the crest of the hillock and reflected by small looking-glasses positioned to reflect and move the light further down. "A whole asama lived here," I murmured. All the better to scavenge from. "There's nobody here, we can stay the night."

Though it smelled and was barren of anything to eat, there was a clean well dug into the very bottom of the hut I was able to scratch a full ladle of groundwater from. "It smells," Mi'hal̆ē commented. "And you're still drinking it," I notified, ready to take her to the ground and wrestle it down her throat. She picked up the ladle carefully and wrinkled her forehead. "There's *stuff* in it," she began but at my stare she quickly sucked down most of it and held her hand over her mouth to keep from retching, holding the remaining sips out to me to finish. Not feeling quite so brave now, I tossed it back and gagged.

Others passing through would also be sure to stop and investigate the hut, so we didn't build a fire but found a good deal of blankets and clothing to pile atop us that night. Though warm enough, as I lay by my sister I felt suffocated and coldly sweaty and got up to prop the door open a bit, sighing in relief when I could see the stars in their silent watch above us. Slipping back under the covers I was glad to hear Mi'hal̆e's soft gurgling and I pushed her over onto her side and closed my eyes.

But when I awoke, I heard my own distant voice, my bruised body shifting periodically for a few groggy moments to find yet new sore spots upon me before my eyes opened. As I looked up and focused on Mi'hal̆e's black, staring eyes, I saw the sun was already high in the sky.

I opened my mouth to speak but saw her face drawn in hunger and confusion and she sat scrunched up on the pile of blankets with her arms around her knees, staring blankly at me as I pulled myself up painfully from the ground. The dew-pot sat outside the doorway and our sack lay open near me, the little darū melon had rolled away, the bag of grain had spilled to the floor and the striking-box was overturned. Mi'hal̆e looked down, ashamed.

"I thought you," she said timidly but didn't finish the thought and didn't meet my eyes. "How long did I sleep?" I asked, hoping we hadn't wasted too much time in one spot. She shook her head. "I thought…" she whispered and then held up three fingers. I balked. "Three hours?" Her eyes crinkled and she shook her head. "Days!" I exclaimed. The dhana covered her face. "I didn't think you'd wake up!" she wailed.

Picking up the striking-box and the melon, I placed these carefully back in the bag and leaned up against the wall. "I didn't feel too great when I laid down," I murmured, trying to figure out how Mi'hal̆e had kept out of trouble while I slept rather than what she would have done had I not woken at all. "You found my surprise," I nodded to the spilled grain. "Did you like the fruit?" She shook her head barely, pointing to the sack. As I carefully picked up the grain, I saw she hadn't touched the dūūcerfrūt. "It's okay, I'm fine," I said. "Help me pick this up so we can get going."

Mi'hal̆e got on all fours, wincing as she pushed herself up.

"What's wrong with your foot?"

She bent her knee and held her feet up for me to inspect. "It's all funny-looking," she said, clearly still unsure if I was here to stay. But we didn't have time to comfort each other. I sat down, picked up her foot in my hand and inspected it in my lap since she'd taken off her stockings sometime as I'd slept. She was right, the skin had begun to break down where holes had ripped in the stockings and had a strange mottled look to it.

Tearing off the hem of my dress, I wrapped it tightly over the hole and looked around in the daylight. In the evening light when we'd arrived, I thought I'd seen furniture somewhere and there it was: a stool where a dhana would have stood to reach the clothing-pegs, an empty table set for the evening meal. Jumpers and skirts lay tossed about, hanging from bedposts and chairs haphazardly and shoes scattered the floor. I'd assumed the hut had been left peacefully when the rains stopped but now I had second thoughts about that. All the more reason to leave *now*.

When I found a blue dress about Mi'hal̃e's size and a little pair of shoes, I left her to change while I snooped around to find something just a bit bigger. Satisfied with a clean, orange-colored wrap thicker than my own filthy shift, I stripped off inside the doorway, cringing at my own scent on the clothing I tossed aside. The continual hunger and thirst, the exhaustion and pain was nothing for me compared to being continually *dirty*. Well, couldn't be helped.

After I pulled off my foot wraps as far away from my nose as possible, I tore a thin blanket into strips by my teeth and re-wrapped them. Not used to wearing shoes to begin with, I passed over a pair of strapped sandals that would have fit me nicely, stretching my toes in the new, soft fabric. I was shocked at how much cleaner I felt already in new clothes. Feeling somewhat more presentable, I went to fetch Mi'hal̃e.

She sat so still I could have walked right over her. In the new dress and her old jacket, she sat with her bare knees and purple flowered shoes. "They're not mine," she said flatly. She twitched and whinged about, pulling at the sleeves of the dress and scratching underneath the skirt. I smirked. "At least they're clean." Her look was not one of gratitude but of annoyance.

"They're only things," I reminded her. "Remember the most important thing. We've got a long way still, so the most important thing is you need shoes to walk in."

Gingerly she pulled herself up and followed me. "You look stupid," she said finally. I ignored her.

The new shoes didn't exactly speed us up. While Mi'hal̃e stopped every hour it seemed to rub at blisters under the wraps I wound around her ankles, they did seem to correct the limp she'd developed. I knew it was painful to walk, even I felt the stress of hunger and dehydration to a degree. But there was enough plant life feeding somehow off the groundwater under the ÚadaÚadẽ's smooth dry surface to keep us going and we stopped only to sleep under any cover we could find over the next two weeks.

We continued on slowly and silently towards Ashetaer until a grove of fir trees appeared in the distance. Working our way towards it, I became suddenly aware something was watching and kept this to myself, thinking the colorful new clothes were a very visibly bad idea. When we settled inside a tree hollow that evening I murmured in bad temper, "Winter was late, then warm, now back again just in time for spring," Though we were now better off than we'd been in some time; both closer to the city and better prepared for the elements, I was still sour. "One dreadful season that can't even make up its own mind,"

Our nightly rituals had gone on as usual, with Mi'hal̃e now checking on me before we lay down, just in case. "I thought you said you were going to protect me," she finally said with considerably less ice in her voice than I expected. "Sometimes you have to grow into your intentions," I said.

To my surprise, she nodded in understanding, just glad I was still there to answer her.

In the morning we pressed onward as I kept an eye out for whomever seemed to have their eyes on us. When Mi'hal̃e walked into a low bush and snagged her new dress so badly I had to rip it to get her out, I stood lecturing her to be more careful until I looked closer and realized she'd found a berry bush. The intoxicating joy of finding food again was almost too much to bear. She leapt up and down unaware of the pain in her feet, rejoicing over the handfuls of berries left on the bush. It barely mattered, even those few were enough. I wouldn't allow us to eat the grain or the nearly dried dūūcerfrūt if we could find food in the wild.

I divided the spoils between us, gazing at my berries and counting them out in my other palm. Mi'hal̄e was undecided of how to eat them; all in one gulp or one by one. She decided on one by one and picked up her first, laying it squarely in the middle of her tongue and smiling ear to ear.

I compromised and sucked a little on the sweetness and then crunched the rest of the soggy berry and swallowed with a flourish. I put away the rest of the berries in my dress pocket, praying soon we would stumble onto another bush. Mi'hal̄e grinned at me weakly as I looked up to return the smile but felt my face fade into a flat, pale stare at something behind her. I motioned to her to get behind me but instead she turned around and came to face with a dhana just her size with all the marks of a NaÓma.

He was clothed in rags about his middle and painted with slashes of black and white. His ears were lashed behind his head with some rough ties and rows of fine, sharp points protruded from above his rounded middle, bones. The arrow pulled back in his bow was aimed right for Mi'hal̄e's forehead and I flinched, cursing myself. This was all my fault. For a moment I'd been careless.

Cutting through the crisp, flat air was the sound of the shallow suck of his breath, stopping time just enough for me to realize just how alone we were, just how important the next moment was and if I focused all my heart and mind, how much power I had to alter it. So, these were the hollow eyes I'd felt upon us. But by the shine of them, it was clear he was afraid. He was more alone than we.

There was a sharp *crack* of twigs under my foot as I leaned forward to clasp Mi'hal̄e's hand in mine. I meant to push her and yell for her to run in one swift movement but before I could speak, she'd moved away from me and towards him and gracefully put out her hand. In silence Mi'hal̄e offered her berries over to the enemy.

His eyes never left her face. Nostrils flaring, he snatched them like lightning and stuffed them in his mouth. We both stared as he chewed noisily, waiting for a next move. The dhana swallowed and slowly reached around to his back, giving me time to pull Mi'hal̄e back to me just as slowly, keeping my eyes on him. He pulled out a flask of water from his hip-bag and handed it to us. With no reservation and the same uncontrollable craving, we both sucked in earnest on it.

"Give it back," I hissed to Mi'hal̄e before she could empty it, though I'd have rather given up my own tail. She handed it over and the dhana turned and ran from us as I puzzled where he could have gotten so much water and where the rest of his tribe must be hiding. Unsure how to proceed, we hid up underneath a nearby patch of thorn bushes, the type the small wild things hide under in the hollow spaces for protection but had long abandoned. It wasn't easy getting in there but without knowing who was in the woods, there was no other choice.

We lay silent and shivering cramped up under the thorns for hours until I was sure the dhana was gone and there was no-one else coming. But still, I didn't know where *he'd* come from. Then I pulled Mi'hal̃ẽ out and cuffed her ears for acting irresponsibly. "He had an arrow to your head!" I scolded.

"I wasn't scared," she said quietly.

"You should be! He wasn't any older than you and he was ready to kill you!"

She said nothing, knitting her brow in concentration, not fear, stopping to pull a ragged breath and as she did so the shine of life dawned in her eyes as anger.

As I studied her, I wondered what the destiny of the Guardian of Indūsa would be, what additional sacrifice there would be for her when I was gone. I realized how sick we had become, both of us covered from head to foot in rashes and bites and we suddenly looked so *old*. I knew with grim certainty that there would be an end, that some morning our eyes would not open any more. What if there wasn't anyone left alive in Bri'ẽn? Shaking my head, I knew there was no time for such doubts.

"We have to go on and stop playing at nonsense. How am I going to protect you if you keep pulling stunts like that? It's only by Mī'ắ's own will we got out of that!" I said defensively.

"He was hungry," she said in a wavering tone. "He didn't want to hurt us. He just wanted to eat. I gave him my food so he didn't have to do anything bad to get it. And, and we got water. Doesn't that mean anything?"

I wasn't sure exactly, but she continued. "You said we'd take care of each other. It was my turn."

Somehow, I did understand. I was the Guardian of a Guardian; my own tasks were unknown to Mi'hal̃ẽ as hers were to me. The most important thing was not to keep her from hers in doing mine. Perhaps I would have to put more trust in her to help me do just that.

ée'shī
23

bending time
ur'choú-én tagōlō

I T would be weeks later before I realized that very day we'd unwittingly come so close to R'rundū village we'd have been able to cross into Adanandū in just over a week's time. But not knowing exactly which way the Naóma dhana had come from, I started off in what I *thought* was the opposite way, hoping to make a sort of loop back if we didn't encounter anyone else in the next few days.

After we passed out of the woods into a flat, gentle glen, it was only a short hike up to the small plateau before us. Scrambling up first, I didn't know how narrow the ground was below me or how close Mi'hal̆e was behind me until she came crashing past and I lost my footing, sending us both rolling down the steep slope one over the other. We collided together in a cloud of breath and dust, cushioned by the sack crushed up underneath me.

"Let's do it again!" said the voice under me and I rolled over to let Mi'hal̆e up. "Race you!" she giggled and ran out of my grasp. I couldn't help but follow and we pitched down the slope this time with purpose on our sides, rolling like beetles to the sound of our own laughter. "Again!" Mi'hal̆e squealed and beat me up to the top. "Again!" she turned around, this time on her own. When she flip-flopped down with a whopping great brush burn on her elbow I decided it would be the last time.

"Enough," I pronounced and pulled her up to standing, smoothing out my own clothes and adjusting the sack across my shoulders.

"Oh!" Mi'hal̆e exclaimed and I grabbed her shoulder, ready for anything lurking. But there was nothing to be seen all the way to the horizon but sparkling blue. "Is this the sea?" she wondered aloud but that was impossible. "It's not water," I murmured and let her go, toeing at the ground to disperse the sparkling sand at our feet. "It's salt!" I realized, alarmed that such a thing had formed so far into the wet, humid south. "It's called a *salt flat*. It means it's been very dry here a long time," I explained simply, unsure of how I could use it as a landmark.

"Béanda," Mi'hal̆e breathed, eyes wide. Then without warning she ran out past me and skipped over the salt, twirling around and around until she fell down in a happy heap. "I'm sitting on diamonds!" she called, waving at me. "T'surundē!"

I shook my head at her. "Get up. There's no where to stop here and anyone can see us against the sand. No more time to fool around." As I walked by, I grabbed her by the collar and pulled her along. "Tastes good," she said as she stumbled along licking her fingers.

"Don't eat things off the ground," I said, knowing how stupid that sounded *now*. I could feel her making a face at my back, but I was too busy pulling down my headscarf over my eyes to block out the blinding reflection of light off the sand. As I noticed the air growing quieter I turned around and saw Mi'hal̆e some ways away trying to do the same thing. I ran back to her, fixed her scarf and dragged her along until she pulled back and tried to bite my hand. "Keep up," I warned and left her to her own devices. But this proved to be the wrong idea.

By the time we made it to the other side of the salt flat to the foot of what looked like a rock table, it was almost sunset and I had resorted to consulting the map again. What I thought I saw was the worst possible thing. While there was no salt flat on the map which confirmed my feeling that it was a more recent development than even F'ala knew, the only rock table on this side of Drīdū led right into the Dhanga'lara Land Bridge. I stopped in my tracks, frozen as I stared at the rise of rock before me. Surely not. We couldn't have backtracked *that* much.

"What's wrong?" Mi'hal̃ē piped up, licking her lips. "Are we lost?" she asked astutely.

I didn't answer, trying to decide what to do next, where to settle, which way to go.

"*You're* the one with the map," she noted and I made my decision, pointing to the line of rock that jutted out of the edge of the flat. "Sit right there and don't move. I'll be back in a little bit."

"Where are you going?" her voice took on a note of panic and I turned around to still her. "*Don't raise your voice.* I'm just going up over the rock to see what's on the other side. I'll be right back so just sit here and don't move. Don't call any attention to yourself, do you understand? Just sit here and… play with the diamonds or something." I waved my hand and was off to pull myself up over the evening-warm rock wall.

While not all that steep, it was no easy climb and I came out onto the smooth table with a collection of new scratches and bruises only to find my biggest failure looking right at me: what *was* the Dhanga'lara Land Bridge, a rock formation once bridging this side of Drīdū to Adanandū over a deep, long-dried out channel. But the rock was gone, crumbled and fallen and left behind was only the wide gulf between one cliff and another. This was why F'ala had said not to come here under any circumstances. There was no way to the other side short of growing wings or hiring someone else's. Out of the question. Even if we'd wanted to hire a darna, clearly no-one lived here anymore.

I sank to my knees, somewhat dizzy just gazing out into the expanse. We couldn't even climb down and then back up the other side; the walls of the cliffs were so smooth we'd have nothing to hang onto and no rope to pull ourselves up. We were now probably months away from where we needed to be and it was *all my fault*.

You're a really shitty navigator, you know that?

I pulled my knees up to my chin and sat staring, despondent and uncaring that the sleepy red sun had sent long shadows scrambling from the little rocks here and there across my feet. The sudden chill in the air didn't move me, but eventually I became aware that Mi'hal̃ē hadn't come looking for me and this was extremely unlike her. I turned and climbed back down the table, panicking just a minute when I didn't immediately see her.

"Nā, where are you?" I called softly, but got no answer in the dim light. "Nā!" I shouted and almost knocked myself over when I stepped on her foot lodged between the shallow stones. She lay against the rock, asleep at an odd angle, her head lolled to the side as if her neck had gone limp. "Nā, wake up Mi'hal'e," I shook her to no avail. "Nā, *wake up!*" I shook her harder, knocking her head this way and that as she fell out of my grasp onto her back. *What's that?* I wondered and swiped my fingers across her lips at something crusted there. *Sand?*

Salt!

"Did you eat it?!" Enraged, I shook her again. "How much did you eat?!" But when she didn't wake, I laid my head down to her chest. *Still breathing.*

Helpless, I pulled off her jacket and loosened up her dress, feeling her slippery, sweat-soaked chest. "*Pín'shah!*" I swore, sitting back on my heels. I frantically pawed through the sack, looking for the dūūcerfrūt but came up empty; they'd dried to husks. "Ah! *Pín'shah!*" I shouted in rage, throwing the sack down and burying my face in my hands. "*I don't know what to do!*" I went on to no-one, but when an answer came back to me, I couldn't get off the ground fast enough.

"Why not ask?" the polite voice inquired. I whipped around, my eyes straining, and when I saw him sitting not a few feet away my first thought was not who he was but how had he gotten there?

The g'ealach tilted his head. "If you don't know, ask. What else can you do?"

I was paralyzed, entranced by his somehow-familiar face, terrified we'd been found. Small, round and happy-eyed, the g'ealach's ears were scarred in such a way... I jumped up and threw my arms around his neck. "Hor'e! It's you!"

He laughed and cuffed me on the head with a paw. "You've got yourself in a mess haven't you, ēdandha? There's no way around it," he shook his head with good humour.

"She's been eating salt, maybe all day," I confessed. "She's breathing but I have no idea what to do and I don't know where to get water. She won't wake up," I motioned towards Mi'hal'e's still form. Hor'e left me to examine her, nosing at her feet and hands. "Worst thing to do if you haven't been drinking," he observed. "Why did she do that?"

"Oh, I don't know! She's so *strange!*" I threw up my hands. "She gets the weirdest ideas!"

Hor'e smiled down at her. "She is her *own*, isn't she?" he commented. "But you've got to get going. So here's what I would do if it were me. If I didn't have any means or power to get myself to the other side, I'd ask someone who did."

"Ask someone who does, ask someone who does," I repeated to myself. "You don't?"

He shook his head. "Óōnōúa, can't help you. But aren't there twelve of us?"

I sat down, feeling suddenly rather stupid. There *were* twelve of us, each with a different gift. Our brother A'nō had the most power of us all, being the first Guardian. *Right then, someone who does.* "Ask A'nō," I said to myself with conviction. "Dhindhē," I looked up to thank him, but Hor'e was already gone.

There was only one way to summon another Guardian and it required complete concentration, total mindfulness on the energy of that Guardian. In short, I was rubbish at it. But now the urgency of getting us to the other side of the land bridge burned bright inside my chest and I crossed my legs, sitting up tall with my palms slack against the warm rock underneath me and my tail loose behind me. I'd never seen A'nō in this life, but I knew well the golden luster of his essence from the days when we still roamed the night sky. It was this I pictured behind closed eyes.

I breathed in: *Fly thee to my side.*

I breathed out: *Do not ye delay.*

Over and over I sent out this message until my eyes flew open with a start and I found myself standing in a cave, its walls bright with the voices of Creation, its floor sparkling with the songs of time. In the center stood A'nō the Gatekeeper of Ebūda with a great staff he held against the continual circles of light ever-moving around him. He neither opened his mouth nor looked at me, but I could hear him speak directly into me.

You must be in some big trouble to have summoned me.

"I am! I got lost!"

I know what you did. I want to know what you want me to do about it!

"I have to get us to the other side so we can get back on track. I don't have any way of doing that. Can you give me some of your power?" my voice faded off. I wasn't even sure of what I was asking at this point.

Why should I give you power?

Not expecting to have to explain myself, I blurted out, "I don't know, because you're my brother and you love me?" I felt his laugh ripple through the light, tickling my brain behind my eyes until it ached.

Though it is true that love is the greatest weapon in the wars of the heavens, the name of the Law in the mortal world is Balance. If I transfer power to you in order to alter this world, I must exact an equal payment.

I felt tears immediately prick my eyes in frustration. "But I don't have anything! What can I possibly pay you with?"

He then looked over at me and I saw my brother's eyes questioning, wondering why I couldn't see what he already knew. *I have yet to meet a living being that couldn't afford a miracle.*

A single tear escaped me as I held out my hands to him in earnest. "Then take whatever it is you think I have and get us across to the other side."

He nodded, saying only, *Get ready.* Then in a grand movement he struck his staff into the ground at his feet and opened it, the blaze and sound suddenly displacing and churning around us into a pure crack of light like summer lightning; blinding and fiery.

I heard the words both in my mind and in my ears as the cave faded and with a jerk I woke to the hard ground below me, the cool twilight air chilled me. I turned immediately to Mi'hal̈ē and grabbed her, hoisting her with all my strength onto my back, unsure of what was to happen now, but resolved to keep us together.

The air became thin, strange to smell and the sky blanched, though it was now nightfall. As I looked down, I saw the ground below me falling, tsō, *we* were floating up! Still unconscious, Mi'halē drifted up away from me and I pushed myself through the air as if swimming to grasp her ankle. Using my own weight to pull her back, I quickly whipped off my headscarf and tied it around my shoulders and hers so that her chest was snug against my back. But below us, the rocks had begun to move.

Flailing my arms, grabbing at the air, I tried desperately to steer us forward as the rocks around us rose, merging together into a thick, arched formation. For a moment it seemed time stopped, and we floated high above this activity. But then I realized the landscape around us hadn't stopped at all. Below us, the sun rose and set, over and over. Shadows fell across the rocks, migrated and faded. Plants rose up from the salt flat, its blue-whiteness melting into green and just as quickly, fading back into that unclouded hue. "*Time*," I whispered, the notion dancing on the edge of my awareness.

I looked out across the horizon and saw tiny villages rise up from sand, to fall back down under flames. Miniscule análong danced, their music twisting up into the sky to break into shards and litter the rocks. Hadim sprang out from corners then seized and vanished into dust. Voices sang and shouted, cried and silenced until suddenly we began to float down and as my feet touched solid ground I heard once again in my mind the words "*Get ready.*"

I stood at the edge of the cliff, looking left to right at the channel below me, now flushed in clear flowing water parted here and there by little riffles where the waves laughed and flowed on. But in front of me a solid bridge of rock stretched over to the other side, to Adanandū. And all around this, all that could be seen began to move in a circle, melting and surrounding that stretch of rock to form a clear tunnel around it. Now I knew what I had to do.

Run!

Hoisting Mi'halē up on my back, I leaned over as far as I could without falling, put my head down and leapt onto the bridge, running with every ounce of strength I had until I reached the other side. Stumbling as soon as I cleared the bridge, I fell onto the dry, red ground cutting a gash into my knee. Bleeding, I pulled myself up and untied Mi'halē as she flopped onto the ground and rolled over, stretching into consciousness. She licked her lips as her eyes pried open.

I stood painfully and looked back, stunned to see the same dry, desolate channel we'd first come to the night before. *The night before?* It was now mid-day and if the world could be trusted, by the face of the moon peeping over the western sky I'd swear it was a month ago. I blinked and rubbed my eyes to make sure I saw what I thought I saw. "*Time*," I breathed again.

"Time? For what? Where are we?" Mi'halē questioned, her eyes focusing on the gap between where we now sat and where she last recalled. I looked her over and marveled at how bright her eyes seemed, how pink her cheeks bloomed. As if, as if the last month had never happened at all. Now it made sense, A'nō had bent time somehow back to before the Dhanga'lara Land Bridge collapsed and then folded it back to the present. The future?

I looked at my hands, captivated and pleased at their smooth backs, devoid of the scratches I'd gotten climbing up the rock table. A sudden sharp twinge reminded me the gash on my knee remained and I rubbed at it absently. I couldn't explain it, but clearly we had lost some of our own time in the process and it seemed to have done us nothing but good. We were both stronger, less damaged by the elements. *Less damaged by stupid things we may have eaten on the way.*

"How much of that salt did you eat?" I glared at Mi'hal̈e and she ducked her head before answering, "A lot. But it tasted good. And I'm all sparkly inside now!" she grinned.

I rolled my eyes. "Never do that again. *Water* is what you need, not salt." Electing not to tell her what had happened in the salt flats, I thought to myself, *Sparkles won't matter when you're dead.*

Mi'hal̈e rolled her eyes back. "So, where are we?" she asked again.

"Where we're supposed to be," I answered, and she smiled.

And it was true, we were now in Adanandū, well over halfway to Bri̇́en. So why did I, for the first time in my life, *feel utterly terrified*?

mi'hal'ē
24

growing into one's intentions

súan-én dashō na'éēshle
ta óō

I didn't know what had happened between the moment I lied down on the smooth rocks beyond the salt flat and the moment I sat up on the other side of the Dhanga'lara Land Bridge but whatever it was, it had left Éē'shī changed. *Scared*, somehow. But she wouldn't speak of it, and so I only had my imagination to fill in that story.

It was only a few days before we came to the town of Naulrū through the dry, red prairie marked by skeletons of brush and scutches of dead grass. The nights were cold but Éē'shī said a fire out here would only start a bigger fire so we slept back to back on the ground against any windbreak we could find. But I found I didn't feel the cold so much, in fact, since we'd left the land bridge. Actually, I felt a lot better than I had in weeks. The dead grass filled me in a cramped sort of way, and I sucked on one of the gummy dūūcerfrūt Éē'shī had hidden in the sack. And with these little sundries my head had the freedom from trying to fill my stomach to think. And to talk.

"Have you ever seen snow?" I wondered aloud as we sat on a gentle swell under a cloudless sky and studied the rows of neat huts in the distance that made up Naulrū. We stood to move on before Éē'shī answered.

"A long time ago," she observed absently. "It can't anymore though. The ground is too warm; it would just melt as soon as it fell."

"But still, what was it like?"

"It's said that snow is made of the tears of stars and that's why no two flakes are exactly alike."

I sighed happily, entranced. Then, leave it to Éē'shī to spoil things. "Snow is so cold it hurts," she went on, shivering dramatically to show me.

"How could something so beautiful hurt you?" I challenged, dismayed.

"Beauty is a quality that is in every living thing because each one carries a grain of the image of its Creator within it. It's a small word used to describe things that are lovely to the eyes. But because everyone is different and unique from each other, you can't say that beauty is the *same* quality in everyone," she looked back to make sure I was listening. "So, to one, snow may be a source of hope; to another, a source of pain."

"So," I began, my mind chewing on her words, trying to reach the conclusion she held out to me. "So, some análong might see me and be scared, but some might be hopeful?"

"Sort of. I mean that true beauty isn't something you can see only with your eyes so be careful with your words. Make sure you look hard to find the beauty inside all."

I thought of something else. "Is there ugliness in everyone too? Like when you want to do good but do something bad no matter how hard you try. Is there sort of an *ugly* bit in us; a bit that can't be good all the time?"

Éē'shī nodded. "There is. And as beauty is individual, so is evil. Everyone has their own temptations."

"Then we are *equal*? It that the word?" I tried it out.

She looked back and stopped for a moment to explain. "Beauty and evil, sorrow and joy are parts of life. They make us equal; no one can escape them. But hate and malice are things we invent ourselves. Those things are chains and they make us equal too for we are all prey to them. When someone treats us badly it feels like a chain choking us. And when they stop or we get away from them, the chains fall away. But we must always be careful that we don't carry on a wish to do the same to someone else, to wrap them in the same chains."

"Why not?" A little of someone's own medicine seemed logical to me. Most of the time I wanted the rest of the world to know what it felt like to be feared and separated. But deep inside what I really wanted was to be accepted and I wished I didn't. So, I listened carefully because the explanations I'd been given all my life of why I should treat others kindly had always seemed thin and one-sided.

"Because it seems like its power, doesn't it? To get even with someone and make them hurt too? But if we really look inside our hearts, I think we'll see that we don't really want to hurt anyone. We just want it to *stop*. And if we do repay someone with evil, we'll just be adding links to the chain that hurt us to begin with. That isn't power, it's allowing someone who hurt us to make us just like them. *Mercy* is the word you want. Mercy is when you have the power to hurt someone who hurt you and you use that power instead to be true to your own heart. Being true to who we are no matter what, that's the power we all come into the world with.

So, promise me something. Promise me you'll never give your power away for something so cheap as someone else's anger, or their spite, or their hatred."

Thinking on this, I was amazed at the idea that I may have some sort of power buried deep within and even more, that I may have the authority to use it. All my life I had been completely powerless, unable to do as I wished or go where I wanted. I was in *awe*. How much wider the sky seemed, how much broader the distant mountains now that I knew this.

"Sé Lamsáa is to the west," Éē'shī changed the subject and pulled me along to follow through a thicket of high reeds. I could see a faint wagon-tread some feet away and I said, "From all that growth I know that was a road, but nobody's been on it for a while. Right?"

Éē'shī nodded. "Well done. We'll follow it from here just in case anyone still comes this way. I think we'll end up going parallel to Sé Lamsáa and then we should hit Dináa."

I followed along, the names of the towns and villages and landmarks meaning nothing to me. Over the next weeks boredom plagued me as we spent the days tramping down the reeds under our feet, following their bends and turns to stay hidden. Everything before me was brown and pale, only when I looked out into the unbending sky could I see a grand motion, continual and just beyond my sight so that I could never see it with my eyes but rather inside in a silent place. And though I could only hear around me the constant *slash-crack-crashing* of dry reeds being snapped in half and trampled on, inside I heard the words beyond sound I had come to know as Mī'á's voice: *I am here.*

I was comforted in a way over the next few days by this and found myself to be agreeable until the reeds thinned out and we came to a grassless expanse of sandy soil where nothing could be seen to eat or drink or hide under. The sun seemed hotter than it had in days and I was uncontrollably itchy. Éē'shī had stopped several times as we made our way across the sand to pull me along as I tried in vain to scratch the sole of my foot.

Then in the flash of one second, everything that had seemed so dead and flat inside me, the story of the last few months of my life came alive with no warning and ripped through me as if it were a wild hadim leaping through my skin. I yanked away from Éē'shī. "I can walk by myself!" She reached out and slapped my elbow. "Then *walk*!" she snapped, stunned.

But I couldn't contain myself any longer and I stopped and picked up the first thing I saw, a small rock, and threw it as hard as I could, not aiming for her but not trying to miss either. "What do you think you're doing?" Éē'shī threw the sack down on the ground and flailed, trying to grab me and dodge me at the same time. I screamed without thinking, as loud as I could, the sound reverberating between my ears into my back teeth until Éē'shī's hand roughly clamped my mouth shut as she hissed into my ear, "Are you trying to get us killed? *Someone will hear!*"

The snap of a dry branch in the distance seemed to confirm this and she grabbed the sack and me and ran without looking where she was going. We hadn't gotten many steps before Éē'shī's foot stumbled on something and she pulled me back sharply behind her. "*S'bonala?*" I asked but she only hissed and looked down to where her foot had left a little break in the ground.

"Wha...?" she whispered.

We stood transfixed as the ground began to crumble below us and before I knew what was happening, it gave way. In a cloud of sandy dust and pebbles I fell straight through! Éē'shī thrashed her arms wildly, grabbing at me and the air but caught only a falling stone in one hand and my dress collar in the other, tearing it in one clean rip.

Stopping with a terrifyingly painful jolt, my feet swayed heavily below me and I looked up, clutching at Éē'shī's legs to hoist myself up. But she kicked at my hand, a scowl on her face as I saw her mouth to me, "*Stay still!*" An impossible thing to do over the roar of earth collapsing in around us, making way to a giant cavern held up along the edges by copper columns and rusted metal plates barely supporting the remaining ceiling. As we landed in a heap on a sort of platform cushioned by dirt we could see that the cavern sprawled out as far around us and I tried to lift myself up to see but was knocked back down by my body trying to expel all that grime out of my eyes and nose and mouth in rattling coughs.

Far below us, enormous glittering spikes bigger around than my waist jutted up from the floor of the cavern and above these, little square dwellings had been carved into the rock walls. Here and there platforms and broken bridges stretched out from one side to the other to connect these. But the drop below was dizzying, and I couldn't help but to reach out and grab Éē'shī 's tail to steady myself. She thrashed her legs at me again but lost her grip on the narrow stone ledge she'd held on steadily to and we plummeted straight down, the wind sucking up out of my chest in a painful squeeze not helped by her tail tightly wrapped around it.

The sack we'd been carrying weighed Éē'shī down faster than me and as I felt her tail squeezing me to get leverage, she grabbed at mine as I passed her up in the air and pulled me down tightly to her. *"Hang on!"* she yelled but I could barely hear her through the slapping of my own ears around my head in the wind.

Wham!

Éē'shī spat as we stopped against something solid. A sour, greenish liquid forced its way up out of me onto the floor, burning the inside of my nostrils. She pulled me up by the arm and my legs found wobbly ground below them. I looked around, clinging to Éē'shī's waist. We'd fallen straight into a wide, deep bucket of sorts, suspended by a thick rope and wooden hook. I tried to look out to the right to see just how far down we were but my weight tipped the bucket to a full, unsteady swing and Éē'shī swore as she pulled me to her, back to back, wrapping her tail around me again.

"I've got to tie you up before you get us both killed!" she hissed, pointing down to the spikes not so far down now underneath. "Now stay still and let me figure this out!" I stamped my foot in frustration and rocked us once more but couldn't break free from her tail. Now that we weren't going to fall right to our deaths I wanted to see!

"Well look at this," Éē'shī murmured. "This is En'chan'tén!"

"Ahn-shaan-tyen," I repeated.

"It was an underground city built to hide innocent prisoners. You won't find it on a map."

I pulled my ear in thought, wondering what an *innocent prisoner* was exactly.

Éē'shī studied the handle and rope above us and without warning, grabbed my hands and wrapped them around the bucket's handle. In one smooth motion she jumped up and then snapped it out of the hook and grabbed onto the bucket's brim around me. My stomach immediately dropped and I screamed, the cold sweat of terror pickling my cheeks. We went soaring along the rope line, the speed of it stealing my breath out through my nose and my fingers weakened to quaking jelly. "Don't let go!" Éē'shī shouted needlessly over the airstream, pulling her tail now so tightly against my middle I thought she'd slice me in half!

"Aaaaaaah!" my voice came bursting out of my throat with a stab. And then just as suddenly as we'd gone flying away in our bucket, we lurched to a stop as its handle stuck on a patch of knotted rope ended by another hook and we swung forcefully back and forth against the knot.

"Aaaaaaah!" *Bump!*

"Aaaaaaah!" *Bump!*

"Aaaaaaah!" *Bump!*

"*Ouch!*" Stop.

I was launched over the rim and couldn't move. But Éē'shī did. She pulled me off of the handle and carefully looked about us at the vacant city of rocky dwellings and roads below, now visible between the beautiful yet deadly crystals. "*Ndendrōs.* They grow in hot caverns where there's a lot of salt in the soil," she nodded at the razor-sharp columns of clear, glittering rock. Now that we had reached the city's center, I could see shafts of light streaming down from portholes in the bits of ceiling still intact above us. "They're sort of underground salt flats where the salt can just grow wild."

"Like the salt hills we used to go to," I observed.

Éē'shī squinted her eyes and surveyed the spectacular ruins. "Exactly. But it's abandoned in here now." True, I heard no singing in my ears and smelled no hearth-smoke in my nose. "How do we get out of here?" I whispered, my words swelling in the silence around us.

"Same way we got in. We fell down. We need to fall *up!*" Undaunted, Éē'shī motioned for me to grab on to the bucket's handle again and my backbone tensed beneath my skin as I thought of soaring again. Grabbing the sides, Éē'shī jumped up and launched the bucket over the hook it hung from and in a hard jerk over the rope's knot, plunged us on a steep angle downward.

My mouth opened wide to scream and I could feel it passing through my throat but the wind in my ears drowned my voice as the bucket flew so fast along its line that everything around me blurred into one streak of muted color. When we stopped this time the bucket pitched forward and threw Éē'shī out but she was still attached to me by the tail and I was able to help her back in. "This isn't *out.*" I worried when my voice came back, and I saw that we'd landed on a little bridge of sorts. There was nowhere to go but over it.

"We can't go where we can't go, so we'll go where we *can,*" she pointed out and I followed across the threadbare bridge, looking down through its boards at the cold, shining ndendrōs glittering meanly back at me. It was only the thought that I'd rather not die with a stake of rock through me that kept me going forward. Still, my brain wondered if it would taste like melon if I could get a lick.

At the end of the bridge sat another little bucket like the one we'd left behind just waiting to be of service; its handle attached to a much thicker rope and a set of pulleys visible way above us. "Going up!" Éē'shī called as we climbed in and she worked to yank on the rope and pull us up. "Help me!" she hollered over her shoulders and I pulled along with her, my arms burning with the effort.

Pull, pull, squeak, pull! Slowly we worked out way up, passing empty dwellings with mournful window-holes and silent roofs, ownerless shreds of clothing strung across the gulf. At the very top we came to a narrow platform and another hook. Éē'shī shoved me out and pulled herself up out of the bucket, letting it drop down to where we'd started with an echoing *bang* and a shower of fine dust.

Éē'shī looked around. "Let's see," she spied a small opening off in the distance and looked down at the edge of the platform to yet another bucket and line. "Almost there." This time I climbed in and tightly held the handle. Éē'shī put her hands outside of mine, gave a mighty push and jumped in behind me as we took off flying. By now my body had adjusted to the drop and a fragile thrill took over me, creeping up from my chest in little trembling fingers into my throat and pushing its way out of me in a long "*Eeeeeeeeeeeeeee!*"

The stop on the other side of the cavern wall was rough enough to push us back swinging for a bit before finally coming to a stop over another platform so tiny it barely held the bucket's width. Éē'shī carefully turned me backwards and transferred our sack to my back, then pulled herself up out of the bucket and bent backward to pull me onto her back. Bolted there to the wall was a narrow ladder and we scrambled onto it, Éē'shī climbing up quickly and pushing open the dusty porthole with a loud *cr-i-i-i-ick*. When we put our feet onto the hot, sandy land above, Éē'shī said pointlessly, "Step lightly."

I rolled my eyes deep back into my head and looked back down at the vast hole in the earth like a starving mouth waiting to eat us back up. Happy to be back above, I wasn't quite sure how to say sorry for trying to (not trying to) hit her in the face. I saw in a stroke of clarity what she meant about using my power. I was trying to punish her for what had happened to me when I was actually angry at someone else. Disappointed in myself, I felt my face pinch as if I would cry.

I have to grow into my intentions.

Taking a breath, I thanked Éē'shī for getting us back to solid ground. "You're really strong," I noted, thinking back to when she asked me if she was strong enough to be a Guardian.

But again Éē'shī seemed scared *after* we'd escaped. "Not strong enough," she murmured, and walked on, leaving me wondering as I skipped along to catch up.

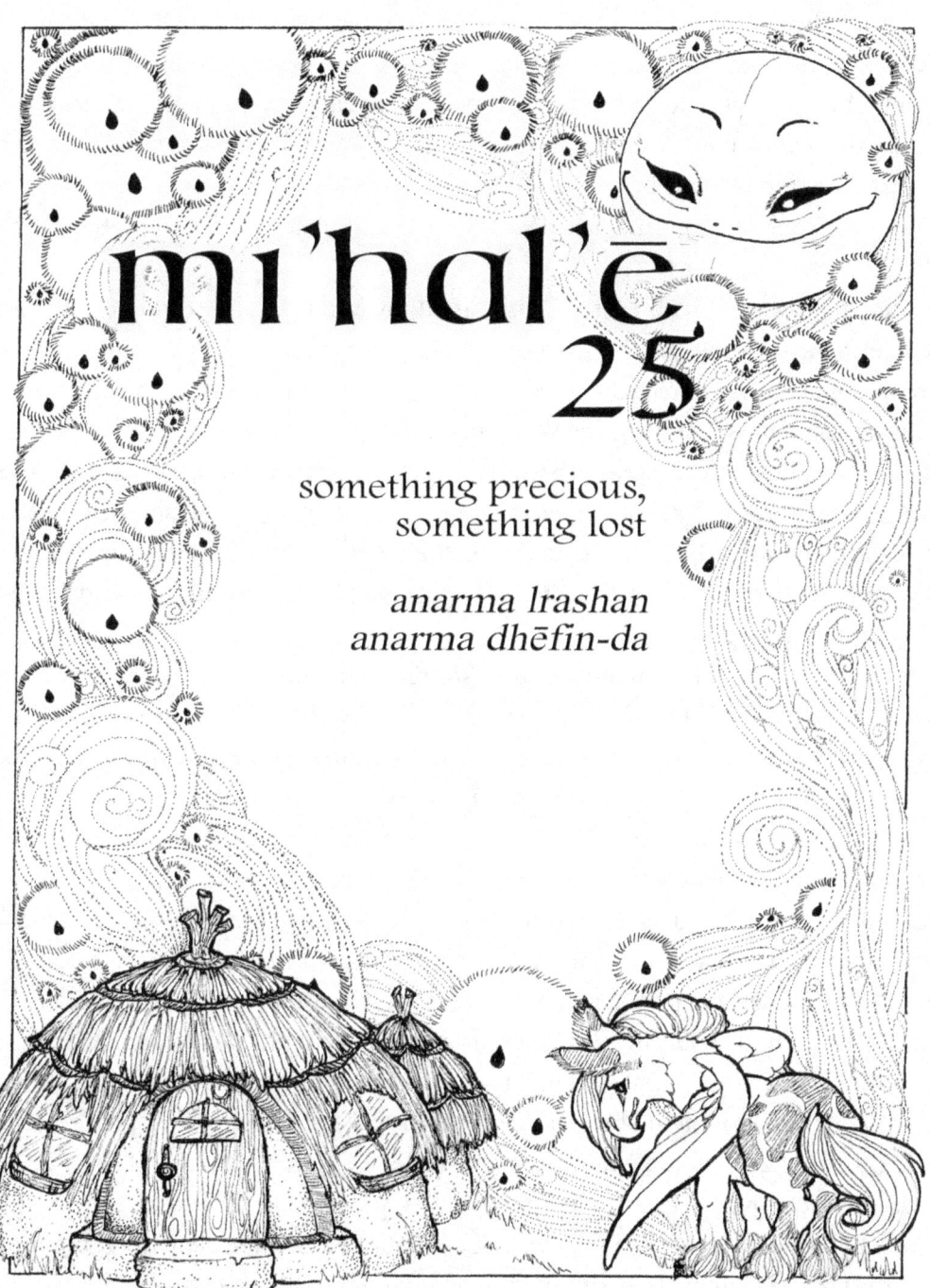

mi'hal'ē
25

something precious,
something lost

anarma lrashan
anarma dhēfin-da

*T*HE sky was still purple when I woke.

My back was sore right between my shoulder blades where a tree-root softly broke the earth below me and I shifted, sniffing at the distant smoke coming from Dináa village. We had come into the ghostly Acai'bhis forest six days before and Éé'shī noted the smoke over the horizon that told of análong still living there. By the color of the smoke she decided there might be food being cooked there and if so, she was willing to venture in. But I must stay as far behind as possible, as I had always done in Pōcarū. I would be invisible.

But for now, I lay and let my mind wander. The early chill made it easy to pretend I was home in the twilight…

Working the fields was difficult in itself without all my blunders and some nights when Dandhō came back late she would flop over her bed in exhaustion and I would lay on the floor and take her big hand in my small ones and trace the lines of veins and scars, marveling at the differences between us, observing the sameness, knowing she was much too tired to bat me away.

Absently I rubbed my hands, feeling the sharp cracks at my knuckles, feeling the emptiness between them. Éé'shī shifted beside me under the dry leaves, creating a loud shuffle of little snaps and rustles. It couldn't be helped; the trees had shed their leaves long ago to diminish their need for water. Now they were bare and brittle, just as we were becoming. Again, I studied my hands, their fine covering of hair disappeared.

Dináa was further from the Acai'bhis than Éé'shī realized, and before we left the forest she took the knife from our sack and made a hole in the trunk of a large tree, inserting a stiff, hollow reed into it. Sitting up underneath it, she sucked slowly on the end of the reed until a thick but reliable flow of liquid dripped down and we were both able to drink a bit of the bland sap. "This tree is almost out of water. The sap is nearly thick as resin," Éé'shī muttered as she held up our nearly-forgotten canteen to fill it for the first time in who knew how long.

She gathered up the sack and started off to Dináa but I lingered for a moment. "Dhindhē," I said softly, knowing we had taken some of the tree's own life-blood to keep ourselves going. The great being shook its crown and creaked as it slowly bowed its lowest and smallest branches to me. As I reached up and took ahold of one, my skin glowed and sparkled with gold as it had when the onandals had said goodbye, and this force traveled up along the tree's branches, bathing it in the same sparkle before fading away. For a moment I became aware of the old hardwood's dim spirit reaching out and then receding. Letting go, I waved goodbye and ran after Éé'shī to catch up.

It was amazing how lively I felt and as I began to skip beside Éé'shī, the two days of walking to Dináa seemed to take only half as long. "There," Éé'shī pointed as I dawdled, dragging the toes of my shoes in the dust to make lines. In between the rolling hills lay Dináa completely hidden by a high, wooden wall unlike any we'd ever seen. "Over those hills to the north should be Lake Óngalora," she murmured. "I imagine it must flood here; the ground is pretty low. That must be why the wall's so high."

It made sense, for as we came nearer the open gateway into the village was clear to be seen and could be raised or lowered unlike most villages that were built open to walk through. The stale stench of smoke still hung in the air but there were no other signs from the outside that anyone remained within, and there were no openings in the wall to see into. "I'm going in," Éē'shī announced and handed me the sack, pointing to a nearby depression in the ground to sit in. I dropped down, close to the wall so I could hear but comfortably low enough not to be seen.

I closed my eyes for a moment, straining my ears to hear anything but after a few minutes of the bland hum of a far-off wind my mind began to wander and I shifted around in my space, looking for something to entertain myself with. Finding nothing but a few errant twigs, I sat upright when a sharp ribbon of light washed over the ground and I rolled over expecting to see the familiar outline of a cloud.

At home, I watched the sky every day for the pudgy, rolling clouds who held not just rain but surely the answers to where I came from. Their fat, white, smiling faces whispered to me every morning by the windowpanes, unlike the thin, wispy streaks over the fields too busy to stop and have a chat with me. So, the flavor of disappointment on my tongue was sharp when I saw the cloud was made of acrid smoke now billowing over the eastern side of the wall. "Éē'shī!" I exclaimed, then threw myself back down into my hiding space, flattening against the hot earth when I heard a voice that wasn't hers.

Carefully, I pulled up just enough to peep over the turf. To my amazement, a few yards away dirt could be seen flying up out of the hill in metered spurts.

"I can't believe it," someone mourned. "A'ma's gone. A'da's gone. I'm an orphan!"

The dirt stopped suddenly and two g'ēalach emerged and sat down, gazing stoically back at a deep, fresh hole. After a while, one put her head on the other's shoulder and said, "We must all become orphans someday. Either our parents leave us behind to go into the next life, or we leave them behind in this one."

And I would have understood right then if Éē'shī hadn't grabbed me from behind, clamping her hand over my mouth to silence me. "I've got something you're going to like," she whispered and together we scrambled out and down the slope to avoid being seen. "What's in the bag?" I asked, spying the cloth in her hand. "You'll see," she smiled mysteriously.

As soon as we'd crossed out of the slopes and into higher hills, she sat down and opened the bag. I gasped as several moldy buns, a flask and a tin full of dried fruits came tumbling out. "First," Éē'shī handed me the flask. "It'll help you stand." So, she'd noticed how shaky I felt when I stood. Though I didn't want her to know, I was relieved she did because it scared me to think one day I might not be able to get up at all. I contentedly slurped at the metallic-tasting liquid. "What is it?"

Éē'shī shrugged. "Found it. Doesn't smell bad so we should be good."

I stopped mid-swallow and handed the flask back to her. She shook her head and pushed it back. "Drink it."

For the first few weeks we'd made our way away from the hut, hunger made its way through me with the force of a storm-wind, puncturing my stomach with cramps so hard as to fold me in two. Its angry, impatient nature didn't limit it to just my middle but allowed it to spread out into my joints, demanding with every snap and prick that it be answered with food. As time went on it didn't care what constituted as food as long as its howl was replied to, and my mind became completely satisfied and indeed, giddy, over sucking on stones or loosening my teeth on bark.

Yet eventually even hunger lost its strength and its power declined to a continual, hard pinch throughout me that took no rest, as if it were some sort of compromise between us. The moldy buns, though musky and unpleasant to the tongue, satisfied us both for long enough to make me think all would be fine in the end.

The next day we started off late to begin with and Éē'shī wasn't happy. In the last vestiges of morning we emerged from over the crest of the hill at the heat's peak to a vast, sunken plain the color of dark cream. As far as we could see, the dusty, smooth land was divided into deep, searing cracks which became smaller and more intricate as they neared the tufted edge where we stood. Nothing seemed to have ever grown here, except the cracks radiating outward as far as one could see.

"Lake Óngalora, once." Éē'shī fidgeted with the hem of her dress, something I did all the time but had never seen her do. When she didn't pull me along impatiently, I stepped gingerly along the lake bottom. Entranced with its smoothness, I reached down and tried to push my finger in a solid square between the cracks but found that the top was covered in fine dust and not the mud I thought it was. The land had dried to rock.

I couldn't help but to smooth my feet along back and forth, skating forward with glee. But Éē'shī saw nothing novel about it. She hung back, eyes huge, as if the cracks might swell open and swallow her into the very sod. It struck me that she was afraid, and Éē'shī was *never* afraid. Unsure of what to do, I gave a friendly wave to her, beckoning her to catch up with me. When she didn't respond I ran back as she would have done, grabbed her by the arm and yanked her on to the other side where I let go and the both of us tumbled onto the bank. Dazed, she sat up and shook her head.

"My turn again," I reminded her, and she nodded faintly. I ducked my head, trying to meet her downcast eyes. "You're not scared, are you?" I asked. "We've got bread and water and fruit, what more do we want?" My cheerful voice annoyed even me.

"I don't know what it is," Éē'shī said slowly. "Ever since…" she sighed. "I wasn't scared, that's the thing. *I wasn't.*"

"Dandhō says only idiots aren't scared of anything and only liars say they aren't," I chirped on, dusting myself off and twirling around to pull Éē'shī up. She dug her heels into the embankment and pulled hard on my elbows to right herself.

"It was a lake-bed," she said quietly. "We crossed the narrow point, but it stretches on and on. All that water just done. So much time, just gone."

And in that second, those two words, *time* and *gone* came together in my mind and I recalled the words of the two ǧéalach outside of Dináa: *we either leave our parents behind for the next world, or they leave us behind in this one. We all must become orphans.*

I knew logically it was likely that the Naóma had taken over the lands behind us, that most of Drīdū was by now probably destroyed under their evil deeds. But somewhere in my heart there was the little belief, shining and pure, that Dandhō and Little Dandhō were still working the fields and tending the shop and going home at night to the hut without me. It wasn't until that moment that I put these pieces together in that wretched flood of understanding that I realized the lonely little hut wasn't behind me waiting for me to return.

My insides stilled and became heavy, too exhausted to bear one more certainty. For as Dandhō once said strangely when I found the picture by her bed turned toward the wall, loss was a thing never felt so keenly when it happened, but only *after*.

"I'll never see them again, will I? My asama is gone." I stared at Éē'shī, waiting to make sure I was right. I'd learned so many lessons of death; how different creatures died, what we did when they died, the clothes we wore and the words we said. I would learn the emptiness it left behind, that unfillable hole that made little pictures in my mind and tricked me into thinking there was something behind me to go back to even if we'd now been gone so long, I couldn't properly remember what I wished to go back to.

I would learn that death was never final; it demanded to be acknowledged every day in case we should forget it had ever transpired. And now this was the final lesson of death that would seep into me, pressing down on my very bones: that regardless of love or hate in this world, death, like birth, came without our permission.

Éē'shī answered, "Not in Ebūda. You cannot see them again here."

I stood fingering my empty pocket, angry I'd been so foolish all this way. Every time I saw Little Dandhō's sparkling, phantom smile in the morning rays of sun, every morning I woke up sure Dandhō's ghostly fingers pressed into my palm, every step I took truly believing the hut trotted behind me were only reminders that I didn't know anything about anything.

"Are they like the lhēsha?" I choked out, climbing clumsily onto her lap. All trace of fear now gone, Éē'shī snapped into her old self and held me tightly. "Shě'á, they're like the lhēsha. There was a purpose for each of them to be in your life. They were the first part of your journey."

We rocked back and forth for a long time, long enough that eventually my eyes slid shut and the tears gummed around my throat into a pleasant, hazy feeling. Though my heart felt empty, the heaviness of exhaustion weighted it into apathy so that I was able to quietly drift in my mind, all the happiness of earlier dissolved.

Everything goes. My ah'sha had said that, and she would say it now.

Once she told me this story: When she was a dhana the village teacher said to her, "Look at the river. Look at all the análong washing. Can any of them say to it, go the other way Great River? Turn around and leave Drīdū! Tsōl. Even if all of them stood side by side with swords and arrows, they could not stop its flowing. Yet even one day the river will dry and wither."

Then he said, "Look at the moons over the sea. Can you say to them, fall down from the sky Tsāi'ín! Move to the west, Gōl! Tsōl. Even if all the análong built the tallest tower they could not reach the sky to pull down the moons. But one day even those will crumble and fall."

But when Dandhō was sent to the Palace in Bri'én, she was taken to the highest place by her teacher who said to her, "Look down over all the city. See its spires, its marketplace, the dhana at their lessons, the servants at their work. But one day, these things will vanish. For all things pass. No thing goes on forever, not least the análong."

Then Dandhō drew a long breath on her pipe and sat back against the hot doorstone and said, "*As long as nature endures, so will the análong. But nature has her limit and when she has reached it, then so will the análong reach theirs. We are not everything; there were those before us and there will be those after.*"

Perhaps she was trying to say something larger about life but now as I saw her in my mind drawing on her pipe all I could think was that she was wrong; we were everything. Éé'shī and I were all each other had left. My tired thoughts slowed, and I begin to fall into a dreamless pit, hearing my voice deliberately ask, "Are you my dandhō now?" And her voice echoed back above me, "Now."

And when I finally looked up again hours later, the flat pale sky had diffused into a dark, warm purple and over the dim I could see the silhouette of Éé'shī gazing out over the border, protecting us as she did night after night.

There was a crack in my heart, a fracture that had silently worked its way open along the way to Bri'én by a trickle of sadness that had grown into a stream of tears unwilling to pour over. I'd been cracked and opened like an egg, and I lie staring at the starless sky, emptier inside than hunger had ever left me. Lost.

Ah'sha…

She would have told me that sadness was nothing to hide from, but an indicator that something precious had been lost. How fitting then that the southern meaning of ah'sha was *precious*.

éē'shī

26

the cost of balance

m'rintsle ihn énshen

1 wasn't afraid; that is, I hadn't been.

Before we'd crossed the Dhanga'lara I wasn't bothered by sorrow or danger because I knew the ending of this particular story and I was at peace with it. Once we reached Bri'én I would hand Mi'hal̊e to Rā-alta and my time in Ebūda would come to its end at some point soon after. I wasn't concerned with the when or the how, knowing my siblings before me had done the same to lead up to this very moment.

But despite the short boost of energy from the experience of crossing to the other side, I became ever more aware of my own body and its limits. My legs twitched and cramped where they hadn't before; my chest hitched and twinged. My mind wondered if something was wrong, if I were perhaps dying right now, before schedule? The ache in my jaw from chewing on grasses and twigs traveled up behind my eyes to settle deeply in my ears and gave me shivers. Even the little cracks in my fingernails seemed to foretell of disaster.

What had A'nō taken as his payment? I began to wonder, embarrassed that Mi'hal̊e had to get me across Lake Óngalora. I thought it must be my courage until the next day when we set off again after the terrible realization to Mi'hal̊e that her asama were dead. Now her footsteps were heavy, wistful, and her eyes dead of their usual spark. Hauling herself up under the weight of such loss and pulling me along dazedly through the empty village of Enúalaeiá was courage. All the steps of my life had been arranged; there was little unknown to me except the few insecurities I had that I'd muck things up. Courage had never been required of me.

Could I have been accused of apathy, that distant cousin of bravery so often mistaken for its twin? Perhaps it'd been so easy to pull Mi'hal̊e along through whatever came at us because I really didn't care what happened outside of me. After all, I knew my own temporary nature. Only Mi'hal̊e had to survive to bring caémba. I was the Guardian, not the star.

Tsō, I decided. Apathy wasn't the price of the passage into Adanandū, it was *confidence*. Confidence, because where before there were calm, sensible answers now a million questions arose inside me each demanding an immediate reply. How could I have known so absolutely only a few weeks ago that no matter what happened I would finish my task? Now from the moment I awoke I couldn't stop from wondering, *how can I?*

"Ée̊shī!" Mi'hal̊e exclaimed, yanking me out of introspection. She pointed at the wide expanse of land surrounding us as we stepped out from the village's boundaries. Beyond the stretch of clean flatlands a faint blue swell could be seen emerging, ephemeral in the smoke that rose from what lay before us: the remains of the Bashō fields.

The very bones in my legs seemed suddenly hollow and I dropped to my knees, shaken. The small stuffs of food and clothes we'd found in Enúalaeiá did nothing to fill or warm me now as I gazed in mourning at what were once the proud and mighty Bashō trees. Tubby and squat, their enormous trunks tapered high above into intricate little branches, crown-like and laden with the soft puffs of cotton famously gathered every year to make cloth.

The weight of their spirits still hung in the air as we neared them in shock, stepping gingerly over both the dry, sharp grass and the arbitrary scorch marks from old fires ridding the world of who-knew-what.

It took us most of the morning to reach their remains and we stood staring for some time, Mi'hal'ē trying to reconcile what she'd heard F'ala tell her of this important field with the wreck of fallen branches and splintered trunks littering the area. In an act of particular offense against the aná-long's beliefs of trees being the grandparents of Ebūda, someone had alternately taken a hatchet to or burned most of the trees here, smashing their delicate crowns and robbing every bud of cotton. "The grandmothers have fallen," I breathed in disbelief. "The grandfathers have died."

"Ōna'a'ma, Ōna'a'da," Mi'hal'ē echoed, grasping my hand tighter. If anything were to frighten me into turning back from Bri'én, this was it. For I wasn't part of this world, but during my time in Hala-Asal I came to respect the Bashō if only on the strength of the beliefs of the análong. I too found myself believing that they were sacred and untouchable by evil. I too had had confidence in the steadfast things of this world.

I pitched myself forward, holding out a hand to Mi'hal'ē, hoping to keep busy and focus on something other than my foreboding fear. "Come on, get up on my back and I'll carry you a bit." She climbed clumsily onto me and held onto my neck and I managed to stand precariously, balancing both her and the sack I now tied around my waist.

The great hill of Bri'én still watched from deceptively far-away in the haze of smoke darkening the air around it. Only those coming to the city to trade come through the Bashō forest so there would be the outlines of well-traveled roads on the other side to follow and there were, albeit now faint.

All roads must lead to Bri'én, I thought and staggered along under my sister slowly, telling myself I must help her now that her heart had become so very heavy and the way may be even harder in the city. It was my turn again.

Along the road we stopped to camp overnight in a dusty depression where the road seemed to disappear. But in the morning the fog wasn't as heavy and looking up, we discovered we'd stopped under a scattered row of abandoned, squarish huts propped up on stilts, rising up ghostly from the parched land. Upon the bottom of each hut's stilts dark ragged rings circled, matching the stale patterns on the ground where water had once receded slowly to its end. There was no way to scale the poles to reach shelter from the sun but as we reached the end of these structures, we camped a night underneath them, the air punctuated by the soft swish and crunch of thatch sheaves slowly coming undone above us in the breeze.

Mi'hal'ē was up first the next morning, staring out before us at the near-wall of fog. "Why is it so dark?" she asked but I couldn't say, other than to suppose there was still enough water in Bri'én to evaporate and saturate the air. This made sense. While most análong were subject to the generosity of the skies for their everyday water, the city had its own water collection saucers that drained down into the Cāilon to be pumped back up by manual cycles through pipes into the city for bathing and washing. The city itself was built on a hill, but the saucer system was built into the chain of smaller hills surrounding the city to funnel runoff water. If nothing else, we could expect a bath and a drink once we reached the Palace and found Rā-alta.

Yet, the air smelled stale rather than humid, and as we walked on it became thicker; so much so that it ate up all sense of distance. I couldn't help but yelp when I stepped down and found my foot sinking slightly.

We squinted our eyes to make out the wilted stalks of an inlen forest, their eerie, thin trunks folded over in half. While it seemed they had given up, sweet relief flooded over me as I recognized we were probably less than a day to the city. Under the shade of the canopies, a few standing trees had curled upward against themselves in the beating sun to allow gentle shafts of light to leak through and dapple the ground. I tried to enjoy some of the golden afternoon light dotting the slender peeling trunks, but my comfort was over as soon as it began.

We were indeed close to the city, but we must pass through the inlen forest and so many of the vast, round canopies had fallen that they covered the ground like a gruesome carpet. My stomach lurched with unexplained nausea, my palms broke out in a thin sheen of sweat and I found that foreboding sense of doom press against my chest. I felt as if the very ground would open up and eat me.

"Don't look down," Mi'halĕ said calmly.

"What?" I said too loudly.

"They're really weird," she nodded in agreement to my unspoken thoughts. "Here, take my hand and don't look down." When I hesitated, she grabbed my hand roughly and pulled, warning, "Remember all that stuff you promised me when we got to Bri'ĕn? All the toys I could have? Well I do so let's go."

I allowed myself to be led along, repeating *go, go, go!* over and over in my mind with my eyes half-closed to reach the opening of the forest where we came abruptly past one of the water collection saucers perched lonely atop its little hill. I sniffed; flat. "Listen," I stilled my sister and we stood straining our ears. "I don't hear anything," she said. "We should," I thought aloud, "The na'bōmens are really loud."

Mi'halĕ shrugged and I pulled her back up onto my back. "Nearly there," I promised and forced myself to weakly go forward. My mind begged for rest and my body screamed for it, but I could not stop. I recognized the smooth, wide path from the water collection saucer leading up to the outer gate of Bri'ĕn so surely I could make it that far. If I made it there, I could go on into the city wall and higher still, to the Dhang'r where Rā-alta was waiting. We only had to find an alley to shelter for the night unseen.

My feet screamed out hot against me, a trickling feeling running down my legs tortured me to take off my wrappings to check if it was sweat or blood or both, but I couldn't stop now. I knew there would be a gatekeeper to contend with ahead, but I put this out of my mind until we actually came to the place. *One thing at a time,* I reminded myself over and over; we hadn't come this far to be turned away by a mere gatekeeper.

"Pull your scarf down over your face," I said to Mi'haľē, "Stay still and pretend you're sick."

But when we came upon him, he'd already met his end and I moved on as quickly as possible, for on top of the striped pole the gatekeeper balanced on to call out his warnings clung his charred remains to sing no more, and the gate hung open in the wind. The upper portion of this creaked randomly, making old silvery sounds as the stagnant air hung about its intricate bars. The delicate metal chains swaying haphazardly and the shine from its famous crystal beads were no longer lustrous but harsh to the eye.

I felt Mi'haľē's grip tighten on my neck and I kept my head down, feeling the cold stain from their reflection spread over my ears as I edged my way in. Blurry voices remained here in my memory, the calling of greetings underneath the metallic passageway and cartwheels mingled with bells and footsteps. But I shook this from my mind and hefted Mi'haľē back up between my shoulder blades, listening for something material; hearing nothing but the low hum of vacancy. Where was this fog coming from?

Now the wrappings had begun to unravel on my left foot, but I walked on with purpose, steeling myself for anything else unexpected. From over the outer wall little could be seen curls of weak smoke coming up from here and there but the feeling inside me sunk deeper and deeper as I neared the inner wall's entrance and heard the solid, booming beat of a solitary hand drum in the distance; the hallmark signal of the Naóma.

Just inside the inner wall surrounding the great city where the Serdaga marketplace once flourished, I lifted my head up and sniffed the air, listening to the past, to drops of the echoes of morning voices and happiness still lingering over forgotten toys in the street. Transposed over the grey arches and dim stone hung brilliant stretches of dyed cloth na'dhana once ran their fingers through, so bright I could remember them with open eyes.

Here and there between lonely blackened windows I caught the memory of trinkets and laughter caught in the panes, joyful tears frozen on the glass. The sacred city was like no other place in Ebūda; and because I had been given a different task than that of the others, I was allowed to watch Bri'én from afar live a life all its own with a different song and cycle of festivals and customs found nowhere else. And just as the magic and joy within the hilled city could never be replicated, neither could its evil. It was a balance that must be maintained, or the Elders knew that the city would fall.

Sprinkled on the wind I could hear a faint tinkling coming from the door-chimes of huts and shops half-burned, and though I still heard that ominous heartbeat of the NaÓma somewhere waiting for us, I feared we'd come upon a city of the dead, a soundless grave devoid of Ebūda's continual song.

"Óōnóúa," I breathed in apology.

Mi'haľē slipped down onto her own feet and stared around silently, straining against my hand heavy on her shoulder to keep her close by. "Where are they? Where are all the análong?" she whispered. "Isn't this the great city?"

I nodded slowly, murmuring, "It's here somewhere, still." Shě'á, somewhere in the Book of Moon, my brothers Sada and Narū kept the chronicle of the análong. But here lie a city unrecognizable to me.

Where there had once been sections of clean road winding through spiraling scarlet temples and mysterious gardens there now lay the crammed, burnt ruins of makeshift huts with interconnected roofs in every available space. My grip on Mi'haľē's hand tightened when I realized there was no visible way up into the main city but through this grey, never-ending smaller city of ruin. It was now that I would've welcomed shoes, but at least we'd made it thus far. I shivered, knowing that the Palace would be heavily guarded to keep the Elders safe if the rest of the city had fallen so low. How would we get past that? Would I be able to simply wave Rā-alta's ring to gain admittance as F'ala had promised?

Rā-alta had to be out there, there was no other alternative. "Is anybody in there?" Mi'haľē asked, pulling on my hand to point to a darkened block of huts. "Tsō," I replied. "This is the Cāilon-da, the slum. Just hold on to my hand and try not to think about what's under your feet."

My thoughtless direction was easier said than done for as soon as the ground below us began to squelch, my stomach turned up into my throat. The stench immediately enveloped us and I knew without doubt that not only had análong very recently lived here amongst the broken bowls and blood-soaked bits of cloth sticking up from the ash; if we looked in the blackened doorways we would see that they'd recently died there as well, slumped unceremoniously where their lives had stopped.

"Keep up," I pulled my sister along, trying to spot some sort of direct route out into the city proper. After sliding through what seemed miles of faceless, nameless streets etched out in the slop below us, Mi'haľē and I exited the Cāilon-da which I could tell by its remnants had only grown more crowded during clashes with the NaÓma who must have forced the residents downward from their homes higher up on the protected hill of the Dhang'r.

As we finally walked into the light out from under the maze of dark roofs, Mi'haľē gasped and stopped to gaze around, her hand pulling from mine to point at a circle of red-lacquered, heavily ornamented roofs. "Look at all the red!"

I nodded, leaning down to rub my knees in relief. "The city has many names: Rūa an Gaú: *the red city*, Béanda an Gaú: *the beautiful city*, Hingshoú an Gaú: *the shining city*. These are temples, just like F'ala's shrine. Look at the doorways and around the bottoms of the walls. See all that extra wood? It's padding to make sure nobody touches the red paint."

"Because red is the color of blood and life and holiness," she intoned, listlessly running her finger around the doorframe before moving away, uninterested.

I guided her away from a round glass dome in the street fitted in gold casing I guessed was an entrance down into the Cāilon underground. We turned down into a covered alleyway and silently walked side by side under its curved eaves, intent on spotting anyone else before they spotted us. As a doorway became visible on the right, I pulled us both in thinking it a shortcut to the street parallel.

Inside we opened our eyes to adjust to the soft light peering in through the rough, open window-holes, the air's dust making the streams of low light patchy and iridescent. The walls were smooth, somewhat like the walls of F'ala's hut but these were blackened at the base with curling paint, its sheaves sloughing off towards the high ceiling where tiny little scrolls of ash still clung. Outside, I spied the little covered coves below the windows where birds had huddled, leaving their evidence of white marks trailing down below.

Exiting from the far doorway we did indeed cross over to another street, stone-laid between a row of round thatch huts blackened by flame. The absence of the na'bōmen's steady creaking became suffocating. The anticipation of a voice, a drip, something other than the intermittent thrum of the hand drum still in the distance overwhelmed as did the pervasive fog.

Oblivious to this, Mi'halē stumbled on beside me breathing shallowly through her open mouth. In and out of the streets we wound our way around thatch and roundhouses, coming closer to the smoke hanging over our heads somewhere in the vicinity of the drum.

In the labyrinthine maze of huts, we passed under the long, skeletal spirals that once were the frame of the upper road traveled by darna messengers and their carts, covered in dead vines and curled, black flowers. Like the tree-huts of Peridūr where darna dwelled, here the pillars where the crumbling system began were built around the trunks of large trees hollowed out near the base for northern travelers to lodge in. Somehow, looking down at this from my comfortable space in Hala-Asal they seemed so small and quaint but from here the enormity of them seemed to remind me yet again of how small I was, how fragile. Helpless.

"How do you know where we're going?" Mi'halē asked quietly without looking up. "The Palace sits at the very top of the city, so we have to keep going up." I explained, then looked around for a doorway to hole up in for the night.

A small row of roundhouses that were typical of the centerlands sat at the end of the next alleyway and the state of their dilapidated rooftops told me just how long it'd been since anyone had lived in them. Like the graveyard those months ago with its smooth ground, these too bore the hallmark of time passed, time lost in wandering. Or perhaps all these things had occurred even back when we slept peacefully in F'ala's hut. Or, maybe even before.

I looked through each hut, searching for one with something soft and dry to lay on and luckily found a small bed. We shared a few of the dried fruits left from our sack and lay down warily but happily, thinking only of how wonderful it would be when we reached the Palace. Because regardless of what devastation lay before us, we both thought without doubt that our suffering was near its end.

The cold, late afternoon light streamed through the small holes and cracks in the hut's domed ceiling, reminding me of starlight and I rested my head against the wall before slipping down onto the old mattress to close my eyes. The last thing I recalled was a cold breeze blowing across my face as I slipped into a restless sleep, oblivious to my quest. It was the deep, animal-like roar of a bōmen that wrenched me awake.

ée'shī
27

a lullaby of drums

imtrit ihn na'adum

RUE to my suspicions, we did come upon someone.

There were so many little open squares hastily plundered and left to rot, we were able to pick up the spoiling dregs of what had been left behind the closer to the Dhang'r we came. But instead of easing the ache deep inside us or bringing strength to our weakened limbs, the food came right back out as if it were poison. "Slow down," I advised, pushing a flattened dūūcerfrūt out of Mi'hal'e's hand. "We'll be there soon, and the Elders can help." *And they must*, I thought, taking note of the swollen, weeping red cracks on her arm visible as her jacket sleeve slid up.

Tom-tom-tom-tom!

The distant hand drum was no longer distant but striking out the heartbeat of the survivors left in this quarter of the city.

The air became old and thick and rank and I pulled the top of my dress over my face and indicated Mi'hal'e do the same as we shifted through as quickly as possible. Suddenly I heard muffled voices coloring the grey air. Pulling Mi'hal'e to my side, I wedged us up inside a narrow corner between two huts to scout out who the sound was coming from.

The voices became louder. Mi'hal'e sat down on the ground and pulled her knees up as I stood to see if I could determine the direction of the sound. Carefully and silently I pushed Mi'hal'e in through a broken window and motioned for her to stay put. With great difficulty, I climbed the little ladder to the roof and pulled myself up the thatch that had begun to collapse down one side.

Below me could be seen a small band of NaÓma, the skeletal, painted warriors who had terrorized all Ebūda had somehow infiltrated the sacred city. There was one emaciated g'ealach, face painted white and a necklace of teeth around his neck. Two darna, their wings raggedly hacked off at the scapular stood watch behind him and beside them a heavily scarred shanár had two young she-dogs cornered. The item in dispute was a bucket of brackish water.

I couldn't turn my eyes away as the she-dogs defended their water with a broken broom until one of the NaÓma managed to kick it away from them and the four closed in and beat the both of them with fists and feet, one blow after another. A sound of disgust escaped my lips, but it was drowned out by the terrible screams as each blow thudded rhythmically, pounding into my chest as if they'd been launched directly on me.

I pressed my hands to my mouth so hard I thought I'd break my wrists, crouching behind the rooftop until the sound stopped altogether and I recognized the sounds of greed coming from the NaÓma when they took their spoils. Turning away, I discovered Mi'hal'e silently peeping over the roof as the awful, demonic rhythm of the hand drum started up to announce their victory to anyone who remained to hear.

Unconsciously, my mouth filled with saliva as I watched them finish off the entire bucket greedily. I could see their glutinous eyes had lost all sign of their shine; all sign of life itself. They didn't even turn when a small figure snuck out from under a collapsed roof behind them armed with a fitted bow and sling. A sharp sigh beside me confirmed that this was the same dhana from the forest, the dhana Mi'hal̈e had given her berries to.

With great precision he quickly shot the NaÓma nearest him square in the neck and reloaded his bow, shooting the next two just as quickly with the deadly aim of a hunter. The beat of the drum stilled among the dying cries around it. Refitting his bow and kicking away the fallen drum from his first victim's hand, he faced the last NaÓma and spoke for this last one had regained his balance and taunted the dhana as if he were too coward to kill him. "Go ahead pinūpi, we took you in and fed you and now you would kill us. Who's going to take you now?" the last sneered. The dhana looked at him coldly and aimed at his throat. "You showed me all of Ebūda, and then you destroyed it. And are you so uncouth to kill and then drink with warm blood on your hands?"

Instantly the NaÓma fell onto the pile of his dying fellows, the sneer fading from his lips as the arrow's tip plunged into his voicebox. For a moment more I watched the dhana rip the drum to shreds, then smear his body paint off in the water bucket's remaining drops before kicking it violently across the square. I pulled Mi'hal̈e down below the edge of the roof and strained my ears to hear him leave before I could allow us to move on.

Mi'hal̈e put her arms around my shoulders from behind. "I'll carry you when we get down," I whispered. "I can walk," she said back and pulled away. After some time, I heard a loud pop and carefully I looked out over the thatch again. Here and there I saw shallow pools of stale blood and bits of rancid cloth and I realized the dhana had rolled the bodies atop one another and set them afire.

Immediately I threw up over the roof without warning from the smell of decay. Mi'hal̈e pressed her nose into my side. Swallowing the slick liquid fire inside me, I wasn't sure I could go on. The urgent questions began to crowd into my thoughts again. What if there were more NaÓma ahead? It was one thing to know such horrors were out in the world, another to see them before me. *I don't think I can make it to the Palace,* I suddenly thought and froze. My legs grew heavy; paralyzed. *How am I even going to get back down?*

Mi'hal̈e's little hand snaked up through the crook of my elbow and yanked until I lost my balance, sliding down through the thatch and down the ladder in one bungling move to the hard sod of the alley. Mi'hal̈e followed close behind and fell directly on me in a bone-jarring huff. She pushed herself up precariously, her clothes black with ash, her face deeply scratched along the cheek. My back seized up painfully and I didn't want to get up.

Lying for a moment, I uttered, "If we get separated, you've got to keep going. Don't look for me, don't wait for me. Just keep going up and stay out of sight. You can't pass the Palace. Understand?"

"Where are you going to go?" Mi'hal̈e's face blanched.

"Promise me!" I said in a stern voice F'ala would have been proud of.

"I promise," she said sullenly, watching as I pulled myself up. Working our way through the alley and as quickly as possible, we wriggled through another small passageway into another covered alley where the street took on a definite slope upward. Behind us, a small voice could be heard, clearly cutting through the thick smoke rising out of the lower streets.

"Éé'shī!" Mi'hal̆ē whispered.

We stayed low but doubled back just far enough for a clear view of what might be following. I listened, the sound was very close, so close I could sense it forming into words. Singing. There was singing in Bri'én. I stood against a signpost, catching sight of that remaining dhana through the crumbled doorway of a hut. He came slowly towards us, dragging his bow brokenly behind him, singing:

Ē-da ta óō	*my warm feeling…*
Seúana shūc-én	*the light season passes*
Cúana-én áng nō na'temat lālai	*taking our breaths away*
Dōr dhemm ta óō endō tīshan	*back to the dark we came from, so let my last*
Éh an dhūmāi an	*sight be a happy one,*
Ta cī'úa nāroú	*I will remember*
Ē-da ta óō	*my warm feeling*

And I looked down quickly to blink my eyes so I could keep the image of him in my mind forever. Because in one swift and deadly thud, a soft gurgle sounded, and then there was no more song. I heard no struggle, no cry. Silence descended around us again as my weary eyes lifted and the NaÓma still stood behind him holding the blade. I stood fixed to my spot, the warm wetness splayed across my face and dress. Only when I heard the clink of the blade as it hit the stone beneath him did I realize I was visible through the doorway.

"Don't look, just *run!*" I cried behind me and ran back to the alley, my heart thrumming its way through my ears.

I pushed at her to go backwards, screaming, "*Go!*" But when she saw the dark stains upon me, she grabbed my hand, biting into it hard and turned to run away from me, her eyes wild. "Mi'hal̆ē!" I screamed. But she'd already made it out of the alley and out of my sight. I had no hope of catching her.

Footsteps thudded upon me from behind, so I ducked under a pile of rotting wood to hide, holding my breath, screaming inside my mouth when I felt tiny bugs crawling on my arms as they wondered what sort of creature had invaded their rightful kingdom. But even after the NaÓma passed, I didn't move. After the sun set over the alley, I didn't move. And after I realized Mi'hal̆ē wasn't coming back and I knew there was no way of finding her in the dark, I still didn't move.

For a time, I did nothing but sit, watching small rivulets of fresh blood run down beside me from things outside my hiding place I wouldn't allow myself to consider; the occasional, otherworldly screech of a single bōmen reminding me I was still alive. And then again, the thrum of the drum penetrated the still.

After a time I imagined perhaps it was not the drumbeat of death but maybe the old drums of Bri'én beating from the festival days I'd once watched when young she-dogs walked about in long robes and gave lanterns to the na'dhana who came to claim their scrolls from the Halls of Learning. And then I thought perhaps I could even hear the ancient, ever-present thrum of Ebūda's creation song I longed to hear again. But perhaps my mind had run away with Mi'hal'ē down that alley after all for now who could be left in the city to beat the drums or intone those sacred notes?

Finally, I looked upward and cried to the heavens, "Why was *I* given this task? I'm so small, I can't finish!" But in the same breath I cursed myself for asking such a pointless question for I had chosen to become the Éē'shī of now. I had known as a star I was the weaker of the two of us. I had known I couldn't bring about the caémba, that's why Mi'hal'ē bore that burden even though she couldn't remember. Was I too weak even to finish out these last few days?

Not what you think you can do. What you must do.

When I did pull myself up in the dark and into a hollowed-out shop to collapse in my own filthy mess, I don't know how long sleep took me, only that a drumbeat lulled me off into it. When I woke it was day, and I collected myself to walk again. Now I was haunted and comforted only by that very thought: *I chose my task. I chose to be born as Éē'shī and those who weren't afforded a choice had been able to complete theirs already and in the appointed time to bring about my rebirth.* Surely then I would be able to finish in some way. Even if this was only foolishness, it was enough to help me go on anew.

Walking was becoming burdensome up the slope of the hill to the Dhang'r; my knees ground and slipped under the skin. But upwards I walked to the long winding lanes of Bri'én's deserted avenues. Through the grey, lonely squares and alleys and markets I picked my way, sucking at the few dripping outside taps I could find that the na'bōmen had helped push water through the pipe system.

Finally, I came to the end of the lower city and stopped to rest at the top of the upper wall at dusk to look out below me. The squarish buildings were made of thick clay, dotted with tiny cube-like windows. These were splashed with the deep blue of the Ebūdean flag whose tatters trembled in the still air over the domed temples below me and from the turrets and domes of the Palace emerging in the haze above me. The eerie white na'bōmen circled the Palace just farther down on the crest of the city's dome, their intermittent song of decay now become the only song I could determine from Ebūda, for Mi'hal'ē's was still being written.

I stood watching all these when a voice, too young but much too old, startled my thoughts. I did not turn; the creeping tingle in my nose told me another one of my siblings was nearby. Beside me

I could feel the rustle of fabric and a silvery dhana stepped up beside me to look out over the view as well. Her long ears tapered and trailed along the ground and she was strongly familiar: Āe'rū, the Guardian of Death who had been reborn again as a dhana and stripped of her famous beauty.

"Elder sister," I greeted, and she bowed back, clutching her scythe gracefully. "Have you come for me?"

"Of course not," she tutted. "Much too busy to cart a sibling off. You can walk your own self when it's time." She was still direct and snappy, which brought an odd comfort in itself. "Look down over this city and see what the análong have done to each other. This world is only misery now, it's fear. Since the days we were put over them, the análong have been tested of their true natures. I've watched the drought come, the control of the land go to the few who frightened the many, the division of them against each other and the atrocities brought in its wake as they gave in to their apathy and ran to every other corner for help. What profit does it give us to help them?" she questioned me.

"It isn't for our profit, it's for our punishment and you know that," I pointed out, realizing I'd also wrestled with myself over what seemed like a very good point now and again. If I couldn't find Mi'halĕ, what use was there for me to go on in this? And even if she found Rā-alta, what if Mi'halĕ failed altogether? Those awful questions never seemed to take a break in my mind. Even though I had the most knowledge of the Guardians, I had no window to the future to help me answer my own questions.

She tutted in disgust. "I'm busy. Didn't you notice all the dead lying around?" she motioned to several dhana laying side-a-side to my left in the grass. "And don't you have our sister to find?"

"I'm going, I'm going," I muttered and shifted the nearly empty sack higher on my shoulder. When I looked back I saw Āe'rū walking away speaking to someone I couldn't see. I gazed for a moment at her and then went on, taking little breaks up the ever-inclining hill as I needed to catch a weak breath.

I hadn't gone far when I came to a very narrow alley where I could hear something whining in low, hushed tones in the shadows back beyond my line of sight. The sound waned as I got closer and an unbearable odor overpowered me as I came between the walls. In the dark, just barely in view, I squinted to see a small figure lying in an unimaginable state. Something; someone had maimed the creature beyond recognition.

Something in me sucked inward violently as if to turn myself inside out. Though I had seen birth, death and all of the atrocities of old wars throughout the ages in my form of detachment as a star, everything presently mortal within me was repulsed by the condition which this living thing had been left in. For as I looked again quickly, I realized that it yet remained bound in this world alive. And in that moment, I recoiled from it in fear rather than looking to it with compassion.

Do you see what the análong do to each other? Āe'rū's words echoed in my mind as the little thing gurgled fluid suddenly and stared into nothingness, its very breaths thin as parchment. Still, it stared into the dim and somehow held onto life as if lacking the words to ask for death. Apathy and hate had come together on this very spot, making its dark mark felt on my very skin.

"Āe'rū!" I screamed and whirled around, shamed into a run back out of the alleyway and right into her.

"You called for me?" she said blankly, sickle in hand.

"Something in there," I gasped, clutching my middle, "Take it with you!"

"I cannot."

"Why not?" I choked on my own spit, "Go look!"

"Go to your business and let me to mine," she said, her tone dropping to anger as she turned to go, but I grabbed her by the shoulder with a shaky grip, my own anger rising over my revulsion. I raised my fist to her. "So do it! Death is your business, have you no mercy?"

"Save your strength. I do not exist in flesh as you do, and you cannot hurt me. While you quarrel with me our sister is running about alone. I know the time of every análong and I will remind you that we are neither such things as humans, nor angels, nor animals, nor demons but Guardians who take orders. And *you* cannot give another Guardian such an order," Āe'rū said calmly and walked away again, fading slowly into smoke.

"But I have *will!*" I snapped. "I have *freedom!*"

She called back faintly before disappearing altogether, "All living things have *will*. If you are so intent, *then do as you will!*"

My heart pounded into my throat so loudly I could hear nothing else. I wouldn't be seen by mortal eyes, I knew, but nothing escaped the orbs of our brother Hor'ō-cō, the witness of all Ebūda. No deed was uncatalogued in the Book of Moon.

I'd been so powerless to stop the suffering before me until this moment. In my mind I suddenly saw F'ala talking to Mi'hal'ē in the loft one afternoon in that life we'd led before. "*Everything we do has a consequence. There are good consequences, there are bad consequences. Sometimes a bad consequence has to happen to make a road to a good one. You're not always going to know ahead of time how things will turn out; all you can do is make your best choice with what you know. Always look for the most important thing.*"

Because the name of the Law in this world is Balance, echoed An'ō. I didn't exactly understand, but I trusted something about these words was true and greater than I. So, I walked with heavy feet back to the alley and picked up a weighty stone. The blow was quick, and I ran as I had never before. No longer did I hear the drumbeat or the bōmen or the wind, the silence descended on me if the ancient melody of Ebūda silenced to abandon me in punishment.

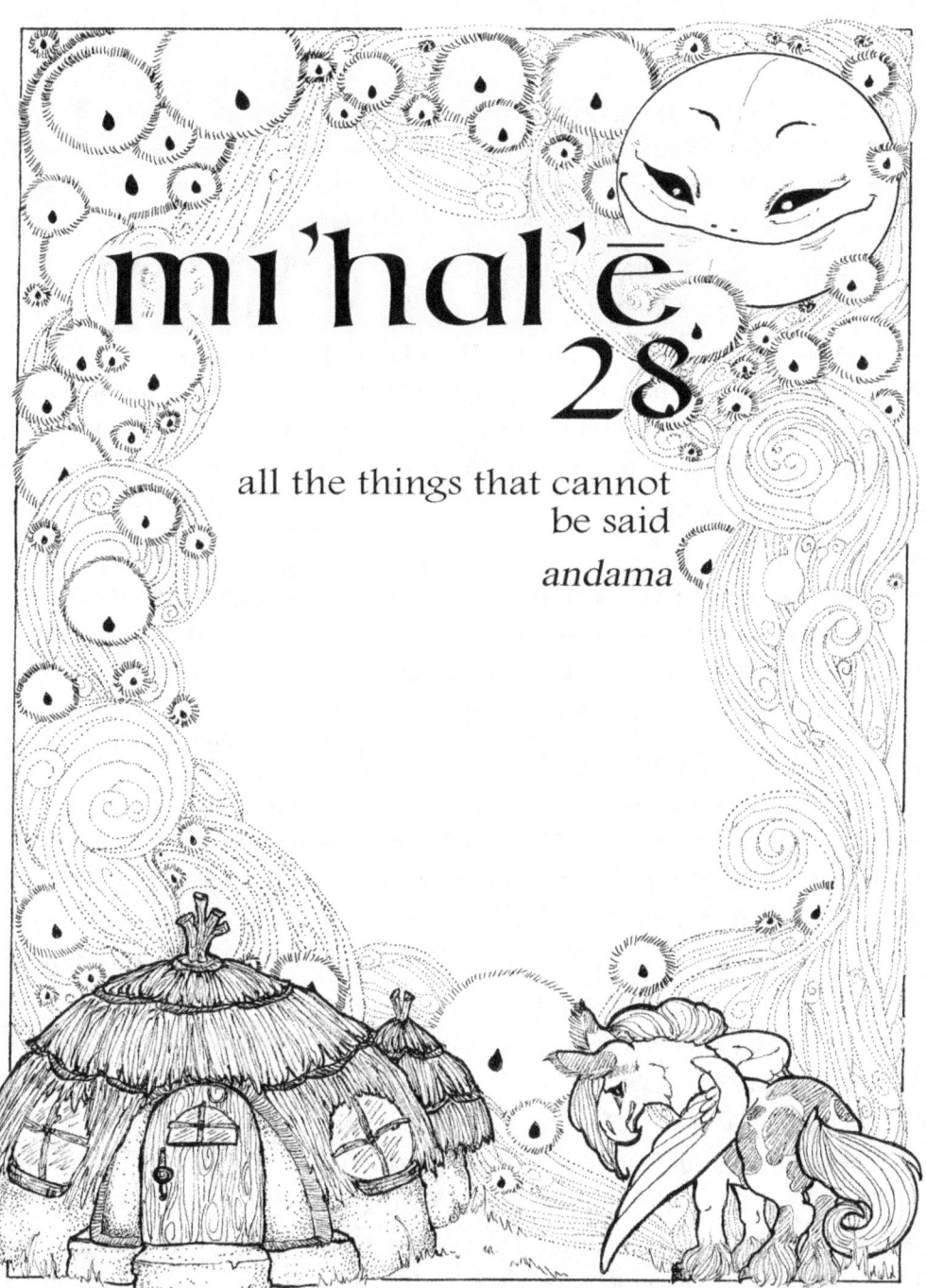

mi'hal'ē

28

all the things that cannot
be said

andama

WHY did it shock me that I was alone now when I'd always been alone in my own skin?
I didn't mean to run away from Éé'shī. The understanding that *this* was the thing that Dandhō had sheltered me from and then sent me out into threatened to tear my thoughts into shreds. I knew it over and over, but I didn't *feel* it until I saw one análong kill another outside the safety of my own imaginings. At first, I thought perhaps I didn't see what I saw, maybe this was what *dreaming* was. But when I saw the blood splashed across Éé'shī's face, how brilliantly red it screamed against her somber skin, my mind froze as my body awakened.

It had become clear to me back when looking out at the vanishing edge of dried-up Lake Óngalora that there was something past what my little eyes could see, that like that constant awareness of motion beyond the trees that I knew to be *Mīʾá*, my awareness had been based entirely on what I could perceive to be in front of me in the scope of my physical vision. The certainty that something else lay beyond that awareness, that something real and tangible out beyond had teased me since my days locked up in the little hut. I was so sure then that there were things I didn't know; wonderful things being withheld from me. But these were only hopeful guesses. Now I knew with certainty of their substance. Now I knew the greatest of evils lay beyond me as well. The most perilous things were the ones I couldn't yet see.

So, my legs took off as if they could outrun the horror, as if perhaps there were some tiny corner still out there that death hadn't yet touched, where the clothes we wore and the food we ate and the beds we slept in weren't stolen from the dead. There had to be, and it had to be where Elder Rā-alta was! "Up," I said to myself when I realized Éé'shī wasn't behind me. "I have to go up."

Though I was aware I was moving upward through the streets, I walked into things, fell,

Didn't notice that darkness had fallen until the nightly chill set into my arms and I looked in earnest for that corner to curl up in. Finding an empty doorway at the end of an arched alleyway, I crawled inside and curled myself into the mildewed straw, listening to the playful clinking of windbells from another doorway. But that dear emblem of summer only made me cry.

After a while I knew I was completely alone. The faint noises in the distance vanished and the air became clearer and thinner, with just a faint breeze washing over me now and again. With some bravery I peeped out of the doorway to gaze at the sky and found the muted outlines of moons peeking up over low rooftops; the washed-out bodies of a few straggling stars. I wouldn't allow myself to think Éé'shī was dead.

"Éé'shī isn't up there, she's *out there*," I said aloud and jumped at the sound of my own voice unanswered. Longingly I looked up and studied the sky, feeling a pang of guilt. "Dandhō, Little Dandhō, I know we're not under the same stars anymore. I know you *are* the stars now. You're looking down on me right now. But what if Elder Rā-alta is there with you too? Can't you tell me somehow? And Anshē," I suddenly hitched in a deep, tearless sob, covering my eyes. "And Rāca."

Éē'shī told me once that there was a place where stars talked to each other as if they were alive. Now I prayed this was true because the stars were beyond what I could reach and now they seemed to wink at each other as if sharing the secrets to everything I didn't know and dared me to jump up and ask them. Surely Rāca was there tumbling through clouds, surely that twinkle to the right was Dandhō scolding me from above for running away and losing Éē'shī. That's what she would say if she were here now, and this was how I knew that my prayers were answered, that my asama, all of them, were still with me as long as I could find the stars. Pulling my knees to my chest I rocked myself back and forth gently. The windbell stayed itself suddenly, out of thought for the dead.

When the sun rose the next morning and the haze fell again over the city, I picked myself up and went on, straining to lift my legs up high enough to climb as the roads turned to carefully laid stone twisting higher and higher. Eventually the alleys parted and as I came out onto a sort of wide street made of smooth white stone, I stepped out onto it cautiously and was immediately spotted.

For a split second I thought Éē'shī had caught up to me and I turned towards the movement but then froze, paralyzed. A stranger! Impossibly thin, yet swollen, her eyes were dull and wide under the faded cap she wore over her ears. I tried to back away around the wall into the alley, but she quickly ambled over to me and grabbed my wrists over my jacket, careful not to touch my skin.

"*Samaan!*" she screeched, her eyes melting into a wild, aimless joy. I squirmed away from her, horrified enough I was afraid to bite her. "Let me go!" I shrieked back, recognizing the northern pronunciation of that awful word, *samanē*.

"I've caught you now- you must grant me a wish! Give me wings so I can fly far away to the ancestors! Don't suffer me to live!" her voice, rough from disuse suddenly spiraled upwards into a sort of howl and I spat at her face, hitting the ground sharply when she dropped me. It was enough time to jet past her and up the white road as she collapsed behind me and fell into a useless heap, bawling, "Samaan... let me fly far away!"

But as I scrambled away, I ran right into a wall of thick smoke and dropped down under it on my hands and feet to crawl in the fresh air. I crawled along the street for a good length until the crown of my head hit hard into something made of stone, so hard a gasp expelled out of me before the pain struck and the last bit of my resolve crumbled into angry tears.

"*Where is this stupid Palace?*" I screamed, patting my head to dull the sting. I pulled at my ears and rolled over on my back to kick out, screaming Dhandhō's favorite expletives as loud as I could. If nothing else maybe Éē'shī would hear me and find me.

No answer came and when my head dulled to a manageable twinge, I turned back over onto my belly and carefully leaned up. I felt along with my hands and realized I'd hit my head against the bottom of a stair. The long staircase led up to an immense set of round, intricate doors now visible for the smoke's path was high over me. I sat back on my feet, amazed at the dulled but enormous jewels set into every stair spelling out the syllables of words in Dala-oúam.

So, the Palace. Looking up from the ground, the Palace was much too large to comprehend its true shape, protected by tall spires and wide, arched windows. Around the bottom I could make out the forms of plants shaped into all sorts of creatures and designs and stemming out from its outermost circle were the still, pale triangular fans set atop tall, thin poles. *Na'bōmen.* The wall of smoke which had made it impossible to see the Palace from below hung in the air just underneath these fans as if it dared not creep any farther to be shredded by their lethargic blades. Now it seemed a cloudy blanket obscured everything behind me.

I couldn't move. I'd screamed out every ounce of energy I had left, leaving me too weak to go on. My body burned from the inside out, radiating heat from a tight, hot knot in my middle. The days of sweating as I'd climbed through the city had left a million tiny itches marching their way across unreachable places; my eyes burned from the smoke. Yet it felt as if the very force of my life was leaking in icy streams from my nostrils against my will. I leaned back against the stair.

"The one time you listen," Éē'shī's weary voice startled me from behind.

Relief washed over me at the sight of her, but I could only say "Óōnōúa," quietly in apology for running from her. She pulled me gingerly to my feet and knelt painfully before me to climb onto her back. Weakly I fell forward, and she molded my limbs around her, rising unsteadily to ascend the staircase which proved shorter than it looked onto the Palace grounds. "I thought I'd never see you again," I whispered into her neck but Éē'shī didn't answer. She glanced at me before hoisting us up over the last stair and I saw in her eyes something dark I knew I couldn't ask about and neither could she tell me. *Andama.*

Sliding me off to the ground, Éē'shī took my hand in hers again and led me through a macabre garden of bizarrely smiling topiaries, their faces and limbs haphazardly burned off or laying on the ground uprooted and naked. Dozens of these garden sculptures twisted and merged into each other across the courtyard; fantastical overgrown creatures turned dark, crisp and mournful.

Though there were many doors scattered around the Palace walls in many different forms, the great entrance was through a large blue wooden door built into an enormous round window, ornate with metal ornaments and spiraled trappings. It creaked open at Éē'shī's very touch and we entered with a gust of wind ushering us at the heels. Just inside the great door, I studied the domed ceiling, impossibly high, painted in a dark glassy red and carved with the names of Elders in Dala-oúam. Around their names were impressed little spirals and golden stars. Immediately I spied Elder Rā-alta's name but said nothing.

"We can't waste time looking around," Éē'shī urged, tugging me along through the first long narrow hall where smaller, even narrower halls and rooms connected off to the sides. The hall suddenly widened and opened out into a soaring, domed room surrounded with tall, clear windows looking out onto lively gardens that now stood grey and mocking. On the inside of the dome were painted circular designs similar to the outside door which spiraled and continued across the ceiling outward into six smaller hallways.

"They lead to six schools, each dedicated to the study of a principle of the faith. Cīama, hashama, caémba, porāma, sāama and andama," Éē'shī explained.

Each of these narrow arms opened up to another small circular room stained all in red with a desk and chair for study. From the ceilings hung trinkets and tiny windbells slowly turned in the dormant air, the words of the análong fallen in the dust covering the little round windows.

Turning left, the hall led into a small plain blue room which connected into another small room filled with many figurines made of silver under a rounded ceiling of colored glass. On the other side we came to a very airy open space where square windowpanes allowed light to flood in on both sides, but in the pale afternoon it took on a sad tone rather than the satisfied mood of a day well-spent. On one end there were long, polished wood benches and on the other side, thick striped blankets like those that we used to sit on and cover the hut windows during the cold season.

In the middle of the hall, the floor was inscribed in a circle and to the sides one could see there had been gardens and fountains outside, but these were now cracked and brown. As we walked through this hall my feet slid softly on the smooth marbled floor and I noticed a rack hanging on the front wall where robes of orange and purple hung. *The First Hall of Learning,*" Éē'shī read aloud from an inscription on the wall.

In the next hall we came upon nothing at all but a few box-like tables and broken writing supplies like those Dandhō used in her work. This hall held the inscription *Second Hall of Learning* upon the far wall and an overturned pot of ink in the corner voraciously swallowed the light coming in from the many rows of frosted panes. I stopped to peer in but Éē'shī pushed me on and I tripped, falling on the smooth floor of the next room.

The echo of my knees cracking on the floor disturbed me more than the pain. Or perhaps it was the gasp behind me from Éē'shī echoing from the high ceiling. Pushing off the floor, the first thing my eyes rested on were the paintings on the wall, portraits that made up a long mural of nine análong in colorful red robes walking with their staffs. "Elders," Éē'shī's voice lowered to a soft whisper and she put her hand out to me without looking back. I took it, my eyes trailing back along to the last Elder in the line. She was young and had kind eyes and for a moment I relaxed in relief but followed Éē'shī in silence to a set of winding stairs.

I felt fussy and overwhelmed and sat down on the bottom stair, refusing to move. Éē'shī sat down beside me, refusing to carry me again. "Five minutes," she said, "then we're going up."

"How are you going to know when it's five minutes?" I asked.

Her brow knitted in irritation. "It's five minutes, get up."

At the top of that stair the landing smoothed out into a sort of tunnel inlaid with thousands of bits of glass. Fascinated, I ran my hands over this and found it was bits of looking-glass. I laughed at myself, remembering how long ago I'd been so silly with Dandhō's little hand glass, not recognizing my own face. Gazing at my fractured face as I walked through the tunnel, I saw an unrecognizable mask looking back. This little Mi'hal'ē's pink cheeks were faded to nothing, her eyes were impossibly large and dull, the skin around them marked with red and the mouth cracked and scabbed. Her cheeks were angled, not round, and her ears drooped. I'd watched slowly as Éē'shī had lost her strength, as her face had closed off and her limbs became sharp and weak. But somehow, I gave no thought to my own transformation, believing it to be deep inside with no outer mirror.

We left the tunnel both in deep thought and barely noticed the catacombs of rooms we passed by, clearly quarters of some kind and seemingly empty. Éē'shī opened one of these and carefully searched it, finding an untouched table of food and some plain undergarments. She held these out to me to strip off my clothes and change out of. "I look stupid," I commented, waving my arms in the bleached undershirt hanging well past my knees.

"You smell better," she shot back and handed me a piece of fresh bread.

But I was too weary. My mouth hurt, the teeth soft in my gums and the gums badly inflamed. The thought of having to chew it turned my stomach; my throat ached to swallow. I'd once thought only of food and that time was past. There was nothing tempting about it anymore.

"There's soup, I'll help you," Éē'shī looked around for a spoon and found it. She sat down in the heavy wooden chair at the table, pulled me up onto her lap and gingerly spooned the thick, yellow liquid into my mouth. Holding me there until the nausea passed, she quickly ate the bread herself and we continued through the maze of rooms until they ended abruptly at a very small door, just Éē'shī's size. I looked up at her and without hesitation she opened it and went ahead through, coming almost immediately to a wide stone staircase.

Up the stairs we trod, wiping our feet off as we went, for the dust was so thick it lay like icing. The muscles in my legs pulled and strained, all of the strength sifted down and spiraled into sandy weights in my feet. Éē'shī looked back to make sure I followed and I scrunched up my face, determined to make it up the steps after her by myself. But the height of them was too much and I bent over, putting my hands on the step before me and pulling myself up one leg at a time to finish.

At the top between the parapets the stone levelled off and spread out into long, raised colonnades, marked every few feet by wide, empty pools stained red as if they'd once held blood. I wanted to look away, yet the pools so looked like hungry mouths open and waiting to eat us that my eyes followed them as I went, just to make sure they stayed put.

At the end of every row there stood a small stone hut punctuated by a sad little flag reduced to shreds and as we passed through the narrow walkways between the pools Éē'shī pointed out that this place was called Nēshorē and was the center where red cloth was dyed in those same pools for use by the Palace.

Dandhō had always insisted I keep my nose to myself but Little Dandhō taught me a little curiosity made the day go faster so I spied into the nearest hut's crude window and stood transfixed by what was inside.

Bones. Clean bones.

Dandhō had once drawn an análong's skeleton for me, showing me how we all looked the same under the skin right down to the bone, but seeing it upfront, knowing by that drawing that this was an análong, I thought immediately she must have left out something. Particularly fascinating was the fact that this poor fellow's delicate bones had become disfigured from its legs and lay against the dirt floor like scattered tiles. And so, I stood staring at them, that horrible rushing feeling of knowledge came springing up from the back of my skull, trying to tell me something I didn't want to hear. "Tsōl!" I said to my myself, pushing my eyes in so hard with my fingers I could see stars bursting.

"That's what happens when you nose about," Éē'shī reminded me, her voice breaking the movement and it melted back into the dark of memory inside me. She grabbed my hand firmly, but not unkindly, to go.

Down the wide stairs on the other side we descended to a high dome of polished gold, outfitted with a large skylight right over the top. Under this dome stood a series of doors, each carved with the name and face of one of the twelve Ebūdean moons. "Is that where Elder Rā-alta lives?" I asked, feeling the heavy yet sparkling sense like dying embers that something was going to be revealed to us.

"Try the doors," Éē'shī ordered and ran to the nearest but couldn't get the handle to budge. Hanging off the handle of the next with all my weight, I fared no better. I didn't notice Éē'shī had slipped around to the other side until I heard her cry out in a strangled scream.

I sprinted around the dome and stopped before a different door, narrow and faded and red. Compared to everything else we'd seen in the Palace, it was very plain and old, but outside this door lay a g'ealach wearing an ornate harness and headdress. His eyes stared out into nothing; his limbs skewed strangely. The paws had been cut off him and strung from his neck. "It didn't just happen," Éē'shī said, looking down at the ground, her mouth covered with her hand. "Whoever did it is long gone."

I stepped over and noticed the deep scratches at the bottom of the door, the matching red under the disembodied claws. The great headdress still fastened under his chin lay akimbo, its long blue feathers reaching out as if all the joy left in him were leaping out to escape his death. "*Say*-yoo," I slowly pronounced the name carved into his harness.

"He tried to get this door open," Éē'shī observed. "Something important is behind this door."

"How are *we* gonna get it open?" I scoffed.

She didn't answer but tip-toed around the g'éalach and studied the bottom of the door. Then with one hand she gave it a little push and it opened with a groan, revealing a cavernous room illuminated just barely from above. Behind her, I couldn't see anything but stale fog. It was the stench that came out like a force that knocked me back.

In one movement we both pulled our collars up over our noses and peered in, trying to make sense of what we saw. The awareness of something large loomed and after some time, the fog thinned, and we saw a great pile of black, cruelly shaped figures reflected in the polished flooring. Death had come before us, blazing out a trail of suffering, taking with it the very one we had come so far to find. All nine bodies had been burned; the charred remains of their faces contorted into silent everlasting screams. And around the black figures strange yet familiar shapes had been painted onto the flooring. "NaÓma?" I asked aloud, needing to fill up the void somehow crowded by their silent screams. Éē'shī's face twitched.

"*Ha-* what do we do now?" I persisted but she wouldn't answer. "Éē'shī?"

Slowly she backed away in shock, unblinking. I followed at a distance, but she continued to follow the wall beneath the dome around until she collapsed at one of the moon-marked doors and put her head between her knees in silence. I stood for a while watching the sky, wondering if I should go back down to find a room to sleep in, knowing Elder Rā-alta was gone yet hoping if I didn't ask it might not be true.

The sun began to set and Éē'shī pulled herself up stiffly and walked off, leaving me to scramble to follow her. Back across the parapet, past the empty dye pools and down the stairs she hurried. "You're leaving me!" I yelled in panic, but she only sighed hopelessly.

"You can't leave me!" my hollow shrieks echoed as we came back through the little door into the maze of rooms and I heard them rise higher and higher in pitch until they curved downward in a defeated arc into a sort of prayer. "I want to go home," I sobbed.

Looking up through my swollen eyes I saw that Éē'shī had stopped and leaned against the wall, wearing the expression on her face I had come to know as *acceptance*. Pained and exhausted but resigned that she could do nothing but let me cry. It wouldn't change anything, and it wouldn't hurt anything and for this I was unsure if I should be angry or thankful. Eventually the tears gummed up in my throat and I stood licking them away from my cheeks. Éē'shī reached out and grazed her fingers over my ears quietly for a little while, staring out into the dark hall before us.

"You know, I'm sad Elder Rā-alta is gone. I am. I-I'm quite sad," I said simply, thinking the air was becoming polluted with the rising whispers of the dead. "She looked kind. From the painting, I mean."

Éē'shī murmured. "I am too."

"*Andama*," I said softly, twisting my fingers against themselves just to feel the skin. How strange now, all the words in this world constricted and dulled and only the breadth of silence could translate between us the story of our losses. Éě'shī nodded. "Let's find somewhere to sleep."

But when we'd come back through the little door, we'd turned the other way and soon found the rooms ended in a short walkway which opened into a wide, shallow depression tiled with fading bits of fired clay. The short wall around it held an elaborate sculpted pūra of silver. Its body contorted into a triumphal arch; its mouth open, hungry, empty. "Water would have poured out from there like a fountain," Éě'shī pointed to it. But the real centerpiece was the round base fitted in the middle of this fountain.

Onto it a colossal clockwork orrery rose encircled with painted metal balls on thin poles representing the twelve moons and their metal orbits circling a casted metal Ebūda. On its base was marked out each season in carved pictures and Dala-oúam strokes and the ailing mechanism could be seen which turned to slot the balls into their seasonal positions by way of a long wooden handle along the bottom. Its impressive size was outweighed by the nightmarish peeling of its paint and the aimless, rusty gears and springs hanging out here and there as if it had been gutted. And its empty bezels where jewels once shone now looked out like hollow eyes over the hushed world below.

Yet the night was warm and over the far side of the wall we could see the Palace dropped off abruptly; its arbitrary design ending to overlook the city. Pulling each other up to sit on the wide flat stones, we relaxed a moment when we saw the placid face of Dhoisa serenely gazing back, her eyes just rising over the horizon. We sat, looking out over Bri'én, gazing at the coal-black rooftops and ruins from which rose curls of the last whisps of smoke washed almost white in Dhoisa's light. The heavy, intrinsic web of time stretched over the city, weighted with dust and thoughts and ancestry. I wondered when it would be our turn to rise to the sky.

Creeeeaaaaaaak! Eeeeeeeeeeeeeeeeeeeaaaaark—Grrriik—Griiiik eaaaaaaarrrk! Hroooooo!

A wind picked up and caught the blades of the na'bōmen around us, forcing their unused blades to wake and echo the mournful cramps of our stomachs. Perhaps they were mourning the loss of their city.

Weeks ago, I woke in the middle of the night crying and Éě'shī, somehow knowing my thoughts patted my back gently and said "Now you think of your ah'sha all the time; your head is filled with every moment you spent and every moment you hoped to. But one day you will put her away in your heart just as you put away your doll. And then you will only bring her out to play in the light of memory and no longer in the shadow of mourning."

But I was a dhana and that night I laid there and cried for me; for the days I would be without her, the times I would look down to only my own little shadow on that dusty ground, the times my hand would only have its own little fingers to curl around. Later, oh so much later, I stopped crying for me, and began crying for *her*, for the days she would never see, and this was when I knew I was no longer a dhana.

Now I looked over to Éē'shī and wondered if the moons knew, if the sounds of the na'bōmen mourned the days coming when she too would be gone from me, and I slipped my hand in hers, surprised to find she resisted me.

She pulled away, curling up into a ball, her ears sticking out oddly from over her hunched shoulders. "My purpose was to make sure you survived, to bring you here. And here we are, and Rā-alta is *gone*… and now I just don't *know what to do*."

"Come here to do what?" I asked longingly, not expecting her to answer. After all the dead we'd passed, all the senselessness and violence we'd seen, I wondered why was I the one who had to survive? I wanted to live, but in the world I knew before everything disintegrated into something no-one could fix. While the world behind me had never belonged to me, neither did the shapeless structure of the one before me.

The tickle in the back of my mind suddenly niggled at me, the golden light dimly illuminating the backs of my eyes. Immediately I clamped down on it but then I paused, wondering if there was something vital it was trying to tell me. My biggest fear had always been drowning in it, becoming lost in that hidden knowledge so keen to make itself known. But Éē'shī and I were going to die, it was only a matter of time now and my body was so very tired, it was no longer afraid to stop.

High on that wall I sat and closed my eyes, breathing in to still my thoughts, breathing out against their anxious protests. "*Why am I the one that has to survive?*" I asked myself, sitting still and quiet until the light grew and drowned out the darkness behind my lids, bathing me in a sparkling glow where the words emerged before me stroke by stroke in Dala-oúam. *Namsal nūl tū an lhéoran: Because you are a Guardian.*

Suddenly I felt my rear-end sore and cold on the wall as if I'd been dropped and I looked over to Éē'shī but she hadn't moved or even answered me.

But because it had come from inside me, the words seemed true in a way no outsider's could and I sat repeating them to myself over and over before I could utter the request for proof:

"I'm a Guardian, aren't I? That's why I have to live, isn't it?"

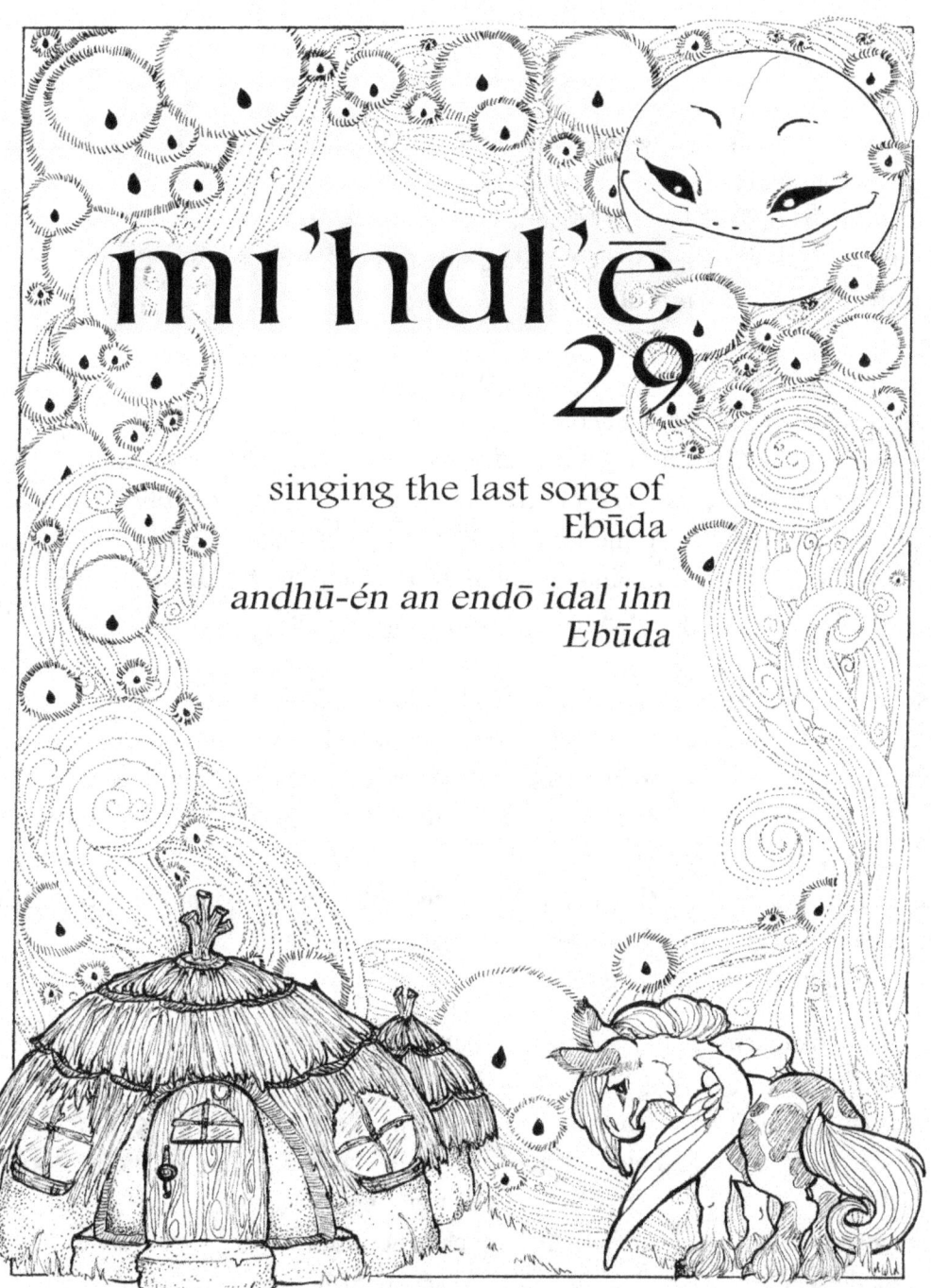

mi'hal'ē
29

singing the last song of
Ebūda

*andhū-én an endō idal ihn
Ebūda*

"Do you know, sometimes…sometimes I hated you. For who you are." Éē'shī looked up over her knees and I saw her face was swollen, her grubby cheeks cut deeply with furrows of tears.

I nodded, stunned. "Me too, for who you aren't," I replied truthfully.

"I was so scared you'd never figure it out," she wiped her face and lowered her legs to dangle beside mine.

Why you never belonged, and never will! chimed in that little voice I thought had gone to sleep when my toes went numb.

"It's why I never belonged," I echoed aloud.

Éē'shī nodded. "But if you're not a Guardian," I reasoned, "How can I be? You said you weren't strong enough to be a Guardian, but…"

"I am."

I stared at her for a moment, the rush of confirmation darting through my mind. "*I knew it!*" I shouted and pushed her backward playfully. "I knew you were!"

Momentarily surprised, Éē'shī pulled herself back up to sitting and burst out laughing, slapping my cheeks lightly as I reached out and pulled at her ears. Stopping to get our breath, we smiled at each other, *knowing*. Then she became serious. "But you, Mi'hal'ē, you are the *last* Guardian."

The last Guardian. What did Dandhō say about the last Guardian? It seemed like another lifetime when we sat in the stuffy loft going over the order of the Guardians again and again. Why hadn't I paid better attention?

"The last Guardian is the one who brings caémba," I heard myself say, all momentary relief at the discovery crashing down under the weight of that hefty task. "How am I going to do that!"

Éē'shī pulled my head down into her lap. "We'll worry about it tomorrow. Sleep."

I desperately wanted to ask her how I was going to do this thing no análong had managed to do but as my head lowered, my eyes became too heavy. In that thin night air, I curled up as best I could against the cold, watching across the sky as it brimmed with the faces of moons peering down at us, rocking back and forth gently to the words on the wind.

Éē'shī, *my dandha*, had found a song to sing.

Bala crē ast nūl ada'chē	Look, cry if you want
Ta cī'úa a det celēl	I'll stay the night
Ha- mēshan ē a'ma tīca'én na'shechi	Where is the mother bringing the sweeties?
Ha-mēshan ē a'ér samala-én mah shēgon	Where is the father, standing at the door?
A'ér ta ah tsōl	I am not father
A'ma ta a tsan	I have no mother
Ta cī'úa a det celēl	I'll stay the night
Shāe ē ōshē an prā-á nē	it is all one can do.

Mlēsan ma énts'rū cad'hē	Silence has come now
Ta cī'ua det cishda dhit	I'll stay again, then
Ha- mēshan a na'ur'sa la'lāi'én la'bū'da	Where have the flying birds gone?
Ha- mēshan a na'daú s'cúela do	Where have the cities fallen to?
Isa dhana ah ta	I am only a child
Isa g'ada ah ta	I am only newly born
Ta cī'úa det cishda dhit	I'll stay again, then
Fē'loú ōshē na'ur'sa a la'lāi-da	after all the birds have flown.

When my eyes opened, I was no longer laying across Éē'shī's lap but curled up stiffly on the ground under the orrery. Above me, the ghostly, off-colored light which slid over the outline of the city was broken only by the slow, steady creaking of the na'bōmen and the strange, fixed gazes of the moons invading the daytime sky.

"Éē'shī?" I whispered, breaking the calm. When she didn't reply I whispered again, louder. Stretching my stiff neck, I looked out to the left and caught sight of her gazing back at me serenely; silently. Éē'shī stood as she had the first day I met her; her proud eyes watched me watch her and I heard my voice, thin and trembling wisp out of me. "Do you think we're the only ones left?" It seemed the question hanging over us.

Éē'shī nodded her head and answered, "Probably." She reached out to help me up and we made our way back through the Palace now that daylight streamed in through its halls to light our way. Stopping just long enough to help ourselves to another laden table of stale food, we filled our sack for the first time in ages and hauled it down the great, jeweled stairs between us and out into the stale streets. No longer afraid of being hunted, we stood and looked down over the endless routes into the lower city, unsure of where to go.

Then, before it could be decided, a sickening, hollow crack roared out from beneath us and I was thrown forward. Jumping up out of the way, my feet scraped along the jagged edge of the stones pushing up beneath me and I scrambled to leap over the fast-crumbling rock to reach Éē'shī and grab her hand.

Her mouth stretched wide, but I couldn't hear her words over the explosion of stone splitting and falling upon itself as a thick crack opened and raced down the steep hill towards the marketplace, dividing it in two. There was no time to think; the Palace steps behind us had fallen in on themselves, creating a chasm we had to cross before they disintegrated into rubble. We clutched at each other, skipping clumsily to any surface left around the edge of the rapidly forming hole, ducking at every noise.

Éē'shī's hand snaked out to grab my arm and yanked me to her, her tail tying us both together tightly. "Look!" she yelled over the din and I whipped my head around to see a fine crack run itself all around the lower city, precisely slicing the outer wall of Bri'én in two so that at once it slid down into the ground, taking everything inside the lower wall with it.

"Tsō- tsō- tsō- *tsōl*!" I screamed, scrubbing my eyes with the heels of my palms. "I don't want to see!"

In one slick movement, Éé'shī pulled us up to the eave of a low-hanging roof and roughly pinned me to its tiles. "You are a Guardian and this is our penalty: *to see*. You *must* look; you *must* see what you did and what you could have done, what was and what *could have been*!"

"But the city! Everything's being destroyed!"

She wouldn't let me go but her voice became soft. "*Everything* goes, *everything* passes. Remember, we don't belong to this world."

"But it's *mine*," I mourned, watching the sky grow dark. In the distance a flat pounding noise could be heard, and I pulled myself up to sit and survey the roofs in the lower city falling one atop the other in a clear line coming slowly ever-closer. "Why?" I asked, simply and naively.

Éé'shī pointed to the middle of the fray where the great sinkhole was swallowing whole alleys to feed its insatiable hunger. "The Cāilon has caved in. There's no one left the pump the water up to the hill. All those empty tubes have probably collapsed underneath." Then she closed her eyes. "This is the end. Some ends are silent, some are violent. It's the same with beginnings. And sometimes they're the same thing."

I slipped my hand in hers, but fear took a hold on me so tightly my middle shook with a fine, cold tremor and I felt as if I'd spill out of myself. Feeling that I should be brave like a Guardian, I said, "Then if this is the end, I'm happy you're with me."

But when my hand slipped out of hers so smoothly; I didn't even try to hold on as she shoved me to the side off the roof into the soft earth below in a cascade of dust and shattered tile. I heard a dark thud behind me, and I turned to push off of my stomach, blowing the dirt from my nostrils. The faded sack lay beside me, its contents strewn about carelessly. My eyes searched frantically for Éé'shī through the dust. A new but smaller crack had ripped apart the earth just under the hut we'd been sitting atop, pulling down several beside it in a row into a small dune of rubble sandwiched between half-collapsed walls. I stood, leaving the sack behind to cautiously step around the margin.

I gasped as I nearly stepped on the little pink fingers stretching out from under the heavy wooden door.

It seemed in that moment that the na'bōmen stilled their lazy sounds as I screamed pure and clear out over the city. Following the outline of the door I came to her head stretched out free from its terrible weight. "*Īla'úa!*" I screamed louder. Dropping down to the ground next to her, I saw Éé'shī's eyes were open and fixed on me. My short relief became horror; I was terrified to touch her, terrified not to. Her mouth opened, giving me a jolt of hope that perhaps she was not leaving me, that she would get up and we'd run away from this. But her words were chalky and fragile as a thin trickle of blood slid down from the corner of her mouth. "Where is… the sack?" she asked.

The sack? Who cared about *the sack*?

"Get it," she croaked.

"I..." I stammered, then ran to shove everything back into the sack and bring it to Éē'shī, determined to do anything to save her. Laying it down gently beside her, I rifled through it, looking for anything that might help, hoping this was when my Guardian instincts would take over. Why the hell didn't I know what to do?

"The scrolls," Éē'shī coughed and I fetched them to her. "Are there magic spells in them?" I asked, because anything else would be worthless now with Éē'shī's lifeblood slipping out all over the place. "Never lose them," she coughed sternly. "The scrolls are your history."

"Tsō," I jumped up and grabbed the door's frame to pull with all my might, working with my feet sliding in the dirt until I nearly slid under it. "Enough," Éē'shī's voice was tired and impatient. Giving up, I sat down next to her, wrapping my legs to my chest. "You can't go," I sobbed. "I don't know what to do!"

Her tired eyes slipped closed. "No-one does. You don't just grow up and know it all. You've got to figure out the most...important...thing."

I watched her for a moment, feeling for a tiny second that I wished it would be done and over with, just to end all this waiting to die business. "Éē'shī?" I asked. Her eyebrow raised faintly in reply. "Is this the end of my second journey?"

Her eyes opened to say this before she left me: "Tsōl, it's the end of mine. Remember, you're only lonely, you're never *alone*." Then only the ghost of a smile victorious remained in this world on her lips.

"Tsōl," I whispered back, the tears squeezing down my cheeks as I pressed my fingers to my eyes to keep them in. But those little diamonds that had waited all these months to come and do their work now flooded out over me, their little army drenching me in the brilliance of sadness. I leaned over and closed her eyes, then sat with the scrolls clutched tightly in my hand.

And then in an instant all the sound in Bri'én had been sucked away and a strange peace came over the wreckage. I stared into the dusty air, not accepting but at least understanding that Éē'shī knew she wouldn't be with me forever. For a long time, I sat crying beside her still form, touching her hand until it turned icy and pale and I realized with certainty that indeed her eyes would not open again. Above, the sky was crowded with the moons, so close I could touch them, and I was grateful that at least something else survived.

When sound finally seeped back into the world, I could hear the distant pops and groans of things cracking apart and sinking down into the Cāilon, as if the city had picked right up where it left off destroying itself. The hill had simply opened right under the Palace and now pieces of the city fell here and there; whole sections disappeared as if some great giant was playing a haphazard hopping game atop the whole hillside, squashing it under his feet.

I stayed in the alleys as we had done when we went up to the Palace but going down was terribly lonely and seemed to take much longer. Now I had to look out for falling debris above me as well as dodging the ground pitching inward underneath me. And on this side, as the buildings of the Cāilon-da collapsed I now saw out in the open all those left behind who tumbled out of those dark places. The large and small were in all states of decay, their bodies bloated and swollen like festival balls, the color drained out of their skin into the filthy debris beneath them.

My head was too full to be afraid of them, or to wonder what had happened. Like the old Silver Sea, I had swallowed so much sorrow I was too full to hold anyone else's. I walked on, unaware of the exchange of day for night. I'm not sure I did understand how truly alone I was, but the emptiness without Éē'shī surprised me in its very scope and I wondered how something as small as I could contain such a thing so bleak and endless. Again, I found myself larger on the inside, struggling to hold in the heavy darkness of despair inside my frame.

I laid myself down in the middle of a broad, stone street and gazed at the fixed faces of the moons. What did it matter where I lay my head down? What did it matter to be a Guardian but not be able to save anyone? How could a world be saved that no longer existed? I asked these things of the moons in my mind, being too tired to voice them. They were too tired to answer. I may have slept.

When I looked up again, my arms and legs quivered as if they were being shaken. *Get up, Mi'hal'ē, you must get up!* I heard a voice urging. It hurt, this shaking, and the skin on my arms began to pull as I rolled away from the sound and rubbed my eyes, curling up into a ball. Stars burst behind my eyes and I clamped them shut. *Get up! Chūba!* the familiar voice said roughly and the invisible something pulled me up. *Straighten your legs and walk for yourself!*

I stumbled and rubbed my face in exhaustion but was grabbed again and dragged forward until I put my own effort into it. Looking around, I clearly saw I was alone. "Éē'shī?" I called, but there was no face behind the voice scolding me, no hands behind those rough tugs.

"But I don't even know where to start," I admitted, listening to the silence, a stillness which settled over the city as its destruction came to a complete halt. I slid down onto the ground, falling back again against whatever stood to catch me. "I don't have anywhere to go."

Éē'shī was wrong. I am all alone.

The cold of the stone below me seeped up through the thin undershirt I still wore, and I felt around aimlessly for the sack to see if the blanket remained shoved in the bottom. Dumping it out between my outstretched legs, I reached out to catch the larger scroll before it rolled away out of my grasp. "My history?" I wondered and pulled the ribbon off, prying the stiff parchment open to see what that even meant.

I recognized it as Dandhō's very best parchment, the stuff she made sure I never touched, at least not that she ever knew. Its smooth, thick surface felt as if it told its own story under my fingertips; the story of what went into its making. The fine linework scrawled across it made the shape of a large tree: the grandfather tree record of Dandhō's ancestors. I traced along the names of the tree, the raised ink of the branches and leaves and the beauty of it until my fingers came to a name I knew: Mi'halē, written as *Rī Mi'halē*.

I knew from watching Dandhō make these same trees to sell that análong names were written in this way, with the surname first and the given name last. An análong took their a'ér's first name as a surname. Here, around my name were the names of Dandhō and Little Dandhō: Adīī'á Rī (F'ala) and Adīī'á Ādō. But my name was the first name of Dandhō's before mine.

Then I was glad my ah'sha had never said she loved me in the confines of a little word, for this was better than that odd, frail word. This was *belonging*.

I rolled the scroll back up and closed my hand around it, satisfied for that moment as I never had been. Closing my eyes for only a moment, I opened them when I felt something prick my nose. I saw nothing but looked up when I felt another sharp little prick to the forehead, another to my shoulder. Around me dropped tiny, white balls into the thick red-black congealed in long lines across the stone. As they met the surface, the balls dissolved outwards into patterns and then vanished into little dark circles in their wake.

My mouth opened in awe, so wide I couldn't shut it and tears welled within me again, not from despair but out of the sense that this was the beauty I'd been told of long before. For a moment I gained an all-knowing sense, a sense of *andama* because I knew the truth. There was nothing behind me or below me, above me or beyond me. The huts, the birds, the análong slipped into oblivion. Somewhere out there amongst the stars were the lives of my asama; lives which had already come and gone and connected to each other and come together to care for me.

Looking out over the hill, I saw that Bri'én was gone around me in the space of a breath; it had disappeared speck by speck in silence. The little white balls continued to fall from the sky, and I craned my neck upwards to watch them, no longer feeling the stinging cold of their kiss on my face.

"Orū," I murmured at the sky. It had warmed from its odd dark color to a flat white as I understood the full meaning of my color; those many definitions melded into their own complicated beauty. There I lay in the street, hands folded over my middle weakly as I watched the wan sky, looking out over the world enshrined in white, the world dead and drained of color, devoid of the rich stain of life. *My world.*

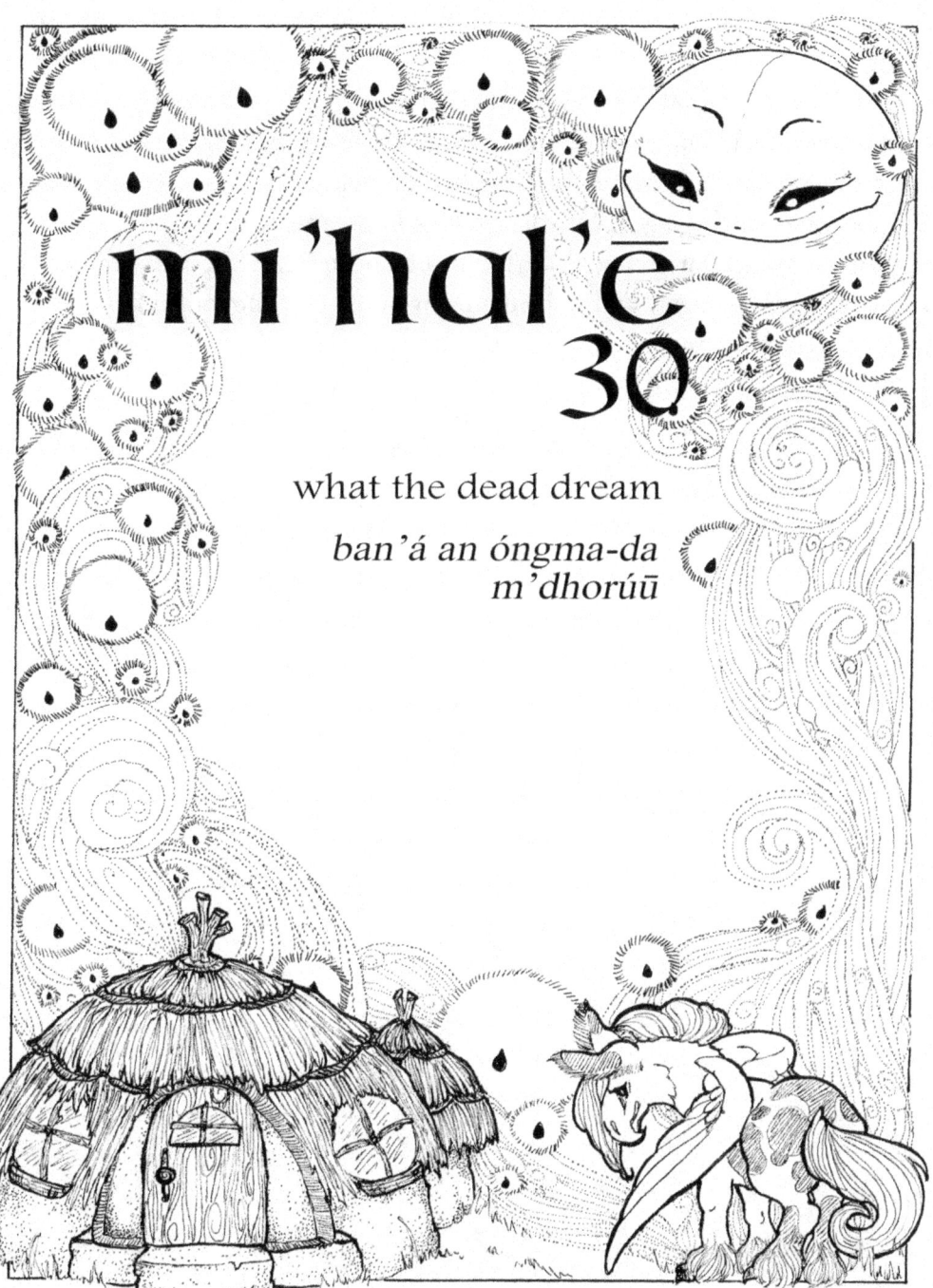

mi'hal'ē
30

what the dead dream

*ban'á an óngma-da
m'dhorúū*

SHE stood leaning on a great sickle, her impatient stare becoming even more so when I noticed her standing there. Her skin, silvery and freckled, made her look older than she must be at only the height of Éē'shī. Her ears tapered down to thin curls that dragged against the ground and she wore a petticoat alone.

"Who are you?" I asked, pushing myself easily to stand.

"Āe'rū," she said without feeling, without noticing the snow around her feet.

"Are you coming to take me?" I asked and she shook her head, laughing. "You're much too big for that now. I'm showing you the way. Come or not, it's all the same to me."

"Oh." Sensing she would leave me if I didn't follow, I hoisted the light sack over my shoulder and stepped forward to go. She turned and walked quickly away. But I no longer felt the cold under my feet, nor did I feel so empty inside. Yet, when I looked behind me and saw a small white dhana in an undershirt slumped over, half-smothered in the snow, I walked on behind Āe'rū, on my own legs.

Then the land fell away and the moons fell. The sky cried; it bled and died. And as it is said amongst the análong, a circle had closed.

āe'rū
31

THIS is the end of Ebūda.

The underworld and all its slaves have perished, and the great golden scales which oscillated from their sweat and toil have ceased to produce the song of this world. It is beyond decay; as the seas disappeared into the fog at its first discordant note, the plains and forests and mountains have disintegrated inward to the splitting apart of the great and lustrous holy city. In the end, all those lowly and despised análong rose up against the NaÓma and took their lives by passing on their malady. For all the might of kings and the wisdom of Elders cannot fight the whims of Nature. So then, the análong fulfilled their own belief in saying that all were equal in birth and in death.

And across Hala-Asal the echoing sound is familiar; for it is the sound of birth.

mi'hal'ē

32

revolution is a whisper

caémba ē an ashurē

ꞺND again, as I'd come six years before, that night I was found on the doorstone of Dandhŏ's hut, I was where before I was naught.

Exactly as I had been created that first day of my being, my limbs were round and strong, and my skin, unbroken. Naked, though not cold, I felt no hunger or thirst or sense of where I might be. But I stretched out luxuriously, testing out my limbs and enjoying the feel of my perfect form as long as I could before I began to wonder if anything else had survived beyond me.

A dense darkness lay all around and blotted out anything to be seen of sky or land and while no ground was visible below me, I didn't fall. I waved my arms around in this living pool of ink to find that it wasn't at all thick as it seemed. Neither night nor day, its tangible weight seemed to *live*. Unsure of how to propel myself forward or backward, I searched the space to find some sort of escape. But when my eyes adjusted in the black, I saw that a small round object floated nearby.

"A'dhā?" I greeted, too frightened to be alone to be cautious. Like moving through water, the object gracefully uncurled itself and turned and I saw that it too was a dhana just my size, with bare skin as black as mine was white; eyes as pale as mine were dark. My heart rose warmly in my throat and I called out, "I'm Mi'halĕ, who are you?"

The dhana looked me over, a cruel smile creeping over his face. "The last Guardian," he spat in words I'd never heard before, yet somehow understood as clearly as I understood my own Dala words. "I know very well who you are."

"I- I'm glad I'm not alone," I stammered, thinking in Dala but now hearing those same foreign words come out of my mouth, feeling their odd weight on my tongue.

"But you are alone," the dhana's voice purred, making me suddenly wary by its smoothness. "Ebūda is gone. If you joined me though, we could be friends. Then you would never be alone again."

I asked, "Where are we?"

"Not where, *when*."

"Then, when?"

"At the time before birth and the time after death; the point of creation and destruction. If one can ever know the difference," the dhana's strange, pale eyes narrowed.

I swallowed, but continued on, curious. "And Ebūda?"

"Naught, like the body you left behind."

I didn't believe it. I could see my body right in front of me and it felt so alive, so *healthy*. "Who are you?" I demanded.

"Sarshēl, Lord of An'dan, that forgotten country outside the Law of Orders." The dhana's face appeared suddenly beside mine. His eyes were scarred around the lids, reminiscent of the markings the Naóma painted on themselves.

"This is the remnant of the remnant, for all things seen are balanced with things unseen and now that the seen has fallen away, we remain in the unseen. No thing, no place, no idea disappears entirely.

It simply becomes something else in Creation. If you must think like mortals do in lines, think of this as the afterward of Ebūda, and we are its inhabitants." he growled as if it were common knowledge. "It is the space of a new world waiting to become."

"If you're the Lord of An'dan, why didn't you save it?" I accused.

He smiled wickedly, drumming his cheek with a finger. "It is true that I have complete control over An'dan, But I was not formed there. Do you know where I come from, little star?"

Something within me lurched and I thought fleetingly that I might rather be alone in this floating world. When I didn't answer, he explained.

"I was once like you, a guardian of sorts in the world of mortals where your kind stood watch from the skies. I stood in the realm of angels and I was sent to humankind to carry out my purpose.

Long before before An'dan was banished outside of the Law of Orders, there were seven of us, and we lived in the third realm above that world of humankind we call *Gaia*.

Created to be lord over the single moon of Gaia, I held the power to heal mortals and the power to kill them when the time came. And it was I who held judgment over them when they disobeyed the Creator. But eventually I fell from my heights." He looked away. I felt compelled to listen.

"In the days when you were nothing but shimmering dust floating above the skies, in those ancient days, I was sent into their world to teach the mortals, for they were very young in the Order and knew not of Law. I walked amongst those little creatures and I was well received, worshipped in fact. So small, so ignorant; they held anything extraordinary as a god in their midst.

And so, I taught them whatever they wanted to know in exchange for their loyalty and sacrifice. My crimes, it was said, were in giving the forbidden knowledge of heaven away, for taking the offering of forbidden adoration, for thinking myself a god. I thought my own desires justified tampering with the timeline of their progression.

You look at me as if I should be ashamed, yet you don't know the value of worship. Look away from me if you dare, if you are without your own stains!" Sarshēl spat. He paused. A strange trickle of sadness crept into my heart as if it knew the story of this falling was familiar to me, but I looked away into the endless darkness, a hollow picture forming before me from his words.

Sarshēl sighed almost wistfully. "I was banished from the Order, Gaia was taken away from me and I wandered through time until I came upon a new master, one also banished from that place, and I was granted a purpose for my allegiance. I was restored to my rightful title as a lord."

"But what kind of purpose could you have in letting my home be destroyed?" I asked bitterly

He continued, ignoring me. "There is a singing throughout the threading of the universe. Each being unconsciously gives forth its song up to the whole of Creation. Even in Ebūda there was always such singing, for it was pulled away from An'dan and sealed away from me by that Guardian, An'ō the Gatekeeper.

Now An'dan is the only place in all Creation which does not sing. All the other worlds and dominions are surrounded by the songs of their lands. But An'dan, being put together from the remnants of all the lands of creation, had no song of its own. It was only when Ebūda was pulled away and made its own country that it developed the very melody which soaked into it and intertwined with the composition of Creation.

I didn't destroy your home. Your *home* stopped singing. It cut itself off to wither and die."

I was entranced by his words, but I pulled back within, unable to stop blaming him for all I'd seen whether it made sense or not. "Then how?"

"The análong belonged to me! Ano had no right to take them! When I found An'dan and was given the power to become its ruler, I made them right up from the dust and gave them life and they worshipped me!"

Those old afternoon stories of the horrors of An'dan I'd once yawned through came rushing back with clarity. "You abused them! That's why Mī'á allowed Ano to save them, why the Guardians were reborn to bring caémba and bring them out of your hands and into the Law of Orders!" I pointed out angrily.

"Is it not the privilege of a lord to be sovereign over his own subjects?" his eyes crinkled in callous amusement.

"Your slaves you mean. And I suppose it is if that's what you believe," I murmured, but recalled Dandhō's offhand observance of the ancient, overthrown kings of Ebūda. "But even so, it doesn't mean you have to be. Forced worship isn't true worship."

"They were my slaves, that's the truth. Your brother Ano put up his barricade, gave them their own speech and law and it was he that taught them to sing in tune with the universe. I've never forgiven him." Sarshēl crossed his arms and leaned back to glare at me.

I looked around me, unsure of what to do next. "If you're an angel, why do you look like me?"

Now his face dipped low and scuttled close to mine. "If we had true bodies neither of us would look like this."

"But I am an análong!" I protested, striking my chest emphatically with my hands.

"You are a Guardian. Whatever you happen to look like, you were created a star and you will die a star," he said pointedly. "To be reborn as an análong, your body as a star could not continue as it was. It would not have survived the shift to enter Ebūda because it is not *of* Ebūda. And now you have died again, spilling over from Ebūda into this unformed place of beginning and ending. Because you do not remember your life before being an análong, your spirit projects the images of what you recall. You see me," he held out his dark arms, "as your opposite. True enough."

"Can I see what you really look like?" I ventured and he stared deeply into me, something concealed rippling faintly behind his eyes. "If it matters," he shrugged.

I felt a slight breeze stirring about my feet and as if light were slowly dawning over us, I was aware that I hadn't been gazing at Sarshēl through my eyes but with another kind of sight. His small black form shimmered and shook, stretching into an enormous circular form of endless dark mass. Great wings of all sizes and shapes stretched out from this, their bones creaking and snapping, and I found myself terrified of the simultaneous opening of thousands of eyes and mouths of every shape and color all over his form.

"Do I frighten you?" Sarshēl's voice purred from somewhere amongst his eyes. Terrified, I lied, "Not at all."

Some of the eyes squinted as if laughing at me. "Good. Beauty is individual, after all."

The reminder of Éē'shī's words about beauty struck me and I could feel my face close inward, the heavy feeling of loneliness pulling down on me. As if he'd noticed, Sarshēl ruffled his feathers, the tips of his multitude of wings caressing the air around me as if to comfort me.

"We are the last standing, you realize. The fate of what this new world becomes is up to us. We can take any fashion you like for nothing has been formed here yet. You would only need wish it.

Now it is no secret that we serve two different masters, is it? When I was banished from the world of mortals, I heard the voice of another power in Creation, that power the heavens call Destruction, or Chaos. It has many names, but whatever you call it, it restored to me the power I used to create the análong. Then my rightful sovereignty over them was ripped away from me by your thieving Guardian brother.

We are all servants to our own masters, you to yours and I to mine. When they are done with us, our time is over. Your master is one of light; that power you call Mī'á. Mine is a one of darkness. This makes us adversaries; rivals. Yet we are exactly the same, make no mistake of that. We have no place with such creatures as análong. *We* are not so lowly."

"I do! I might be a Guardian but... I'm an análong too..." I murmured, suddenly unsure of what that meant, or if one could truly be two things at the same time.

I heard his laughter ripple over me in an eerie wave I felt creep right under my fingernails. "You were certainly as necessary to Ebūda as was I; light and dark are requirements for the balance of mortal realms. And so we are the remains of our own worlds, but we can be the founders of a new existence." Sarshēl's eyes opened wide and I wasn't sure where to look.

"I just want to go home. I just want my family back," I shook my head, trying to make sense of all this talk of dark and light and existence.

"Do you?" the eyes squinted here and there, examining me. "You seem to think I annihilated your little world single-handedly when I assure you, that was not the case at all. You want to go home to your little family, yet you have no idea what they were capable of. You might not be in such a hurry if you knew the truth," he teased.

I didn't want to know, and I instinctively curled my knees up to my chest as if I could protect myself from it. But something deep inside me twitched and grew into a wide longing to know and I felt myself powerless against it. "What is the truth?" I heard myself ask quietly.

Sarshēl loomed so very close to me but I couldn't feel that warmth of proximity and I wondered if he truly hadn't any presence at all. Or maybe it was I who'd lost mine. "Oh, my child, let me show you. Gaze into the lives of those análong you pine for," he boomed and I looked in the direction of the closest eye which bulged and expanded until I was caught in its movement and my mind drew into its rings and collapsed as if I were being pulled into it by the beating of his wings around me.

* * *

Immediately the space around me fleshed out and filled with a lightness, and I knew I was in Ebūda but in another time, an older time when the air sparked with a life before my own. Before me stood five elderly análong dressed in the red and gold robes of Elders. They spoke in low tones and to the side I could see the small dark figure of Sarshēl as I'd first seen him, whispering unseen to all but me into the ear of the tallest figure, his sharp little fingers curling around the Elder's shoulders.

"The end is coming," someone in the group said aloud, "And we must make grave decisions. The last Guardian is coming, the one who will bring our downfall. When the Guardian comes, what will be done with her?"

"Who can change the fate of a Guardian? It should be decided when the time comes," another answered.

But the Elder who had listened to Sarshēl said to them, "We will wash our hands of that. Beyond all, the Council must be maintained. When the time comes, if the NaÓma wish to kill her, the Council will not interfere. Is this decided?" There was an uneasy murmuring among them that nothing could be sincerely decided until Elders Anan, Corin and Rā-alta returned, but that they agreed to keep the meeting to themselves alone.

The walls grew and stretched, changing until I could see we were surrounded by the Palace walls and on a great throne sat that first Elder speaking to a servant alone.

"The NaÓma ask for an offering for protection when they reach the city," he reported.

"An offering?" The Elder said smoothly. "Oh, I see. There's gold we could offer from the Palace stores."

The servant looked uncomfortable. "Sir, they ask for something more… portable. More *disposable*."

The Elder nodded behind his gnarled hands clasped over his chin. "They're asking for payment. I expected no less. Then send a servant into the Cāilon and command two hundred slaves for this offering. Take only the healthiest, the strong and the young."

"But sir, they're likely to-"

"How it is my concern what happens to a slave? The Council must be preserved at all costs. I don't need to tell you that you cannot refuse the order of an Elder and expect to live."

The servant bowed and left the room. From behind the throne another Elder slipped out of the curtained hall and stood by it, commenting. "In the end we don't need the Guardian to beg for our souls. The NaÓma will find her and they can take care of it for us."

* * *

"They wanted you dead before you even came into the world," Sarshēl hissed into my ear as the inky black returned abruptly around us. "They thought you were useless!"

"What did you say to him?" I demanded as the distance grew between us again and I could properly see all of his terrible eyes and mouths again.

"It didn't take me long in the ancient days to find a way past Anŏ. The route of dreams is an open one, a road traveled back and forth between all realms. Speaking to the análong was cumbersome in that way, certainly, but not impossible. A bit like, dropping breadcrumbs. Análong are very much like humans that way. They hold a degree of malice in their hearts naturally; of selfishness and greed, impatience and apathy. They are easily influenced to follow those desires.

Dreams aren't the only gateway however; there are many unseen ways into the heart, as I was made to make use of when the Guardian Lān closed that venue.

And so, I merely repeated that Elder's own fear and selfishness back to him and he let me right in. He chose to listen and act on his own weaknesses for he was arrogant enough to think that I would make good on the promise to save the Elders from death and give them souls. They thought they could bargain directly with me for power and circumvent the Guardians and their own deal with Mǐ'á. To save his own skin he would have had you put to the death."

"Shut up," I warned, clenching my fists. "How could *you* promise to give them souls?"

"I wouldn't pretend to try," Sarshēl's voice coddled. "I have power, but not so much as that. But you never met those Elders, did you? All dead by the time you got to them. Before you go tutting at me, perhaps you should consider those you knew best. Not all you might have thought them to be. As I said, not one of them is without some degree of evil; all of them desperate to be saved. It's been thousands of your years since I touched an análong and yet, none remain, do they? A famine, a drought and they all go to pieces tearing each other limb from limb!"

I'd seen it myself, and I didn't need to see any more. "No, I don't want to-."

"Open your eyes and look, Guardian!" he roared, and I was pulled to him again to see the visions in his wings before I could protest.

* * *

In the last evening's light, I recognized Dandhō bent over a bed. Thin and crooked, her ears dropped in exhaustion and her head was oddly bare. But it wasn't my bedside she sat by; it was a strange bed in a strange hut. I could see with great surprise she'd taken off her arm-bands, those colorful bits of cloth she never spoke of, and under them were swollen, white scars eating down deeply into her speckled blue skin.

She gently woke the old sleeping análong laying there tangled in the thin blankets and waited for him to register some sort of recognition. He put out a faded, bony hand to her and rasped, "Are you my daughter that left those years ago and never returned to me?"

Bowing her head, the same Dandhō who'd boldly sent me into the forest answered him, "I am Adīí́á Rī who is called Ta- F'ala. Are you my father who never sent for me?" The old análong's nod was so slight I nearly missed it.

"I am dying just like the rest of the Pōcarū," he whispered.

Dandhō pulled herself up with difficulty and returned from another room with a damp cloth to press to his forehead. To my great horror, I saw the char-like lumps swollen and sickly on her neck.

"No," I whispered, the ugliness that would be her death overshadowing the actual loss of her. "Don't worry A'da," She gave a brittle smile. "We all are. I was gone so long because I was busy taking care of some things. But now I'm here to take care of you."

The old análong's face smiled gently and I watched a little longer at the real first peace I'd ever seen upon Dandhō. And it drifted around the room until the whole place faded away into silver sand floating about me.

* * *

"She finally went to see her father," I murmured.

"On his deathbed!" Sarshēl exclaimed, his feather's trembling angrily. "What kind of daughter waits until her father's last breath to come to his side?" he demanded.

I really didn't know what sort of daughter would do that; I'd never been a daughter. Sarshēl pressed on, gathering his wings closer around me as if to suffocate me. "And look at him! He left her behind, all alone in the city when her mother died. He chose her sister over her, he abandoned her! What kind of father forgets one of his children?"

"I don't know, I…" I stammered, for I'd never pondered the stories of Dandhō and Little Dandhō much before me. I reached out and took what was handed to me, not considering there may be much more beyond what I could see.

Sarshēl's laugh was slow and winding into hysteria. "Secrets. I wonder, how many more secrets are there? I wonder how well you truly knew your little family?"

My lower lip wobbled precariously, an old familiar threat of tears. Sarshēl pounced on this and a wave of his deceptive smiles rippled around me. Clenching my fists, I resolved not to be taken by his lies.

"I know they loved me, my ah'sha and all," I replied stiffly.

"So sweet, this idea of love, so...simple. But I wonder, how much stock would you put in a murderer? Can you really put faith in the word of someone that dangerous? What sort of love is that?" his voice pondered.

I could feel my face warm in frustration as a cold trickle of fear tickled me. "I don't know what you're talking about."

"It's interesting, isn't it? I promised you the truth, and I intend to deliver. I just think it's interesting that your *ah'sha* never mentioned it."

"What do you mean?" I asked, willing myself not to listen but still irresistibly curious.

"Those bands on her arm. I wonder why she wore those?" he baited.

"Scars," I murmured.

"I wonder how she got those scars. I wonder why she never told you about them?"

It wasn't a lie that I wondered the same thing. This time, when the eyes opened and the wings pulled, I willingly allowed myself to be swallowed up. I wanted to see.

* * *

I blinked to clear my vision, but it was very difficult to see anything but the outlines before me. The small shack's door was open, illuminated by ribbons of light cutting through the humid, heavy air. I turned my head and saw in the distance, a glass dome far above where light poured in and bounced off great round mirrors fixed far above me in the rock's walls. It was this light that traveled through what looked to be a sort of underground city and in the mirrors, I could see the moving shadows of those high aloft walking by. It made the eerie light move like water, waving back and forth across the simple dwellings and the silhouettes of nondescript streets.

But here and there were flashes of golden reflections; the moving sparkles of large, moving wheels and gears, the steam of water being pushed up through the thick pipes traveling upward. I shuddered. This was the bad place, the Caīlon.

A movement caught my eye and I turned back to the open door. Cautiously I walked through into a small room fitted with a bed and table. I couldn't make out what laid on the bed but the feeling that someone was there frightened me. The room smelled rank, like old metal. No, I knew that smell. It was blood. There was someone standing in the shadows, just beyond my sight and I crept closer, reminding myself that this was someone else's memory; my body wasn't really there. Nothing here could truly hurt me.

I heard it before I saw it. A sound repeating; deep and cruel. The movement; constant and punishing. An adult and a child. The child looked older than Éē'shī but younger than Little Dandhō and I didn't know what was happening, only that it hurt. He was hurting her.

I couldn't scream. My voice wouldn't rise high enough to come out of me but died in a fat, worthless lump in my chest. Then everything stopped in one rough thud and he moved away, but the dhana didn't move from the bed. Behind me, a movement, something smaller than I. I jumped back to see.

Unaware that there were three of them in the room, the little voice asked "*Ha-* are you ok, Rī?" In the dim, I saw this small child snatched up off her feet faster than she could scream. The older child, Rī, pulled herself up off the bed in a jerky motion and rushed over to the table, grabbing what lay there in the gloom.

The voice from the shadows was low and dangerous as he growled, "Stay out of it, dhana." But Rī held her prize from the table over her head. "Don't you dare touch her," she threatened, but he only laughed from the shadows. "I own you two. I'll do as I please with the both of you."

Because it was so dark and so fast, I saw only the glint of the knife blade slashing through the air. Rī grabbed at the smaller child with her other hand, pushing her roughly out the door. The struggle was quick and hard; the screams intensified, the crack of Rī's head against the wall shocked me. She waved the knife with all her strength. He yelled, "I'll kill you!"

But he didn't. He couldn't.

An odd, sucking noise cut his screams short as he fell backwards against the table. I could see his neck and chest darkened, the stain growing as he stopped moving completely. Rī dropped the knife, clutching at her arm to splint it against her ribs and she turned and ran into the street. "Lec'shii! Lec'shii!" she screamed, but the street was empty. Near the end of it I saw her pause in the stream of light shining from above for a moment looking frantically for the smaller child. The hem of her dress was dark and bloodied; her arm streamed scarlet down onto her foot-wrappings. I ran and caught up to her and as I did, a noose of rope fell down from the glass dome far above and caught her up right from the ground.

Immediately I was also caught up from above and now I stood in the marketplace, squinting in the light. I shaded my eyes and looked around, searching for Rī and saw her being pulled out of another open dome from the ground a few yards away. There, a shanár merchant had pulled her up by the rope, lifting her high over his head in one strong motion. I ran forward and stood nearby, ashamed that I was mesmerized by the pattern of blood splashed over her legs and arms. The merchant put her down and looked her over.

"What's your name?" he asked.

Rī stood with her good hand out to feel, unable to open her eyes at all in the sunlight. She answered, "Nothing, sir."

"Who do you belong to?"

"No-one, sir."

"That's like to fall off. What happened to it?" he studied her bloodied arm nearly dangling from just below her shoulder.

Rī said nothing and clutched at it tighter, but I could see she was shivering under the hot sun.

"Then if you are without a name and without a master, I'll call you F'ala," he said. "I have many na'dhana and I've been looking for a servant for the little ones. You can sleep in the storehouse and my eldest is about your size so you can wear her old things. Let's get the arm fixed first. Come on, no one's going to miss you." And he took her by the other shoulder and pulled her along through the unconcerned crowd, as if it were so easy to rewrite a life.

I followed for a little while, watching her look back again and again to that spot she'd been rescued in. Then my steps fell onto nothing and I found myself once again floating in the company of Sarshēl. I touched my own arm as I thought of what I'd seen, understanding now that Dandhō's bracelets hid the proof of the day she'd killed another análong, the day she lost her name. "Dandhō was a slave," I murmured, stunned.

"She was nothing but a liar," Sarshēl's many lips curled up in glee. "She lied about her crime to be taken in, lied about her status as a slave to become the Ta-, lied to Rā-alta to get her status back by taking you in. She wasn't fit to carry the water of a Guardian and she knew it."

"It's not true," I hissed. My thoughts became muddled as I strained to remember what I knew to be true. Or what I thought I knew.

"A murderer's reward is to be executed!" he roared.

"Yes," I said softly. Yes, the law of Ebūda was written that a life demanded a life. But I'd been fortunate that Dandhō had taught me well that no matter how noble the hearts of the análong, no matter how high their ideals, reality proved a poor mirror. The truth was that the demands of the city to be fueled by the labors of the Cāilon far outweighed its desire for justice to all its dwellers. Even so, that truth didn't excuse brutality.

"If she'd been executed," I continued softly, "I would have had no one."

"Does that wash out her crime? If she had been punished as she deserved someone else may have given you a better life," Sarshēl pointed out cleverly.

A familiar fear traced its cold fingers around the back of my head and seeped deeply into me. I couldn't turn away from this knowledge that I'd lived my whole life with a murderer. Yet I also knew the ambiguous nature of words; that strange way a word had of showing a different side of itself in the mouth of one whose intent it was to use it to their own purpose. Angels... demons...

"She saved that child," I said, carefully trying to steer my memory away from what I'd seen. "He would have hurt her too."

"A master's privilege over his property," Sarshēl declared. "It is no different than my own privilege over the análong."

I closed my eyes. My mind felt thick, the thoughts heavy and hard to sort through. I knew of the buying and selling of análong; I knew Dandhō had kept me from that same fate. And I knew that there was no escape from that life, that the child she saved most likely never breathed fresh air again. That Dandhō had been saved from it was … a miracle. I didn't know her reasons for lying, who could tell what went on in another's heart?

But one thing was very clear in my heart: I'd been taught the dangerous truths, the secret knowledge of Ebūda and by it I knew that we each carried the light of Creation within us, not one more than the other. "Porāma," I whispered. "Cīama."

"Words, words; worthless, worthless lies," Sarshēl's voice lowered. "Are these little sayings what ties you so strongly to the dead?"

"I don't know why anyone does anything," I said, "not even myself sometimes. But I know that none of us is above another. I know that we all do things, good and bad."

"A Guardian is a thousand times superior to an análong; a Guardian is not shackled by any mortal law! If we join together, we can free ourselves of our masters of light and darkness and form our own world, write our own law! We will be the masters of a whole new existence!" Sarshēl half-implored, half-threatened. "Think of it, a world where you never have to hide, where you'll never be alone. Where you can use your own power as you were born to do!"

It was more than I could bear. The promise of a life free to walk outside without striking fear in the hearts of all who saw me, the assurance of a day working in the fields liberated from the terror of being seen, the panic of being taken away or sold or killed. Such a hope was beyond anything I could imagine and yet so strongly alluring my imagination couldn't resist trying to. If I had that power within me to create such a place, shouldn't I at least take a closer look?

In that space between my eyes, something familiar flickered, something quick and bright, but not threatening. The glimmer that had intimidated me all my life now beckoned, calling to show me something, to show me everything. And then I allowed it to overcome me, the true understanding that I was a Guardian. It was just as I'd feared, the sensation of wings beating within me, and a barrage of images, feelings and words. Without my permission, I felt them all molding together into a definite path swirling about me in a circle moving so fast it threatened to crush me within it. *All things*, the words rushed out. All things right, all things wrong; the words, the very wonderful and awfulness that was *me*. And with a thrust I clamped my eyes shut and brought it all to a halt, gasping for breath.

"See how marvelous you are!" Sarshēl beckoned, as I made myself stand firm against the mighty, rushing waters of knowledge. I had grown so much since the first time six years ago when it burned into me. I was now able to contain it; no longer did it have the power to annihilate me under its weight. No longer could the beating wings push at my understanding; they but tickled and illuminated that which was already there. It was no longer in a strange, detached way that I would accept that I was a Guardian.

Even so, what Sarshēl proposed seemed too simple, deceptively simple. How could I possibly make something out of nothing?

"First though, caémba," I stalled, hoping I would figure it out on my own. "If I agree and stay with you, if I do, I've got to bring caémba first. That's my purpose."

The lips of his many mouths pursed in pity. "You poor child, I thought you knew! There is no such thing as caémba of course. That's only an análong dream, a wish to be equal to humans. One cannot be human if one is born an análong, the same as a star cannot be an análong. It is the curse of mortality, to constantly want more than one has. You don't need to take my word for it, look around you! Are there lines of análong waiting to be handed their souls like bowls of soup? Are there armies with swords and shields waiting to fight for a revolution?"

I didn't need to look. Sarshēl was truthful of that; there were only the two of us left and I was being childish in thinking I could just turn around undo what had been done.

"That's right," his eyes suddenly surrounded me, scrunching up with false empathy. "You were all alone all your life. No friends, no real family, no opportunities. How could they accept you when you were only a stranger amongst them, the color of death on every inch of you? How could they love a constant reminder that one day they would fade into the ground and never wake again?"

I sank down into myself, the pressure of it weighing on me. So many times, I thought there were no words in the world to describe the emptiness, that complete dejection that came from knowing that while I was like every other análong in every other way, the reminder in my own skin served was constant, permanent. The truth was, I'd died ignorant and half-loved and utterly, utterly a foreigner. I was, in fact, friendless.

Yet I couldn't accept that they were gone, that I'd be better off in this nothing-world with Sarshēl than with those I had so hoped to be my own. The air around me stirred and Sarshēl flew back, hovering in the distance. His eyes blinked randomly as he studied me and I could feel the restraint he put upon himself. "But with an equal, you'd never be alone again," he promised once more.

"Why are you in such a hurry for me to decide?" I wondered aloud.

Sarshēl didn't flinch. "Every Guardian has power," he purred. "By virtue that you were once a star, your power didn't disappear just because you changed form. But I imagine nobody told you about that. Nobody told you about that power you could have used all along. Not your so-called family, certainly not your *ah'sha*."

"Stop it," I warned. "It's not your right to call her that."

"I'm not beholden to the customs of mortals! You've been nothing but a fool. I'm embarrassed that you'd believe you were nothing but a soul-less, powerless análong child. Don't you have any idea of what you can do?" I was immediately aware of the beating of many wings, the sudden wind skipped up around me and beat against my face so that I had to turn away to breathe.

"No." That tiny word pressed out into the dark seemed to suck all of the air out from around me. "I don't want to join you," I said with a bit more confidence.

"*WHAT!*" It was more an accusation hurled at me than a question. The air that had disappeared resurfaced and came at me with gale-force, blowing me head over heels a good distance. In less than a second Sarshēl caught up with me and surrounded me in his wings like a cage, the mouths taunting me now with bared teeth, the eyes casting a reddish hue momentarily before sliding back into their ambient hues. "I'm sure you're just tired. You only need to give it a moment of thought," his voice soothed.

"No," I repeated in a measured voice.

"Clearly you haven't been paying attention," Sarshēl's voice tempted, a feather caressing my cheek. "Stay with me, choose to reign with me. Only a fool would choose to die now, just at a new beginning."

"Is that what's going to happen? If I don't choose, I'll just, disappear?" I wanted a straight answer.

"All things created have their end eventually," he admitted. But, seeing my hesitance he went on. "Do you know how your precious F'ala died? In filth, alone, degraded. Not like us; nothing like us! We never need to truly die if we join together."

"But you said created things-"

"*MAKE YOUR CHOICE!*" Sarshēl's large right wing sharply stuck me in the face and I felt tears spring up hot to the back of my eyes. But he controlled himself long enough to ask, "Haven't you ever considered that this is all there is? That all that knowledge you've held so dear is nothing but ideas? You want the truth but you're too immature to hear it."

Suddenly I lunged at him and screamed with all my being, the sound becoming so gradually loud in my ears I couldn't tell when it melted into a grief-stricken silence. Even my eyes shook with such rage I thought they'd fall right out of my head. I felt crushed under my own weight suddenly; legs trembling with the uncertainty of my future, my past. The understanding that nothing was as I'd expected it to be, that reality was far beyond my imagination drowned me and I was utterly at a loss as to what to do.

"You can't shock me now," I growled. "I've already seen that the world hides behind a mask. I've already lost everything I had. Whatever truth you're trying to prove to me isn't going to change who I am."

If he's so powerful what does he need you for?

That little voice, that mean little version of myself who'd been silent for so long called up from my feet. And for a moment I thought she meant that I wasn't worth needing, but then I listened again, really listened. When I heard the words repeated, I heard them differently. They weren't pointing out my shortcomings, they were pointing out *his lack*. What did he need me for? If he was a powerful lord who had formed the análong in the ancient days and given them life, why couldn't he just make this new world himself? If I died here on the spot what did it matter to him?

He dangled a truth in front of me, but it wasn't the entire truth. How did I know we really were alone, that my family wasn't out there and that there wasn't still something even beyond what I could see? *Oh ah'sha, tell me what to do*, I prayed.

Remember the most important thing.

"No," I repeated, curling up to protect myself from Sarshēl's angry attack.

"Then you will die here, do you understand? *You will cease to exist.* There will be no chance to change your mind, no way to go back," he said carefully, uneasily.

Letting down my guard slightly, I considered. I'd never had the life I longed for, and what did I do to deserve that? Didn't I deserve at least a try? If I was so above the análong, wasn't I entitled to go on? In some way I supposed I should be grateful Sarshēl had shown me that much.

Don't be stupid, he doesn't care about you or what happens to you.

You're right, I thought down to my feet. *Sarshēl doesn't care about anyone. He lost Ebūda because he didn't care about his own creations. I don't know how this works, but he can't go on without me. Can't go on…*

"And you'll cease to exist too, won't you?" I called out. "That's why you need me. This is your punishment, isn't it? You lost Ebūda to my brother and you've been getting your revenge all these years. But now Ebūda is gone and your master is done with you. Your time is over."

Then I was aware of being totally and utterly alone; alone in a way much deeper and more terrifying way than any I'd felt in all my life, even after Éē'shǐ's death. "Sarshēl!" I shouted, but my voice fell flat. I waved my arms and legs about but couldn't propel myself in any direction. "Sarshēl!" I screamed, my back arching as I forced the sound out into the thin air until something seemed to break around me and I came face to face with the abundance of eyes and mouths and wings that made up his true form.

"I do hope you enjoyed that because that's what it's going to be like forever if you don't take my offer," he sneered at me. I didn't answer, instead glaring back to inspect every bit of him until I found a tiny little eye amongst the glares of rage hidden deep in the feathers peering out from their safety. Reaching out, I gently pulled back the little wing to reveal its clear surface. Fear looked back at me.

Remember the most important thing…

"I've made my decision," I said, the words etching their way across my mind, threading out from the tapestry of all those words of those already gone before me.

I was loved. I was given food while my family went hungry. I was watched over in the night on the roadside. I was given the knowledge I needed for this very moment. I was given a rightful place on the grandfather tree. It was not for me to judge or pardon what happened before me; it was for me to write the story of my life from the words that flowed into mine from the past. I knew what it meant to be a Guardian, and I wanted to be more. I wanted to live even in these last moments, to make my own choice and use my own power.

What is the most important thing?

Ah'sha sent me out into a dangerous world and nothing could take the sting away from that. But now in this uncertain moment, I could see a glimmer of why. As I didn't know the dangers that might still be ahead of me, or the consequences of what I would choose to do, I had to make a choice based on the belief I placed in the universe. Like that hope ah'sha had placed in me to survive for this very moment, I had to do my best and only my best.

Belief grows into faith; faith grows into certainty. But we start with hope.

The wings softened and all of Sarshēl's eyes focused on me alone; piercing, hopeful. "Excellent! I knew you would make the right decision!"

"I have," I waved my hand from side to side. "And this is where I shall end," I explained as his many eyes bulged open in shock. "*We* will die here. We're already dying. That's why you're in such a rush for me to join you. You want to save yourself."

"So, you choose to punish me!" the eyes stretched and began to melt grotesquely together. "You choose to kill me, when *I* would have saved *you!*"

"You're right, I do have power I've never used. And you're also right, I am a Guardian. All my life I was a foreigner. The world hated me, it feared me, it made me invisible. But it was my family who reminded me every day that I did belong, that the differences between me and them were out shadowed by the similarities.

My power in is making my choice, and what I choose is to rule no-one but myself, to prevent a new world where you can have any influence on anyone else. I choose not to help you give your own power away for something so worthless as the hate of your master," I said.

Sarshēl screamed in fury. "How dare you speak of my master, you know nothing!"

"I know that no análong is entirely good, not even me. But I also know no being is entirely evil, and that includes you," I stared purposefully at that one tiny, fearful eye and it shuddered closed, melting into the soup of color now pulling in the teeth and feathers of Sarshēl's once frightening but magnificent form. "But you gave the good part of yourself away to your master. You told me yourself, you chose the master you wanted to serve. I can't undo what you've done to yourself."

"Choose what you will then! Murder me!"

I bowed my head, exhausted but ready. "Every action has a consequence. I accept the consequence."

The strike to my chest was so fast it took the breath from me and I gasped as I tried to dodge the sharp fists of air which formed out from underneath Sarshēl's congealed eyes and beat against my head and back so hard I couldn't tell what direction they came from. His skin seemed to absorb all the air around him while mine seemed to leak my own weak spirit outwards like the fine smoke of incense. The pain was unimaginable; it stretched to every pore of my body and I bit the inside of my mouth to keep from crying out. I arched toward him, seeing my own blood in my mind before it spilled from the sharp pinyons of his wings as they cut through my middle.

"What are you doing?" my voice croaked out, the pain all at once sharp and fiery. I looked down and allowed my grief to mix in with the garishly bright blood dripping down my legs. Suddenly they appeared so white, so soft and cold and detached from the rest of me. I was fading away.

"Go from my sight!" Sarshēl roared, his wings stretching out in full like a dark sail. "Don't you dare look at me; I was glorious in ways you could never imagine!"

The pain ceased as sharply as it had begun. A strange calm settled over the air between us and I drew back into my own mind for a moment, unsure of how to move. An oddly unsettled feeling came over my thoughts as if I'd forgotten to do something important and now couldn't recall what it was.

A thin trail of liquid wiggled down my lips as I reached out weak arms to Sarshēl. I caught on to one of his longer feathers and pulled weakly, surprised at how easy it was to bring his evolving form to me. He wrestled weakly against me, piercing me even further but my body had become so disconnected, so faded and detached my mind, it only registered a faint twinge.

Sarshēl's voice rose again, attempting to distance himself from me. I jumped back, pulling him nearly through the gaping hole he'd plunged through my front with those razor-like pinyons. I jumped back again, trying to get my arms around his vacant form as he struggled less fiercely, distracted by the wet feel of blood streaming down my back.

That's not blood. You're trying to make sense of what hurts in your mind.

My toes wiggled their notice and I looked down just as Sarshēl heaved back and rammed across my head with an audible crack.

But I didn't move, nor did I feel the blow. "That's right," I whispered against his wordless screams. "I have no body to bleed. I have no head to be injured. I'm not bleeding, I'm not hungry. I'm not cold. And I'm not fooled by you."

Over and over again, even as he weakened and lost more and more of his form, Sarshēl repeated his attacks and I repeated my mantra until I saw that my skin was fading, the connection between my limbs and torso thinning out.

"Stop fighting," I whispered as Sarshēl's voice thinned out, his form condensing before me, the wings losing their definition as they disintegrated into a fine smoke.

"No-one ever loved you," his voice came back in a sob. "You were all alone."

"No," I said sadly, "You've forgotten that anyone ever loved *you*." Not even this great, ancient being understood the simplest of things. All things belonged to a family. Mine didn't fit, it didn't look like other families or act like other families. But it was the only family I knew and at that moment I felt I would drown in love, yes, disappear altogether in my love for them. The certainty shone bright in that dark, dark place that I wished all the beauty in the world for them, and every heartbreak too, for I didn't want them to miss one second of all that life could give. I was never alone. Just lonely.

What is the most important thing to you?

"I am a Guardian. And I am also an análong. I lived as an análong and I will die as one. I will do as my ancestors did, which is all I can for the dying. And what can I do? I have nothing to give. But because you've forgotten love, I will be the one to love you."

"Who gives you the authority?" Sarshēl tried with every ounce of strength he had left to escape me, but I took a breath and propelled myself forward with all my strength and wrapped my arms around his pulsating form. "*Ta cī'úa éh an an*," I repeated my promise in the Dala words of my people. *I will be the one.*

A biting wind suddenly howled against us with such force I thought it would blow us both to bits, but I could feel his substance. Now I could feel some semblance of form against mine, resisting. The barrier which had held us floating away from each other dissolved and I felt the true sensation of his body weakening, growing smaller and smaller until it condensed and disappeared. I opened my hands, sure to find them empty. But there in my palm rested a tiny, single eye. Its lashes lay gently, like a sleeping butterfly.

"It's alright, I'm here," I said softly, unsure if Sarshēl had the means to hear me.

The little eye opened, and I saw it was clear and bright and filled with tears. "It's ok," I reassured. "You're not alone, I won't leave you."

Drip.

What was that? I closed my palms gently over Sarshēl's remaining eye and looked out into the dark, straining my eyes to see what could have caused the distinct sound of water.

Drip.

"Who's there?" I called, but no answer came.

Drip.

"I don't understand," I opened my palm to speak to Sarshēl but jumped to find it empty, the eye vanished. I turned around but there was nothing to see, nowhere to go. So, this was what the end looked like.

Drip. Drip. Drip.

For all my bravery, my face crumpled into tears and I drew my knees up to my chest, throwing my head back to shout my last words. "I am Rī Mi'hal'ē, the last Guardian and the last análong," I declared. "And as the last act of my people, I forgive the crimes of Sarshēl by my own power. This is the caémba! Let Creation remember us forever for our true selves, not what we were tempted to be.

For what I remember most and above all, is that everything seemed so horribly, impossibly beautiful. And so, I thank them, and I bless them, all that feared and hated me, all that feared my face. For I would not have loved so deeply without them and I would never have wanted for what I already had."

Drip.

Then as suddenly as I'd felt that abject solitude, the awareness of another's presence flooded me and I looked up to see the faint outline of someone familiar. Beside me, I felt Dandhǒ's presence, tall and hot, fidgety and strong and her words began to form around me. "Ah'sha!" I shouted, but there was no answer. Like the memories I'd been allowed to see, she wasn't in my time to be able to hear me. She wasn't speaking *to* me.

"I knew the day I explained to her about hunting that she'd seen me for what I really was, a murderer. No matter what my reasons, I had killed an análong long ago and my hands could never be washed of that blood. What had happened to me could not be spoken of, was never spoken of in society. So, in a way, there was no-one I could ever tell. And besides that, I had left Lec'shii behind me, certain to meet the same fate. I don't know how I could have gone back, but still; I didn't try. I knew that til the day I died.

Rā-alta had no idea when she ordered me to take Mi'hal'ē that I'd made myself less than a slave with the choice I'd made in that moment. But somehow despite my incompetence, Mi'hal'ē was so smart, so quick, so clever. I wrote to Rā-alta to tell her but couldn't make myself send the letter. It seemed every good thing I wanted to say about the dhana sounded as if I were claiming some sort of part in it and I knew that couldn't be. Nevertheless, even when she disobeyed, I couldn't help but be proud. Proud, and terrified because Rā-alta was right. This dhana was a Guardian; everything we'd ever hoped for."

I reached out blindly to grasp her hand but found only empty space. "No, ah'sha, I didn't do anything," I cried. "Because you loved me, this is how I grew."

Drip!

That distant sound of water continued, becoming insistent, yet it remained beyond my vision. My ah'sha had gone.

Drip! Drip! Drip!

But then I heard the singing of Dala words. One voice, thin and clear from above dropped the first tone on my head like the ring of a bell.

...ōshē ē ūrn ihn ūrdū...all is full of light

The singing swelled and grew from above me, below me, around me, within me! A multitude of voices intertwined, rose and swirled; the words of the song becoming the beat of a drum inside me.

...caémba ē ashūrē ... revolution is a whisper

A chill made its way up my arms, giving me hope that the end had been delayed, that perhaps my family remained somehow for me to find them. The words seemed familiar, as if the song were from so long ago.

...na'dan'shir ē tēmat...*creation is a breath*

...'s aói ī-nen dō arēl...*and love, the path to eternity*

...hōtō- an pín ihn an gaú nūa ē tī'shē ...*see, the seed of a new world is come!*

As the voices rose around me and spiraled upwards, I heard my own joining them to form a wall of sound that held me and rocked me gently. My eyes slid shut as I listened, and I felt warmth wash over me. I felt the longing to see my family once again, but it had become a different pain, the sweet pain of memory. Now as I sang from a place buried within, I felt a new pain for Sarshēl. How he must have missed his own people, for didn't all things separated yearn to return to their own?

...ōshē ē ūrn ihn ūrdū...*all is full of light*

Higher and higher the melody rose until finally I could hear it no more, only a new warm wind whistling gently in my ears. But long after I could still feel the words now part of my being.

Slowly the wind died and around me, there shone a bright light, burning through my eyelids and bringing my senses back in a flash to feel the crisp stamp of it on my skin. My hands clasped as I felt the outlines of my limbs fill in with the pure golden light left to me by the onandals.

My eyes opened tentatively but I could no longer see anything past the golden glow surrounding me. Only when I thought about moving did the impression of standing return to me and I felt the sensation of something lapping heavily against my legs.

"Water," I whispered in awe, struck by the irresistible wish to put my hands in it and splash. Bending down, I gave in and dragged the tips of my golden fingers in the brightening water. Dismayed, I couldn't feel its coolness or its refreshment. Still I played, hoping for some sort of connection to manifest, pausing to look up only when a bit of color swimming atop the rippling water caught my eye.

And then I saw them, the children of Ebūda coming towards me through the water. Tens and thousands splashed and danced towards around me in their colorful clothes waist-deep in the calm waves, clapping and smiling at me. Some rode on the backs of others, some skimmed the water with their wings.

Their names soared through my mind: Tenādha, Endhē, Nūshca, Endorē, Laata, Lāca, Ants'ala, Nīdha, Pōra, Naftah, Līcah, Dashorē, Ahnūc, Ahrē, Ne'talē, T'hī, Dhem'sha. Then they came faster and faster until they melded into a solid blur of sound and I was surrounded in an enormous, warm circle of laughter as the children pulled me with them out into the sea, where far off in the distance a faint white glowing line appeared; an edge. But as they splashed on in one formation toward it, I found my steps becoming heavy and exhausted. When I reached out to them for help they passed me, nearing the golden shore pulling up from the sea, stretching out into a valley.

I was again, alone.

Tears came, slipping down my face. All of my sorrows fell, adding to the water, stopping only when I saw the dark reflection of ten figures approaching, holding out their arms. Beckoning.

"A miracle," I whispered.

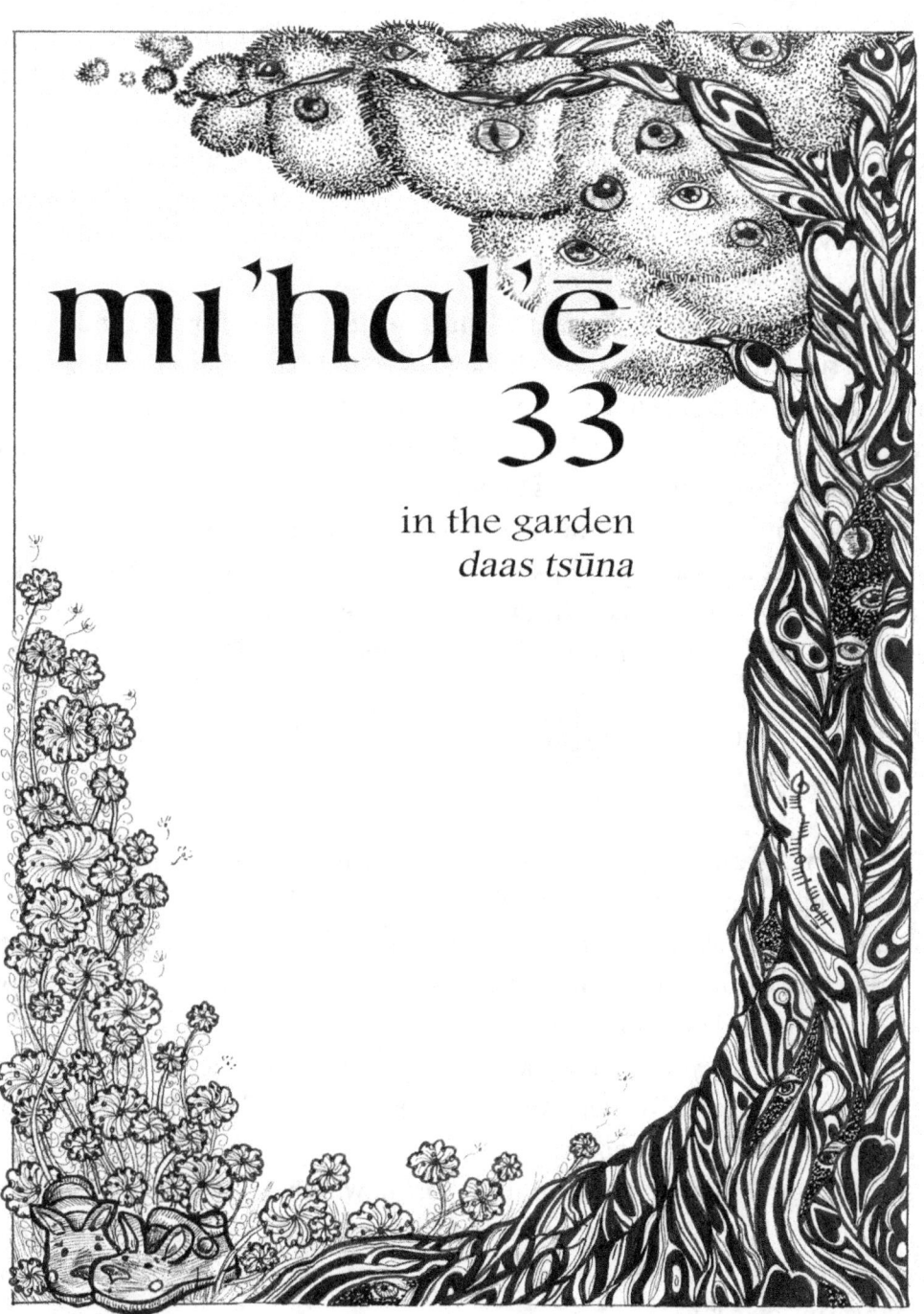

mi'hal'ē

33

in the garden
daas tsūna

1'D never noticed the design carved into the door-handle, nor that it was anything but plain, curved metal. Now I studied the crude marks curiously before pushing on it to open.

"I'm home!" I called more to the hut than anyone, bursting in through the common room like I'd always been told not to, catching my foot in a rug and dancing awkwardly across the floor into the sleeping room where my flailing hands pulled down the door-curtain in one clean rip.

"Graceful," a delicate, familiar voice observed. Pulling the curtain off my head, I saw Little Dandhō sitting on the bottom bed, her hands clasped over her knee. She shrugged her shoulders as she laughed and I launched myself at her, knocking her back onto the mattress with the force of my embrace. I wiggled against her, overjoyed.

"Come on, we've got to go help in the garden," she extracted herself from me and pulled me along outside where the sun streamed down through the trees onto the most beautiful garden I'd ever seen. Overflowing with melons and every other good thing to eat, it sparkled with the drops of a recent shower. The air, singing with the hum of bees, smelled rich and warm. And the very soil, happy after its years of mourning, glowed under flowers brighter and greater than any ever grown there before.

"You can help me tie up the vines," a strange voice said. I turned and saw that Little Dandhō had left me to join several others in breaking up new soil in a distant patch of the garden I didn't remember. Indeed, I'd never seen these strangers either, yet they seemed familiar to me in the distant way my mouth recalled a pleasant taste. I took the string from the owner of the voice and recognized her instantly: Elder Rā-alta.

I stammered, "I'm-" but she waved gently and nodded. "Rī Mi'halĕ. And I'm Rā-alta, your big sister."

"My big sister?"

"Mi'hal' ē!" My name came happily from the melon patch and two figures ran to me, hand in hand. I would have known them anywhere: Éĕ'shī and beside her, Āe'rū. We grabbed hands and twirled around in a circle, falling down in fits of laughter until the other strangers came to surround us, leaning on their hoes and shovels or sitting on overturned baskets. "How do I know you?" I picked myself up and dusted off my dress, inspecting each.

Éĕ'shī grinned. "These are your brothers and sisters. There's me," she made a proud face. "Āe'rū and Ădō you know. Rā-alta you've met. And all the brothers: Hōrŏ-cō, Horĕ, Lān, A'nō, and the twins Sada and Nārū. And Úă'la is coming."

I waved shyly to the figures clothed from the waist down, then followed Éĕ'shī to work on the vines. We tied them up to poles, feeling the hot sun on our backs and the cool breeze in the air and everything seemed so bright, so alive. "Why don't I remember everyone?" I asked suddenly, feeling I should recognize my own kin.

"Try," Rā-alta said, looking over from her work with a kind expression.

I stood very still and closed my eyes, breathing in the pleasant scent of the garden. Then I felt the sudden flowing of expansion inside my mind, awareness threading out beyond me in little trickles like young roots reaching for water. Images flew past me, glaring and pungent and memory eclipsed me, blending past and future together so that I felt the embers of starlight in my chest from long ago as I begged Éē'shī to trade places with me and allow me to save the análong. There, the tender wishes of childhood grazed past my cheeks as a new face looked into mine that I hadn't yet met.

It took me that long to grow into my intentions, I mused.

"Everything was so small to me," I said. "How could it have ever been that small to me? In all my life here everything was so big, so far, so forbidden. But I do now remember looking down from the heavens, with you."

"Yes," Éē'shī said softly, taking my hand and squeezing it. "When we were stars."

We worked on for a while, the sun never seeming to move from its comfortable place, but no-one complained of weariness. I was astonished by my own strength. How long had it been since I'd worked in the garden? Surely hours must have passed until the eleven of us sat down outside the storehouse to take a drink from the water pump. Rā-alta fussed over me, smoothing out my dress and wayward ears. On my other side, Éē'shī leaned over. "Did you bring them?"

"What?"

"The scrolls. I told you not to lose them. Have you got them?"

"No," I scrunched my up my eyes in dismay. "How could I bring them with me here?"

"Don't be silly," Éē'shī swatted at me and pointed down.

I looked down and discovered two scrolls beside me. The larger I knew was the grandfather tree. But the smaller I didn't remember at all. Examining it, I realized it was the scroll I'd never looked at; the letter Éē'shī bid me to take when she died because it was part of my history. But the names *Cicūri* and *Rā-alta* were written on the ribbon, not mine. I gazed at it dumbfounded, then handed it to Rā-alta. She leaned forward and took it gently, unrolling it to read. I glanced over her shoulder to read along.

My dearest Rā-alta,

I regret you may not read these words in this life, and that I never had the courage to say them. But my own life's breath is running out and I can never enter into the next one without you knowing. I can only hope that fate will deliver my truth to you. Do have any idea how much I've missed you these long years?

I never meant to leave Briën forever. When we parted I was so lost, I went on to do things that would shame you if you knew of them. I stayed in the city for several years, closer to you than you ever knew. But by then I was nothing. I'd lost every shred of dignity. For this reason, I returned to Drīdū, but I never forgot your tears outside the Palace that day when we were na'dhana. And every day we spent apart, I thought of the words I needed to say.

After I became Ta-, I too collected all the news I could of you from messengers coming through Pōcarū. Not a day went by, I didn't think of you. No matter what I may have ever said or did to the contrary, I was so proud you became an Elder. If anyone was born for it, it was you.

When I arrived in Bri'ĕn that day, I was overwhelmed at how much time had passed, stunned by how beautiful you had grown. And I was anguished over what I had missed. For when I saw you look at Sa'úū I realized it wasn't my shame that kept us apart. It makes sense now that if there was a way to forgive who I had become; your gentle heart would know it. Tsōl, what separated us was that while my heart was owned by you, yours was promised to him.

Did you have any idea when you asked me to take the dhana that I would have done anything you asked? Is that why you chose me? Because everything I did for her, I did first for you. And in return you gave me the one thing I never knew I wanted: a daughter. Forgive me that I fell in love with a Guardian. Forgive me that I loved you; that I will always love you.

Your Rī

With that, she rolled the letter back up and held it to her heart, closing her eyes. "Are you alright?" I whispered, and she hugged me with one arm. "I only wish she would have told me all that time ago."

"But how did it even get here?"

"Through love. Because lies bloom and fade. And evil, like a flower, has its season and then withers. But truth endures forever."

"Then this is my ah'sha's truth?"

"Yes. That she loved me. And that she loved you. And look what love has done." She waved her hand over the beautiful garden. "It has given us a *tomorrow* where before there was none."

And as I gazed at the lush garden fat with vegetables and flowers, the barrel full of sparkling water under the pump, the bulging storehouse and the deep blue sky, I thought to myself there was nothing else I could possibly want in that moment. That is, until my gaze floated down to eleven pairs of feet, feet of every color and shape. And I realized something was missing.

Jumping up, I ran through the garden to the front of the hut and skidded to a stop at the doorstone. No pipe. No boots.

I'd never been good at growing things and the joy I'd felt at my little melon patch's success was ruined when two plants withered unexpectedly. She'd said that day in the garden, "*My wish for you is that you would always want for something, that your joy would have a drop of sadness in it so that it*

may be full." And I threw down the shovel and bawled, "*That's a terrible wish!*" But her face washed over with the look of one who has learned from experience the things words cannot teach us. She said, "*It's a wish you'll understand one day better than me. Now pick up that shovel!*"

"I understand now. You're the thing missing, ah'sha," I whispered with a sweet, satisfied ache. "My most important thing." I sat down with a flop against the door, cradling my head in my hands. "Won't I ever see her again?" I wondered aloud in despair.

A valiant voice rang out from up the path into the fields before me. "When the world was gold, and brindled, the sky! Doors, standing open, their gilded thoughts belied!"

From behind the hut Ééʾshī came running to the end of the path, exclaiming. "Úáʾla!"

I joined her half-heartedly and we stood and watched as the stalks of grain parted and flowed like water to reveal the figure of a tall análong, both male and female, made of the elements of the shanár, the darna and the g'éalach. Delicately featured with a face painted for war, her skin shone like diamonds, her muscles rippled smoothly to carry her with strength, and her hands wielded an enormous golden sword. Thrusting it into the ground before me, she kneeled. "I am Úa'la, the Guardian of Revolution. It is time for us to decide."

We followed Úa'la into the garden again, and here where there had been a great growing garden now opened a pool of sparkling water. Around it, my brothers and sisters grasped hands. Úa'la raised the sword, then looked at each of us.

"Once we were stars over Gaia, which is called *Earth*. We fell and were reborn in Ebūda outside the Law of Orders. By our sister's struggle with the fallen angel Sarshēl we have fulfilled our deal with the heavens and the análong are granted their request."

"It's done," Rā-alta smiled at me. "You've passed your tests. You proved that one born as an análong could rise above the worst evils of their own people and carry out the best of them."

"I don't think I did," my head felt heavy, defeated.

Rā-alta smoothed over my ears and kissed me. "You are the Guardian of Hope. You brought hope to the one análong in all the world I chose to take care of you. And her love guided you and taught you. And when you were faced with your rival, you carried that love and passed it on. Everything you see here, the sky, the trees, you, I. All possible because you were the one. There was a circle bigger than any of us, and you closed it."

"All mortal things have will," Úa'la continued. "And all mortal things wish to return to where they come from. But this is not revolution, for revolution always moves *forward*. The análong believed that when they were given souls, they would return to Ebūda; a perfect and restored Ebūda. And they have received their souls, but they will go onward. For Ebūda has had its time."

"But where will they go?" I asked.

Úa'la smiled, lowering the sword to wade into the water. "To join the spirits of humankind waiting to be born."

"Come on," my sisters urged, and we followed each other into the water. One at a time, Hor'ē, Lān, A'nō, and Sada listened as Úa'la whispered something into their ears. Then they reached down into the water without looking back and let it sift through their fingers as their bodies melded softly into the water's rings. I gazed on, transfixed as the reflection of their eyes grew larger and larger and the colors of their skins melted away completely on the top of the water and the ripples turned dark as if they had swallowed them each up.

At the water's edge stood Hor'ŏ'cō and Nārū, their heads bowed.

"Are we going to join the spirits of humankind?" I whispered to Éé'shī. "If you want," she said in a serious tone. "No one can force you to."

But as my sisters each smiled at me and then disappeared into the water, I stood behind, stalling.

"Can't you tell me if I'll ever see my ah'sha again?" I implored. But Úa'la declined. "No one can tell you that, little sister. We can never know the will of another, mortal or immortal. You must make your own choice if you are to go on or not, just as she has had to make hers. All you can hope is that in the next life you will find each other."

Still I hung back, unsure if I wanted to spend another lifetime chancing that I might not fit in, that I might never see my family again in any shape. Sensing my indecision, Úā'la told me to pay attention. "Our brothers have chosen not to go on."

Hor'ō'cō and Nārū clasped their hands together and bowed to me, thanking me for all I had done. It felt funny, not being able to truly understand what I'd actually done and then being thanked for it by a stranger. "We have seen the most vile nature of all things mortal and we do not wish to see it again," Hor'ō'cō declared. "As the witnesses of Ebūda we have given our testimony to the heavens against those who have defied the Law. Now we choose eternal rest."

Úā'la nodded with a tender look, then held out both hands to grasp two heavy books which appeared in the same way the scrolls had materialized. "These are the memories of the Guardians of Ebūda; the chronicle of the análong which is called the Book of Moon. May they be inscribed with the lives of these two witnesses and never be destroyed. For we should not suffer Time to remember them by what we wish had been, but by what truly was."

Then the sky parted and funneled down, pouring its blue into the pages of the books and Úā'la placed them onto the ground and ran the golden sword through them both, crumbling them into dust. As I watched this dust scatter onto the top of the water and turn it to liquid gold, I saw that only Úā'la and I remained still, now under a sky of star-scattered night.

"But I've only just met you all! I've only just got here," I whined. "Why must I choose now?"

Úā'la's strong painted face softened to me. "This place is made up of the wishes of the Guardians, the desire for the ordinary. Without all of us here, it will become unstable and crumble. The wishes of our siblings have gone on with them. Remember, rarely are wishes just handed to us. There's some chasing-after involved; some work."

Chasing-after, I thought. *Wait for me, I'm coming!*

And I reached down into the water, watching as my arms dissolved into pure, sparkling gold.

mi'hal'ē
34

illusory

m'samacala

O NCE I had a beautiful dream, a dream of who I was *before*. I was made of every color, every song, every tear, every laugh. I was light, I was joy, I was snow. I danced without feet and flew without wings. I was a star.

And then I fell a long way down. I became sorrow and I bled despair. Struck and burnt, I ached for those I never knew, drowning in the memory of a time before.

Then finally I awoke from these dreams, for this is what they were: illusions. And sometimes when I woke in the night, I wondered if they'd ever happened at all.

naats'ūcē

35

tomorrow, and another
amhar 's andap

1 "ITADAKIMASU!"

Nastuki clapped and eagerly dug into breakfast without waiting for her parents to begin.

"Slow down, you'll choke," her mother admonished but her father grinned vaguely over his rice bowl at her healthy appetite. Natsuki clapped again and thanked her mother for the meal, "Gochisousamadeshita!" before dashing off to her room.

"Late is no way to start second term!" her mother lectured after her.

Pulling on her school seifuku and grabbing her bookbag stuffed with her favorite pens and note-books, Natuski paused only long enough at the counter to grab the bento her mother had packed. "Doumo!" she called in thanks and raced out the door and down the narrow path to meet her friends by the mountain rock overlooking the sea. Her older sister Kiyoshi had already eaten and left, prob-ably to catch up with her friend Hoshi. The two inseparable girls were in high school and started earlier than Natsuki and her friends in the junior high.

"Ohayō Natsuki-chan!" Hiraku and Aneko waved emphatically from the meeting rock. "Hisas-hiburi!" she called back. It had been almost two months since the end of the first term and Natsuki had missed them both terribly. The girls stood a moment opening their bentos and admiring the snacks their mothers had sent for their first day back. Immediately Aneko offered to trade her sweet bean dango for Natuski's persimmon.

"Hey, don't trade it, give it to me!" An annoyed voice shouted from further up the path. Natuski looked up to see her tall, lanky sister and her delicate friend gazing down at them. Natsuki shrugged and traded her fruit, sticking her tongue out to Kiyoshi. Her friends murmured "Ohayō, nii-san!" and politely bowed.

Kiyoshi snorted in amusement but said nothing more. Hoshi took her arm and pulled her on. "Come on Kiyoshi-kun, we're already late." She waved over her shoulder to the girls and they noted with interest the new charms hanging from her mobile which matched those hanging from Kiyoshi's bag. Hiraku clasped her hands and did a little hop. "*Kawaii!* They're both so cool!"

Natsuki rolled her eyes and the girls continued on, reaching the school not quite late but definitely not on time. Quickly slipping out of their shoes inside the doorway and into their indoor uwabaki for the day, they took the back three seats and pulled out their notebooks, standing up to greet their teacher at the class monitor's signal.

As was her nature, Natsuki immediately sat down to an open notebook and turned her attention out the window. Aneko poked her in the ribs, looking past her where the morning mist was rising from the sea. "*What are you looking at?*" she motioned with her hands. Natsuki was about to sign back "*Nothing!*" but stopped when a sudden streak of movement caught her eye in the schoolyard.

A boy on a bicycle came racing in, tossing his bike to the ground without locking it properly to the student bike rack. He haphazardly ran back to grab the bento he'd dropped in jumping over the

naats'ucē

35

tomorrow, and another
amhar 's andap

1 "ITADAKIMASU!"

Nastuki clapped and eagerly dug into breakfast without waiting for her parents to begin.

"Slow down, you'll choke," her mother admonished but her father grinned vaguely over his rice bowl at her healthy appetite. Natsuki clapped again and thanked her mother for the meal, "Gochisousamadeshita!" before dashing off to her room.

"Late is no way to start second term!" her mother lectured after her.

Pulling on her school seifuku and grabbing her bookbag stuffed with her favorite pens and note-books, Natuski paused only long enough at the counter to grab the bento her mother had packed. "Doumo!" she called in thanks and raced out the door and down the narrow path to meet her friends by the mountain rock overlooking the sea. Her older sister Kiyoshi had already eaten and left, prob-ably to catch up with her friend Hoshi. The two inseparable girls were in high school and started earlier than Natsuki and her friends in the junior high.

"Ohayō Natsuki-chan!" Hiraku and Aneko waved emphatically from the meeting rock. "Hisas-hiburi!" she called back. It had been almost two months since the end of the first term and Natsuki had missed them both terribly. The girls stood a moment opening their bentos and admiring the snacks their mothers had sent for their first day back. Immediately Aneko offered to trade her sweet bean dango for Natuski's persimmon.

"Hey, don't trade it, give it to me!" An annoyed voice shouted from further up the path. Natuski looked up to see her tall, lanky sister and her delicate friend gazing down at them. Natsuki shrugged and traded her fruit, sticking her tongue out to Kiyoshi. Her friends murmured "Ohayō, nii-san!" and politely bowed.

Kiyoshi snorted in amusement but said nothing more. Hoshi took her arm and pulled her on. "Come on Kiyoshi-kun, we're already late." She waved over her shoulder to the girls and they noted with interest the new charms hanging from her mobile which matched those hanging from Kiyoshi's bag. Hiraku clasped her hands and did a little hop. "*Kawaii!* They're both so cool!"

Natsuki rolled her eyes and the girls continued on, reaching the school not quite late but definitely not on time. Quickly slipping out of their shoes inside the doorway and into their indoor uwabaki for the day, they took the back three seats and pulled out their notebooks, standing up to greet their teacher at the class monitor's signal.

As was her nature, Natsuki immediately sat down to an open notebook and turned her attention out the window. Aneko poked her in the ribs, looking past her where the morning mist was rising from the sea. "*What are you looking at?*" she motioned with her hands. Natsuki was about to sign back "*Nothing!*" but stopped when a sudden streak of movement caught her eye in the schoolyard.

A boy on a bicycle came racing in, tossing his bike to the ground without locking it properly to the student bike rack. He haphazardly ran back to grab the bento he'd dropped in jumping over the school fence. "Shin'ichi's such an airhead," Aneko whispered. "First day back and he didn't even bring his books."

Natsuki grinned as Shin'ichi vanished out of sight under the school awning. For their first year in the junior high his father had bought him the new bike and since the first day of first term Natsuki had plotted to ask if she could ride on the back of it. Hiraku said she should just ask to borrow it for a weekend and then all three of them could have a turn. But while she wouldn't admit it to her friends, Natsuki didn't want to learn to ride it. She just wanted to ride on the back of it.

Now the second term had started, and all the children were back in their seats, fidgeting to tell each other of their holidays off and to trade new pencils and pass notes under the class monitor's nose. From the back of the room Natuski smiled, gazing still out of the window, her head cradled in her palm.

Suddenly her heart felt big inside of her, full of love for this life around her. In a few hours she would eat lunch with her best friends, and later on leave school with them, gossiping all the way back down the mountain path about all the stories they'd heard over the school day and eating their snacks. She would go home and change out of her school seifuku and into the jinbei clothing she wore to join her parents and sister and neighbors to work in the tea fields high behind her house picking the delicate leaves to be rolled and dried. Then they would come home tired but happy to a late meal prepared by her sweet old Obā-san and to argue over a television show before bed.

Natuski smiled. Today, she might ask Shin'ichi about the bicycle. Or maybe tomorrow.

Yes, *tomorrow.*

The Book of Moon: An Loúr ihn G'éalach is an allegory of mental illness in childhood. Characters and events are based on the author's experience as a child and teenager growing up with a mental illness. It was written with the intent to help create awareness of the isolation, discrimination and stigma experienced by the mentally ill in their everyday lives.

For more information, please visit www.thebookofmoon.com

K. Rose Quayle is also the author of *Look Left, Walk Green: a Shocking Tale of Losing the Past and Choosing to Gain the Future.* When she's not writing you can probably find her hanging out with her chickens, making lists of stuff she's probably never going to do and losing puzzle pieces.

Not necessarily in that order.